These
Bones
Were
Made
for
Dancin'

By the Same Author

MURDER: THE MUSICAL
THE BIG KILLING
THE DEADLIEST OPTION
TENDER DEATH
BLOOD ON THE STREET

By Maan Meyers

THE DUTCHMAN
THE KINGSBRIDGE PLOT
THE HIGH CONSTABLE
THE DUTCHMAN'S DILEMMA

These Bones Were Made for Dancin'

A SMITH AND WETZON MYSTERY

ANNETTE MEYERS

DOUBLEDAY
New York London Toronto Sydney Auckland

PUBLISHED BY DOUBLEDAY
a division of Bantam Doubleday Dell Publishing Group, Inc.
1540 Broadway, New York, New York 10036

DOUBLEDAY and the portrayal of an anchor with a dolphin are trademarks of
Doubleday, a division of Bantam Doubleday Dell Publishing Group, Inc.

Library of Congress Cataloging-in-Publication Data

Meyers, Annette.
These bones were made for dancin' : a Smith and Wetzon mystery / Annette
Meyers.—1st ed.
p. cm.
1. Wetzon, Leslie (Fictitious character)—Fiction. 2. Smith, Xenia
(Fictitious character)—Fiction. 3. Women detectives—New York (N.Y.)—
Fiction. I. Title.
PS3563.E889T48   1995
813'.54—dc20   95-909
                                                                     CIP

ISBN 0-385-47653-1

For
Russell Perreault,
my champion, my friend

My thanks to Larry Katen, Sharon Villines, and Leah Ruth Robinson for strategic information; to Howard Weiss, for letting me peep into his wallet; to Dolores Bullard, Cathi Rosso, Linda Ray, Ann Ledley of Actors Equity, Paul Moore and Sally Gifft of United Scenic Artists, Deene Rudofker, Kathy Schrier, and Philip Rinaldi. To Helen Lahey, Executive Director of Theatre Authority, and her assistant, Anna Louise Soetje. To Joan Fisher. To Wally Monroe of the Actors Fund, and Harvey Sabinson and Irving Cheskin of the League of American Theatres and Producers. To NYPD Detective Ray Pierce. To Detective Tom Natale, Senior Firearms Examiner, NYPD. To Dr. Marina Stajic, Director of Forensic Toxicology, and Dr. Robert C. Shaler, Director of Forensic Biology, both from the New York City Medical Examiner's Office. To Dr. Michael Levy, Clinical Assistant Professor, Cardiothoracic Surgery, State University of New York at Stony Brook.

To the amazing Peg Caldwell-Ott, forensic anthropologist, consultant to the Chief Medical Examiner of New York, who gave me the idea for this book by saying that a dancer's bones are different, and also generously gave technical advice. To Dr. William H. McDonald, Associate Director, Criminal Justice Center of John Jay College for Criminal Justice.

Any errors in technical detail are completely mine.

My thanks also to Chris Tomasino, my agent and friend. To Judy Kern at Doubleday. To Kate Miciak, an editor to die for. And especially to Marty, who sees everything in its rawest state and tells me the truth, always.

"The show's still big; it's Broadway that got small."

—DONALD G. MCNEIL, JR.
"ON STAGE, AND OFF"
New York Times

"Swimming pools on stage, vendors selling T-shirts and baseball caps, that's what my life in the theatre has come to."

—CARLOS PRINCE
CHOREOGRAPHER, *Hotshot: The Musical*

MEMORANDUM

To: Carlos Prince and Leslie Wetzon
From: Nancy Stein, Assistant to Mort Hornberg
Date: November 14, 1994
Re: *Combinations, in Concert*

Congratulations! Phyllis Reynard (score) and Medora Battle (book) have waived royalties on basis of two performances.

If more performances are contemplated, we'll have to work out some kind of arrangement with the Dramatists Guild. I'm waiting to hear from Davey Lewin's brother, but don't think there'll be a problem.

So, we're on. Mort asks that we keep this as quiet as possible so that he can make a big splash announcement.

I just want to say how thrilled I am to be working on this project with you.

Chapter One

THE SHOOTING BEGAN AS WETZON TURNED HER KEY IN THE LOCK. TWO SHOTS, one after the other. She pushed the door open with her knee.

"Major Strasser's been shot."

The two most important people in Wetzon's life were lying on the floor of her living room in semidarkness. Even the dog, Izz, draped like a little white rug on Silvestri's chest, seemed mesmerized as the movie came to an end.

Then Silvestri, Carlos, and Rick said in unison, " 'Louis, I think this is the beginning of a beautiful friendship.' "

As Bogart and Claude Raines walked off into the night, Wetzon leaned around her door, put her finger on the doorbell, and pressed hard.

"Yipes," she heard Carlos say, and Izz began to bark. Silvestri sat up and peered at her.

"It's only I, gentlemen, come home from a long, cruel day at the Markets. Pray, don't get up." Wetzon set her briefcase on the floor and hung up her coat. It had been a moderately successful but hideously long day. She'd arrived in Philadelphia in time for a seven-thirty breakfast at the Warwick, hustled the broker out, and had a second breakfast at eight-thirty with another broker. Testified in an arbitration hearing at ten. Lunch at twelve, another at one, another at two, and drinks at four and five and quick, run for the New York train, all that club soda sloshing around inside her.

So it wasn't hunger that brought her into the kitchen but, rather, the glimpse of the Zabar's bag on the counter, the contents of which would be Carlos's and her dinner tonight. They were working on the arrangements for *Combinations, in Concert,* a two-performances-only revival of the landmark musical to benefit the AIDS group Show Biz Shares. Sniffing, she unpacked Scottish salmon, smoked whitefish and carp, niçoise olives, crème fraîche, bagels, a small roll of goat cheese. The large container of shrimp bisque she emptied into a saucepan. The fragrance was lyrical.

When she came out of the kitchen, the lights were on, the television was off, and both Carlos and Silvestri wore sheepish grins.

"Birdie, darling." Carlos tucked back the cuffs of his black silk shirt. "You never told me Silvestri is a film buff."

"Didn't I? It must have slipped my mind, as it were, my being in the trenches every day with my crazy partner, who's decided she'd rather produce Broadway shows than headhunt on Wall Street."

"That won't last." Silvestri had regained his composure. He rarely exposed his sentimental side, even to her.

Carlos agreed. "When the Barracuda sees it's neither glamorous nor lucrative, she'll go right back to Wall Street, where she belongs."

Silvestri came slowly toward her, and now he slipped his hands under the jacket of her blue pinstripe and pulled her to him. "Mmmm, you smell good."

"Essence of vitriol," Carlos said. His voice died off in the kitchen.

"*Moi?*" Wetzon giggled. "*Non-non-non.*" Her Gallicism got lost in Silvestri's lambswool sweater, turquoise, like his eyes.

He kissed her cheekbones and each eyelid. "I'm off," he said, slinging his pea jacket over his shoulder. "And I'm taking Izz." He scooped up the squirming Maltese, whose pink tongue slobbered over the cleft in Silvestri's chin.

"She's getting to be a regular. You ought to give her a percentage of the winnings, you know."

Silvestri had begun to take Izz to his weekly poker game—boys' night out—always conducted at his apartment in Chelsea. The tradition had started when he saw that the little dog distracted the other players just enough to give him an advantage.

Although he'd been spending most of his time at Wetzon's place, Silvestri held on to that Chelsea apartment as if it were a prize. It was rent-controlled, he said. Where would he get another like it in the City these days?

Who said you'd have to, Wetzon always wanted to respond, but didn't because they were still a little wary of each other. Neither wanted to get hurt again.

"Ciao, Carlos," Silvestri called; Carlos answered him in kind.

"Ciao?" *Ciao?* What had gotten into him, Wetzon thought as she attached Izz's leash to the hook on the little dog's collar. "Now be adorable, Isabella," she instructed, kissing the little pink snout. She walked with them out to the elevator.

"Hey," Silvestri said casually, "are you free for lunch tomorrow or Wednesday?"

"Not tomorrow. Smith told me to hold all day tomorrow for a surprise." Wetzon groaned. She'd almost forgotten. There was no telling what Smith had cooked up now.

"Wednesday, then?"

"Sure. What's up?" She looked at him curiously, but his face told her nothing. He was in his Lieutenant, NYPD, mode. "You never do lunch."

The elevator arrived, doors opening. Three people on it looked expectant.

"I want you to meet someone." He scooped up Izz, got on, and as the doors closed, said, "I'll call you. Hold Wednesday."

Her heart did a pirouette, then a back flip. His mother! She was finally going to meet the fabulous Rita, who lived in Forest Hills and had put herself through law school after Silvestri's father, a cop, had been killed while trying to break up a 10-64, a domestic dispute. Rita Silvestri had found her calling in legal issues pertaining to women, in particular battered women.

Wetzon went back into her apartment and closed the door. "I'm going to get out of these *shmattas*," she called to Carlos. She shed her Wall Street skin for leggings, sweatshirt, and socks bulked around her ankles, and made for the barre in her combination living room–dining room.

When she'd redone the apartment after the flood two years before, she had opened the space, exposed the beams in the thirteen-foot ceilings, and removed the arches endemic to prewar buildings in Manhattan. Her contractor friend, Louie (Louise) Armstrong, had installed Wetzon's barre almost where it had been in the dining room, which they'd eliminated, and backed it with a wall of mirrors.

She stood in front of the barre and did a *plié*. The woman in the mirror still looked like a girl, gray-eyed, thin of face, and sharp of chin. Stretching her neck, Wetzon saw no wrinkles. Her ash-blond hair hadn't changed color, though here and there she spotted a thread of white. It was long again, barely grazing her shoulders, but she hadn't put it back in the dancer's knot on top of her head. She would, she told herself. Eventually.

The tremorous excitement she'd felt when Silvestri had made the lunch date was abruptly tempered by caution. She wasn't ready—true. She was too young—not true. In a few months she'd be forty. *Plié, relevé.* Sweat appeared on her upper lip.

"Birdie! We have a ton of work to do." She hadn't even heard Carlos, but there he was sitting at her dining table surrounded by platters of food and legal pads.

She grinned at him in the mirror and soft-shoed over to the table, dropping gracefully into a chair.

Eighteen years ago both Wetzon and Carlos had been part of a landmark musical, one the *New York Times* had called "a cold, but admirable musical about relationships that will be for Broadway what *Carousel* was in its time, an event that changes how audiences perceive musicals forever." Such praise could kill, and this time it did. As is often the case, so-called "landmark" musicals like *West Side Story* and *Company,* to name two, are never as well-attended as the crowd-pleasers like *Cats* and *Grease. Combinations* had run for barely a year, never at capacity. It had been Wetzon's and Carlos's first big show together.

Over the years the people connected to the original company of *Combinations* had had more than their share of tragedies: Roger Battle, the co-librettist, had died of heart failure not long after the show closed. Davey Lewin, the director-choreographer, had died of AIDS four years ago; Larry Saunders Lawrence, one of the dancers, had succumbed to it a year ago. After Larry's death, Carlos had had the idea of bringing together all the remaining members of the company for two performances in concert during Christmas week as an AIDS benefit. He would stage it with Mort Hornberg, who'd been Davey's assistant eighteen years earlier on *Combinations,* and Mort, Carlos, and Wetzon would produce it, with all the profits going to Show Biz Shares, a nonprofit organization that helped AIDS victims from all parts of the theatre community.

"We'll do it together, Birdie," Carlos had proposed. "Think of it, you and me, dancin' again." His excitement was infectious. Wetzon was in.

One by one she'd tracked down almost everyone still living who'd worked in the original company. Even Bonnie McHugh, who had a TV sitcom now, had agreed to take her old part.

The only one Wetzon hadn't found was Terri Matthews.

"That doesn't make any sense," Carlos said now, spreading crème fraîche on his toasted half-bagel and topping it with a slice of salmon.

"I tried Equity, AGVA, AGMA, AFTRA, even SAG. No listing. I tried NYNEX. I even tried the Actors Fund. Odd, isn't it? Don't you remember seeing her at auditions?"

"Not really, but that doesn't mean anything."

"Wait a minute." Wetzon had an inspiration. She picked at the whitefish with her fingers. "Wasn't Terri leaving the business? Didn't she inherit some money or win the lottery or something? I seem to remember she always talked about opening a dancing school in Cincinnati."

"Good grief, not where the tall corn grows?"

"That's Iowa, silly," Wetzon said. She wiped her fingers on the napkin and went to the phone. "Listing in Cincinnati for Terri or Theresa Matthews." She spelled the name out. "It's a private home, or it may be a dancing school. . . . Do you have other listings for dancing schools? No. No. That's not right. . . . Thank you anyway. Wait— give me that number."

"Whatcha get?" Carlos demanded, even before she'd hung up the phone.

"Nothing, but I have the number of a school called Ballet Broadway—"

Carlos choked. "Give me a break, Birdie. Terri would never do that."

Wetzon shook her finger at him. "Behave yourself, snob." She came back to the table and sat. "Someone there must know her. Terri's a hometown girl and a dancer. She can't have disappeared off the face of the earth."

I have an exclusive! The lovely Bonnie McHugh is returning to Broadway to re-create her starring role in the musical *Combinations,* where she was discovered by Aaron Spelling almost eighteen years ago.

And while our clever little Bonnie was being coy, I have managed to find out there's to be a concert version of that wonderful show during Christmas Week as an AIDS benefit.

Is our Bonnie testing the waters for something bigger?

—CINDY ADAMS, *Live at Five,* NBC-TV
TUESDAY, NOVEMBER 15, 1994

Chapter Two

"Birdie, I just heard Cindy Adams announce our show on Live at Five to millions of viewers!"

"How could she know? I thought we're all supposed to keep our mouths shut so that Mort can announce it."

"Did you know, darling, that Bonnie was the star of Combinations? *Get it?"*

"Got it."

"Well, Wetzon, what took you so long?"

Madison Fiske's succulent Southern tones flowed into Wetzon's ear. He had just opened a boutique office for Hayden Ross in Palm Beach and was filled up to here with himself. And he had some cause because the huge wire house had, up to now, never opened a boutique office, preferring to stock sixty and seventy brokers in each of its many branches. Size equaled savings. Still, the fact that they'd chosen "Mad" Fiske to manage was a miscalculation of epic proportions, and had to be attributable solely to the fact that he looked good in a suit. *Plus ça change, plus c'est la même chose.* On the Street, perception continued to outweigh reality.

"I understand congratulations are in order, Madison," Wetzon said. Shortening his name was a no-no.

"I've been waiting for this for a long time, lady. You are the largest purveyors of flesh to this firm. Now I want you to go to work and find me *my* type of brokers."

"Your type?"

"Yes. Your partner knows the type I like. Ask her. We talked about it when I was in New York last week and you weren't around."

It was an accusation. Wetzon's eyes crossed. Smith was terrific at promises, then always dumped fulfillment on Wetzon. She sighed and pulled out a clean legal pad. "Smith isn't here right now, Madison, so why don't you fill me in on exactly what you're looking for."

"WASP types like myself, Wetzon, are the only ones I'd consider for my office. I'm simply not going to hire those other types."

Say no more, she thought. Keeping her tone neutral, she asked, "What other types?"

"You know, the types that are dealing here on the Palm Beach corridor, those New York and Brooklyn Jewish and Italian types. And those neurotic Long Island types."

"Oh, sure, Madison," she said, knowing his list of undesirables ruled out three-quarters of the people in the brokerage industry, and in America, for that matter. It never ceased to amaze her that the Madison Fiskes of the financial community, almost on the endangered species list, still behaved as if they owned the Street.

"And, Wetzon, listen closely. I don't want any fat, ugly people who don't know how to dress or eat."

Wetzon held the phone away from her ear and stared at it. "All right, Madison, how about if I come down there and interview people in person over dinner so I can check out what they look like and how they eat?" She had no intention whatever of doing this and could just imagine the screaming from old-line, conservative Hayden Ross if she were to send them a bill for the expenses. Even a dickhead like Madison Fiske had to see this was not an efficient way of doing business.

But Madison said, "That's a very good idea."

She hung up the phone before she told him something she might regret, and rifled through the stack of message slips on her desk. "Don't hold your breath."

Oh, dear, oh, dear. Assistant D.A. Marissa Peiser had called late yesterday. Little quick pulses ticked off in Wetzon's throat. Earlier this year Wetzon had turned over evidence to Peiser showing that Richard Hartmann, the notorious criminal defense attorney and Smith's current lover, was laundering money.

Peiser had promised to keep Wetzon out of it if she could because Wetzon had gotten the evidence in the course of breaking and entering, an activity that was still illegal last time she checked.

Wetzon sighed. What she needed was a cup of coffee. She went into the reception area, came back with the pitcher, filled it from the shower in the bathroom, holding it out carefully so she wouldn't get splashed, then poured water into the coffeemaker. It was eight-thirty. She'd come in early, having no dog and no Silvestri to deal with. The precious hour between eight and nine in the office was quiet time. Managers were always in early and easier to talk to before the Market opened at nine-thirty. Older brokers still came in early to set up their day and talk to clients as they had done for years, in the days when the Market opened at ten.

The new generation of brokers strolled in just before the Opening and left at the Close at four o'clock. A different kind of ethic now prevailed on the Street—much less service-oriented, definitely a nineties thing.

She measured the coffee into the filter and turned on the machine, then sat down at Max's desk with its healthy stacks of suspect sheets—the biographical interviews of candidates—and opened the bundle of mail she'd picked up on her way in.

Some bills, some checks, and even a few résumés from people who weren't stockbrokers. *Crain's, Barron's*, the *Journal. Registered Rep*, the trade magazine for brokers, who in the early eighties were dubbed by their firms Registered Representatives. A nice change from the old Customers' Man. And yet, didn't Customers' Man imply service? Now they were called Financial Consultants, whatever that meant.

She sifted through the suspect sheets in the tray Max had marked WETZON—HOT.

Max Orchard had been with them for two years now. He was a

sixty-six-year-old retired accountant in gum-soled shoes. Max's short neck, flat chest, and round belly gave him a Tweedledum appearance, exaggerated by the suspenders that brought his pants almost to his armpits.

Madison Fiske would never hire Max, that was for sure, and Smith hadn't wanted to either. But B.B., their previous assistant, was covering work that had been handled by the treacherous Harold Alpert, who'd left them to join their biggest competitor, Tom Keegen. They'd been desperate. So Wetzon prevailed over Smith's protests and Max had been hired.

The coffeemaker began gasping and gulping as it finished its cycle. Outside, tires squealed and someone leaned on a horn.

Six months ago B.B. had gotten married and moved to Oregon to become a vintner, and they had still not found anyone for—

She sat up. What was that? An odd tinkle, like breaking glass, then a thud. The front door. She got to her feet. Smith? Too early for Max, who worked four days a week, eleven to four. She walked to the door and opened it before remembering she was alone. Too late.

A huge fur boulder fell on her, driving her to the floor.

"Jeeze, I'm sorry!" the boulder gasped, sprouting arms and legs but remaining firmly atop Wetzon. "Quick, close the door. You won't believe this, but someone just tried to shoot me."

"Would you mind getting off me and telling me who you are?"

"Oh, of course." The intruder scrambled to her feet, a square-jawed Kathleen Turner kind of blonde, not much taller than Wetzon but at least fifteen pounds heavier. She gave Wetzon her hand and swung to her feet, then shed her raccoon coat, which looked exactly like Wetzon's. "You must be Wetzon." She felt the top of her head. "Migod, where's my hat? It must be out there." She pointed to the street. "Do you suppose he stole it?"

"Your hat?"

"Yes. You know they steal fur hats now."

"They do?" A broker, Wetzon thought. A broker and totally insane.

"Why don't you hang up your coat and come into my office. What firm are you with?"

The woman started laughing. Her mascara lay in beads on her eyelashes and she wore too much blush. The neckline of her black jersey dress was cut in a deep V, revealing fleshy cleavage. "What firm?" she echoed, between laughs. "Yours. I'm Darlene Ford, your new associate."

MEMORANDUM

To: Carlos Prince and Leslie Wetzon
From: Nancy Stein, Assistant to Mort Hornberg
Date: November 14, 1994
Re: *Combinations, in Concert*

Show Biz Shares is arranging with Theatre Authority for letter agreements with the performers. An honorarium of $200 will be paid to each.

Performers will make themselves available for rehearsals one week prior to performance, beginning December 16th.

Although Theatre Authority is designated by Equity to handle benefits, as a courtesy we are keeping them informed about arrangements.

The only fly in the ointment is Bonnie McHugh. She is insisting on her own hairdresser at a fee of $2500. If this is the case perhaps the hairdresser, Brian Fahey (he does her hair on her TV series), can be prevailed upon to donate his talents for the rest of the company.

The other immediate problem: Have you located Terri Matthews? If not, maybe this is the time to find a replacement. Didn't Vicki Howard do the road company?

Chapter Three

"CARLOS, DO YOU BELIEVE THAT BONNIE?"

"She's forgotten her roots, Birdie. Tsk. Tsk. That's what happens when gypsies go Hollywood."

"Yeah, well, Shirley MacLaine remembers her roots."

"Hers and all those others she's made a previous life with."

"GODDAMMIT, SMITH! HOW COULD YOU HIRE AN ASSOCIATE WITHOUT consulting me?"

"Shshsh, she'll hear you." Smith betrayed not one flicker of concern. She hooked a gigantic raccoon hat on the doorknob and stared at it.

"I don't care if she hears. She's a nut case. She says someone is trying to kill her."

Changing her mind, Smith took the hat off the doorknob and tried it on. It was a perfect fit. "Someone is, and don't I just know who."

"Oh, puleeze. Is that a new hat?"

"I'm giving it a trial."

"Wherever did you find her? And what the hell does she know about headhunting? I assume I'm going to have to teach her the business."

"Assume nothing, sweetie pie." Smith had her Cheshire cat smile on full lumen. "Wait till you hear. You'll love it."

"I'm just dying to hear how I'll love it." Wetzon sat down at her desk. Damnation, Smith had steamrolled her again.

Smith licked her lips and spoke slowly, for effect. "Darlene is—correction, *was*—Tom Keegen's latest star recruiter. Trained by our own personal Benedict Alpert, the one and only Harold, and she has outproduced him in less that a year."

Benedict Alpert. Smith had actually made a joke. "Very funny, Smith."

"Clever, I would call it. So what do you say about my star hire?"

In spite of her exasperation, Wetzon was impressed. "Outproduced Harold, huh? How much does she bill?"

"Four hundred thou in nine months."

"Wow! Okay, you got me. I'm impressed."

"I knew you'd love it. It's a *coup.*"

"She looks cheap, though, Smith."

"Is that all you can say? Not 'Thank you, darling Smith'?" Smith's mouth formed a pout. "You never appreciate me."

Wetzon sighed. "I do, I do. You're wonderful. It's a *coup.*"

Smiling now, under all that fur, Smith said, "We'll do her over. She's a table rose."

"A table rose? What the hell is that?"

"You know, a blank tablet."

Wetzon laughed. "You mean *tabula rasa.*"

"Whatever."

"So who's trying to kill Darlene?"

"Tom Keegen, of course." Smith sat on her desk, swinging one long slim leg. She took a bottle of clear polish, Chanel of course, from her handbag and top-coated her fingernails.

"I would think Keegen'd rather try to kill you, or even me, if anyone."

"Oh." Smith's leg stopped swinging while she thought about it. "You're right. I did it. He's trying to kill me." Instead of looking frightened, she looked pleased. And there went her leg again. She pushed the polish aside and blew on her nails.

"No, he's not," Wetzon said. "Keegen's not that crazy. As we know from experience, headhunters are fungible. How on earth did you manage to woo Darlene away from him?"

"Weeelll, I've been hearing about her from some of our clients—you know how they like to torture us about how good our competition is—"

"As I'm sure they torture our competition with how good we are."

"Be that as it may, would you believe we both get our hair done at the same place—Ishi?" Smug was the only way to describe Smith at this moment.

"Since when do you go to Ishi?"

Smith smiled and patted the raccoon hat.

Rubbing her forehead, Wetzon said, "Never mind, don't tell me. It's amazing how dumb I am."

"Some of us have it, sweetie pie, and some of us don't." Crossing one leg over the other, Smith preened. "Anyway, need I tell you it was love at first sight?"

"Indeed?"

Smith frowned. "Not that kind of love."

"Oh, excuse me, I lost my head."

"I had to make a quick decision because Keegen was pushing her to sign a lucrative but confining contract immediately."

"And what did we give her, may I ask?"

"A lucrative and confining contract. And our lovely selves to work with."

"Get real, Smith."

"We gave her the title of senior vice president and fifty percent on every placement she makes."

"Is that all? Are you sure she's that good? Fifty percent of nothing is—"

"Trust me, sugar. Would I put us in a bad deal?"

Wetzon pondered that, pressing Marissa Peiser's phone message into accordian folds between her fingers. Smith was an astute deal-maker. She sniffed out profits as the NYPD canines sniffed explosives. Still, *trust me* always triggered Wetzon's memory of a conversation with a broker in her first year as a headhunter. He'd told her that, in business, *trust me* really means *fuck you.*

"So let's have an itsy-bitsy meeting right now," Smith continued, "and get everything going. If this works, and I know it will, we're going to be able to break through above us and have a duplex office." Smith went to the door, threw it open, tossing her final comment over her shoulder. "And, sugar, be nice to Darlene. She's very nervous about having you like her."

"Nervous about me? Good grief, Smith. I would say the woman's a little on the high-strung side in general. Does she know our new medical insurance has a ten-thou deductible on shrink bills?"

"Oh, you." Smith dismissed Wetzon's words with an indulgent wave and stuck her head out the door, calling, "Sugarplum, come on in here."

Darlene's short skirt, hooked like a sarong in front, revealed chubby knees in sheer hose. The heels on her slingbacks were even higher than Smith's. "Oh," she said, staring at Smith's head, "you found my hat!"

"It was lying in front of our door," Smith said severely. She took it off and examined it. "It's very nice." She handed it to Darlene, albeit reluctantly. "But you ought to have that nasty stain removed."

"What stain?" Darlene brought the hat to her nose, then looked at it and began to tremble. "See, I told you," she said. She offered the hat to Smith, who, to Wetzon's astonishment, backed away, a strange look on her face.

Did Smith already regret hiring Darlene? Wetzon wondered. Well, if so, that made two of them. Smith's eyes glazed over. Dammit, Wetzon thought.

Darlene's voice rose precipitously. "You don't understand. He's going to kill me. Look, Wetzon. Look at this. I'm not crazy. I know you think I'm crazy. You have to believe me."

Wetzon felt sorry for her. She took the fur hat from Darlene's trembling hand and looked at it, then took a closer look.

A singed groove ran like a dark stain across the crown.

MEMORANDUM

To: Carlos Prince and Leslie Wetzon
From: Nancy Stein, Assistant to Mort Hornberg
Date: November 15, 1994
Re: *Combinations, in Concert*

At Mort's request I have enclosed a preliminary budget for
two performances of *Combinations, in Concert,* currently
scheduled for the evenings of Thursday, December 22nd,
and Friday, December 23rd, at the Richard Rodgers
Theatre.

These are very early numbers and subject to change after
our next meeting—reminder—tomorrow—Mort's office, 4:00.

Please call me if you have any questions.

Chapter Four

"*Birdie!*"

"*What?*"

"*I can't stand looking at all these numbers. You look at the budget and let me know what you think.*"

"*Carlos, don't be such a baby. It's simple.*"

"*Darling, simple is as simple does. Besides, I thought everyone on Wall Street is required to learn creative bookkeeping.*"

Silvestri had said Walker's on North Moore and Varick, and she'd given the address to Ahmed, who said "Yes, lady" a bit too quickly, making her antennae twitch.

"Do you know where that is? It's downtown."

A line of cars formed behind them on East Forty-ninth Street, and horns began a jarring melody.

"Yes, lady," Ahmed said again. "Get in, get in or you'll get me a ticket."

Wetzon got in and Ahmed shot the cab forward. Whiplash time, she thought. Yeah, try and collect. Something besides his provisional hack license, posted boldly so a passenger could see it only when she was already sitting in the cab, told her Ahmed had no idea where he was going. Maybe it was when he turned uptown.

"Downtown," she said through clenched teeth.

"I know, lady, I know. I just want to get away from construction."

Maybe there was construction, maybe there wasn't. It was New

York, after all. Sit back and relax, she told herself. She did so reluctantly and closed her eyes. Ahmed could be right.

It was just that she was nervous about this meeting. She wanted to
make a good impression on Rita Silvestri. Hell, she wanted to make a
sensational impression on her.

Think about other things. Yes, what? Tom Keegen shooting at their
new associate? She couldn't even consider it without smiling. It was a
joke. Would he really be that stupid? It did look like a bullet burn, but
who was to say it was?

And what about Darlene Ford? If she was a terrific headhunter,
did it matter that she looked like a refugee from Great Neck, where the
dress code was over the top and women wore sequins on their sweat-
shirts? And Wetzon had called Carlos a snob.

Consider this: Darlene was a gold mine, if you could believe Smith.
They'd been talking for years about expanding their office space. Then
during the real estate slump they were offered the brownstone on East
Forty-ninth Street off Second Avenue, where they had their office, at a
bargain price. And although all the apartments on the four floors above
them were rented, there was always the fantasy that one day they
would combine their first floor and the second floor and make a duplex
office.

Their second-floor tenant, an antiquarian bookseller, had just given
them notice that he was moving to larger space on Second Avenue. If
Darlene was as good as Smith seemed to think, the year ahead could be
a banner year for Smith and Wetzon. And if it was, maybe a duplex was
in their future.

The cab screeched to a stop. She opened her eyes. She had no idea
where they were, and her driver . . . where was he? Ahmed was
standing in the middle of the street waving down another cab. She
looked at her watch—twelve-thirty. She rolled down her window and
shouted, "Dammit, Ahmed, what do you think you're doing?" She got
out of the cab.

"Stay, lady. I get you there in two minutes."

"Forget it." She left a five-dollar bill on the front seat, tucking it under his Koran, and took off. She'd recognized a landmark: directly behind her was Trinity Church graveyard.

She walked the rest of the way to the restaurant, stopping only once to ask directions—of a broad-bottomed woman in the gray pants of the U.S. Postal Service, rolling a big bag of mail on a three-wheeled cart.

When she pushed open the door to Walker's, she was only ten minutes late. She found herself in a late-nineteenth-century saloon— wood bar, etched glass, and all. Perfect. But it was crowded. No space at the beautifully patinaed bar—what she could see of it through all the standees. All the tables were packed with diners, a mix of pinstriped and neighborhood. The din rose up to the tin ceiling and dropped back down on the denizens. None seemed to care.

"Ms. Wetzon? Ms. Leslie Wetzon?"

She turned toward the voice. The man had a thick red thatch, a generous mustache, and sideburns almost to his jawline. "The Lieutenant and his party are in the back room. I'm Casey. Do you want to check your coat?" When she shook her head, Casey said, "Then follow me."

The back room was also packed, but here the tables weren't one on top of the other. Wetzon ran her fingers through her hair, catching a glimpse of herself amid the Art Nouveau design etched in the glass-paneled door as she followed Casey.

Would Rita have—

She stopped abruptly. Silvestri was sitting at a corner table, and the woman he was talking to, whose back was to Wetzon, was too young to be Rita Silvestri. Wrong again, Wetzon, she told herself, feeling the embarrassed flush rise to her cheeks. If this wasn't Rita, who was it? An edge, just an edge, of uncertainty hit her.

"Hi," she said, thinking at once that her voice sounded too loud and filled with phony enthusiasm. "Sorry I'm late." She sank into the chair Casey held for her and shrugged out of her coat. Then she perused her competition while Silvestri smirked at her. At least she thought he was smirking.

"Les, this is Nina Wayne. Nina, Leslie Wetzon."

Wetzon's heart sank. Nina Wayne was beautiful. High cheekbones, luminous complexion, green eyes. She wore no makeup and her sand-colored hair was in an elegant, not-a-hair-out-of-place French twist. Wetzon hated her. When they shook hands, she saw that Nina's fingernails were blunt, short, and unpolished and that she wore no rings.

Giving Wetzon a firm handshake, Nina said, "I've been hearing a lot about you."

"You have?" She shot Silvestri a suspicious look.

"Let's order," Silvestri said from behind his menu.

They ordered burgers with bacon, and fries, and draft beer. Around them came the steady hum of lunch conversation.

Wetzon put her napkin in her lap, making a project of it, then nibbled on a breadstick.

Eyeing both women, Silvestri cleared his throat. He seemed relieved when the beer arrived, foaming in huge glass mugs.

"I understand you're a dancer," Nina Wayne said. She gave Wetzon a warm smile.

"I was. A long time ago."

"And you were on Broadway?"

"Yes. And summer stock and the road."

"You don't dance anymore? How do your joints feel?"

"Fine, thank you, how do yours?"

"Les—" Silvestri began.

Nina Wayne smiled.

Wetzon said, "I take classes and stay limber by barre work at home. Are you a physical therapist?"

"I'm a forensic anthropologist," Nina Wayne said.

Their burgers were presented, lush on oval platters, the bacon brown, the fries thick and crisp. After a brief moment of appreciation, an unofficial time-out was accepted while the focus switched to food.

"Les is making a comeback," Silvestri said. He'd cleaned his plate and was picking at Wetzon's fries. Had Wetzon caught pride in his voice? Naa. Couldn't be. Not Silvestri.

"Really?" Nina said.

"No, not really. I'm doing a two-performance revival in concert of *Combinations,* a musical I was in a few years ago. It's an AIDS benefit to honor three people from the original company who've died."

"Combinations," Nina said. "I saw that when I was in high school."

Silvestri coughed behind his hand and ignored Wetzon's glare.

"Well, then you saw me. I was in it until it closed. Why don't you guys tell me why I'm here? What is a forensic anthropologist?"

"When there's no face or fingerprints, they come to me," Nina said. "My job is to identify unrecognizable—by standard techniques—human remains."

"Nina's a consultant to the New York City Medical Examiner," Silvestri added.

"Well, that's all very interesting." And it was. Somehow Nina Wayne was beginning to look different to her. Was it because she, too, was a woman in a man's world?

The table was cleared and they ordered coffee: two straight, and one decaf for the ex-dancer who was hyper enough without caffeine.

"Les, I asked you to have lunch with us today because I'm working on a case with Nina and thought there's an outside chance that you might be of some help."

"You want *my* help?" She didn't have to say any more. It had always been a bone of contention between them; Silvestri always accused her of butting into police business; now he was asking for her help. Definitely a red-letter day.

Nina Wayne said, "Of course, it's probably unlikely, but I never rule out coincidence, especially not in this city." She paused while the waiter set down the coffee mugs and topped off their water goblets.

Wetzon suddenly felt herself in a maze. "What on earth are you two talking about?"

Reaching under the table, Nina brought up a tan leather briefcase and from it removed an eight-by-eleven manila envelope. She returned the briefcase to floor.

"Les, remember I told you about the skeleton in the trunk?" Silvestri asked.

"The one in the basement of the brownstone in the Village?"

"Yeah. On Eleventh Street."

"Oh, Eleventh. You never told me where."

"It was in the newspapers," Nina said.

Wetzon smiled. "The *Times* and the *Journal* didn't feature it."

"We haven't been able to identify her," Nina said.

"Her?" She was watching Nina's fingers on the clasp of the manila envelope and feeling an odd, undefinable trepidation.

"Yes. A woman. Dead approximately fifteen to eighteen years." Nina slipped some black-and-white photos from the envelope. "Pull your chair around, Leslie, and I'll show you why we asked you here."

Bones, Wetzon thought as she shifted her chair. They were photographs of bones.

With her blunt fingers, Nina pointed to several areas on the bones. "Wear facets on the toes," she said.

"Wear facets," Wetzon repeated. *Right*.

"A large subchrondral cyst on the superior aspect of the acetabulum."

Wetzon nodded, staring at the photographs. *Sure*.

"The pelvis—innominates," Nina continued, intent on the photographs. "Necrosis in the acetabulum."

Wetzon sent Silvestri a pleading look. "Please tell me what you're saying in lay terms."

But it was Nina who responded. "The wear facets on the toes come from hyperextension, which we find in the bones of medieval monks. However, this woman was obviously not a medieval monk. The combination of this particular pelvic cyst and the wear facets on the toes indicates that these are the bones of a dancer."

. . .

MEMORANDUM

To: Joey Greenway
From: Nancy Stein, Assistant to Mort Hornberg
Date: November 15, 1994
Re: Props, *Combinations, in Concert*
CC: Carlos Prince and Leslie Wetzon

The following are the props Mort remembers from the original company. I've gone through the playing script and haven't picked up anything he missed.

    10 prs. of pompoms
    10 top hats
    10 red bow ties
    10 pink neon canes
    1 small drum on a red, white, and blue band
    2 drumsticks
    2 prs. handheld cymbals
    3 whistles on strings
    3 rattles
    1 small accordian
    1 marching band leader baton
    10 miniature American flags on sticks
    1 bass fiddle, with wheel attachment
    1 wedding cake

Chapter Five

"NANCY, I THINK THE ORIGINAL CANES WERE BLACK BAMBOO."

"I know, Leslie, but Mort feels they should have a little more jazz to them, so he's replacing bamboo with neon."

"Did he check with Carlos? I hope so. Carlos is the co-director on this."

There was a dead silence. "I'll let Mort know, Leslie."

FOR A LONG MOMENT WETZON STOPPED BREATHING. THE ROOM BEGAN TO SPIN around her.

"Les?" Silvestri was reaching across the twirling table to her, worry etching grooves in his face. "This was a lousy idea, Nina. Stash the photos and let's just forget about it."

Wetzon blinked at him, trying to see him clearly. He said, "I'll be right back," then got up and made his way to the front room.

Nina reached for the photographs. With a jolt the room stopped spinning, and Wetzon placed her palm on the pictures. "No, wait."

"Are you all right?" Nina asked. "You turned the color of this table-cloth."

Wetzon nodded. "I don't know what happened. It was like some-one walking over my grave. . . ."

"I thought maybe you—"

"Knew her?"

Nina nodded.

"From her bones? That's a little far-fetched, isn't it?"

"A little."

Silvestri set a jigger of booze in front of her. "Take a sip," he ordered.

She squinted up at him. He was unconsciously licking the dribble from the glass from his fingers. "I'm okay."

"Now," he said. "Don't argue."

She rolled her eyes at Nina and took a sip. Single malt. She held the liquid in her mouth, savoring it, then let it slide its warm way down her throat.

Satisfied, Silvestri sat. "Hey—" He'd noticed the photos were still on the table.

"She wants to see them," Nina said.

"I want to see them," Wetzon said. She traded the scotch for coffee and sent Silvestri her don't-tell-me-what-to-do stare. But she didn't look at the photos under her hand. She couldn't. Not yet. "Tell me what you know about her. How do you know it's a woman?"

"Well . . ." Nina looked at Silvestri, who shrugged. "Women have smoother brow ridges, and the pelvis is more splayed than a man's. We start first with defining sex, then race—she's Caucasian—then stature. The wisdom teeth were in and very slightly worn. This makes her between twenty-four and twenty-seven when she died, but the decomposition was extreme. There was no soft tissue to work with. Luckily, the cellar was dry; there was no evidence of water damage, and the trunk she was found in was not porous.

"Christ," Wetzon murmured.

Silvestri pushed the scotch in front of her, and she drank it without protest.

"Did I hear you say *trunk*, Nina?"

Nina looked to Silvestri.

He unfolded his arms and slid the photos from under Wetzon's hand, leafing through them until he found the ones he wanted. Holding them apart, he said, "Six months ago this brownstone at Eleventh and Hudson was bought by an architect and his wife. There was a tenant in a duplex on the top two floors. They began renovating the first three for a triplex. The trunk was in the cellar with a lot of other junk left by previous tenants." He held up the photograph of a large black metal trunk with brass corners, something like the one with which Wetzon had gone off to college, only this one was even more familiar to her; it had touring company stickers on it. She recognized *Cabaret* and *West Side Story*, among others.

Silvestri slid another photo in front of the one of the trunk. Same except now the trunk was open.

She was staring at a skull on top of a clutter of bones. Clinging to some of the bones were shredded pieces of fabric that looked like what might once have been jeans. The skull was topped by dull gold hair.

"She had blond hair?" To her own ear Wetzon sounded cool and professional, but in her gut she felt dread and some odd kinship with the woman, maybe because Wetzon's own pelvis and toes probably had the same kind of stress cysts.

Nina said, "Yes, but not that color."

"It's hard to believe that small pile of bones made an adult person."

"Not so small. I figure her to have been about five feet six inches with a weight of about a hundred twenty-five pounds."

"You can tell all that?" Had she cherished those jeans, Wetzon wondered. Had she bought them stiff and new and molded them to her body in the shower?

Nina nodded. "It's the length of the thigh bone and a mathematic equation: multiply and add and there you have it. Also, we can estimate weight by the size of the belt we found in the trunk."

"The belt didn't disintegrate?"

"It was plastic."

"She had no ID?"

"No."

"I thought people could be identified by teeth now."

"The Colorado dental ID program turned up nothing."

Silvestri handed the photos to Nina Wayne, who slipped all of them back into the manila clasp envelope and returned them to Silvestri. "This is your set. I've got another with me."

Wetzon stared into her almost empty coffee cup. No one spoke, although Nina leaned forward as if she were about to.

Suddenly Silvestri's beeper sounded. "I'll be right back," he said, passing their waiter, who was heading toward them with two pots of coffee for refills.

"Warm you up?" the waiter asked.

"You couldn't possibly," Wetzon said. He smiled politely. "But give it a try," she added. She cleared the huskiness from her voice.

"Well?" Nina said after the waiter had gone.

"Why are her bones just lying in a pile like that? Did someone cut her up?"

"No. There was decomposition to the extent that the skeleton dearticulated. Gravity would pull the bones apart."

"You think I might have known her." It was a statement, not a question.

"It's a vague possibility. The dance world is a small, tight society."

"True, but she could have been a ballet dancer. Then I might not have known her unless she was a star or I had a class with her."

"Try this. Did you know anyone—a dancer—who might have lived on Eleventh Street approximately fifteen years ago? Someone you haven't seen in a very long time?"

"A lot of dancers lived in the Village—still do. It's so long ago. I'll have to think about it. I can ask around. Can you get me enlargements of the stickers on the trunk?"

"Yes."

Silvestri returned. "I've paid the bill," he said. He didn't sit. "I've got to get back."

Wetzon looked at her watch. Two-thirty. "Me, too." She stood and put on her coat.

"Les? See you later?"

She nodded. The unfurled Nina Wayne was taller than Silvestri. Wetzon would have smiled and almost did, but another thought intruded. "Wait," she said, looking from one to the other, "you never told me how she died."

"Oh," Nina said.

Silvestri put his arm around Wetzon and hustled her through the restaurant. He waved to Casey. On the street, midday traffic crawled, people hurried back to work, collars up. It was a nippy mid-November day. Framed by the towers of Wall Street, the Goodyear Blimp floated soundlessly over the Financial District.

A truck backfired, and for just an instant Silvestri froze. He hadn't removed his arm from Wetzon's shoulders. Nina, wearing a long wine wool coat that accentuated her height, joined them.

"Can I drop either of you?" Wetzon asked. "I'm going all the way east on Forty-ninth Street."

Silvestri shook his head.

"I'm teaching at John Jay," Nina said, "but it's easier for me to just get on the subway."

"How did she die, guys?"

Silvestri flagged down a cab and opened the door for her. "She was shot, Les. Someone put a bullet in her skull."

MEMORANDUM

To: Nancy Stein, Assistant to Mort Hornberg
From: Lou Zucker, Acting Manager, Richard Rodgers Theatre
Date: November 15, 1994
Re: *Combinations, in Concert*
CC: Carlos Prince and Leslie Wetzon

When you gave us the budget you forgot to include porters.
Union custodians are required by the parent organization.
This will add $1501 to the budget. Also the General
Liability and property floater will be $250, as estimated.

Chapter Six

"See what I mean, Birdie? Would I know they forgot to include porters?"

"Carlos, dear heart, I wouldn't have known either. We're going to have to accept things on trust."

"Trust, huh. Ever since you told me the Wall Street translation for trust me, my little heart shivers when I hear the words."

When Wetzon arrived back at the office, total chaos confronted her.

Max, who greeted her appearance with obvious relief, was fielding phone calls, a totally foreign element in his voice: borderline hysteria.

Their new associate, Darlene, was blubbering loudly into a clump of sodden tissues.

"What is going on here?" Wetzon demanded.

Smith came out of their office as if shot from a cannon, smoke and all. "A restraining order," she sputtered. "That—that scumbag!" If it were possible, steam would be issuing from every orifice.

Darlene's sobs grew louder.

"Now calm down, everybody," Wetzon said, taking charge. "Let's not lose our heads. No one," she added, "has died." No one here, she thought, has been shot in the head and stuffed in a trunk to rot for fifteen years. "Has anyone called Shirley?" Shirley Boley was their lawyer, a tough, no-nonsense woman with a background in securities law who was a highly successful single practitioner.

The phone rang.

"Smith and Wetzon, good afternoon," Max said. He looked at Wetzon, who shook her head.

Take a message, she mouthed.

"Shirley's on it already," Smith told her. "Darlene, sugar, please—" Smith's nerves were decidedly frayed.

"What exactly are we being restrained from?" Wetzon hung her coat in the closet and went into the office she and Smith had shared since they'd started their business almost ten years earlier. "Darlene, please, come on in here and let's talk about this."

"Shirley said Darlene's not to recruit or try to recruit anyone she talked to at Tom Keegen's. She can't even call them and tell them she's here now."

"Oh, come on, we all talk to the same people. There are no secrets in this business when it comes to the names of stockbrokers. It's how you sell them that counts."

"Of course," Smith said slowly.

Uh-oh, Wetzon thought, knowing her partner so well. An idea of questionable morality was undoubtedly forming in Smith's devious mind. "I suggest that until this is straightened out—and Shirley is great at this, so it shouldn't take too long—Darlene, you go through B.B.'s suspect sheets and pick out people you've never talked to. Onward and upward."

Darlene dried her eyes and blew her nose.

The phone rang.

"Smith and Wetzon, good afternoon," Max said. ". . . She's in a meeting. May I take a message?" He hung up the phone and wrote out a message, then handed it and the previous one to Wetzon.

Wetzon told Darlene, "His suspect sheets are alphabetized in the bottom drawer of your desk. Go through them. If you have any questions, ask us."

Smith interjected, "And, sugar, if you should think of someone fabulous you've talked to that we don't know about, you just give that name to Wetzon and she'll make the call."

"Good grief," Wetzon groaned. Smith was a piece of work, she was thinking as she ushered Darlene—still clutching sodden tissues—from the room, closed the door, and leaned against it. "Have you no shame?"

Smith smiled and inspected her manicure. "Well, I certainly hope we haven't made a mistake. The Tarot said—"

"What do you mean, *we?*" Wetzon flipped through her pink message slips.

"Very funny."

"I'm not laughing. I've just had a dreadful lunch."

"Oh." Smith suddenly became adorable. "Weren't you having lunch with Dick Tracy and his mother?" She always called Silvestri Dick Tracy because she knew it annoyed Wetzon.

"She wasn't there. He brought a forensic anthropologist and pictures of the skeletal remains of someone they found in a theatrical trunk. They think she was a dancer about fifteen years ago and that there's a chance I might have known her."

"Ha!" Smith shrieked. "From a collection of *bones?* Give me a break."

"It was depressing."

"I would think so." With an exaggerated sigh, Smith said, "The cards warned me and I didn't listen. Death came up and then the Tower. I'll lay out a spread for you tonight."

"Do me a favor, Smith, whatever it is, don't tell me."

"If you would only open yourself to the healing qualities of the Tarot, you would be able to deal spiritually with everything that comes your way."

"Like you, I suppose?"

Smith shrugged. "I hope you don't have plans for breakfast tomorrow."

"I don't. What's up?" She reached for the rest of the messages that were on her desk under the marble peach paperweight, a thank-you gift from Laura Lee Day after Wetzon had placed her at Oppenheimer. Damn, there were two calls from Marissa Peiser and another from

Arthur Margolies, Wetzon's lawyer, who also happened to be Carlos's lover.

"We've been summoned to Rosenkind Luwisher for a power break-fast tomorrow at seven-thirty," Smith announced. "Both of us."

"Sounds ominous, but it is probably more of the same thing. They always make this big deal about coming down there and then they do their dog-and-pony show for us on how to sell the firm, none of which is anything new."

"I know, but with what's happening on the Street now, with Pru still smarting from bad publicity and possibly selling out or merging with another firm, and PaineWebber buying Kidder at a fire-sale price —no cash down—we're going to have to coddle our clients. We could wake up one morning and not have any. Cash or clients." She watched the buttons light up on the phone with satisfaction. "Sweetie pie, why don't you get a cab and come pick me up at seven tomorrow?"

"A cab on the West Side at seven in the morning? You have to be kidding. I'll take public transportation, thank you very much."

"Public transportation?" Smith was horrified.

Wetzon grinned at her. "Read my lips, Smith. The subway. Some-place you've never been."

"We'll get a car service."

"Fine." The mental image of Smith being jostled by third world blue-collar workers on the subway at rush hour—hell, at *any* time—was so funny Wetzon had to cover her burst of laughter with a fit of coughing. Then, as Smith was looking fish-eyed at her, Wetzon was rescued by Max's knock.

"Come in, Max, sweetie," Smith called.

Max opened the door. He was beaming. "Dan Buski for Wetzon again. He called twice already."

"Now look at that adorable man, will you, Wetzon?" Smith said, hand on hip. "Doesn't he look absolutely *smashing* today?"

Wetzon nodded. Smith was impossible. She always made a big deal over how chic Max was when they both knew that Max, in his brown suit and gum-soled shoes, was no fashion plate. Today he was wearing

bull-and-bear braces that pulled his pants all the way to what little
chest he had. After Max closed the door, Wetzon shook her head at
Smith. "You're incorrigible."

Smith ignored her. "Dan Buski, huh? He's on the Director's Coun-
cil at Smith Barney. That means his gross production is over seven
hundred and seventy thou."

"Yes, I filed him in the 'unlikely' file; a retail broker, and he's
practically an institution there." Wetzon smiled at her joke.

Smith looked at her blankly, without a show of amusement.

"Hello, earth to Smith, we have two kinds of brokers on the street,
retail and institutional. We deal with retail. Dan's a retail broker. Get
it?"

"Yes, but it's not funny." She motioned to Wetzon. "Why don't you
just pick up the phone and make us rich, sugar."

Wetzon threw up her hands, then picked up the phone and tapped
in Dan's number. "Dan, how are you?" she began, putting a happy
smile in her voice. She sat down at her desk and pulled out a clean
suspect sheet, writing his name on the top.

"Great, Wetzon." Dan Buski had a voice that lived and breathed
Brooklyn, but he was a Harvard graduate with a degree in philosophy.
"It's been a while since we talked."

"Don't tell me you're getting the itch to see what's out there. Actually, it's a good time to test the water. The deals are extraordinary."

"I know what's out there, Wetzon, and it's no better or worse than
what's here. Believe me, it's not perfect here either, but no place is
perfect and I've got a ton of deferred comp. I'd be crazy to move and
leave that on the table. No. I hate to disappoint you, but I'm not calling
for myself. I'm calling for Barbie Sloane. Do you remember her?"

The name Barbie Sloane conjured up murderous thoughts in
Wetzon's mind. Four years ago she had held Barbie's hand and listened
to her problems with her alcoholic parents, her abusive husband, her
branch office manager, her physical trainer, and her therapist. She had
introduced Barbie to Jerry Elias, a manager at Loeb Dawkins, who was
hot to hire her. He had wined her and dined her and arranged for her

to meet all the important department heads at Loeb Dawkins. Barbie gave him a commitment for four weeks hence.

A week later Jerry Elias had called Wetzon and reamed her out. Barbie, it seemed, had joined Loeb Dawkins, but in another branch office with a different branch office manager.

"But, Jerry, I didn't do it," Wetzon had protested. "I'm just as shocked as you are. Eighteen thousand dollars has just been ripped from my hand."

When she'd called Barbie to get an explanation, Barbie told her, "You understand, this is business, Wetzon. I made a business decision." She had gone as a package deal with another broker for more money than Jerry could offer her, and the headhunter who'd put the package together was none other than Tom Keegen.

"Oh, yes, Dan," Wetzon said. "I remember Barbie Sloane very well."

"Well, she'd like you to call her."

"I don't think so, Dan."

"Do it as a favor for me, Wetzon. She's changed a lot. My wife and I are good friends of hers. We met her through the Delphi." The Delphi was one of those EST-type organizations that had recently sprung up across the country emphasizing spirituality.

Sure, Wetzon thought. Spirituality on Wall Street. Perfect. She said, "Why doesn't she pick up the phone and call me?"

"She's worried about confidentiality. She thinks they're checking her outgoing calls. Her trailing twelve months come to about six hundred fifty thousand now. She wants to talk. She's waiting for your call."

Wetzon repressed a groan. "Okay, Dan." She wrote down Barbie's direct number, then hung up. Smith was looking at her expectantly. "Barbie Sloane," Wetzon said in disgust.

"Bitch. Major bitch. Rot in hell, bitch."

"I know. I think I'll pass, if you don't mind. Let her work with someone else."

"What's her gross?"

"Six hundred fifty thou." A long, pregnant pause followed while they stared at one another. Then Wetzon picked up the phone and punched in Barbie's number. "We are whores," she told Smith. "Thirty-nine-thousand-dollar whores."

"Filthy rich ones," Smith said.

"Barbie Sloane," the voice on the phone said.

"Hi, Barbie, Leslie Wetzon." This time she did not decorate her words with a smile. That would be too much.

"Oh, I can't talk to you right now, Wetzon. I've got no sales assistant and I'm doing everything myself. My old one went to Oppie for a lot more money. I suppose I could have kept her if I kicked in some money, but why should I? They hired a new one for me, but she doesn't start till next week. Call me back in fifteen minutes. Use the name Mrs. Weinberg; otherwise, they'll know who you are."

"It'll have to be tomorrow, then, because I'm heading out for a meeting."

"I'll be here till nine tonight. I have a dinner meeting with a client and then I'm coming back to the office. I have to set up a seminar, and I have to do it all by myself. Call me after your meeting. Around eight-thirty."

"I may not be able to, Barbie. Let's leave it for tomorrow." *Bitch.*

"Listen, Wetzon, I know we had a problem before, but it was a business decision you would have made in my place—"

Wetzon held the phone away from her ear and stared at it. Everyone in this business was into self-justification.

"—and I've changed. I don't drink or smoke or do drugs anymore. I'm a Certified Financial Planner now. I work with wrap fees and very-high-net-worth individuals. Lawyers and accountants send me their clients."

"Dan speaks highly of you."

"Dan's a good friend. My best friend. I pray for him." Barbie paused, then hurried on, "I don't necessarily want to move. They treat me very well here. They send me around the country to talk to brokers. It'll take a lot of money to get me to move, but I have to know what's out there, what I'm worth."

Wetzon longed to say, *You're worth shit, Barbie,* but she didn't. Instead, she said, "Fine, Barbie. I'll call you later." She broke the connection. "Talking to that woman is like talking to a fist. And it's in my face."

Smith smiled. "As I recall, that's the name you gave her four years ago."

"The Fist. Yeah. Perfect." She checked her watch. "Oops, four o'clock. I've got to get out of here."

"Where are you going? I thought we'd have a little drinkie after work today. We never seem to spend any time together anymore, and I miss you."

"Can't tonight. Meeting on the *Combinations, in Concert* benefit at Mort Hornberg's office, then dinner with Silvestri."

Smith made a face. "He can't walk in Alton Pinkus's shoes."

"I wouldn't want him to." Wetzon got her coat from the closet, picked up the phone and called Marissa Peiser, got her voice mail— good—and left a message.

"I'm afraid," Smith persisted, "you'll regret your decision, sweetie. I still don't understand how you can reject a successful, wealthy, powerful man like Alton Pinkus for the likes of an Italian cop."

"Drop it, Smith. I will never regret my decision. And if I were you, I would distance myself from Richard Hartmann as quickly as possible, before his trial begins." Two could play at the I-don't-see-what-you-see-in-your-lover game.

"Oh, pooh, there isn't going to be a trial. Dickie has too many connections. It's all political, you know. He's being framed."

"Framed, sure."

"But I did want to talk to you about something personal. I need some advice."

"In a hurry?" That would be the day, that Smith would take advice from Wetzon.

"It can wait. How about dinner tomorrow?"

"Fine. I'm off." Wetzon buttoned her coat and left their room. Max was on the phone doing an interview. Darlene was also on the phone, obviously talking to a broker. Wetzon stopped to listen.

"Of course," Darlene said, "if you were anxious to leave, we would think you had a problem. We only want to talk to *happy* brokers."

Smiling, Wetzon thought, Couldn't have said it better myself. Harold Alpert had done a good job with Darlene. Wetzon waved and left the office. A rush of cold air hit her face; every nerve tingled. She loved winter in New York.

Their doormat was askew, and she stopped to straighten it with the toe of her shoe, dislodging something shiny caught in the mat's bristles. Bending, she plucked it up and rolled it in her palm.

It was an odd-shaped lump of lead, streaked with bits of copper.

MEMORANDUM

To: Carlos Prince and Leslie Wetzon
From: Nancy Stein, Assistant to Mort Hornberg
Date: November 15, 1994
Re: *Combinations, in Concert*

The sizes JoJo wants for the orchestra platforms are not
standard sizes, according to Paradiso Music. I've told him to
talk to you, but both Mort and I feel JoJo should work with
our parameters, given that Paradiso is only charging us
$400, which is a 50% discount.

Chapter Seven

"LESLIE? THIS IS NANCY STEIN. ABOUT THE MEMO I SENT YOU AND Carlos . . ."

"I was going to call you. We heartily agree with Mort that we should work within the least costly parameters. What's wrong with standard sizes?"

"JoJo said the look would be better."

"I guess JoJo thinks this is all about the orchestra. I personally think it's all about dancing. I'm sure Medora thinks it's all about the book . . . oh, forget it. We vote for standard sizes."

NEW YORK WAS A WALKING CITY. SOMETIMES IT SEEMED THAT THE WHOLE Island of Manhattan trembled under the striding feet of its inhabitants and the strolling feet of tourists, who came in droves from around the world to see the sights and rub elbows with New Yorkers. Everyone walked, women especially. Corporate women and secretaries, doctors, receptionists, all wore the ubiquitous white walking shoes and white socks over panty hose. Legs were lean and taut. Bottom desk drawers all over the City were receptacles for business shoes, to be slipped into on arrival in the office.

At this time of year Wetzon normally enjoyed a brisk walk clear across town to Broadway, but finding what might have been left of a real bullet after she'd seen the groove in Darlene's fur hat disturbed her.

The sudden volley of calls from Marissa Peiser, who was working on the money-laundering case against Richard Hartmann, and from Arthur Margolies, Wetzon's own lawyer, none of which she'd responded to, made her uneasy. Peiser had promised to try to keep her out of it, but—there were so many buts.

And there was also the eerie skeleton in the trunk. And the restraining order. Her mind roiled.

She was not enjoying her walk.

When she passed Steve Sondheim's house a block away from her office, she automatically tipped her beret and made a sweeping bow, sending him her respectful obeisance, before continuing on.

In front of every office building on Madison Avenue, a small straggle of smokers stood shivering over their cigarettes. The no-smoking laws had driven them out onto the sidewalks, so they could add to the pollution of the streets.

Paul Stuart, where the best of Wall Street bought its pinstripes and white shirts, not to mention the rest of the wardrobe, had wooden turkeys sporting cashmere scarves in its window, subtly reminding everyone that if Thanksgiving was upon us, could Christmas be far behind? A derelict was using the side window with its rich display of cashmere sweaters as a mirror, adjusting his moth-eaten tweed sport coat, smoothing his filthy khakis, turning sideways, frontways, making runway model overtures to his image.

No one paid attention or even gave his madness a wide berth. It was the theatricality of the whole performance that drew Wetzon's attention. It was what Laura Lee Day, transplanted Mississippian in New York, referred to as a New York Moment.

MORT HORNBERG KEPT A SMALL OFFICE ON THE SEVENTH FLOOR OF THE SARDI Building on West Forty-fourth Street, in the heart of the Theatre District.

She was not looking forward to this meeting. Carlos had promised her that she would have very little to do with Mort, but promises, promises . . .

From where Wetzon stood waiting for the light to change, she could see the marquee of the Palace Theatre, just a few blocks uptown, where Disney's *Beauty and the Beast* (the musical) was still running to the chagrin of the not always silent theatre community. Considered a don't-worry-about-the-cost retread of the movie, hyped out of sight by buckets of Disney money, *Beauty and the Beast* was spurned by the Tony voters in 1994, the year it was nominated. The show displeased everyone, it seemed, but an audience that did not normally attend theatre—these days, most of the world. Even those few for whom theatregoing was a family tradition had been driven away by exorbitant ticket prices. And those who paid the tab wanted to be dazzled with the spectacular for their money. *Beauty and the Beast* was flourishing, playing to packed houses every night.

Across Broadway on Forty-fifth Street, at the Minskoff, was *Sunset Boulevard,* yet another Andrew Lloyd Webber extravaganza, this time of an American film classic. It was a raging success, but Wetzon's Theatre friends were very ambivalent about Webber and his pageants. He had thrust himself down Broadway's collective throats and made them grudgingly accept him because he brought in big audiences and, therefore, big money.

But they'd drawn the line at Disney. The circus atmosphere at *Beauty and the Beast* was created by Mickey Mouse's great merchandisers. You had clothing, records, books, ad nauseam, hawked at you from entrance to seat.

At the Shubert, *Crazy for You* was still limping along, attracting audiences, and across from the Sardi Building, *Kiss of the Spider Woman* played on, the title role going from Chita to Vanessa to Maria Conchita. Farther west, the beautiful old St. James was still home to *Tommy,* although it wasn't playing to full houses anymore.

The changing times on Broadway were one of the reasons there was so much interest in *Combinations, in Concert,* which was part of the old Broadway, a time when ticket prices were affordable and new plays were rarely overproduced to please a show-me audience paying between seventy-five and eighty-five dollars a ticket. A price that theatre people themselves—performers, the production staffs, and theatre owners—would never pay.

The walls of Mort Hornberg's reception area were covered with posters of every show he'd worked on; hit or flop, each had its place without apology. There were two knobless doors in the far wall, both tightly closed. In fact, the room seemed vacuum-sealed, probably because Mort loathed being bearded in his den. Once, legend had it, he had to be cajoled and threatened before he would come out of his office and shake hands with an investor who had just written him a check for a hundred thousand dollars.

Sitting at a small desk talking to herself was a young woman, her neck tilted at an odd angle under a curtain of long blond hair. She moved her head to look at Wetzon, her hair shifted, and a tiny phone appeared wedged between shoulder and neck. "Well, I'm sorry," she said into the phone, all the while munching on sunflower seeds from a Baggie. A blue-bound script lying open on the desk was peppered with pieces of the shells. "Ah, sure." The young woman affected an upper-crust British accent. "Would you care to leave a message. He's just not in the office right now." She lifted a corner of the script, scattering the detritus, and wrested from beneath it a pad of message slips. After jotting down the message, she extracted the phone from the curtain of hair and hung it up.

It was a performance easily as fascinating as the derelict's in front of Paul Stuart's window.

"I'm Leslie Wetzon," Wetzon said.

"Yes?" There was not even a glimmer of recognition in the woman's eye.

"The four o'clock meeting about *Combinations, in Concert*. Would you tell Nancy I'm here?"

"What did you say your name was?"

"Leslie Wetzon."

The young woman picked up the phone and pressed a button. "There's a Leslie Watson here for a four o'clock meeting." Her English accent had slipped badly. She managed to sound like a poor imitation Billie Dawn.

One of the vacuum-sealed doors opened and Nancy rushed out, her shoulder-length earrings quivering. "Oh, Leslie, you're early! Mort's still in an important meeting and Carlos isn't here yet."

Everything quivered on Nancy, except her hair, which couldn't because it was in a buzz cut. She wore a long black skirt that quivered to mid-calf, black high-heeled boots, and a black lace bustier, from which her bosoms quivered under a belted black cardigan. In her hand —red nails two inches long—a large black looseleaf binder quivered.

She was an exclamation point in every way.

"Is there a place I can make some phone calls?" Wetzon asked.

"Of course." Nancy gave Wetzon a lip-quivering smile. "You can use my desk." She swept Wetzon through the door and pulled it closed behind them—there was, Wetzon noticed, an inside knob—until they heard a dull click. "Do you want coffee or something? A diet soda? The fridge is in there. Help yourself. I'll be in the back room. I have to check some figures for Mort."

"I'll be fine," Wetzon said. She felt a certain amount of sympathy for Nancy. She'd replaced the cool-headed Sunny Browning, who was now producing her own shows, as Mort's assistant. Working for Mort, juggling his demands, his moods, his abuse, would surely make even the sanest person quiver.

She sat down at Nancy's desk, picked up the phone, and called Silvestri, waiting a long time till he came on the line. As she told him about Darlene and the lump of lead, she could literally hear him growling. When she finished, he said, "Jeezus, Les, why didn't you report it right away, when it happened?" He sounded hassled and impatient.

"Because, dammit, I just found this thing fifteen minutes ago . . . accidentally. It popped out of the doormat when I moved it." Why did he always make her feel as if she'd done something wrong?

"But the hat—"

"It might not have been a bullet, and Darlene is a little paranoid."

"I'll have Metzger call you when I can get hold of him." Artie Metzger was Silvestri's old partner at the Seventeenth, the precinct under whose jurisdiction Wetzon's office fell.

"I'm not in my office. I'm at Mort Hornberg's."

"Then you call Metzger. Gotta go, Les—"

"Silvestri, wait. When will you be home tonight?"

"Late." The phone crashed in her ear.

"Yeah, good-bye, sweetie, honey, darling," she said, cradling the phone. So much for dinner. Next incarnation, no cops, please. But Silvestri's late night meant she would have the evening to herself, which wasn't all bad. She was looking forward to reading *The Waterworks*, the Doctorow book that she'd picked up yesterday in paperback.

Nancy's desk was in obsessive order. Projects were lined up in individual wire baskets, each in a black binder, each labeled. A stationery box was marked COMBINATIONS, PHOTOS. A computer equipped for CD-ROM, complete with speakers, sat on an extension perpendicular to the desk. It had a blue screen and hummed. The perfect accessory for a musical director's office.

Wetzon rose and checked her watch. Carlos should be here any minute. There was no sound from behind the closed door she presumed led to Mort's office. Intrigued, she put her hand on the knob—she could always excuse herself—and opened it a crack, just enough to see Mort lying on his back on a red leather sofa, his mouth open, sound asleep. She suppressed a giggle and closed the door.

The walls around Nancy's desk were covered with framed photographs taken in the course of all the different shows. She saw pictures of Mort *sans* the beard, when he still had hair on his head, before he'd begun wearing his signature cap. There were several shots from *Combinations* rehearsals. A very young Leslie Wetzon in tights and leg warmers, Rog Battle's arm slung over her shoulders. The cast party in Boston, everyone looking tired but happy, for the reviews had been wonderful. Terri and Mort puckering up for the camera. Rog and Medora, Medora's hands gesticulating, the light catching on her hammered-gold bracelet. Foxy at the piano with Rog and Davey and some of the company. Others in the background. Carlos doing the drum number. A cast photo, posed, with everyone holding a prop. Rog and Medora conferring with Davey over some plot change, Medora looking haggard.

Wetzon sat down at the desk again and called Arthur. Those days were thrilling to look back on, but thrills, from her experience, never came free.

"Arthur Margolies." Arthur's calm, reassuring voice flowed over the phone lines.

"Arthur, I'm glad I caught you."

"Caught, nothing, Leslie. I'll be here at least half the evening."

"Oh, good. I'm widowed, too, tonight, so your young man and I will console ourselves with each other somewhere nice."

Arthur laughed, then paused, cleared his throat. Uh-oh, she thought, here it comes.

"Leslie, something's come up with the Hartmann case."

"I figured, Arthur. Peiser has been trying to get me. What is it?" Why was she asking? Didn't she know? Didn't she feel it in her bones? Bones. No, she didn't want to think about bones now. Hartmann had threatened her. That was enough to cause the shudder that ran through her.

"Yes, well," Arthur said, "I'm afraid you're going to have to testify before a grand jury."

MEMORANDUM

To: Carlos Prince and Leslie Wetzon
From: Nancy Stein, Assistant to Mort Hornberg
Date: November 15, 1994
Re: *Combinations, in Concert*

Enclosed is a copy of the agreement with Boomer, Inc., for them to supply the sound equipment for the period of one week. Rental charges are $8000, plus labor, $850, on pairs of four crews, with additional labor billed at 10% net.

Chapter Eight

"Boomer, Inc.? What's that?" Carlos frowned over the latest memo.

"A sound company, I guess. You would know more about this than I would. Is it a new company?"

"Very new, methinks. I wonder if it's one of those companies that some producers set up with inventory so that they can rent their own productions sound equipment and lighting equipment and make the money on both ends."

Mort Hornberg sat up and rubbed his eyes. "Leslie, darling, where's Carlos?" He reached into his pocket, sprayed his mouth from a small container, then got to his feet and gave her a kiss.

"Important conference, Mort? Cannot be disturbed? Let the peons cool their heels."

"I need my beauty sleep," Mort said plaintively, smoothing his jeans and adjusting the contents of his Jockeys.

"Don't tell me the heir's keeping you up late," Carlos said. He was holding a Diet Coke, leaning elegantly against the doorjamb, one leg crossed over the other. "Hi, gorgeous." He gave Wetzon a sultry wink.

"No, not little Maudie." Mort shook his head. Maudie was his two-month-old daughter. "Maudie's wonderful. It's Poppy. She's driving me nuts. I thought if she had a kid, she wouldn't nag me about staying home and talking to her." He screwed up his baby blues, looked from Wetzon to Carlos, and said with all seriousness, "Don't ever get married, pallies."

Carlos rolled his eyes at Wetzon.

"Where's Nancy?" Mort hollered, changing the subject. He took his seat at his desk and threw his legs up on it. Nancy materialized behind Carlos. She was still fused to her black binder. "Oh, there you are," Mort said. "Get me some of my stuff, there's a good girl."

Wetzon said to Nancy, "You take care of Mort and I'll do me."

She followed Nancy into a tiny closet kitchen compact with cabinets, counters, microwave, two electric burners, a small sink, and a full refrigerator with an icemaker.

"The club soda?"

"In the fridge." Nancy poured a dark viscous liquid into a glass.

"Don't tell me he's still drinking that crap—what's it called again?" She grinned at Wetzon without quivering. "Fernet Branca."

"Right. He always called it his Jewish boy stuff."

They returned to Mort's office exchanging conspiratorial smiles. Mort still had his feet up on his ormolu Louis someteenth or other desk. Carlos was stretched out on the sofa.

The women took the red leather chairs. Opening her black binder, Nancy started writing.

Good grief, Wetzon thought, no one had even started talking yet.

"Okay, gang." Mort took a swig of the Fernet Branca, grimaced, and patted his lips. "Let's go over everything. Is the company set?"

"Everyone but Terri Matthews. No one knows where she is," Wetzon said. "I even called some dancing schools in Cincinnati. No one there knows her."

"Oh, she'll turn up," Mort said, waving his hand in dismissal. "There's going to be a big story about us in New York magazine. Wanna bet she surfaces?"

"Yeah, but it's too late now. I spoke with Vicki Howard this morning," Carlos said. "Vicki did it on the road. She was thrilled, as you would be if you were married to an accountant and living in New Jersey with four kids under the age of ten."

Mort laughed. "Good. Cast's complete. Nancy will work out a

schedule for the week we have them. I'm cleaning my calendar for the whole week."

"I should hope so, Mort," Wetzon said. Mort was notorious for saying he'd do something and then chiseling away time. Over the last few years he'd developed the habit of leaving a show in progress early and letting his assistant—whoever that might be—do the work.

"Don't be such a smart-ass, Leslie. I always keep my promises," he said defensively, brushing the dandruff from the shoulders of his pale blue cashmere. "You stay on top of the company, and I'll give you a show."

Wetzon bristled. He really thought what he did was more important than what anyone else did. She watched Nancy's nose practically press the pages of the black binder. The woman's forefingers were faintly jaundiced. She was a closet smoker.

"Maybe Nancy can send out a nice thank-you to each cast member confirming dates and schedules," Wetzon said.

Nancy nodded. "I have one prepared. I figured I'd send them all out at the same time."

"Next on the agenda: Joel Baby thinks he has some interest from Gary Kaminsky for a TV documentary. What do we think? It could be very attractive."

Joel Baby was Joel Kidde, Mort's agent, Carlos's ex-agent, who probably represented most of the gorillas whose jungle was Broadway. Carlos had fired Joel after *Hotshot: The Musical* opened last year.

It was the only thing Carlos and Smith had ever agreed on: that it was a conflict of interest for one agent to represent several, sometimes all, of the conflicting creative talent and even the producers on a Broadway show. Yet it happened all the time.

"Do you mean attractive for us or for Show Biz Shares?" Wetzon asked.

Mort didn't respond. He leaned back in his chair and contemplated his Tonys, which sat on a shelf to his right. He looked as if he was counting them. He probably was.

"I thought—" Carlos sat up. "I thought we weren't in this for the money."

Mort smiled sheepishly. "The TV people will reimburse Show Biz Shares for all costs."

"Okay," Carlos said.

"Listen to this, darlings." To emphasize how serious he was, Mort took his Gucci loafers off the desk and sat up. "They'd like two free airings. After that, they'll pay a percentage of all earnings to Show Biz Shares."

"A percentage? What kind of percentage?" Wetzon asked. She was waiting for the other shoe to drop. With Mort, the other shoe always dropped.

"Fifty-fifty. We—the three of us—will get ten percent collectively of their fifty."

Clunk. There was the other shoe. "That's disgusting, Mort. They should take ten or fifteen percent and the rest should go to Show Biz Shares. We shouldn't take anything out of this. This isn't about making a profit."

"I agree with Birdie," Carlos said in a voice like steel.

THEY HAD DINNER NEAR LINCOLN CENTER AT PICHOLINE—WHERE THE MENU was Mediterranean and the décor country French with a dash of so-phistication—having agreed not to comment on Mort's revolting be-havior until the California Cabernet Sauvignon had breathed enough to be tasted.

Finally, after a long sip, Carlos drawled, "I do believe, Dear Heart, that Mort and your partner have something in common."

"In common? Are you kidding? Mort's just like Smith. We're going to have to watch him and the Exclamation Point—Nancy—carefully." She picked at the picholine olives, then broke off a chunk of focaccia and dipped it into the olive marinade and demolished it. To the waiter she said, "I'll have six bluepoints, the halibut, and a green salad."

"Sounds good to me," Carlos said.

After the waiter left, Wetzon asked, "What do you suppose she keeps in that black binder?"

"Maybe she's got an assignment from the *Observer* to write a dishy exposé on all this."

"Well, she certainly writes a good memorandum, but does she have to keep telling us she's Mort's assistant? What could be in that black binder."

"Let's steal it and find out." Carlos gave a good imitation of the Shadow's laugh, and they were still laughing two hours later in the cab driving uptown. When they reached Eighty-sixth Street, Carlos paid the driver and they both got out. "I'm going to walk the rest of the way," he said. "I need the air." He kissed her on the cheek, giving her a bear hug. "Nighty-night, Birdie."

"Wait, Carlos." They stopped in front of her building, where the night doorman, Mario, was flirting with 2A's teenage daughter. "Didn't Terri Matthews live in the Village?"

"I don't know." He wrinkled his brow. "Come to think of it, I used to run into Terri at Balducci's." Although he'd been living with Arthur on West End Avenue for years, Carlos still owned and rented out his loft on West Tenth Street. "I remember I walked her home once. She had two huge shopping bags of food. She lived around the corner from me, somewhere on Eleventh Street."

MEMORANDUM

To: Carlos Prince and Leslie Wetzon
From: Nancy Stein, Assistant to Mort Hornberg
Date: November 16, 1994
Re: *Combinations, in Concert*

A coup: Marty Richards is going to let us use the backdrop
from the revival of *It's a Bird . . . It's a Plane . . . It's
Superman,* which will still be in the Richard Rodgers before
it loads out for the road on December 26th.

Chapter Nine

"How about that, Birdie? Isn't that a great backdrop?"

"I hate to tell you this, Carlos, but I've never seen the show. It was way before my time. Actually, I was a child when that show was first done on Broadway."

"Ha! You were never a child. But take it from me, it had a wonderful backdrop of the City skyline."

She didn't know what woke her. The elevator maybe, or a car alarm. A siren. Whatever it was, she was wide-awake. She stretched and looked at her clock. Two-thirty. Silvestri was lying on his side, turned away from her, Izz curled up in the small of his back like a fur hot-water bottle.

The whole apartment smelled like an Italian kitchen, of garlic and sausage. Silvestri had come in late, and in a much-improved mood, with a greasy bag of calzones from John's.

He grunted in his sleep. Amazing. Two calzones—he'd brought the second for her and she'd wisely refused—and two beers and all he did was grunt in his sleep. She would have had lunatic dreams and would have been wide-awake at two-thirty. So now what was her excuse?

She leaned over and kissed the back of his neck and inhaled the sexy mixture of sweat and garlic. When he didn't move, she eased herself out of bed.

Winter intruded through the two inches of open window with explosive little wind gusts from the north that rattled the wooden blinds.

Izz raised her head, looked at Wetzon, debated whether it was worth disturbing herself, then snuggled deeper against Silvestri.

Taking the Doctorow into the living room, Wetzon situated herself under the afghan she and Carlos had crocheted backstage during the run of *Chicago*, and the custody of which they now shared. The words danced on the page, broke up, came back. But when she closed her eyes, the trunk appeared and she was wide-awake again.

So that was it. She'd been trying all afternoon, all evening, to drive it from her mind, but it wasn't working. It had nudged her awake and now wouldn't let her sleep.

She rose, wrapping the afghan around her, and got a glass of water, drinking it slowly as she stood in the open space at the entrance to her living-dining room. She loved this room with its earth colors and Stickley pieces and the old sunburst quilt wall-mounted over the sofa.

Silvestri's attaché was on the floor next to the marble-top table. She sat down on the rug and laid the case flat. When she opened it, the manila envelope with the crime scene photos was right on top of his clean shirts in their laundry package.

She opened the clasp and slipped out the photos. Gruesome. She felt like a voyeur. Yet, she couldn't put them down. She shuffled through them slowly as if looking for something. She didn't know what.

Each photo was labeled EVIDENCE, CRIME SCENE UNIT, with a case number; at the bottom, an M (for what? Murder? Mayhem? No, more likely, for Manhattan), the date, and a centimeter scale.

The trunk again, closed. Open. Another photo of the open trunk, this time minus the bones. Clothing, rotted. A photo of the items from the trunk, each laid out and numbered. She looked at these closely. What was this? It looked like a jagged piece of ceramic tile. On the edge of the break, and above it, in script, the letters *To*. It was a long time before she could move.

Finally, Wetzon got to her feet and padded over to the floor-to-ceiling bookcases. She had a flea market antique magnifying glass, which she never used, somewhere on one of the shelves. Ah, there. She picked it up and brought the photo to the dining table. Laying it flat under the light, she held the magnifying glass over it. Her hand shook. *Someone who didn't know would not recognize it in the condition it was in. . . .* She had because she had one just like it.

She was shivering when she returned the magnifying glass to the bookshelf. Then the search was on. She found what she was looking for two shelves down and one over, took it off its stand, and brought it back to the table. She placed it next to the photo.

It was a ceramic tile with the *Playbill* cover, the bright magenta logo of *Combinations*. Davey Lewin, the director, had given everyone in the cast one of these with a personal inscription.

Wetzon's said: *To Leslie, a miracle of combinations, with love from Davey.*

MEMORANDUM

To: Carlos Prince and Leslie Wetzon
From: Nancy Stein, Assistant to Mort Hornberg
Date: November 16, 1994
Re: *Combinations, in Concert*

Attached is a copy of the revised budget, which includes worst-case scenario for box office. It doesn't include anything for sound and light rental.

Chapter Ten

"SEE," CARLOS SAID, "I'M RIGHT. MORT IS RENTING US BACK HIS EQUIPMENT."

"Well, I don't know, m'love. That would be really weaselly if it were true. If he owns the stuff, the least he can do is donate it to this production."

"Don't count on it, Birdie."

"Oh, yeah? Well, don't think I'm not going to bring it up at the next meeting."

"LET'S DO IT," TERRI SAID.

"We have less than an hour." Leslie Wetzon, girl dancer, slipped her feet out of her tap shoes and flexed them, then put on her Keds.

"But we're so close. Come on." Terri grabbed her hand and they ran down three flights of stairs to the stage door.

Rain, billowed by the wind like sheets on a clothesline, swept Tremont Street. It rained like that in Boston more than anywhere else, at least it seemed that way to Leslie, who was a veteran of two Boston openings, both road companies. *Combinations* would be her third and the first headed for Broadway.

They'd been rehearsing for ten hours straight, stopping only for the breaks required by Equity. The tech had dragged on and on until everyone—cast, creators, production team, even the stagehands—was cross-eyed with fatigue. Tempers were dangerously short. JoJo and Rog Battle had almost come to blows because JoJo kept giving the sing signal at the wrong moment and killing a laugh. It was JoJo's first show as conductor–musical director, and his mentor was Foxy Reynard, the composer-lyricist. Not a bad mentor for a rehearsal pianist to have. Foxy had spotted JoJo on his motorcycle—he looked like one of Hell's Angels, tattoos and all—on her last show and plucked him out of oblivion. She had made him part of her deal. Joined at the crotch, Carlos said.

Surprise, surprise, Foxy came down on JoJo's side in the squabble between JoJo and Rog. Davey, that rare director who never seemed to get tired or flustered, had rushed in and called a break. Which was why Leslie and Terri were standing at the stage door at the tail end of the performers' stampede from the theatre for the local eateries. The long hours and the tension always stimulated actors' appetites.

Ohio-born and -bred, Terri Matthews had the golden glow some lucky blondes are born with and, even more lucky, keep as adults. It was as if there were a pale light under her poreless skin. A tiny dusting of freckles crossed her snub nose. She was fresh and pretty, and oddly sexy. Leslie had seen JoJo's eye rove to Terri, but nothing had happened, at least not as far as Leslie knew.

They flew through flooded streets, gazelles leaping puddles, dancers released. Soaked to the skin and laughing, they arrived at Filene's and squeezed past those shoppers gathered under the awning on Washington Street to keep dry. They made for the basement.

After a fast tour, up and down the aisles, they began to pick at the racks, holding clothes on hangers up against themselves, waiting for the other to comment. Terri found an ivory silk suit, very fitted, trying the jacket on over her leotard.

"What do you think?" she demanded.

Tilting her head, Leslie said, "Beautiful. But ivory? I'd never have the guts to wear something like that."

Terri gave her a rueful smile. "I never say never anymore. Besides, I might have a special occasion to wear it."

"Hey, you and Peter have decided—" Peter Koenig was an actor and Terri's most consistent boyfriend.

Terri said no more, but looked I've-got-a-secret mysterious.

They went back to rehearsal, stopping only once to pick up burgers and Cokes, Terri with her ivory silk suit, Leslie with a blow-the-budget Chanel suit—one small tear in the lining—in the same magenta as the *Combinations* logo.

At the stage door of the Shubert, Terri turned to her, glowing, and said, "God, that was fun, wasn't it?"

Tears rolled down Wetzon's cheeks. "Yes, it was fun, Terri," she murmured. "A hell of a lot of fun." *Combinations* had been a critical hit; they'd been comrades through the wars, all of the company. Then they all got swept up in the business and other shows and lost track of one another. Wetzon took her tile and the photos and curled up on the sofa.

She stared at the photograph of the skull and the bones in the trunk. How could this have happened? But wait, maybe it wasn't Terri at all and she was jumping to the wrong conclusion. Then Terri's husky voice surrounded her. *Didn't anyone miss me?*

In a business where careers came before mates, friends, and children? Well, not very likely.

Terri had told everyone out of the blue that she was going back to Cincinnati to open a dancing school. Which was probably where she was right now. Wetzon tissued the tears from her face, but the dread and the guilt she couldn't blot away.

Having turned so deeply inward, she didn't hear the *click, click, click* on the wood floor and was shocked when, ready or not, she had Izz, the white fur ball, in her lap joyously licking her face. The tile flew from her hand and hit the floor with a smack like the crack of a rifle. Izz shuddered. In slow motion, like the opening of a flower, the tile began to splinter from the center outward, till its face became a mass of spidery lines.

"What the hell was that?" Silvestri said. He stood where the hallway met the living room. "It's three o'clock and you're—"

She looked at him in his Jockeys, barefoot, hair on end, and waves of laughter clogged her throat. Then, without warning, the tears came.

"Les?" He was sitting beside her, holding her. "You want to tell me what's going on?"

She leaned against him; the urge to laugh was utterly gone. She could never remember feeling so desolate. Izz got off the sofa and sniffed at the shattered tile on the floor, circling it.

"That's what woke you," she said. "Izz knocked it out of my hand."

"Did you have that dream again?" Silvestri said, dismissing the tile.

"No." Two years had passed since she'd been shot, and she'd suffered post-traumatic-stress disorder. With therapy, she rarely now relived the moment in her dreams. "I couldn't sleep. I was thinking about the girl in the trunk."

Silvestri's eyes went to his attaché on the floor, open. "It's my fault. I should never have brought you into this. Come on back to bed." He pulled her up, but she shook him off and bent to inspect the tile.

The entire face had cracked, but when she nudged it with her finger, it didn't separate.

"Look at it, Silvestri. Then look at the crime scene photo with the items lined up, from the inside of the trunk, I guess." She sighed and went into the kitchen, took a metal spatula from a drawer, and returned. Silvestri was crouched, looking at her tile. She said, "You were right to bring me into this." She slipped the spatula gently under the tile and lifted it, holding the overlap in her palm.

Silvestri rummaged in his attaché and pulled out one of his freshly laundered shirts. Removing the cardboard, he dropped the shirt back into the case. "Put it on this, Les."

Wetzon nudged the tile onto the cardboard and set it on the dining room table, then retrieved her magnifying glass and the photo.

"Show me," Silvestri said.

"This is why you were right to bring me into it. Davey Lewin gave each of us a tile with the logo of the show and an inscription. I'm not sure anyone would have spotted this, Silvestri, except someone from the original company of *Combinations*."

"What does this have to do with *Combinations*?" He was looking through the magnifying glass at the photograph. In a moment he would see what she saw.

"Look at this and now look at my tile." She watched him; the moment came quickly.

He set the magnifying glass on the photograph, put his hands on her shoulders, her back, stroking her. She let him take her back to bed.

After a time she said, "We've been looking for her, for the concert performance. No one's seen her or heard from her in years. It's awful that this could happen." She was suddenly extremely tired, as if someone had pumped oatmeal into her veins. She pressed her cheek against his chest. "We are all to blame for this."

"Okay, you think you know her, but why don't we wait till Nina checks it out?"

"Maybe it's all a big mistake. She could have given the tile to someone." But even as she suggested it, Wetzon knew that was highly unlikely. Actors, especially dancers, clung to memorabilia. Sometimes memorabilia were all they had.

"Who was she, Les?"

She chewed her lip. Giving a name to the bones would make it so. "She was one of the dancers in the show. We were roommates on the road, sat next to each other in the dressing room. Her name was Terri Matthews."

MEMORANDUM

To: Carlos Prince and Leslie Wetzon
From: Nancy Stein, Assistant to Mort Hornberg
Date: November 16, 1994
Re: *Combinations, in Concert*

The rental of the sound equipment will cost $8750, plus an estimated $925 in labor, for a total of $9675. They are not charging us for freight, which is estimated at $3500.

If this is okay with you, please initial and return.

Chapter Eleven

"I'm not initialing this, Carlos, and don't you do it either. No initialing anything till I talk to Mort."

"Your wish is my command, Dear Heart."

At dawn an icy drizzle glazed the City with a brilliant sheen.

She had given Silvestri the names of the original cast and production team—everyone she could think of—and the phone number of her friend Ann Ledley at Actors Equity Association. Silvestri was on the phone talking to Nina Wayne as Wetzon left.

How many people, Wetzon wondered, as she climbed into the waiting car, just drifted out of your life over the years? People you liked —and even disliked—whom you would never see again. Your lives came together intimately for a short time, then separated. You thought about them in passing, if at all. When was the last time she'd thought of Terri?

The family unit—for that's what it was—of a musical came together of necessity. There were usually a mother figure and a father figure. Intimacy was almost instantaneous, especially if the musical went on the road, then it dissolved when the show closed or you left one show for another. And that was understood, accepted.

This morning she was glad for the anonymity of the car service. The driver, young and bearded, wore a small gold crucifix earring dangling from one earlobe. He was intent on jumping traffic lights, racing through the Park. He growled and grunted at the crosstown bus, a

Con Edison truck—parked where else but smack in the middle of Columbus Avenue, where they were excavating a major crater—and general traffic that didn't move fast enough for him.

She wanted to tell him that rushing through your life meant you missed moments of serenity, people you were fond of who were there one moment and gone forever the next. But she didn't. He wouldn't have understood. She looked out the rain-scored window of the car and tried to remember the closing night party of *Combinations* seventeen years ago, the last time they'd gathered together as a family, in Tavern on the Green.

The driver double-parked in front of Smith's building on East Seventy-seventh Street, got out, and talked to the doorman. Smith, of course, was late. It was already seven-thirty, which meant the odds were against their on-time arrival for breakfast. Smith favored the grand, if tardy, entrance, maintaining that the most important people never showed up anywhere on time.

"I could call them and tell them to start without us," Wetzon said, *sotto voce,* when Smith strolled out ten minutes later.

Her partner evil-eyed her from under cocoa-shadowed lids, and flicked a fifty-dollar bill that looked as if it had just been minted at the driver. "This is yours if you get us to the Rosenkind Luwisher Tower across from the World Trade Center in fifteen minutes."

"For godsakes, Smith, what year is this? No one does that anymore. You're insulting the man. He could lose his license."

"Ah, lady," the driver purred, watching Smith in his rearview mirror, "now you talking my language."

From under hooded lids, Smith's eyes were gleaming. A smug smile said it all.

"Without killing us, if you please," Wetzon added as the car shot east to the East River Drive. She could feel herself slipping from fair to foul.

During even a drizzle in New York, gridlock was a given. Traffic backed up the minute streets became wet. Who knew why? No one ever slowed down, and in wet weather fewer walked. Maybe more people used cabs and car services, putting more cars than ever on the clogged streets. Whatever the reason was, the driver didn't get his fifty-dollar tip and Smith and Wetzon were late.

The Rosenkind Luwisher Tower rose some sixty-eight floors, with the brokerage now occupying the top twelve. It had once been Luwisher Brothers' alone, but Luwisher Brothers had not survived the spate of mergers and acquisitions after the '87 Crash and had needed a quick influx of capital. Rosenkind Partners, a group of high-stakes raiders, had furnished the capital and taken over the firm.

"You're dawdling, Wetzon," Smith called. "There's the elevator—grab it."

"Dawdling? Dammit, Smith. Who made us late? Next time I'm taking the subway and I'll meet you."

The elevator was paneled in tufted brown leather and programmed to go directly to the fifty-sixth floor. When they got on, it said, "Good morning. This elevator goes only to Rosenkind Luwisher Brothers. Please choose your floor."

"The usual?" Wetzon asked.

Smith put her gloved finger on the shiny brass square that read 67. "The executive dining room," she said as if in response to the digitized voice. The elevator rose softly like a helium balloon.

When they got out, Wetzon saw nothing much had changed. Oh, yes, maybe the color of the carpet, which was now a pale olive-green, and the walls, which were off-white with a hint of olive. The ambiguous Georgia O'Keeffes were gone. In their place were the distorted visions of Francis Bacon, an artist Mike Rosenkind collected. Rosenkind liked the references to him as a collector of fine art when articles about the firm appeared in *Forbes* and *Fortune*.

The sixty-seventh floor soared into the sixty-eighth, over which a skylight projected a sense of eternity, just the thing for a brokerage firm. Maybe Calvin Klein had stopped by to make a deal and had been inspired.

Where once there had been a real tree that grew hydroponically, reaching up two stories to the skylight, now stood a gigantic Botero sculpture of a chubby man, rear view, naked on a ladder, commissioned by that famed collector of fine art Mike Rosenkind. The sweeping marble staircase where Wetzon had found Carlton Ash's body four years earlier remained as it was.

Under the skylight on the sixty-eighth floor, the executive dining room was circled on three sides by windows overlooking Lower Manhattan and the Financial District. Despite the heavy drizzle, the Statue rose through the mist, her torch a beacon.

Tables were covered in white linen, and the entire atmosphere was subdued and proper, graciously reminiscent of the Old South; the waiters were elderly black men in black suits and white shirts, reminding everyone in the real world that Wall Street, bless its avaricious heart, remained consistently in a time warp.

"This way, please." Neil—managing director—Munchen's assistant —led them to a closed-off section. They saw at once that this wasn't an intimate breakfast.

In the small sea of faces, Wetzon quickly recognized their ex-associate, Harold Alpert, and the tubby little man with him must be . . .

"Tom Keegen," Smith muttered in Wetzon's ear. "Let's go." She tapped Wetzon on the shoulder.

Neil's assistant's eyes widened.

"Wait a minute, Smith. Let's hear what they have to say. It must be important to get us all here like this."

"Come on in, girls. Y'all have your coffee," Doug Culver, one of the managing directors, said. "We'll begin shortly."

"Girls?" Smith looked ready to explode. Wetzon took her arm and steered her to an empty table, which already held a pitcher of orange juice, a pot of fragrant coffee, and a basket of muffins and croissants. "You are not being cool," Wetzon said through a clenched-teeth smile.

A waiter handed them a short menu—pancakes, waffles, eggs, omelets, fruit, and oatmeal.

"I couldn't eat a thing," Smith said. "I would choke."

"Try." Wetzon perused the menu.

"Oh, very well. I'll have the grapefruit sections, the farmer's omelet with a side order of sausage well done, and four pieces of seven-grain bread, well toasted."

Wetzon looked at her partner with amusement. Smith could put food away like a linebacker, do no exercise, and not gain an ounce. "I thought you would choke," she teased. Smith glowered. Wetzon ordered a toasted bagel with cream cheese on the side.

Minutes later, Doug Culver rose. "I want to thank y'all for comin' today on such short notice." He spoke in a slow drawl, which meant if you didn't keep your wits about you, he would stick a knife in your back while spreading Southern charm as seductive as redeye gravy. Thick-waisted, a good ol' Georgia boy, Doug had a placid exterior and slow smile that belied a sharp mind with an uncanny instinct for self-preservation at any cost. Only he and Neil Munchen had survived from the team that ran Luwisher Brothers before the takeover. "I'm sure y'all know each other, so introductions aren't necessary."

Wetzon was looking around when it suddenly struck her that she and Smith were the only women in the room. It was at this point that their breakfast arrived.

"We here at Rosenkind Luwisher Brothers," Doug Culver continued, "as we approach the year 2000, believe that we must position ourselves to take advantage of the changes that will occur on Wall Street. We estimate that there may be perhaps only ten firms that will make it to the end of the twentieth century. We expect to be one of them." He paused here to let all this wonderful information sink in. "With that in mind, we're goin' to do some restructurin'."

Wetzon nudged Smith with the toe of her shoe. "Here it comes," she whispered.

"We feel we have a great story to tell, and if you tell it right and get these guys—from the top firms, of course—down here to talk to us, we can close them."

Right, Wetzon thought. They all said this. Each firm truly believed it was unique. (She had once commented to a Loeb Dawkins manager that basically all of the large firms were the same in what they had to offer brokers. What made the difference was the manager. Unspoken was the fact that managers fell like pins to a bowling ball, as everyone in the industry knew. But this manager had taken exception. "There is no firm on the Street of the quality of Loeb Dawkins," he'd declared. Wetzon had agreed, "You're absolutely right.")

"So," Doug Culver said, "we're goin' to hire an inside recruiter."

The room got so quiet you could hear someone pouring a packet of Sweet'n Low into his coffee.

"What does this mean to us?" The man who spoke had a young face under curly white hair.

"Who's that?" Wetzon asked through a mouthful of bagel.

Smith looked up from her omelet. "Howard Rivkin."

"Oh, that's Howard Rivkin. The brokers like him."

"He's pond scum," Smith snapped. "They all are."

I guess we are, too, Wetzon thought.

"It means," Doug Culver continued, "that y'all won't have to work as hard—"

"Something smells rotten here," Smith muttered. "Since when do they worry about how hard we work? I think they've invited us here to—"

"Cut to the chase, Dougie," Wetzon called. When he looked in her direction, she gave him her most charming smile.

"Ah, Wetzon, I knew I could count on you to keep me from wanderin' off the subject. The net-net is, we are makin' a change in our policy with recruiters."

Wetzon surveyed the room. Everyone was trying not to look at anyone else. It was like the Last Supper, only it was breakfast. A fuck-you breakfast. A cut-off-your-balls breakfast.

"We have given this much thought, as you can imagine—"

"Of course you have," Smith said in a voice dripping with sarcasm.

"And we feel that the six percent you get is too high in these difficult times, so we are goin' to cut your fees."

Smith rose like the Valkyrie. "In your dreams, Doug Culver."

Culver released a benign smile like a soft burp. "To four percent."

Smith turned to Wetzon. "Do they owe us any money?"

Wetzon shook her head. She stood beside Smith. "What do you want to do?"

Smith began moving and Wetzon rushed to keep up with her. Only after they were on the elevator did Smith answer Wetzon's question. What she said was, "Rape, pillage, and burn!"

MEMORANDUM

To: Carlos Prince and Leslie Wetzon
From: Nancy Stein, Assistant to Mort Hornberg
Date: November 16, 1994
Re: *Combinations, in Concert*

JoJo says he doesn't think we have to pay vacation or holiday premium to the *Combinations* musicians, but he didn't seem to want to confirm it with the union. Mort thinks you should do it. I'd appreciate your getting back to me on this.

Chapter Twelve

"PERFECT. OF COURSE, YOU'LL DO IT, CARLOS."

"You're volunteering me? I'm afraid of Local 802. They always say no and they're not very nice about it. I think you should do it."

"I might get really angry and say what I think."

"Oh, all right, I'll do it."

SMITH THREW HERSELF OFF THE CURB, WAVING FRANTICALLY AS ONE CAB AFTER another crawled by, occupied. Of course, there were no cabs to be had, which only added to Smith's ire. Wetzon was more philosophical. After all, the subway was the most efficient means of transportation in New York, and if Smith would only stop fighting it, she would see it was true.

As for the treachery of Rosenkind Luwisher, loyalty was a rare and unappreciated commodity on Wall Street. The fact that Smith and Wetzon had kept the firm on as a client through all the bad years counted for nothing. Headhunters, a manager had recently informed Wetzon, were a dime a dozen, and the firms would deal with anyone, even—as Smith succinctly put it—pond scum, if pond scum could introduce brokers.

Not one firm had ever stopped dealing with a headhunter who was caught putting brokers in with one hand and taking them out with the other, something that Wetzon would never do.

Honesty and honor had no payoff these days on the Street.

"You might help, you know," Smith snarled. She stepped back on the sidewalk in a fury. "They can't do this to me."

"They, whoever *they* may be, have nothing to do with our not being able to get a cab." Wetzon dipped into her handbag and pulled out the coin purse that held her subway tokens. She extracted two and held them up. "If we use these, we'll be at Grand Central in fifteen minutes. And we'll be dry, too."

"I'd rather die."

"Fine. I'll give you a splendid funeral." Wetzon turned up her collar, opened her umbrella, and began walking toward Broadway and Wall, the closest stop on the Lexington IRT, number 4 and number 5 trains.

"You're not going to leave me standing here alone," Smith howled, fixing two gaping women lugging Odd-Job—Closeouts with Class—shopping bags with her most malevolent stare.

"Count on it." Wetzon moved off.

She was halfway down the block when she heard, "Wait!"

Turning, Wetzon saw her partner coming on quickly. "I'd like you to know that my mission in life has always been never to set foot in that black pit," Smith said plaintively.

"It's really not as bad as you think, Smith. At least there are fewer panhandlers." Wetzon was moderately sympathetic. She was perhaps the only one who understood that her glamorous partner was a fragile soul, of which even Smith was unaware. And as often as Smith made her angry with her outrageous behavior, Wetzon always knew it was a cover for some peculiar insecurity.

They descended newly tiled and fairly clean stairs, went through the new turnstiles designed to wean riders from tokens to magnetic cards, which most New Yorkers, being chronically adverse to change, had rejected out of hand, preferring the reliable token.

A train was coming in as they reached the platform, and when the doors opened, a swarm of people pushed off. "Come on," Wetzon yelled over the noise. Two men, a woman holding a stroller with a screaming, chocolate-dripping child, blocked the doors. Wetzon gave Smith a push and got her on the train.

"Why do you stand in the door and not let people on?" Smith complained.

"Get a life, bitch," the woman with the stroller snarled.

"Oh, for pitysakes," Smith said.

As luck would have it, the train was crowded. No seats and hardly any space on the poles and bars to hold on. When the train lurched forward, a fat woman fell against Smith, the slice of pizza she was eating barely missing Smith's sleeve.

"Are you all right?" Wetzon asked. Smith actually whimpered; she had a dazed look on her face. Culture shock.

"I have seen hell," Smith said. And that was all she said until Fourteenth Street, when the car emptied out and a new, more aggressive group pushed their way on. All the while, Smith, eyes firmly shut, was trying to make herself as thin a line as possible so as not to be touched, brushed, or jostled. It was hopeless.

"Ladies and gentlemen," a voice said. "I am asking you to be charitable. Help me out here. See my child. We are hungry." The man was gaunt, with a haunted expression on his face. He pushed the child—a painfully thin little girl with frightened eyes—forward. The child had a brace on one leg and held a metal cup for coins, which rattled when she shook it. "My wife is in the hospital, and I've lost my job. I do not want to rob and steal, but I will if I have to. I'm asking you to help me not go bad."

"Awg," Smith said. "I thought you said—"

Wetzon shrugged and clutched the bar over her head. She could have taken out a paperback—she had one of Patricia Highsmith's Ripley books in her briefcase—but she felt, as Smith's mass transit mentor, she'd best keep her eye on her. "Don't make eye contact," she murmured. "Read the ads." A mistake. The ads were mostly in Spanish, advertising condoms, hemorrhoid treatments, and drug rehabilitation.

The child suddenly picked Smith out of the audience and pushed the cup at her. Smith's expression changed in miniseconds, from horror to fury. "You can't fool me," Smith said, looking down at the cup with disdain. "This is nothing but an act."

When the child burst into tears, the entire population of the car began to hiss. It was in the nick of time that the train tore into Grand Central, ending the journey from hell.

"AND SMITH FELT SO SULLIED BY RUBBING ELBOWS WITH THE *CANAILLE* THAT she had to go home to shower and change." When Wetzon finished her narration, Laura Lee was laughing so hard tears clung to her extended lashes.

"Xenia Smith on the subway. What's wrong with this picture?"

They were sitting in Starbucks on Eighty-seventh and Broadway, Laura Lee with her latte and Wetzon with her decaf double espresso. Their high stools were set in front of the big window, giving them a view of the passersby. While it was only six-thirty, it could have been midnight, but the lights from passing cars illuminated the sidewalks and streets, as did those from the shop windows all along Broadway. Broadway, the main drag of the Upper West Side, was as busy in the evening as it was during the day.

Two briefcases and Laura Lee's violin case were propped up at their feet. Laura Lee's music teacher lived on Eighty-seventh and West End, so she and Wetzon had taken to meeting like this every Wednesday, when Laura Lee came for a lesson.

"As for your erstwhile client, Rosenkind Luwisher," Laura Lee said, running her hands through her short brown-spiked-with-gold hair, "it's about derivatives, you know. They fell out of bed with them. They've taken a major hit."

"Derivatives? What about them? You've lost me."

"Well, darlin'," Laura Lee said, blotting her lips with a napkin, "I understand that tomorrow's *Journal* is goin' to have a blowout story on it. Rosenkind Luwisher is havin' to bail out one of its funds to the tune of three hundred mil—"

"Good God." Wetzon set her cup down.

"They are also goin' to reimburse customers who got caught in what they advertised as a safe investment by shorin' up the fund. Can you imagine sellin' people on derivatives as a safe investment?"

"Well, no, because I've never understood what they are."

Laura Lee grinned at her. "Listen, darlin', they started out simple. Everythin' on Wall Street starts out simple. Derivatives are just securities derived from other investments, like when mortgages are lumped together and sold in pools. Then, as so often happens, people begin to get creative. They shuffle, cut and slice, reassemble, and people lose tons of money. The SEC gets mulish when what is advertised as safe proves otherwise. Get it?"

"I'll never get derivatives, but the rest is perfectly clear. So this is not restructuring for the next decade, it's plain old belt-tightening."

"They have to cut costs somewhere, and you're it."

"Yeah. We're just a rung above branch office managers." Wetzon drank the last of her espresso and looked out the window. A little girl pumped past on a small two-wheeler with training wheels. Her father walked beside her carrying a big shopping bag from Citarella, an upscale fish and meat market on Broadway in the Seventies. "Look at that. I don't believe it."

"What?" Laura Lee peered out, her eyes following Wetzon's pointing finger.

"That little girl and her father. They're the ones who were begging on the subway today—the poor child with the brace on her leg. I can't believe it. I hate it when Smith pronounces the worst and then is right. And they were really good, Laura Lee. They fooled me."

Laura Lee laughed. "That child's daddy's just another entrepreneur, darlin'. The world's full of them. Why, we even have a dustin' of them on Wall Street." She finished her latte, gathered up her briefcase and violin, and waited for Wetzon, who was buying biscotti and having a half pound of decaf espresso beans ground.

"There're even a few of them in the The-a-tre," Wetzon said.

When she unlocked her door five minutes later, Silvestri, in T-shirt and jeans, was on the phone making notes on a pad, as if he'd been there all day. He waved to her with a bottle of Beck's as she hung up her coat. Izz was jumping and dancing as if she hadn't seen Wetzon in years.

In the kitchen, water in her stockpot roiled. Fettuccini lay on the counter and an interesting-looking sauce *sans* tomatoes simmered in a pan. A big bowl of salad greens and tomatoes sat on the counter, along with a crusty sesame-glanced semolina bread from Carmine's. An egg yolk floated in a small bowl.

When Silvestri hung up the phone, he found Wetzon sniffing his sauce. "What are you going to do with the egg?" she asked.

"Toss it over the hot pasta."

"Mmmm. You're hired."

"Oh, but I think you should try me out first," he said.

She ran her finger from his throat to his waistband very slowly. "What a nice idea."

Catching her hand, he pulled her to him. The phone rang.

"Oh, shit," she said. He pushed aside her hair and kissed the back of her neck.

"Whoever it is will leave a message," Silvestri said, unbuttoning her blouse.

In the background her answering machine went into action. A man's voice, full of a kind of phony cheer, said, "Hi, Leslie, this is Peter Koenig. I'm back in town with *Tacoma Triptych.* . . . In case you don't remember me, I used to go with Terri Matthews."

• • •

MEMORANDUM

To: Carlos Prince and Leslie Wetzon
From: Nancy Stein, Assistant to Mort Hornberg
Date: November 16, 1994
Re: *Combinations, in Concert*

Great news! We just heard that a piece about the show will lead off the "On Stage, and Off" column in tomorrow's "Weekend" section of the *Times*. He spent an hour with Mort last week, so we were keeping our fingers crossed.

Chapter Thirteen

"Did you see that, Birdie? He spent an hour with Mort last week. Do you think Mort mentioned he had two partners?"

"Not on your life, darling. Believe me, he'll take all the credit for everything. But of course, if something goes wrong, it's 'By the way, I have two partners in this fiasco.'"

"So what do you think? Shall I call him?" Wetzon broke off a chunk of bread and sopped up the few droplets of the sauce that remained on her plate.

"Why not?"

"We don't know if it's Terri yet, do we?" She cleared the table of the empty plates, went into the kitchen and put them in the sink, returning with a tray holding her Melitta coffeepot, two cups, and a plate of almond biscotti. "Do we?"

"So it's *we* now, is it?" Silvestri laughed at the face she made, then said, "No, we don't know if it's Terri Matthews."

"When will we know?"

"Maybe soon. Maybe never. We need medical records, dental records. We've got the police in Cincinnati working on it with Nina." He tasted the coffee. "This is good."

"Starbucks. Did you talk with Ann at Equity?"

"Yeah. She was helpful. The last year Terri paid her dues was 1977. She left no forwarding address, and after *Combinations* closed, she had no other contact with the union that anyone knows about."

"No medical bills?" Wetzon dipped one of the biscotti into her coffee, then let it melt in her mouth.

"No."

She looked down at her plate and sighed.

"Les?"

Raising her eyes, she saw his so-very-familiar face, as familiar as her own. His dark hair was getting wispy in front. The sharp line of his jaw was softened by the shadow of a late-day beard; the small dent in his chin kept its own shadow. She asked, "Are you ever afraid, Silvestri?"

When he loved her, his eyes were turquoise; when he was angry, they became gray. They were turquoise now as they studied her. He had not answered her question.

"Of course," he said. "Only a fool is never afraid, Les. A little dose of old-fashioned fear is a good thing. It makes you think twice before you rush into something."

"I never used to be afraid. I used to just forge ahead, trusting that everything would come out all right."

"Don't I know it." He smiled at her.

"Silvestri, I'm certain that was Terri in the trunk. Someone killed her and got away with it because we were all so self-involved. She was killed twice. Once by a gun. And again by everyone who knew her."

"Les, why don't we wait till we get a positive ID?"

"Then I'll call Peter tomorrow. I don't feel like talking to him tonight anyway."

"Did you talk to Metzger?"

She'd almost forgotten about Darlene's shooter. "No. I'll do it to-morrow. I promise."

They loaded the dishes in the dishwasher and cleaned up the kitchen. Silvestri poured the rest of the coffee into his cup and sat down on the sofa to watch *Double Indemnity.* Wetzon went to bed.

As exhausted as she was from the day, she slept badly, waking and dozing. Muscle cramps attacked her calves, her arches; her toes felt the pressure of the quilt. She was sleeping tense. She got up while it was still dark, pulled on leggings, a sweatshirt, and leg warmers, and did a slow but thorough workout at the barre, all the while accompanied by the refrain of Terri's husky voice saying, *Didn't anyone miss me?* Toweling the back of her neck, Wetzon refused to question whether the sweat came from her sorrow or the workout; she stopped, sat cross-legged under her barre, back against the wall, and meditated until Izz climbed into her lap.

She made coffee, gave Izz fresh water and dry dog food, and got into the shower.

The list of things to do grew: return Peter Koenig's call, return Marissa Peiser's calls, call Metzger, talk to Carlos and find out if he talked to Local 802 as Nancy had requested, and on the lighter side, rape, pillage, and burn Rosenkind Luwisher. It would be a long day, topped by dinner with Smith, always a strain and a half.

Half-dressed, she sat on the edge of the tub and dried her hair, then put it up in a topknot. It was just barely long enough. There was a time when she'd never been without the dancer's do, but that was before the shooting that had grazed her scalp. The bullet had burned a path through her hair so that it had to be cut back almost to the scalp.

She stopped in the middle of applying mascara. That's why the burn in the fur hat had caught her attention and held it. That's why she was avoiding calling Metzger.

The newspapers were stacked on her doormat. She scanned the headlines. *Voilà* the piece on Rosenkind Luwisher, just as Laura Lee had said there would be. It was the lead story in the *Journal*, positioned on the right of the front page. Big news. She read it while she swallowed her vitamins. Orange juice with a coffee chaser.

The *Times* covered it also, on the bottom of the front page, to be continued in the "Business Day" section. She wondered if brokers would consider the announcement an excuse to leave Rosenkind Luwisher. Maybe. Maybe not. All the firms were constantly hijacking one another's brokers, showering big producers with money if they came on board. Money and perks: beautiful offices, sales assistants, sophisticated computer systems, expense accounts. The bottom line was the deal—how much can I get?

"The Metro Section" of the *Times* had nothing on the skeleton, but why would she think there would be? She felt as if she were holding her breath, waiting.

When she put on her coat, Silvestri appeared, showered and shaved, dressed in a suit.

"Leaving you the *Times*," she told him.

"Early appointment?" He touched her topknot lightly, not commenting on it but noticing it.

"Couldn't sleep." She avoided his eyes. "Call me if you hear anything."

"Okay. I'll be late tonight."

"I'm having dinner with Smith." She settled her beret carefully over her topknot, scratched Izz under the chin. The phone rang, eliminating any thought of long good-byes, but Wetzon waited, hand on the outside door, to see who it was.

"Nina, yeah." Silvestri listened, not saying anything. Then, "No, it's okay." More listening. "Oh? Well, let me know. I'll be downtown all day." He hung up and looked at Wetzon.

"Well?"

"Nina's going out to Cincinnati."

MEMORANDUM

To: Sammy Weiss
From: Nancy Stein, Assistant to Mort Hornberg
Date: November 17, 1994
Re: *Combinations, in Concert*
CC: Carlos Prince and Leslie Wetzon

Confirming arrangements for Commercial Liability at .099 per patron. Don't we also need to be covered for:

1) property floater on lights and sound equipment
2) Workers' Compensation
3) General Liability

Would this coverage be available through the Nederlanders?

Chapter Fourteen

"DARLING, DOES BEING A CO-PRODUCER MEAN MY MAIL HAS TO BE SODDEN with floaters and liabilities?"

"Floaters, you say, Carlos? Let's get Silvestri in on this. Sounds like a job for the NYPD."

"AW, WETZON, WHERE AM I GOING TO GO AND MAKE THIS KIND OF MONEY?" Charley Whiting whined.

"Almost anywhere. Charley, maybe this is the perfect time to make a change," Wetzon said. "With your trailing twelve over half a mil, you could get yourself a really nice package . . . say in the neighborhood of two hundred fifty thou." She could hear Charley breathing in asthmatic gusts.

"Listen, Wetzon, I'm going through an ugly divorce. I still don't understand it. My wife knew I was a *putz* when she married me twenty-three years ago. Why is this suddenly bothering her now?"

"I'm sorry to hear that, Charley." Scratch him, Wetzon thought.

"What good would it do me to move and collect a big check? She'd take at least half of it. And this firm has stood by me all the way. They've shown me how to hide my income from her—"

Wetzon wished him good luck with the divorce and squeezed three referrals out of him before she hung up. Charley Whiting *was* a *putz*. He had just told her he was hiding money from his wife and that Rosenkind Luwisher was helping him. Well, lucky for him he'd dropped this on Wetzon. She considered what brokers told her confidential and privileged. Too bad others in her business didn't.

She made a note to update Charley in three months and filed him in her March folder. He was the last of the brokers Max had qualified for her. It had been a tough day, but she'd actually persuaded six Rosenkind Luwisher brokers to interview. Cheers for our team.

Smith had spent the morning making business development phone calls and had gone out to see clients in the afternoon before she ended the day with her weekly manicure. The pressure was on Smith now to develop new clients, and on Wetzon to pull brokers out of Rosenkind Luwisher.

Darlene was working Atlanta and Boston, though Shirley Boley had assured them that the restraining order preventing her from talking to any brokers she'd talked to while in Keegen's employ wouldn't stick. So all the wheels were greased and the pistons were working. Except that she'd gone out for a sandwich and Mel Wallach, a Bliss Nordeman manager, had called from a pay phone on the street. His secretary was on vacation. Where was he supposed to meet Barbie Sloane for lunch? By the time Wallach called, he was already twenty minutes late. Max had checked Wetzon's datebook, where she always wrote the time and place of each appointment, and told Wallach where to go.

"Great," Wetzon said when she got back. "The Fist doesn't want to meet, gives us a hard time because Mel wants to do lunch, and now he's late."

There was no word from Silvestri about Nina Wayne's trip to Cincinnati, but it was too soon anyway.

Wetzon had agreed to meet A.D.A. Marissa Peiser for coffee at five, and after that, dinner with Smith. Grumbling, she went into the bathroom, took her hair down, pinned it up again, reapplied lipstick. When she returned to her desk, she saw by the little lights that both Max and Darlene were still working the phones.

She was edgy. The Andy Warhol drawing of the fat roll of dollar bills was hanging slightly crooked on the wall. She straightened it. Out their back window the garden looked a little forlorn, as did most gardens in winter in New York. A melancholic sigh drifted from her lips.

No more of that, she told herself. She picked up the phone and called Barbie Sloane, using the name Mrs. Weinberg, as Barbie had instructed. She was put on hold with a rather pleasant tape of something from *Peer Gynt,* then the sales assistant came back and said, "Ms. Sloane will be right with you." Back on hold, the name of the melody teased her memory. Was it "Anitra's Dance"? The music stopped abruptly.

"Hello." Barbie's voice was dark with a kind of cautious paranoia.

"Hi, Barbie, this is Wetzon." Her greeting was brimming over with good humor. Wetzon the phony, she thought. Wetzon the phony said, "How did lunch go?"

"Well enough, I guess. He's a nice man. But I never like to take lunch, and he was late. I don't know why I was there. I don't need the extra stress."

Wetzon held the phone away from her. The Fist was at it again. "It doesn't hurt to talk, Barbie." And there was no way that Mel Wallach could ever be described as a nice man.

"Right, Wetzon, but frankly, I don't know why I'm talking. I'm perfectly happy here. They treat me very well."

"You know, Barbie, you're absolutely right. Maybe you should stay where you are."

"Well, I'd be a fool not to look, Wetzon. I owe it to myself to know what I'm worth out there."

"How did you leave it with Mel?"

"He's sending me a packet of material and we'll talk again. But I'm too busy to do anything now. I'm training a new sales assistant and—"

There was a knock on Wetzon's door, and Wetzon cut Barbie off before Barbie could list her whole itinerary yet one more time. "Why don't we talk after you've gone through the material Mel's sending you?" Wetzon hung up. "Come in."

Artie Metzger, the tall, angular detective who had been Silvestri's partner at the Seventeenth, stuck his head in the door. "Busy?"

"Never for you." She jumped up and stood on tiptoe to kiss his cheek. Metzger, with his solemn face and the deep bags under his eyes, always made her think of a basset hound.

"You're looking good," he said.

She grinned at him. "Yeah." He was one of Silvestri's poker group, so she didn't have to say more.

"Whatcha got for me?" Parking himself against Smith's desk, he took out his pad.

"We hired a new associate from a competitor. Her name is Darlene Ford and she started on Tuesday. She literally fell in the door and claimed someone had taken a shot at her."

"A nut case?"

"So I thought, but lo and behold, her hat had a burn line in the fur, and when I left the office later in the day, this popped out from under the doormat." She handed him the twisted lump of lead. "Silvestri says it's a bullet."

"Did you hear anything?" He rolled the deformed bullet around in his palm.

"Not a thing. What kind of bullet is that?"

"Probably from a rifle."

"Rifle?" Wetzon was rattled. "Are you kidding? In the City?"

Metzger shrugged, as if nothing could surprise him anymore.

"Listen, Artie, Tom Keegen is not that crazy. He was Darlene's last boss. She thinks he's the one who's after her."

"Let me talk to her."

Wetzon opened the door. Max was sorting his suspect sheets into stacks. Darlene was off the phone and making notes. "Darlene, will you come in here, please?"

She sent Darlene into her office and said to Max, "Can you stay another fifteen minutes while we have our meeting and cover the phones?"

His eyes followed Darlene, then came back to Wetzon. "Of course."

Closing the door, Wetzon said, "Darlene, this is Detective Metzger. He wants to ask you some questions about the shooting."

Darlene became all twitches and nervous smiles. Metzger settled her in Smith's chair and leaned one elbow on the filing cabinet.

"Oh, dear," Darlene said. She pulled at her skirt, which was too short to begin with and was now creeping up her thighs. She played with a strand of her hair, fingered the gold chains around her neck, scratched at her hose with frenched fingernails.

"Ms. Ford, I just want to ask you a few questions," Metzger said.

"Okay." She chewed on her lower lip and looked at Wetzon, who nodded.

"How did you get here on . . . ?"

"Tuesday," Wetzon offered.

"Tuesday." Metzger made a note.

"I took a cab. I live on East End Avenue. It's always easier for me to take a cab. I can get one in front of my—"

"Okay, then what?"

Darlene looked confused.

"Did you pay the driver before or after you got out?"

"Oh. Before."

"When did you hear the shot?"

"I didn't. I had my hand on the door when my hat was knocked off my head. I heard a ping, as if something hit metal. My daddy is a lobbyist for the NRA; I am very comfortable with guns. I knew what that sound was. You see, he said he'd kill me if I came here."

"Who?"

"Tom Keegen, my ex-boss."

"I hardly—" Wetzon began.

Metzger held up his hand. "Give me Keegen's address and I'll have a little talk with him."

"I'll give it to you," Wetzon said. She wrote it on a piece of memo paper and handed it to Metzger.

"I want to take a look around outside." Metzger tucked his pad away in his inside pocket. "And I'd like to see that hat. Do you have it here?"

Darlene left the room and returned with the hat, which Metzger inspected, then handed back to her without comment.

Wetzon followed Metzger outside. It was cold. She hugged herself as she watched him poke around near the doorframe. He stopped suddenly. "See here?"

"What?" She leaned around him. He was pointing to a deep dent in the metal door above her head. "This may have been the ping she heard."

"Damnation." Wetzon clutched her arms and shivered.

"Let's go back inside." Metzger sounded distracted.

Inside, Max was taking his coat out of the closet. He was about to close the door when Metzger stopped him. "This yours, Leslie?" He picked up the sleeve of Darlene's raccoon coat, then dropped it.

"No, Darlene's."

"Don't you have one like it?"

"Something like it."

"Do you need me?" Max asked, not very anxious to leave.

"No, good night, Max. Thank you." She shooed him out. "Do you want some coffee, Artie? I can't predict the flavor. It's the bottom of the pot."

"Couldn't be worse than ours." He poured himself a mug. "Come on in here and close the door."

She looked at him, trying to figure out the sense of the message she was getting from him.

"Sit down, Leslie," he said.

"Artie, what's—"

"Sit." Metzger pointed to her chair and took a sip of coffee. She turned her chair away from her desk and sat.

"Tell me what's up with you," he said, as if it were a social occasion.

"Oh, well, let's see," she said, playing along. "Carlos and I are producing a concert revival of a show we did in '76, as a benefit."

"What else?"

"I may have known the woman whose skeleton was found in the trunk. Do you know that case? Silvestri's working on it."

"Yes. Go on." He was waiting patiently, taking sips of his coffee.

"Oh. I'm going to have to give grand jury testimony against Richard Hartmann."

"Ah," Metzger said, as if he'd finally heard what he wanted. He set his mug down on top of the filing cabinet and seemed to be considering his next words carefully.

"Oh, Artie, come on—" Then out of some deep recess of her brain came the name of the piece from *Peer Gynt*. It was "Aase's Death."

Metzger said, "Leslie, it may not have been Ms. Ford the shooter was after."

MEMORANDUM

To: Carlos Prince and Leslie Wetzon
From: Nancy Stein, Assistant to Mort Hornberg
Date: November 17, 1994
Re: *Combinations, in Concert*

The load-in may have to go into a third day. We have it scheduled for Tuesday and Wednesday so that Thursday can be used if necessary. The estimated cost of the third day is $12,500. Due to the volume of sound and lighting equipment, Ellis says the electrics will go from 8 to 12 people.

Chapter Fifteen

"Birdie, darling, now don't lose it. We'll talk over how to handle Mort, and then you can do it at the meeting."

She gnashed her teeth. "Right."

ALTHOUGH THANKSGIVING WAS STILL A WEEK AWAY, THE CITY WAS ALREADY dripping with Christmas decorations. It was tiresome and cynical. It was a New York tradition that on the Monday following Thanksgiving the City and its inhabitants plunged into an orgy of Christmas buying, dinner parties, cocktail parties, brunches, open houses, and general festivities. Trying to ignore it was like holding back a tidal wave with the palm of your hand. For Wetzon, Christmas season only became official with the lighting of the tree in Rockefeller Center during the first week of December.

She'd suggested the coffee shop on Lexington in the Fifties with the inappropriate name, Broadway Diner. No one Wetzon knew went there, so it was perfect. It was also on the way to Fresco, where she was meeting Smith for dinner.

Slightly spooked, she walked up Second Avenue, looking over her shoulder from time to time, remembering Metzger's suggestion that she vary her routine. Was someone watching her? Had one of Richard Hartmann's "friends" decided to help him out?

A bearded man in a blue baseball cap and a shabby I ♥ NY sweat-shirt pushed a grocery cart past her. He wore grubby jeans and new white Reeboks. On his hands were bright yellow rubber gloves. His cart was spilling over with aluminum cans in plastic bags. He parked in front of the trash basket on Fiftieth Street and began foraging among crumpled bags, cardboard and Styrofoam containers, and pizza crusts.

In swift succession he plucked a dozen or so cans from the clutter, adding them to his collection before moving on to another trash basket on the next corner.

He was another New York entrepreneur, taking advantage of the fact that most people in the City didn't bother getting refunds on the five-cent deposit the state required on all carbonated beverages in cans and bottles. A nickel? Give me a break. Not worth the trouble. This attitude had spawned an industry for the homeless and unemployable, who became territorial working certain neighborhoods. She knew that somewhere in the City there was a redemption center called We Can that collected all the cans and bottles and paid the pickers.

The Broadway Diner was lean on diners at this hour, so it was the ideal time and place to meet and not be seen. At present there were more service people than customers. In the smoking section an elderly man read a foreign-language newspaper filled with big black Cyrillic lettering. An overflowing ashtray of stubs not quite extinguished created a mini smoke screen around him.

The only occupants of the nonsmoking section were a man and a woman in the seriously old category. They were having an early dinner of meatloaf and mashed potatoes.

Wetzon requested a table as deep into the restaurant as possible, away from the plateglass window. She ordered coffee and waited.

"That's not what I said," the old woman complained. She was tiny, slightly hunched, with a small beak nose. She poked at her meatloaf with her fork but didn't taste it.

"What?" the old man said. His hair was gray and he wore horn-rimmed glasses too small for his face. He spoke louder than necessary.

"I said," the woman raised her voice, "that you're deaf."

Wetzon smiled and let her mind rest. It had been almost two years since she had last seen Marissa Peiser, and now here she was rushing in, hair flying. The Assistant District Attorney's straight brown hair was still shoulder-length, but it had a definite tint of red. The belt on her black raincoat dangled loose from its torn side tab. A black leather shoulder bag and a scruffy briefcase completed the picture. She shook Wetzon's hand.

"What?" the old man said.

"Forget it," the old woman answered.

"What?"

"A little golden-oldie background music," Wetzon told Marissa.

"Thanks for meeting me," Peiser said. "I'll have black coffee," she told the waiter. "And a toasted bagel." She looked at Wetzon. "I haven't had lunch. Do you want anything?"

"More decaf." After the waiter left, Wetzon asked, "Should I have something stronger?"

"Maybe." Marissa shrugged out of her coat, and it lay half on the back of the chair, half on the floor. She was wearing a gray suit with a red silk blouse that tied at the neck in a steinkirk. The bow drooped. She took a crumpled tissue from her bag and blew her nose. The expression in her eyes was of concern mixed with decency. Wetzon liked her. She felt Peiser would never lie to her.

"So what's this all about?"

"I think we're going to have to call you to testify before the grand jury. I'm sorry."

"So am I. It means I can be prosecuted for burglary."

"We'll give you immunity. I'll work it out with Arthur Margolies."

"That's okay, but there's something else that's not."

The bagel and fresh coffees arrived as Peiser was pulling a yellow legal pad from her briefcase. She set the pad down, broke the bagel in pieces, and took a bite. "What?"

"What?" The old man raised his voice again.

"I said, ask him about the discount. Oh, never mind."

Marissa ate and Wetzon watched the old people pay their bill and leave. She was almost sorry to see them go; they'd provided comic relief.

"Someone took a shot at one of my employees on Tuesday. Just

missed her. I found what was left of a bullet. A detective came in today
to talk to us. He thinks the shot might have been meant for me, because she was wearing a raccoon coat similar to the one I own."

"Hartmann?"

"Who else? He may have found out you're calling me to testify."

"He wouldn't do it himself, but he knows enough people," Peiser
mused. "He's just trying to scare you off."

"He's succeeding. Talk to Detective Metzger at the Seventeenth."

"We'll protect you."

"Thanks a lot. How? Let's not kid ourselves. You can't. I'm not
going to go into hiding. I have a business to run. When will you need
me?"

"Right after Thanksgiving."

"I can hardly wait."

Marissa reached for the check. Her hands were chapped and there
was an ink stain on one finger. "I've got to get back to my office."

"Are you still seeing Riccardi?" Riccardi had been the detective on
the Brian Middleton murder, when Wetzon had first encountered
Peiser.

Peiser smiled. "Cops and A.D.A.s are a good fit. Yes, we're together. You and—"

"Silvestri. Together."

They shook hands again on the street and parted, Wetzon turning
west to meet Smith at Fresco. Night had closed in while she and Peiser
sat in the Broadway Diner, and now a cold wind whipped debris about
in little eddies.

She hadn't called Peter Koenig, which wasn't like her. She always
returned phone calls. Unlike Smith, who made a fetish of not. She'd
call him later when she got home. Why had he chosen this time to
reappear, she wondered, just when Terri . . . ?

She remembered him fairly well. Peter Koenig was one of those
really nice guys that girls didn't marry. Tall, with dark hair, he always
struck Wetzon as sincere—maybe too sincere—and hovering. The hovering she remembered distinctly. She suddenly flashed on Terri's an-

noyance when he had arrived in Boston during rehearsals. What had Terri said? "Peter doesn't let me breathe."

Girding herself for another foray into Smith's narcissistic world, Wetzon opened the door to Fresco. Huge planters filled with purple kale guarded the entrance, but the first, immediate, and overwhelming sensation was the noise of conviviality. It blasted out at her from around the bar, and although it was early, from the restaurant itself. She was checking her coat when she heard Smith call, "There she is now."

She turned slowly. Who was Smith with? If it was Richard Hartmann, Wetzon would be out of there in a trice. Wetzon squinted into the sepia light. Smith was doing one of her seductive slouches into a tall dark-haired man, graying attractively at the temples. The man smiled at Wetzon and held out his hand as if he knew her.

Frowning, she stepped toward them, then hesitated. Good God, she thought. She did know him. It was Peter Koenig.

MEMORANDUM

To: Carlos Prince and Leslie Wetzon
From: Nancy Stein, Assistant to Mort Hornberg
Date: November 17, 1994
Re: *Combinations, in Concert*

Just a reminder that the half-page ad will be in the *Times* this Sunday, the 20th, at the cost of $33,642, plus artwork and mechanicals at another $4,000.

Tickets for both Thursday and Friday performances are $250, $150, and $90. Please let me know how many to put aside for you.

Chapter Sixteen

"*Birdie?*"

"*Yes.*"

"*Did you see these ticket prices?*"

"*Yes.*"

"*A little steep, don't you think?*"

"*If you're bringing a whole entourage, my love, it certainly is a little steep. Me, I'm ordering four for each night. That's a cool thou, but I'm a working girl.*"

"*I may have to become one to pay for my tickets.*"

"I knew you'd want to see him, sweetie pie," Smith gushed.

"Mort's assistant gave me your office number," Peter said. "And when I called, I got Xenia."

Xenia? Wetzon smiled. "You look great, Peter. Are you joining us for dinner?" He was drinking a martini, with an olive, no less; he was Rip Van Winkle and had slept for seventeen years.

"No, I'm afraid not. I have a tech in about a half hour. I just wanted to say hello. And I was hoping you could give me Terri's phone number."

"I'm sure she can," Smith said. "Excuse me for a minute." Her wandering attention had focused on a group of diners who were just arriving. No doubt she'd seen someone she knew. Fresco was a table-hopper's delight.

"Amstel Light," Wetzon told the bartender.

"I figured Terri'd be coming in for the revival, if she wasn't here already."

"Don't tell me you lost track of her."

"Well . . ." Peter looked embarrassed. "Sort of."

"How come?"

A raw flush started at his collar; it worked its way up to his cheeks. "She broke it off between us, then I got into the Seattle Rep. When I wrote her, my letters came back marked 'Moved, No Forwarding.'" He looked at his watch and drained the martini. "Gotta go. Can I have her number?"

"I don't know where Terri is, Peter. We haven't been able to find her."

He looked stunned. Or was it a performance? Wetzon wasn't sure. "What do you mean?"

"I mean, no one seems to know where she is—"

"I've got to get out of here, Wetzon." He put some bills on the counter. "But I want to talk some more. I don't understand about Terri."

"Neither do I, Peter. Why don't I call you in a day or so and we can get together when we each have more time?" Out of the corner of her eye she saw Smith on her way back.

"Good idea, Leslie," Peter said, then called to Smith, "Good-bye, Xenia. You're a doll."

"Bye, sweetie, good luck with the show." Smith blew him a kiss around Walter Cronkite and an elegant woman who had just walked in the door.

When Wetzon pulled out her American Express card, the bartender flashed two tens at her. "The gentleman left more than enough," he said.

"The gentleman paid for our drinks, *doll*," Wetzon said to Smith as they were led to their table amid a few nods and waves from the other tables. All around them Wetzon recognized faces familiar from broadcasting.

"He's quite nice for an actor. And cute, too." Smith smiled and appropriated the chair facing the dining room. She began spooning the white bean spread on a garlic cracker.

"Yes. For an actor." The dining room was bright, a welcome relief from those restaurants that gave diners pseudo-intimacy by turning down the lights so you had to peer through the flickering flame of a votive candle to see your dinner companion and your food. About her dinner companion, Wetzon wasn't concerned, but she did want to see what was on her plate.

They took their time ordering and finally, after much discussion, chose a bottle of Chianti and the white bean-and-potato soup, sausage and tomato in a fennel crust, and rigatoni with garlic and broccoli rabe, intending to share everything because the portions were voluptuous. The important decisions made, they settled back, content.

"Well, now," Wetzon said, eyeing her partner. "Business development agrees with you." Considering how hard Smith was working, she was vibrant.

"It does when I can shake assignments out of the trees. Marley Straus is opening a branch in Boston, and we're going to stock it for them."

"Now that's what I like to hear. Darlene is already working Boston. Let's let her run with it."

The wine arrived, and after their glasses were filled, they toasted each other. Smith proceeded to decimate the crackers and move on to the slices of crusty Tuscan bread, then signaled for more of everything.

"What was it you wanted to talk about?" Wetzon was feeling somewhat mellow after the first few sips of wine. "Leave me some bread, will you?"

"Did you see Barbara Walters?"

"Yes, I did." Wetzon's impatience began as a faint itch on the ball of her foot and then spread rapidly. Smith was going to draw this out so that it ruined the entire meal. "Just say it, please."

Smith lined up the sesame crumbs with her fingers and moved them back and forth on the white tablecloth.

"Is it Mark?" Smith's son was in his first semester at Harvard.

Beaming, Smith replied, "Oh, no, he's doing so well. He loves it. He'll be home next week. And of course we'll be at Mort and Poppy's for Thanksgiving, so you'll see him."

"Oh?" Wetzon was surprised. Smith knew Mort only slightly, and Mark knew him from working as a gofer on *Hotshot* last winter . . . but still . . .

"Why are you so surprised? Doesn't everyone do Thanksgiving at Mort's?"

"Well, everyone in the Theatre."

The first course was served. Wetzon picked up her spoon.

"I'm having a problem with Dickie." Smith blurted it out over the soup.

Wetzon set her spoon down. "What kind of problem?" She raised her glass to her lips.

"He's very controlling. I never noticed that before."

"Controlling? Richard Hartmann? No kidding."

"He doesn't seem to understand that I have a lot of admirers."

Smith had put on her Cheshire cat smile, so Wetzon began to wonder what else was coming. "Somehow I can't get a picture of you waiting in the visitors' section with the other gun molls at Sing Sing— or wherever they send him after he's convicted."

"Read my lips, sweetie pie, they will never convict Dickie. He's got important friends everywhere. Not my kind of people, of course. They're a bit too rough around the edges for me. And," Smith added brightly, "I do feel I need to broaden my horizons. Don't you agree?"

Although she understood all too well the kinds of friends the slimy Richard Hartmann might have, Wetzon had no idea what Smith meant by broadening her horizons. "Let's not talk about him anymore, please. I was afraid you might set me up and have him join us tonight. I'm glad you didn't." She pushed her bowl toward Smith. "The soup is delicious."

"Oh, I'd never do that, sweetie pie." Smith took a spoonful of soup. "God, this is good."

"But you surprised me with Peter Koenig."

"Well, I thought you'd be glad to see him. He said you were old friends."

"I was a friend of his girlfriend, Terri Matthews. The one he's looking for."

"And you told him how to reach her." Smith pushed the crusted sausage-and-tomato affair across the table. "Try some of this."

Wetzon moved a portion from Smith's plate to her bread plate. It amazed her that she could still be hungry. "I couldn't tell him how to reach her because I don't know."

"But I thought you were having a reunion of everybody—"

"We couldn't find Terri. Remember I told you about the bones of a dancer they found in a trunk in the basement of a brownstone in the Village?"

"How could I forget?"

"I'm afraid it might be Terri."

"Not really?" Smith sat up suddenly, very interested.

"You see why I couldn't tell Peter that, not yet, not till they know for sure. And if it was Terri, she was murdered."

Smith took a tiny notebook from her tiny bag and began jotting something down.

"May I ask what you're doing?"

"Bones of a dancer, you said. It would make a wonderful movie, don't you think? I just made a few notes."

"Why?"

"Well, now that I'm in show business . . ."

Wetzon waited until the empty plates of the first course were cleared away. Then she said firmly, "But you're not in show business."

"Oh, but I am, babycakes."

Wetzon cringed inwardly. Over Wetzon's protests Smith had invested a portion of their pension money in *Hotshot: The Musical* last year. It was not that Wetzon didn't want to invest in Carlos's musical, it was the fact that the investment was in their pension that bothered her.

Investing in Broadway shows and expecting to get anything back, let alone see a profit, was like buying a thousand lottery tickets and expecting to win.

But they had gotten lucky. With the show still standing room only, they were now seeing profit checks every two or three months. And Smith, whose antennae were attuned to money, was looking at the Theatre as fertile ground.

"Smith, investing in a play doesn't put you in show business."

"Oh, I'm not talking about that."

Their pasta arrived already divided into two bowls, and they dug in. "So enlighten me. What *are* you talking about?"

"*Combinations, in Concert,* sweetie pie." She spoke slowly, as if she were talking to someone dim-witted. "Joel Kidde and I are going to produce it for Ted Turner."

"You're what?" Wetzon lowered her fork slowly, ordering herself not to stick it into Smith's hand as she reached once more for the bread basket.

"Why are you looking so shocked, sweetie? Didn't Mort tell you?"

"He mentioned there was interest, and Carlos and I blew him off. So you can't do it."

"We really don't need your permission, sugar. Foxy and Medora have agreed, and as authors, you know they make those decisions."

· · ·

Is Mort Hornberg finessing a twofer on Broadway? Hornberg
is producing a revival of the golden oldie of the seventies,
"Combinations." The landmark musical will be presented in
concert for two performances, Thursday, Dec. 22, and
Friday, Dec. 23, to benefit Show Biz Shares. "Combinations"
fixed in theatre history the names of Davey Lewin, Roger
and Medora Battle, Phyllis Reynard, and Lewin's assistant
director, Mort Hornberg. Included in the original company
were Bonnie McHugh, who shortly after the end of the run
was tapped for the long-running TV series, "Bonnie and
Joe," and Carlos Prince, the director/choreographer.

The performances will bring together all the living
original performers and will honor the memory of Davey
Lewin, Roger Battle, and Larry Saunders Lawrence, a cast
member.

Aiding and abetting Hornberg as producers of
"Combinations, in Concert" are Carlos Prince, and Leslie
Wetzon, one of the orginal dancers. Prince and Wetzon will
be re-creating their roles in this production.

Tickets will go on sale at the Richard Rodgers Theatre,
on Monday, Nov. 28. Part two of the twofer are rumors that
the performance will be televised. Mort Hornberg said,
"There's a lot of interest from the networks, and we're
considering everything, but nothing is definite."

Chapter Seventeen

"HI, THIS IS LESLIE WETZON, ONE OF THE ORIGINAL DANCERS," WETZON SAID. "I hope I woke you."

"Birdie." Carlos's voice was still thick with sleep. "What time is it?" A crash followed.

"Hello?"

"I dropped the phone."

"I'm waiting."

"Do I detect a derisive note, Dear Heart?"

"It's utterly possible. Did you see yesterday's *Times*?"

"No."

"I'll wait." After a minute, while she did *demi-pliés* at the barre, she began to hear the crackling of the newspaper. "Do you see it?"

"Shush, I'm reading."

"Didn't you get my messages?"

"Oh, didn't I tell you? Rocco rushed me up to Boston to look at *Pin the Donkey*, which is unsalvageable, by the way. Got in too late. Didn't check my machine. You're not letting me read."

"Read. And, by the way, you didn't tell me."

"Jesus H. Christ!"

"Yeah. Furthermore, it's actually been sold to Ted Turner. Joel got Foxy's and Medora's okay to go ahead. Mort, the mealymouth, has agreed, and guess, just *guess*, who will produce it with Joel and Mort?"

"I have no idea. Hit me with it."

"Xenia Smith."

"Awk!" Carlos made a strangling noise and dropped the phone again with a noisy clunk. Or maybe this time he threw it. When he came back on, he snarled, "Hang up. I'm calling that two-faced worm."

"I have this feeling this is going to break down to division of labor. Because Mort's office was going to handle the business end and Nancy was acting as general manager, he divided everything sixty-forty, with darling Mort getting sixty. I remember very clearly that he said all artistic decisions would be made by the *three* of us." She reached for her exercise mat and unrolled it. It took Izz less than a second to lay claim to it.

"Hang up," Carlos growled.

"Think of it, we'll be working for my partner, Dear Heart."

"Awk!" Carlos hung up in her ear.

Wetzon lay on her mat thinking, Izz on her chest trying to lick her chin. Smith and Mort. They deserved each other. She'd like to walk away from both of them. No—she'd like to murder both of them.

"You finished with the phone?" Silvestri asked.

"Yikes!" The receiver, still nestled between Wetzon's shoulder and chin, rolled off the mat and bonked on the floor. She raised her eyes and contemplated him upside down, his face getting closer and closer —till their lips touched.

"Hey," he said.

"Hey," she said. He was wearing his good blue suit, knife-creased trousers. "Got a meeting?"

"An appointment with Medora Battle. What kind of name is that?"

"Medora or Battle?"

"You have to ask?"

"Sounds Greek to me."

"Greek, huh? Okay."

"Could I be the Shadow and listen?"

"Work on it." He stood. "How about some breakfast, Izz?" He and the dog went into the kitchen, Silvestri returning solo with two mugs of coffee. He handed one to her and leaned against the barre while she sat cross-legged on the mat and sipped her coffee.

"Then what?"

"Phyllis Reynard." The receiver gave an angry buzz, then a digitalized voice began to give orders. Silvestri reached down and cradled the receiver. "You sounded pissed, Les. Who were you talking to?"

"Carlos." She sighed. "It's a long story, and I've got a rehearsal and you've got an appointment." She stretched her legs out in front of her and raised one slowly to her nose.

"Want to tell me about it over dinner?"

"Yup. And you can tell me all about Foxy and Medora."

"Foxy?"

"That's what everyone calls Phyllis. Wait till you meet her. I should be home by late afternoon." She took her coat from the closet, nuzzled Silvestri, then left the apartment.

She heard the phone ring while she waited for the elevator, and went back. Silvestri held the phone. "Carlos," he said.

She took the phone from him. "So? I'm on my way to the studio."

"I couldn't wait to tell you. Mort sold us out."

"Surprise, surprise."

"He said the contract has a clause giving Show Biz Shares a percentage of any TV sale, which translates to a minimum of twenty-five thousand dollars, and Show Biz Shares agreed."

"And if we put up a fight, they lose."

"Exactly. Listen, Birdie, what if we kick in our percentage to Show Biz Shares?"

"Now you're talking."

"That's only one of the many things I love about you. It's never the money."

"I wouldn't go that far."

"I have just one more thing to say to you."

"What?"

"This cannot and will not go unavenged."

"I'm with you all the way, Zorro."

"Later, *guapa*."

THE REHEARSAL STUDIOS ON WEST SIXTY-FIRST STREET WERE IN AN OLD warehouse building, where open spaces, high ceilings, and huge windows lent themselves easily to the dance. Special, forgiving wood floors had been laid and the walls whitewashed. Everything was bare-bones efficient: dressing rooms, lighting, water fountains. And the very air bloomed with the splendid musky sweat of dancers dancing.

She loved it. When she entered this world, her persona changed. Her walk was different; she was taller. Her body found its Zen.

The elevator was crowded; from under jackets and sweaters, legs, legs, legs, multicolored, long and slim. Wetzon's toes stretched irresistibly to point, arch high, inside their Easy Spirits.

On the fourth floor, piano music came from an open studio. Wetzon, shifting her coffee container from hand to hand, stopped to watch a professional ballet class being taught by a formidable woman whose small stature was enhanced by a mountain of black lacquered hair. She was keeping time with a cane.

Someone said, "Excuse me." And Wetzon moved aside to let Gelsey Kirkland through.

Ha, over the hill and still dancing, she thought. Let that be a lesson to you, Leslie Wetzon.

She opened the door to the smaller studio and saw Carlos sitting on the floor, back against the wall, a Starbucks container between his outstretched legs. He was talking to someone sitting at the piano, back to Wetzon.

"Birdie," Carlos said. "Look who's here."

Phyllis Reynard, known to theatre insiders as Foxy, turned and smiled at Wetzon. Her face was a sculpture of perfect lines, symmetrical, deep, elegant. So elegant in fact that the name everyone called her seemed incongruous, even insulting. A childhood name that stuck. Her hair, once black, was now iron-gray and feathered around her face.

When she held out her hand to Wetzon, silver bracelets, a dozen perhaps, sang.

The hand Wetzon took was small but strong, with long, tapered fingers. "Foxy." They touched cheeks. "What a nice surprise." Wetzon dropped her shoulder bag and the sack containing her tap shoes and towel on the floor and set the coffee container on the studio upright. Her coat she laid over the nearest barre.

Foxy wore black gabardine trousers, a heavy silver belt with a large turquoise stone, and a red turtleneck sweater. A black pea coat, not the kind you get from an army-navy store, rested on her shoulders.

"I kidnapped her," Carlos said, answering Wetzon's unasked question.

"Yes, and I'm going to be late." Foxy's voice was smokey. She checked her watch—a black-faced Movado with little diamonds—and ran her fingers lightly over the keys, as if she couldn't sit at a piano without touching it. "I've got a meeting."

"Oh," Wetzon said, "and here I thought you were going to rehearse with us." She shook her tap shoes from the sack and kicked off her sneakers.

Foxy smiled and all the wrinkles moved in harmony. "Carlos and I were talking about the TV sale."

Wetzon put her feet into her tap shoes and buckled the instep straps. "We were surprised that we were presented with a done deal." She raised her eyes to Foxy, who was still sitting on the piano bench teasing the keys, and saw a touch of something—embarrassment? defensiveness?—quickly surface and fade away in her dark eyes.

"The money was good, and we can all use the money. Besides, Show Biz Shares will get a nice piece of it."

"But no one was supposed to profit from this."

"From what I've heard, Leslie, you're not averse to making money."

"Oops," Carlos said. He stood gracefully, then bent from the waist to pick up his container of coffee.

"That's true, Foxy." Wetzon also stood, eyes shooting daggers at

Carlos. "But not when I'm donating my time and energies to what I thought was a charitable enterprise." She leaned back against the barre, flexing her toes, then brushing, *click, click, click.*

"Oh, please, Leslie. Believe me, this way everyone makes money. I promise you Show Biz Shares will not be unhappy." Foxy smiled again, slipped her arms into the cashmere pea coat, and looped a black-and-white silk scarf around her neck. Her soft black loafers hardly made a sound on the floor.

"Birdie," Carlos said, "give it up. We lose this one."

Wetzon sighed. "Foxy, wait—"

Foxy's shoes came to a stop with an odd squeak. She turned back.

"Okay, truce," Wetzon said. She did not want to make an enemy of Foxy. Life was too short. Besides, there was an outside chance that Foxy might remember something important about Terri. "I wanted to ask you something."

Foxy smiled and the wrinkles undulated.

"Terri Matthews," Wetzon said.

"What about her?"

"You remember her?"

"Of course. She sang like an angel."

"Yes. I suppose you heard that we haven't been able to find her."

"She's probably somewhere in Middle America, with a husband who bowls every Friday night and two and a half children." Her tone was scornful, even as her words dismissed Terri as banal.

"You didn't like her?"

"How can you say that?"

Carlos threw his arm over Wetzon's shoulders. "Now, girls," he said.

"I can hear it in your voice. What if something terrible happened to her?"

Foxy's eyes almost disappeared among the wrinkles. "Things happen to girls like that." She was icy—no, glacial.

"Girls like what, Foxy?"

"Birdie—" Carlos squeezed her shoulder.

Wetzon brushed him off with a shrug. "No, Carlos. I want to understand what Foxy's saying."

Foxy's eyes blazed. "And I want you to understand, Leslie. Bad things happen to girls like Terri who can't keep their hands off things that don't belong to them."

THE MAGIC OF THE GOLDEN YEARS ON BROADWAY.
RE-CREATED.

Mort Hornberg, Carlos Prince, Leslie Wetzon
Show Biz Shares
in association with the Nederlander Organization
present
The Original Broadway Cast

Tommy Brown
Joan Fisher
Vicki Howard
Kenny Klein
Bonnie McHugh
Margie Nicholson
Carlos Prince
Bob Rosen
Steve Sedlet
Leslie Wetzon

Direction by
Mort Hornberg and Carlos Prince

Choreography by
Carlos Prince

Music and Lyrics by
Phyllis Reynard

Book by
Roger and Medora Battle

Orchestrations by
Howard Haines

Musical Direction by
JoJo Diamond

Original Broadway Recording
Eggplant Records

Tickets on Sale Beginning Monday, November 28th, at 12 Noon
Telecharge: (212) 555-6200 or Richard Rodgers Theatre Box Office
Tickets: $250, $150, $90
Two Performances Only: Thursday, Dec. 22 and Friday, Dec. 23

Chapter Eighteen

"Whaddaya think, Birdie? It looks pretty good to me."
  "It looks pretty good to me, too. And pretty official."
  "Not getting cold feet, are we?"
  "We wouldn't dare."

Wetzon spent the first half hour confirming appointments; Mondays on Wall Street could be hairy. Most of the crashes had happened on Mondays. And the stock brokers tended to be sluggish on Mondays, after a weekend away from the office.

She had been unable to reach Smith because Smith refused to own an answering machine. So some of her ire had dissipated. And in truth, Smith's behavior could never really be called surprising. If you thought about it, she was right in character.

Terri Matthews and her fate left little space for anything else in Wetzon's mind. More, Wetzon found herself unable to keep Foxy's cold condemnation of Terri from her thoughts. What had Terri done to—

Smith exploded into the office, splendid in a huge camel-colored cashmere shawl, one long end draped over the other shoulder. She wore a matching suit and carried a Brunschwig & Fils shopping bag stuffed with fabric samples, and *dum-dum-dee*-ing off-key the title song from *Combinations*.

"What's all this?" Wetzon snapped, pointing to the bulging shopping bag.

Smith ignored Wetzon's waspishness. "Sweetie pie, I have so much to tell you. I've decided to redo my apartment. After all—"

"Now that I'm in show business . . ." Wetzon finished for her, putting a nasty spin on the words.

"Oh, very funny." Smith unwound her shawl and tossed it on top of the filing cabinet. "I'm in too good a mood to let you get to me." She looked at Wetzon and laughed. "What have I done, broken into that private world of yours?"

Good grief, Wetzon thought. There was some truth in what Smith had just said. She folded her arms. "You have a point," she admitted.

"And from what I see, it's a good thing, too. The Theatre needs me desperately because no one in the Theatre knows how to run a business. Businesses are supposed to *make* money, babycakes, not lose money. Even Twoey—"

"Twoey? Are we seeing Twoey again, I hope, I hope?" Twoey was Goldman Barnes II, Smith's ex-lover, who had left Luwisher Brothers after the merger to pursue his dream of being a Broadway producer. *Hotshot* had been his first show, and he was now the new fair-haired boy on Broadway. The Shuberts—that is, Bernie Jacobs and Gerry Schoenfeld, who owned most of the theatres on Broadway—were falling all over themselves to be accommodating, as were the Nederlanders. And the ubiquitous Rocco Landesman, head man of Jujamcyn, and Twoey were talking about a co-production down the line.

"Well, no, sugar. Twoey seems to be in some kind of relationship with that dreadful Puerto Rican woman who used to be Mort's assistant."

"Smith, Sunny Browning is not Puerto Rican."

"Whatever."

"Then, if it's not Twoey you're toying with dumping Hartmann for, who is it?"

"I told you when we had dinner."

"No, you didn't."

Smith fluffed her dark curls with both hands. "Joel."

"Joel Kidde? How fascinating. I never thought he had one."

"One what?"

"A penis."

Smith opened her mouth to respond, but the phone rang and Wetzon grabbed it. "Smith and Wetzon, good morning."

"Wetzon," a voice whispered into her ear. "The rumor *du jour* is that Dean Witter is buying Prudential."

"No kidding?" Who was this guy? She was trying to match the hoarse voice with a face, saw Smith staring at her, hands on hips. Wetzon gave Smith a broad wink, and Smith made a wringing motion with her hands, sat down at her desk, and began going through her messages.

"I hope you haven't forgotten me," the voice said in an even more seductive tone.

That did it. In all her experience as a headhunter, Wetzon had never met anyone quite like Kevin De Haven. His telephone technique *was* a seduction. "Oh, Kevin, come off it. You know that stuff doesn't work with me."

"What does, Wetzon? Come on, I'm serious here. I want to know."

"Never mind. Are we perhaps interested in making a move?"

"I am entertaining that idea. I hear they're giving money away all over the place."

"Well, let's say there are good deals for brokers without problems. Are you clean?"

"Would I lie to you?"

He'd answered her question with a question. What was wrong with this picture, she asked herself. "What kind of numbers are you doing?"

"Well, you gotta know, it's not like the old days. There's no calendar here."

"My, my, no new issues? No syndicate? How are we doing any business?"

"Very funny, Wetzon. I've got some big clients and they're buying listed stock from me. I'm doing between five and six hundred. But more important, I've cleaned up my act. Not one complaint in three years."

Ah, the answer to the big question. "Well, Kevin, maybe we ought to sit down and talk."

Wetzon wrote in an appointment for a drink with De Haven and hung up the phone in time to see Smith raise her pile of messages and, with a grand flourish, drop them in her wastebasket. She brushed her hands together and smiled at Wetzon.

"How do you know there wasn't something really important in there?"

"If it's that important—"

They both finished her sentence together: "—they'll call back." They looked at each other and laughed.

"Oh, well," Wetzon said, "I give up. Welcome aboard. But the day you put on tap shoes, I'm outa here."

"That's a deal." They shook hands on it. Smith's laughter was infectious. When she was up like this, she was fun to be around. Still, Carlos was right: Smith's behavior was particularly treacherous. After all, weren't they partners? Smoldering again, Wetzon found she wasn't prepared to let bygones be bygones just yet. "But right now I have something very important to discuss with you."

"Oh?" Smith upended the shopping bag of samples on her desk and began picking through them. "How about this on my living room walls?" She held up a piece of taupe linen.

"Very nice. Very expensive. Smith—"

"That's the general idea."

"Are you sure you want to do all that work on this apartment? You've been talking about moving for years."

Smith mulled that over for a moment. "So I have. You know, sweetie pie, you're absolutely right." She placed the shopping bag under the edge of the desk and shoveled all the samples back into it. "Fifth Avenue, or Park Avenue? What do you think?"

"Sutton Place is nice. My friend Gloria lives over there. And, of course, Central Park West is *fabulous.*" Wetzon was playing Little Iodine. She knew what Smith's reaction would be. Smith thought the

West Side was full of out-of-work actors, musicians, liberal Democrats, Jews, and blacks.

"Central Park West is on the West Side."

"It was last time I looked."

"Well, sugarplum, the West Side is good enough for you, but I would just be *lost* over there. There wouldn't be anyone like me on the street."

"Thanks, God," Wetzon said under her breath and was covered by the persistent ring of the phone. When she went to answer it, she saw someone already had. "Smith, I tried to get you all weekend—"

"I was in Westport."

"You didn't answer your phone."

"I was busy." She smiled uneasily, and cleared her throat. "If you must know, I was hiding from Dickie."

"Can't you just break it off with him?"

She shook her head. "It's not that easy."

"Did he threaten you? He threatened me."

"There are other things involved. I don't want to talk about it." She gave Wetzon a nervous smile.

"Jesus, Smith. Well, okay. Just let me know if I can help."

Max knocked, then stuck his head in. "Good morning, ladies. Lieutenant Silvestri is on the phone for you, Wetzon."

"Good morning, dearest Max," Smith said, bestowing a benevolent smile on him.

Wetzon rolled her eyes and picked up the phone. "Hi."

"Les, Nina just called." He sounded odd, gruff.

She sat down at her desk and turned her back to Smith. "It's Terri, isn't it?"

"It's Terri," he said.

MEMORANDUM

To: Carlos Prince and Leslie Wetzon
From: Nancy Stein, Assistant to Mort Hornberg
Date: November 21, 1994
Re: *Combinations, in Concert*

Bonnie McHugh's hair person is Brian Fahey (telephone 213-006-3428). I spoke with Joel Kidde, Bonnie's agent, who said that Fahey has a fixed price and that "We shouldn't try to negotiate with him." It's a take-it-or-leave-it situation, but Bonnie won't do the show without him. Then I asked if Fahey would do all the hair, but Kidde said no. If Fahey does all the hair, he gets a flat $10,000.

So we'll have to get someone with a little more flexibility to donate hair time for the two performances.

Chapter Nineteen

"CAN YOU BELIEVE BONNIE, CARLOS?"

"I told you she went Hollywood. She must owe this Brian Fahey from here to Casablanca."

"I'm for everyone doing her own hair."

"I couldn't agree with you more."

"NICE PLACE," NINA WAYNE SAID. SHE SET HER BRIEFCASE DOWN NEAR THE door. Her face was gray with fatigue, betraying more age than Wetzon had suspected. She took off her coat while Izz circled her cautiously, sniffing at her shoes, then slowly the little dog's tail began to wag.

"I've made coffee."

"I could use something stronger." Her voice was thin and colorless.

"Have you eaten?"

"Not since this morning."

"How about a nice buttery toasted bagel?"

"Oh, that would be heavenly."

"Wine? Beer? Vodka?"

"Vodka with orange juice."

Not long afterward they were sitting in the living room with their bagels and screwdrivers, shoes off, feet up, Glenn Gould playing Bach's *Italian* Concerto. They did not talk about Terri Matthews. It was almost as if they were waiting for official permission to do so.

After discussing diet, calcium and estrogen, the new skirt lengths, the pros and cons of sheer versus opaque panty hose, they fell silent.

"What exactly do you do?" Nina asked.

"I'm a search specialist, an executive recruiter, otherwise known in the vernacular as a headhunter. Which is fine with me. I call stockbrokers and encourage them to interview with other firms. And if the talk takes, the other firm pays me a percentage of what the stockbroker has done or will do. It's all based on supply and demand." Wetzon smiled. "They demand, we supply, we demand."

"It's your company?"

"Yes. I have a partner. We've been in business almost nine years now. Hard to believe. And we have two associates on staff."

"Do you like it?"

"I love it. Most of the time. Do you want a refill?"

"Yes."

Wetzon made another screwdriver for Nina but switched to plain orange juice for herself. As she set the glasses on the coffee table, she asked, "How did you get into forensic anthropology?"

"I started out in Paleo-Anthropology at Cornell. Physical—that is—human fossils. Then I just slipped into it. It seemed like a natural progression, for me at least. I did my graduate work in forensic anthropology at Kansas State."

"Are there many of you around?"

"When I was at Kansas, we were a pretty rare species, but things are changing. There are two hundred forensic anthropologists nationwide now, about forty–fifty of whom are in actual practice; the rest are students and/or scholars and researchers."

"And you teach, too."

"Yes, John Jay, and at Rutgers. I'm only part-time with New York State. I do about fifty or sixty cases a year for the City."

"Sounds like a full-time job to me."

"It is. New York City is a complex urban environment. We never know what we're going to find, and a lot depends on the chain of evidence. I have to be constantly aware of individual characteristics that I can determine postmortem and that may be a matter of antemortem social records: X rays, hospital and dental records."

"Then you're a detective, too."

"Yes. Right from the beginning. My first job is actually to ascertain whether the bones are even human."

Izz gave a hysterical bark and shot off the sofa. A moment later Silvestri's key turned in the lock; he opened the door and Izz danced around with short, excited yips. Silvestri was carrying Chinese takeout in a brown paper bag.

"Sorry I'm late." He took off his jacket, his harness and gun, and got a beer from the fridge.

"No problem, Silvestri," Nina said. "It's the first chance I've had to catch my breath in three days."

"Anyone want Chinese? Shrimp fried rice?"

"No, thanks," Nina said.

Wetzon shook her head.

"Good. More for me." He brought the open cardboard container, two chopsticks stabbed into it, into the living room and set it on the coffee table with a clutch of napkins and the bottle of Beck's. He left again and returned with his attaché, loosened his tie, then took it off and rolled up his shirt sleeves. "Did you show Nina the tile?"

"No. We were waiting for you."

"Take a look at this, Nina." He pulled the photo from his case and took Wetzon's fractured tile on its cardboard base and laid them both on the coffee table. "See that?"

Nina studied it, nodded to Silvestri. Silvestri pulled a stool from under the coffee table and sat down. He began eating the fried rice, using the chopsticks with expertise. "Okay, let's go through it again. I know, I've heard. Tell Les."

Sitting back on the sofa, Nina began. "Terri had an accident when she was fifteen. She fell into an empty swimming pool and broke her left humerus—her upper arm—in three places. The break was so bad she needed extensive surgery. Lucky for us."

"You found the records?"

"It wasn't easy. The hospital was torn down in '89, and some of the records were temporarily stored in the basement of one of the city government buildings and forgotten about. Again, lucky for us, because any records that went to the new hospital pre-1970 were destroyed."

"Then how on earth—"

"A volunteer at the PD, the widow of a cop. She was a retired archivist and she remembered taking a delivery of hospital files and organizing their storage to keep them separate from the city archives."

"There were X rays and they matched!"

Nina nodded.

"I think Terri had family in Cincinnati . . . an older aunt?"

"A grandmother. She died ten years ago. She'd been in a home with senile dementia since 1977."

Grandmother. Gran. Wetzon's brain leaked a memory of Terri on the phone, speaking very gently: "Gran, look in the oven or the refrigerator." She'd turned to Wetzon and explained, "She's lost her glasses again. She panics and calls me. I'm going to have to find her a place where they'll protect her. She forgets everything and I'm afraid she'll set the house on fire."

"Terri had to put her in a home, I think," Wetzon said. "She talked to Davey—the director of *Combinations*—and then flew to Cincinnati from Boston while the rest of us came on in with the show. She was all broken up about it. Her grandmother had raised her. And now she didn't even know who she was." It was like peeling an artichoke, Wetzon thought, because as she spoke, more and more came back to her. "Terri said bringing her grandmother to New York was not an option. She kept hinting that something important was happening in her life. Like the ivory silk suit she bought when we went shopping in Filene's Basement. For a special occasion, she said."

Nina was nodding. Silvestri, on the other hand, had this kind of proud papa look on his face that disconcerted Wetzon. Then it was gone, but their eyes met and held for a long moment.

"I drove out to the nursing home," Nina said, "and spoke to the administrator. Sarah Matthews, Terri's grandmother, died in 1985 not knowing or caring she even had a granddaughter. One of the nurses remembered Sarah as totally helpless. For a year or so before her death she couldn't even speak. No one ever visited her, although next of kin, according to old records, was Theresa Matthews in New York, at 481 West Eleventh Street, Apartment 2R. There were copies of two letters written by the director of the home to Terri about her grandmother's condition in 1979 and '80. Both were returned stamped 'Addressee Unknown.' "

"Then who paid for her grandmother's care?"

"Social Security and some money left by Terri's parents, who died in a boating accident when she was three. There's still some money in a trust account in Terri's name. It's been sitting in a local bank collecting interest for the past ten years."

"I don't get it. Wasn't there a lawyer?"

"The lawyer who had power of attorney for Terri and her grandmother died in 1980. His firm merged with another. The files went into storage at the other law firm. We'll have to subpoena them. They've continued to take their fee as trustees all these years and never notified anyone that Terri was missing."

"The subpoena for their files is in the works," Silvestri said.

"Why didn't this lawyer report Terri missing?"

"My personal feeling is that after his death, Terri slipped through the cracks, and if someone at the firm thought of doing something later on, it wasn't worth the trouble."

"Unethical and fraudulent behavior, I would say." Everyone, Wetzon thought, had let Terri down.

"What else?" Nina said.

"You said she was shot," Wetzon began.

"We found a spent bullet loose inside the skull and a circular perforation on the right occipital bone."

"Does that mean she was in the trunk when she was shot?"

"No. Small-caliber bullets don't usually pass through the body. We know for a fact that she was killed somewhere else because there was no obvious evidence of blood in the trunk. We packed everything up and sent it to the FBI. Their serology people may be able to find something."

"But what about the bullet?" Wetzon said. "Can't that be traced?"

Silvestri shook his head. "For that matter, with the bullet just lying there, we have no way of knowing that's the bullet that did the shooting, or even if it's from a handgun."

"Can't you fit the bullet into the hole in the skull?"

"No," Nina said. "Not very likely, because with time, bones contract or expand, especially after seventeen years and unknown moisture."

Silvestri added, "The only time you can associate bullet to body is if the bullet is lodged in the bone. If it's not lodged in the bone, it could have been in the trunk before the body was placed there."

"So," Wetzon said, deeply disappointed, "we are nowhere."

"Not necessarily." Silvestri set the cardboard container down, had a swig of beer, then took some folded sheets from his inside pocket. Wetzon reached over and moved the almost empty carton of fried rice to the side.

Laying the sheets flat, Silvestri read from them: "Rent-rolls for number 481 West Eleventh Street. The brownstone is five floors and has two floor-throughs on the fourth and fifth floors, then two apartments per floor on the second and third, and a garden apartment on the ground floor. Makes seven tenants, right?"

"Right," Wetzon said. "Plus whoever they lived with."

Nina watched Silvestri with narrowed eyes. "And?"

"No Terri or Theresa Matthews."

"Maybe she didn't live in the building after all," Wetzon said.

"And used it as a mail drop?" Nina frowned.

"I don't think so," Wetzon said. "She lived in the Village somewhere near Carlos, who was on Tenth Street then. Silvestri, didn't Equity have a last known address for her?"

"Yeah: 481 West Eleventh Street, Apartment 2R."

"Well . . ." Wetzon took the carton and began to pick at what was left of its contents with the chopsticks. "How about you just read off the names. She could have used an alias for some peculiar reason . . . like, you know, Georgina Spelvin. Actors use George or Georgina

Spelvin when they don't want to be associated with a play but need the work. Someone used Georgina in a porn film."

"You know that firsthand, Les?" Silvestri was laughing at her.

"Oh me, oh my, and you thought I made all this money on Wall Street, Silvestri," she said, going into the kitchen with the empty carton. She could hear Nina laughing. Wetzon returned with a tray bearing her coffeepot and three mugs.

"Hey," Silvestri said.

"Don't hey me," she said, mock huffy. "What name is on the rent-rolls for 2R in 1976 and 1977?" She set the mugs down.

He glanced down at the sheet of paper. "Poppy Morris."

Wetzon almost dropped the coffeepot. "Poppy Morris? Ged-doudahere!"

"Les?" Silvestri looked shocked.

"You know this Poppy Morris?" Nina said.

"Of course I know her. Poppy Morris is Mrs. Mort Hornberg."

SKELETON IN TRUNK IDENTIFIED

By Jonathan Thomas

The persistent investigative work of forensic anthropologist Nina Wayne and a NYPD detective, Lt. Silvestri, finally paid off when the identity of the entombed skeleton discovered in a trunk in the sub-basement of a Greenwich Village brownstone was established yesterday.

The remains have been identified as Theresa (Terri) Matthews, an actress, last seen on Broadway in the landmark musical "Combinations."

Coincidentally, that musical is being revived in concert with its original cast for two performances on Dec. 22 and 23.

Leslie Wetzon, one of the producers of the new production and a dancer in the original company, said that they had been looking for Ms. Matthews to re-create her performance, but she had dropped out of sight. The two concert performances are to benefit Show Biz Shares and to honor the memory of Davey Lewin, the original director, Roger Battle, the co-librettist, and Larry Saunders Lawrence, one of the dancers.

"We will be adding Terri's name to this," Ms. Wetzon said.

The building's owners, Angela and Barry Zeman, bought the empty brownstone in August, and had just begun extensive renovations when the trunk containing Ms. Matthews's remains was discovered.

Lt. Silvestri said that investigators would interview friends and associates of Ms. Matthews, who was unmarried and lived alone. No missing persons report was ever filed on her behalf. Lt. Silvestri added that while it has not yet been determined how Ms. Matthews died, the case is being treated as a homicide.

Chapter Twenty

"So that's the story," Carlos said. They were in the rented studio again and he was running Wetzon through the "Time Machine" number that she originated eighteen years ago in *Combinations*. Carlos was looking frayed around the edges. "Did you tell me she was shot in the head?"

"She was." She fumbled a step. "Dammit."

"Don't rush it, Birdie. Look, step left, shuffle right, ball change, brush, hop, toe, heel, step right, step left. There you go. 'I think she's got it.'"

Wetzon smiled at the quote from *My Fair Lady*. "They're not releasing it to the newspapers because they don't want to tell everything. I'm only telling you because you're going to swear on your twinkly toes that you will not say a word to anyone about how she was killed."

"This is so depressing, Birdie. I can't stand it. Terri was so lovely in a kind of fresh and clean, milkmaidy way." He watched her moving. "Okay, okay, and two and three, four, five, six, seven, eight."

The syncopated melody of the song surrounded them, bathing them in nostalgia. "I think that's the way she was inside, too. She always had that wide-eyed look—almost like a tourist, as if she were seeing everything for the first time and it was all quite wonderful."

"No, Birdie. Brush right, hop left, toe, heel, drop right, step left. See." He did it and she followed him.

"God, how does Ann Miller still do it?"

"She never stopped. She never decided it would be more fun to pick up a poisoned blowpipe and a poisonous partner and hunt heads on Wall Street."

"Oh, shush. You know I could never have been Ann Miller. Ta-da." She finished with a leap, step, step, stamp. Sweat streaked down her face, frizzled her hair. She sopped it up with her towel. "You see before you an aging body."

"Stop complaining. Let's go through it again."

"You're a slave driver. Can we rest for a minute?"

Carlos stopped the tape and Wetzon shuffled over to her gym bag and pulled out a bottle of Evian, took a long drink, and offered it to Carlos. He drank, capped it, and handed it back.

"Encore," he said. "It'll all come back, you'll see—"

"But will it come back in time? And will I live to see it?" Carlos was so trim, in fine dancing shape, that it was only possible to tell his age from the character lines around his eyes.

"You'll see." He grabbed her and pulled her along with him in a waltz clog around the studio. Wetzon was panting when they came to a stop.

"You're a handsome devil, my man." She hugged him, and he lifted her off her feet and twirled her around. When he set her down, her feet began tapping.

"I love you, too, Birdie." He kissed her and started the tape. "But you're on. Go for it."

She remembered more this time, or rather, her feet did, and by the second hour she had it. Now all she had to do was smooth the edges and throw herself into it with all the enthusiasm and energy of the young Leslie Wetzon, girl dancer, just out of college and in a real Broadway show.

"DID YOU KNOW PETER KOENIG THEN?" WETZON ASKED CARLOS. THEY WERE sitting at the counter in Rumpelmayer's spooning fresh whipped cream into their hot chocolates.

"Just to say hello to. He was always hanging around Terri, but I never got anything sexual between them."

"That's funny. Neither did I." The chocolate was so thick it coated her spoon. "He went out to the Seattle Rep in 1977, and now he's back in New York playing one of the leads in *Tacoma Triptych*. He called me for Terri's number."

"You mean he's never been in touch with her since?"

"That would have been difficult, wouldn't it? She's been a little dead."

"Maybe he killed her and he's covering himself because he read about the skeleton in the trunk."

"Maybe. But I'm more interested in why Terri was living in Poppy Hornberg's bachelor girl apartment."

"Oh, that's simple. It was a sublet."

"Were Poppy and Mort together then?"

"Don't think so, although they probably knew each other. Poppy wanted to get into United Scenic Artists. She was trying to persuade Boris or Ming or Oliver to hire her as an assistant to paint sets and stuff. Her parents had money, so it wasn't a question of salary. I think she finally got something with Tony Walton, when he was doing Mort's first show, but it didn't last long. She put her hooks into Mort, and that was that. It's likely just coincidence about the apartment, Birdie. Six degrees of separation and all that, you know."

"Thank you, John Guare." Wetzon's endorphins had kicked in: a tough, sweaty workout, followed by hot chocolate, surrounded by the restored Art Deco mosaics of the old restaurant. It made her dreamy. "I'm going to have a drink with Peter. Silvestri is talking to him today, and I'm meeting him for a drink tomorrow night after curtain at Joe Allen."

"By yourself?"

"Why not?"

"Why not, doll face? Because he might be a murderer."

"Get real. If Peter murdered Terri, he's certainly not going to do me at Joe Allen's crowded bar among all the tourists."

Carlos drained the grayish remnants from his cup. "I hesitate to ask, but does El Silvestri know you're meeting Peter?"

"I didn't ask his permission, if that's what you mean. And I don't need an escort," she added in high haughty.

"God help us, she's getting bent out of shape." Carlos raised one eyebrow at her and lowered the other eyelid. "Girl, I feel for the poor guy."

She laughed. "Who, Peter Koenig?"

"Oh, no. Someone much more in need of my sympathy."

"Who then?"

"Silvestri. Poor man. It must be a little like living with Miss Marple."

She threw her napkin at him. "Make that Kinsey Millhone, if you please. They're going to talk to Poppy, but they set up the *Times* article to try to blow the killer's cover."

"Oooooh, such cute language. Where did you get it?"

"Osmosis," she said, wrinkling her nose at him. "Everyone, including everyone from *Combinations*, will be at Mort's Thanksgiving party."

"And they'll all be talking about Terri, and the burglary that went bad," Carlos said, shaking his head. "Lordy, lordy."

"It wasn't a random killing, Carlos. It was too orderly. The bullet in the head, the body in her own packed trunk, moved to a sub-basement."

He stopped licking the chocolate from his spoon. "Wait a minute, Birdie, are you implying that—"

"Yes. Silvestri and Nina Wayne—she's the forensic anthropologist —think that Terri's killer was someone she knew well. Maybe someone we all knew . . . *know* . . . well."

· · ·

MEMORANDUM

To: Carlos Prince and Leslie Wetzon
From: Nancy Stein, Assistant to Mort Hornberg
Date: November 22, 1994
Re: *Combinations, in Concert*

Enclosed is another budget, but there are still lots of holes.
Ed Venderose, now that he's joined us, is going over
everything. He says we're over budget on the number of
stagehands. I know these numbers can be revised, but I
think we should wait until after the November 28th
meeting. Let me know what you think.

See you at Mort's party.

Chapter Twenty-One

"CARLOS, DARLING. ED VENDEROSE, DO YOU REMEMBER HIM?"

"Of course. He blossomed from nerdy apprentice to Broadway general manager. He's made quite a career for himself."

"He's a worm, a letch, and a creep."

"But if he's a good general manager, what difference does it make, honey chile?"

"Grrrrr."

AT THE LAST MINUTE, ON A WHIM, INSTEAD OF GOING HOME AND COMING BACK down later to meet Peter Koenig, Wetzon went to the box office of the Booth and bought a ticket for the first preview of *Tacoma Triptych*. The line was short—everybody was waiting for a preview closer to the opening when the show found its legs—and there were plenty of orchestra seats available. Then she went over to Ollie's for a bowl of hot-and-sour soup and an order of spareribs. She was tired, and every muscle and joint complained. No more excuses; she would have to start taking regular classes again.

In the meantime, she had no idea what had happened at Silvestri's meeting with Peter Koenig. Silvestri had stayed at his place last night. When she got home after her rehearsal with Carlos, there'd been a message from him saying just that. No explanation.

Wouldn't you think, she mused, peeling the red flesh from the sparerib, that he would say why? How would it be if he said, "Les, I have to stay in Chelsea tonight because of something or other, but I love you and miss you, my darling"? Sure. Don't hold your breath, baby. And if he did, how long would it take her to lose interest?

She almost laughed aloud. The not-quite-attainable always had more appeal. A maître d' led a couple by and the woman was wearing L'Air du Temps. Terri Matthews, who'd worn that scent, floated into Wetzon's prescience, like the ghost of Hamlet's father. *Didn't anyone miss me?* I'm so sorry, Terri, she thought. I owe you. She looked down at the small pile of clean bones and pushed her plate away. What was the matter with her? She paid the bill, went to the ladies' room, and scrubbed her hands.

A brisk wind blew down Shubert Alley, chasing people into the lobbies of the adjacent theatres—on the Forty-fourth Street side at the south end of the Alley, the Shubert, where *Crazy for You* still ran; and at the north end, Forty-fifth Street, the Booth. At the Booth a small knot of people milled around. First previews were always rough, and theatre mavens were discouraged by producers from attending. Heaven help us, word could get out that a show was in bad shape. And on Broadway a breath of that kind of word was death.

So what you often had was the Theatre Development Fund crowd. TDF would buy up blocks of tickets at a big discount and sell them to its members (membership was a small annual fee) at approximately half the box office price. All of this was underwritten by contributions from the big foundations and the state and national councils on the arts. The practice served as a buttress against empty houses, which were bad for morale as well as the pocketbook.

And then there was "paper": the house was papered when unsold tickets to previews, as well as after the opening, were often given to Actors Equity to distribute to members, and to hospitals for staff.

The Booth was full of paper tonight. Wetzon saw it when she took her seat toward the rear of the orchestra. Actors Equity. Although they tended to punch up the laughs, actors were usually good audiences. They forgave much in the name of Theatre.

She looked behind her as ticket holders slowly took their seats. Standing room was rarely sold to the public during previews. This

space was where the creative and production teams gathered to watch
the show and take notes. It would not be unusual to find the playwright, his significant other, assistants of every ilk, most of the production team, all leaning on the shelf behind the last row of the center
orchestra with their legal pads. Everyone except the director, who usually chose to sit somewhere in the first ten rows. No one had gathered
for the moment; she took off her coat and let it rest on her shoulders.

There was no stage curtain. The set for *Tacoma Triptych* was an art
museum. The play had been a huge success for the Seattle Rep and
had gone from there to the Goodman in Chicago, and now it had come
to Broadway without any assurance of success. This was because
Broadway was big-time and what delighted Seattle or Chicago audiences rarely did the same for New York.

Tacoma Triptych played straight through without an act break.
Good thing, too, because few would have returned for a second act.
The play was tedious. Its pacing was off and some of the performances
were amateurish. Not Peter Koenig's, though. He was impressive. He
had a pivotal role in the first two-thirds of the play, after which his
character admitted to a terrible murder and committed suicide.

It was a chilling scene, and its power froze the audience. Then the
play drifted slowly to its final scene, when it turned out that Peter's
character had not done the murder at all. He had confessed to protect
his stepdaughter. She had not only committed the original murder as a
child but had also manipulated her stepfather's suicide.

An opera without music is what it was, although rumor had it that
the Pulitzer Committee was taking it seriously. With or without the
Prize, how long *Tacoma Triptych* would run in New York was highly
debatable. Still, such a show was a showcase for performers like Peter
Koenig. He would get spectacular reviews, a Tony nomination, and
Hollywood would beckon. People would remember his performance
long after the show was forgotten.

That is, unless Peter had killed Terri. Then nobody would remember his performance in *Tacoma Triptych*. Or, in reality, everyone would
if that was to be his last role.

Wetzon slipped into her coat as the lights in the theatre came up and the cast members began to take their bows. Paper usually ran for the hills the minute the play was over, but this group didn't. They waited for Peter, gave him a standing ovation, and then ran.

She was mildly curious about the author of *Tacoma Triptych*, the pseudononymous M. B. Garfield. *New York* magazine had done a short titillating piece, promising they would reveal the identity of the author after the play opened. Wetzon smiled. It was probably Joyce Carol Oates. Ms. Oates was so prolific it was almost an embarrassment.

Wetzon's eyes took in the standees. Anyone back there in standing room could be the author, for they were all strangers to her. All except for the hulking, redwood-shaped Ed Venderose, the general manager. Ed had been a sonorous-voiced apprentice who delighted in what he thought were hilarious misogynistic jokes when Wetzon was still a gypsy. She saw his eyes flick over the orchestra, pass over her, veer back. He was trying to place her. She turned away from him.

As the curtain calls ended, the group standing in the rear of the house began to disperse. Wetzon came up the aisle thinking about Terri again, her bones, the grinning skull replacing the sweet-faced girl. Pausing, she fit her beret carefully over her topknot. A whispered expletive made her turn in time to notice a tall figure making a real effort to remove herself from Wetzon's line of sight. Although the woman's face was hidden by a slouch hat, it was not hidden enough so that Wetzon couldn't recognize Medora Battle.

"Medora!"

Medora looked chagrined. She played with the belt of her tan trenchcoat. Like Rog, her late husband, Medora was white bread and could disappear in any crowd of Episcopalians, but not in the working Theatre, where ethnicity reigned. Her pale blue eyes rested on Wetzon briefly, then skimmed away, as if Wetzon had caught her with her fingers in the till. "Leslie," she said. "I can't—"

"Well, Leslie Wetzon, I thought I recognized you!" Ed Venderose blocked her. "What are you doing here?" He didn't wait for an answer.

By the sheer force and breadth of his huge belly, he pushed her outside.

Before she had a chance to sputter or flail at him, Wetzon was on the street in front of the theatre among hordes of people. And both Venderose and Medora were gone.

MEMORANDUM

To: Carlos Prince and Leslie Wetzon
From: Nancy Stein, Assistant to Mort Hornberg
Date: November 22, 1994
Re: *Combinations, in Concert*

Please hold Monday, the 28th, at five o'clock, for a production meeting at Mort's office. We have a few things to iron out, including whether there should be a third performance especially for the taping.

Joel Kidde and Xenia Smith, who are producing it for television with Mort, may also be attending.

Chapter Twenty-Two

"Birdie, did you see the memo?"

"Yes."

"I can hear you're in a foul humor."

"Aren't you?"

"I still can't figure out how the Barracuda wormed her way into our project."

"You should have been her partner all these years. Then you wouldn't have to ask a question like that."

"No, thank you very much anyway, darling."

WETZON, FURIOUS WITH HERSELF FOR NOT SWIFT-KICKING VENDEROSE, took herself over to Joe Allen. Who did Ed think he was anyway? She was going to have a few short but curt words with Mort about putting him on *Combinations*. Wasn't Nancy supposed to be general-managing? Now there was an extra salary. Whose bright idea was this?

And what the hell had gotten into Medora Battle? It was as if the whole world were doing some kind of weird, deadly dance.

She sat at the far end of the dark bar and ordered a beer. Some of the regulars still came for the bar, but the restaurant itself was always full of tourists who assumed Joe Allen—its walls covered with posters of flop shows, some in which she'd danced—was one of the theatre world's favorite eating spots.

The bartender was deftly making margaritas while Wetzon nursed her beer and watched the door for Peter. She didn't even know what she would ask him. And because she'd been unable to vent her anger at Ed Venderose, she felt stupid and self-conscious.

Peter chose that moment to appear, and Wetzon noticed again the slick veneer, something he'd lacked seventeen years earlier. She waved and he came and sat next to her. Then to her surprise, he leaned over and kissed her cheek.

The bartender smacked a cocktail napkin down in front of him. "What'll you have?"

"Scotch and soda," Peter said. He began patting his pockets as if looking for something.

Wetzon watched him, not saying anything. The waiter set the scotch and soda in front of Peter. The actor stared at it for a moment before taking a sip. He gave up his search for whatever he'd been looking for.

"I'm having some trouble accepting this," he said suddenly.

"Welcome to the club," Wetzon said.

"How could it have happened? Where were we?"

"Where were you?"

"I had the offer from the Seattle Rep." He took another swallow. "I told you that. I wanted her to marry me."

"And she said no?"

He nodded. "There was someone else, she said. She was going to marry him." Peter turned away from Wetzon, and when he spoke again, she had to strain to hear him. "I'll never forget what she said. She said, 'Don't you want me to be happy?' "

"Who was he?"

"She wouldn't tell me. She said I'd know soon enough. Did she tell you?"

"No. I remember calling her about a week after the show closed. She sounded funny, sort of disappointed it was me, and told me she was expecting another call and would call me back. She never did. And I went out with *Promises, Promises,* and that was it."

"A police detective called me today. I put him off till tomorrow afternoon because I didn't want anything to get into my head before the performance."

So Silvestri had not gotten to Peter yet. "What do you expect? It's a murder investigation. According to the papers, they are going to question everyone who knew Terri. That means all of us."

"I guess I feel guilty," Peter said. His voice was uneven, and when he rubbed his eyes, some fragment of makeup shifted to his hand in a dull smudge.

"We all do." Wetzon worked on her beer. "Saw your performance tonight. It was wonderful."

"Thank you." He radiated pleasure. "Did you pay for your ticket?"

She nodded.

"I wish you'd told me. I would have passed you in."

"It's okay."

"Streisand is buying it. She wants to direct the movie. They're talking to me about repeating the part."

"Nice."

He drummed his fingers on the bar and didn't say anything for a long minute. Then he took her hand. "Look, Leslie, I've been talking this through with Xenia."

"Xenia?" Automatically, Wetzon pulled her hand away, and almost fell off the stool. That settled it. She was going to have to kill Smith.

"She's a very empathetic person, don't you think?" Peter put his hand on her thigh.

"Oh, very." She looked down at his hand. "Do you mind?"

He removed his hand. "The cops will never find whoever did it. We knew her better than anyone—"

"We're talking *murder*, Peter. Terri didn't put herself in the trunk and walk down to that basement."

"No argument. He did it."

"He who?"

"The guy she was in love with. Something must have gone wrong."

"Very wrong."

"And her friends deserted her."

"Hold on there."

"Anyway, I was really glad to hear you'll do it."

"Do what?" What the hell was he talking about?

"Xenia said—"

"Excuse me. *Xenia* said?"

"She said that your company does investigations and that you'd be happy to look into Terri's murder. The killer has to be someone connected to *Combinations*."

"Why?" She banged her fist on the bar, frustrated. "Dammit, Peter. No!"

"I feel responsible, Leslie. I was angry. She rejected me. I had the offer for Seattle and I wanted to get as far away from her as possible."

"The police should handle this, Peter." Depressed, Wetzon sighed and finished her beer. "Why do you say it was someone in *Combinations*? I would have known it. And besides, all the guys are— were—gay."

"Terri told me she had a serious thing going with someone in the company. I hung around outside her building that day for a long time, but no one I recognized showed up." He found his wallet and flipped it open, searching through its crevices. "Oh, here it is." He pulled out a piece of paper, unfolded it, and handed it to her. It was a check.

When Wetzon didn't take it, he put it on the bar in front of her. "So it's a deal?" he said. "Good. I'll call you." When he handed the bartender his American Express card, his elbow brushed his wallet, sending it to the floor. Wetzon got off the stool and picked it up. He hadn't even noticed his wallet was gone. He signed the slip and looked to return the card to its slot, but no wallet.

"You dropped this, I think," Wetzon said, handing him the wallet.

"Practicing another career move?" he asked, slipping the card in its slot and putting the wallet in his inside pocket.

"Not me."

He kissed her on the cheek again and left.

Which is when Carlos emerged from a dark table and sat down beside her. "What's this?" he asked, fingering the check.

"Our retainer. What are you doing here?"

"Protecting my talent. Retainer for what?"

"Yeah, yeah. He's hiring Smith and me to investigate Terri's murder."

"I want you to tell me, Dear Heart, that you said absolutely positively no."

"Can't do that. Smith said absolutely positively yes."

"Laying it off on the Barracuda, are we? And you're not tempted."

"This is not a joke, Carlos. I saw his cards."

"What cards?"

"One card in particular. 'Pistol License.' In his wallet, dammit. I'm talking English. Why aren't you following me?"

"I'd follow you anywhere, Birdie. Just tell me in good simple words."

"A pistol license, Carlos. Peter Koenig has a license to carry a gun."

MEMORANDUM

To: Carlos Prince and Leslie Wetzon
From: Nancy Stein, Assistant to Mort Hornberg
Date: November 22, 1994
Re: *Combinations, in Concert*

I know you would want to hear some good news: the
response to the ad has been incredible. Ticket orders are
rolling in. We'll fill them on a first-come, first-serve basis. At
this rate the *Combinations* benefit will be sold out by early
December.

Chapter Twenty-Three

"GODDAMMIT, WETZON, DOESN'T ANYONE DO A PLAIN VANILLA BUSINESS ANY-more?"

"George, you mean to tell me you don't want brokers who do sexy things—like derivatives?"

"Too much trouble. They head south on a deep breath and we all go down with them."

Wetzon laughed. How true. Recently another major firm had had to cough up hundreds of millions to prop up their own mutual funds, fat with derivatives. Rosenkind Luwisher brokers, especially, were given free rein to develop odd businesses, which usually meant they were not portable. An unportable feast, she thought. "So how about someone doing a million-dollar business?"

"On what?"

"Institutional options to international clients. He's looking for a firm that commits capital to the options market."

George groaned. "Good luck to whoever hires him."

"Then, last but not least, another million-dollar man. Fourth year in production, international business in S and P futures. Rosenkind Luwisher gives him a direct line to the floor of the Merc in Chicago."

"Read my lips, Wetzon. Plain vanilla."

"Well, now that you mention it, I do have a plain vanilla broker from Rivington Ellis. He's been in the business—"

"Which office?"

"Ted Crass's."

"Then he's one of Crass's Criminals, and I don't want him. Try me again, Wetz—" The phone crashed in her ear even before he finished saying her name.

Wetzon hung up the phone. George was probably right. Ted Crass had hired a crew of the hyper and burned-out from other firms, and the brokers in his office had become known on the Street as Crass's Criminals. There were lawsuits up the yin-yang. Wetzon knew it was only a matter of time before Rivington Ellis pulled the plug on Crass, and almost no one would want his brokers. But they would wander around and eventually get hired somewhere because they did big numbers. What? Wall Street police itself? Not in this life.

As for the Rosenkind Luwisher brokers, they were all eager to interview, but no one wanted to talk to them. Plain vanilla was what headhunters and managers on the Street all longed for, but plain vanilla wasn't changing firms these days.

Wetzon pushed the Rosenkind Luwisher folder to the side, uncovering the five-thousand-dollar check that Peter Koenig had made out to Smith and Wetzon. "Damn," she said for the umpteenth time. She was angry all over again. She poked at the check with her pen, took it up, looked at it, put it back.

And it was this opportune moment that Smith chose to waltz through the door. Wetzon rose from her chair ready for blood.

Smith was deterred for only an instant. "Sweetie pie," she bubbled, "I have so much to tell you."

"And I have a few things to discuss with you." Wetzon reached for the check.

"I'll go first," Smith said.

"How could I have thought otherwise? What's so important?"

"Well," Smith said, putting her shawl over the back of her chair, "I'm thinking of getting my eyes done."

"This is important?"

"It is for me." Smith got huffy. "I have to look my best now—"

"Now that you're in show business? Smith, for godsakes, you look wonderful. You always look wonderful."

"Maybe just the little wrinkles around my eyes." Smith had her mirror out and was sending little teasing smiles to her image.

"Why not have your whole face done, so long as you're there already?" Wetzon suggested.

Smith tilted her head. "And my neck. I really hate that chicken skin, don't you?"

"For sure. Hate it. Really hate it."

Nodding, Smith said, "You're absolutely right." She fluttered her fingers under her chin. "How is Darlene doing?"

"Not bad. She's lining up people for Boston. She's working out all right, I guess, but she's so neurotic. Would you believe she wipes her phone down with her purse vial of alcohol a few times a day? I can't see her running this place."

Smith dropped the mirror on her desk. Luckily, it didn't shatter. "Running this place? Are you crazy? *We're* running this place."

"We are? I thought you're going into show biz."

"Well, I'm dabbling. It's okay to dabble."

"Dabble all you want, but maybe we should think about selling the business."

"Selling? You want to sell *my* business?"

"It was *our* business last time I looked." Wetzon leaned against her desk, arms folded, just barely resisting the urge to strangle Smith.

"Oh, for pitysakes. What would you do?"

"What would I do? That's right, Smith, I have no other life except this business."

"That's what I've been saying," Smith said with exaggerated patience. "You limit yourself, sweetie pie. I mean, you've tied yourself to Dick Tracy. You're an appendage. When was the last time he took you out someplace nice?"

"That's beside the point. Silvestri doesn't have to—"

"I rest my case." Smith smiled and made a sound suspiciously similar to a purr.

The outside door opened and closed. Smith cocked her head, then jumped up and flung open the door to their private office. A tall young man stood on the threshold grinning at them.

"Mark," Wetzon said, all smiles. Smith's boy was a handsome man well over six feet tall, and despite his mother and her cracked values, he had somehow grown into a decent human being.

"Hi, Wetzon," he said. He was wearing a bulky black leather jacket and clean pressed khakis.

"My baby." Smith straightened the collar of his shirt, which had disappeared under the weight of the jacket. Her hands lingered on her son probably longer than necessary. Mark was in his first year at Harvard and she was very proud of him.

"Aw, Ma," he said, but he gave her a hug and then reached for Wetzon.

Wetzon hugged him back. He smelled of leather and aftershave. "It's so good to see you."

"I don't want to butt into your day," he said.

"It's okay. We're closing the office early, right, Smith?"

Smith nodded. "Mark and I are going to get a quick snack and do some shopping. Mark needs new clothes."

"No, I don't. All I wear at school is jeans." He winked at Wetzon.

Smith paid no attention. "We're having dinner at Orso with Joel, and afterward Joel's arranged for us to see *Showboat* in Hal's own house seats."

"Excuse me. Hal?"

"Hal Prince, of course. I would think you'd know that, Wetzon," Smith said, giving Wetzon flinty eyes.

"Very nice," Wetzon said.

"Oh, and I got us house seats for *Tacoma Triptych* for Friday, if you want to go, Ma."

"Oh, I don't know, sugar." Smith looked blank.

"A serious straight play, Ma. Supposed to be wonderful."

"House seats?" Wetzon asked. "Do you know someone on the show?"

"Only the playwright's daughter. April's in some of my classes."

"Wait a minute," Wetzon said. "There's a big mystery over who the author really is."

"Well, I know the answer," Mark said, pleased with himself. "Do you want me to tell you?"

"Of course."

Smith frowned. "What are you two talking about?"

"Tell me, Mark." When he paused, Wetzon said, "Okay, tell me the last name of your friend."

"I'll tell you her whole name. April—dum-da-dum-dum—Battle."

"Aha!" Wetzon said. "I knew it! Medora Battle wrote *Tacoma Triptych?*"

Mark nodded.

"What's this about Medora Battle?" Smith said, annoyed.

"I don't understand. Why all the secrecy?"

"Well, all I know is April said her mother's had a writing block since her father died, and was very insecure about writing without her father. It's taken all these years."

Smith looked from Wetzon to Mark. She was out of the loop. "I don't understand what you two are talking about. Wetzon, didn't you have something you wanted to tell me?"

"Yes, I did. I do." Wetzon tucked Medora Battle away on a back burner for the time being and girded herself to deal with Smith.

"Great," Mark said. "I'll just sit out at old Max's desk and make some phone calls." He smiled at Darlene, who looked up from making notes on a suspect sheet.

"Darlene, meet Mark, Smith's son," Wetzon called. "We'll shut down at one o'clock, I think, and reconvene Monday morning. Unless you have any objections, Smith?"

"Fine with me. I want to have a staff meeting Monday morning and make a business plan for the next six months." She gave Wetzon a meaningful look, as if to say, *No more talk about selling this firm.* "Darlene, please call Max and ask him to be in at ten o'clock on Monday."

Wetzon sighed. Once more she was being herded along on Smith's itinerary.

Smith closed the door. "What did you want to talk to me about, babycakes?"

Wetzon shifted back into first gear. And once again Smith had almost managed to drive everything from Wetzon's mind. Taking a necessary moment to gather her wits, Wetzon said, "Peter Koenig." She pulled the check out from under the paperweight and fluttered it at Smith. "Goddammit, Smith, you told him we do private investigations . . ."

Smith managed to squeeze out a smirk. "I did, didn't I?"

"Why?"

"Because we do—"

"Smith!"

"I did it for you, sweetie pie. You were so upset about how this skeleton might be your dancer friend, so I gave you an opening. . . ."

"Oh, Smith," Wetzon groaned. "We can't do this."

"Why not, I'd like to know?" Smith said. "Money is money. It's what I'm always telling you: If they give, you take. If they take, you scream."

MEMORANDUM

To: Carlos Prince and Leslie Wetzon
From: Nancy Stein, Assistant to Mort Hornberg
Date: November 22, 1994
Re: *Combinations, in Concert*

JoJo sent the attached breakdown. He didn't include a
conductor on the payroll because the conductor wouldn't be
a member of Local 802.

Also, he included himself as Leader because one is required.
It's his intention to turn that money back to Show Biz
Shares.

Chapter Twenty-Four

"WELL, JOJO'S MY MAN," CARLOS SAID.

"I'm surprised, I guess."

"He's not as bad as you think he is. Oversexed ain't bad, you know, Birdie."

"Oh, please."

IN THE CITY OF NEW YORK, APARTMENTS WERE LABELED "POSTWAR" AND "prewar," the war always meaning World War II.

Prewar buildings (symbolized in real estate ads as "P/W") were extremely desirable because they usually had large rooms with beamed ceilings, intricately parqueted floors, big kitchens with pantries; some even had F/Ps—fireplaces. Their windows—those that hadn't been replaced because of rotting frames—were double-hung with eight lights, or were the casement variety. Their lobbies were marble-floored, with stained-glass windows, brass trimmings, and ornately plastered ceilings. Those buildings that dated from the thirties were Deco in architecture and design.

Wetzon lived in one of the P/W buildings on the Upper West Side, where they proliferated. Her building dated back to 1922.

But as lovely as these buildings were, they, like people, aged. Parts began to wear out and had to be replaced. Parts like roofs, elevators, boilers, water pipes, plumbing, wiring. Whenever something needed replacement, tenants were assessed according to the number of shares they owned in the co-op. Wetzon had just finished paying off a twelve-thousand-dollar assessment for her share of a new elevator.

Laura Lee Day, on the other hand, lived in a postwar building near Lincoln Center. Her building could not be considered new, as it dated back to the mid-sixties, but it was old enough to have, along with a huge terrace, large rooms and relatively high ceilings. But no picture moldings and no rosettes in plaster, Wetzon thought, as she stared upward.

"I feel detached," she said. She handed the container of black bean soup she'd bought at Fairway to Laura Lee, who emptied it in a saucepan to heat.

Laura Lee had returned that morning on the red-eye from Los Angeles. She looked at Wetzon dubiously. "Um, that's because you don't want to deal with the fact of your friend's murder." She stirred the soup. "I have olive sticks from that divine bakery in Santa Monica, and goat cheese—"

"It's not just Terri, it's everything. I feel as if I'm in limbo. Where are your bowls?"

"Up there." Laura Lee pointed with her nose to the cabinet above her. "What everythin'?"

"Smith—"

"Well, that's hardly a surprise. The surprise is that you two are still partners."

Wetzon grunted. She'd heard it all before. "Headhunting is not as much fun as it was. Duck a minute, will you?" She opened the cupboard over Laura Lee's head and took down two soup bowls. "There've been so many mergers, which eliminate either clients or fertile hunting grounds. Now Rosenkind Luwisher has decided to hire an inside recruiter and cut us out. Firms have tried it in the past and it's never worked."

"So what do you care?" The soup began to sizzle around its circumference, and Laura Lee turned down the burner to let it simmer. "The truth is, Xenia Smith is like some awful relative you're stuck with being related to. But you're in luck."

"How so?"

"She's *not* a relative." Laura Lee set the bowls on a tray with a bottle of sherry and two glasses.

"Laura Lee, do you know what it's like to break up a partnership?"

"It's not easy."

"Yes. Maybe I will someday and it'll be when I want it to happen, but not right now. I'm not ready."

"So you've detached yourself?" Laura Lee turned off the light under the soup and poured it, steaming, into the bowls.

"I guess." The bag of breadsticks was sweating oil. Wetzon shook them out onto the napkin she'd placed in a bread basket, then licked her fingers.

"What about Silvestri?" Laura Lee asked, giving her friend a sideways glance.

"Yes, what about Silvestri?" Wetzon didn't look up. She busied herself with unwrapping the goat cheese and setting the plate on the tray next to the olive sticks. Laura Lee carried the tray into the dining room and Wetzon followed.

The room was really a dining L, but its windows faced out on a large terrace. Twenty floors up brought it an expansive view of the City, looking south and west to the Hudson.

"Darlin', you're havin' a little old midlife crisis," Laura Lee informed her. She moved the bowls from the tray to the linen placemats, which were set with matching napkins and silver.

"Impossible. I had one last year, and one is enough. Don't you know that your body forms antibodies and it can't happen again?"

"Last year was different. You had that post-traumatic stress disorder and it came from gettin' shot. This has everythin' to do with turnin' forty, darlin'. What's with the unemotional Italian?" She poured sherry into the glasses and a dollop into her soup.

Wetzon laughed. "Same old-old. There, but not there. You know. No commitment. Not even a promise. I guess I have a relationship with the only strong and silent Italian in the country."

"You could have had a commitment from Alton Pinkus, and you didn't want it." She put her spoon in the soup and then to her mouth.

"Now you sound like Smith. I would have been some kind of trophy for Alton. That's not me, and you know it."

"I do know it. Let me ask you the big question, darlin'."

"Shoot."

"Would you marry Silvestri if he asked you?"

No sound for a while except the faint slurping of soup being sipped.

"Maybe if he got me at a weak moment." Making an effort to smile, Wetzon set her spoon down, distressed. "I don't know."

"Well, you should."

"What would you do? I mean, if Eduardo—"

"I'm the wrong person to ask," Laura Lee said. "Eduardo and I have a nice arrangement. He stays in his place and I am happy here. It's the perfect relationship. He's had children; he's been married; and I am not interested in either experience, thank you. Of course, you might—"

Aghast, Wetzon said, "You don't think I'm going to have a baby at forty! Can you imagine *me* changing a diaper?"

They stared at each other and both began to laugh. Then Wetzon stopped. It seemed suddenly awful to be laughing about a situation like a midlife crisis, like marriage and children, when Terri Matthews would never have that problem.

"So what's it to be?" Laura Lee asked, putting a thin layer of goat cheese on her olive stick.

"I'm going to find out who killed Terri. That's first. And I'm afraid it's going to be someone I know, someone connected to the original company of *Combinations*. Someone who'll be at Mort's Thanksgiving party tomorrow."

"So, I see we're changin' the subject here. Okay with me." Laura Lee raised her sherry glass to Wetzon.

"Someone's been leading a double life for seventeen years, Laura Lee."

"Maybe it was one of the people who died. Did you think of that?"

"Two of them died of AIDS, and Rog Battle had heart failure. Besides, Rog and Medora—" She stopped.

"What? I'm waitin' breathlessly."

Wetzon thought out loud. "Rog Battle. He always had a girl in the chorus. There was a story that Medora and her mother attacked one of his girls from a previous show on a subway platform. They beat her up pretty badly."

"Tsk, tsk, what sordid lives these Broadway types lead."

"I wonder who would remember that?" Wetzon took a sip of sherry. "I bet Foxy would. Mort might. Rog died right after the show closed. Carlos and I were at Davey's apartment when the call came. I took it . . ."

"You?"

"Yeah. Isn't that odd? It was Medora. For some reason, Davey didn't want to talk to her. I told her he couldn't come to the phone, but then a man came on. It was their doctor and he told me Rog had died. I made Davey take the phone then."

"So Rog Battle died before Terri?"

"I think I talked to Terri after that. I think . . ."

"Was Rog Battle the big dick-around on the show?"

Wetzon snorted. "Big dick-around, huh? I like that."

"Was he?"

"I—no. No. Come to think of it, JoJo was. He was the nervous, first-time conductor. And boy, did he dick around." She paused and grinned. "He even hit on me. But all the time it was very clear that JoJo was Foxy Reynard's fella."

MEMORANDUM

To: Carlos Prince and Leslie Wetzon
From: Nancy Stein, Assistant to Mort Hornberg
Date: November 22, 1994
Re: *Combinations, in Concert*

Re: sound. With some minor substitutions, Boomer Inc. has
come in with a bid of $10,000 for the equipment rental.
They will also charge us for two men to load-in. One will be
at the hourly rate of $35.75 and the other at the rate of $28.
Eddie Venderose says this is a fair charge.

Chapter Twenty-Five

"WHAT DO YOU SAY? TWO LARGE PLAIN, THREE SALADS, THREE BREWS?" Silvestri hadn't even bothered checking the menu on the wall of their booth.

The women looked at each other and smiled.

"Beck's or Amstel. If not, I'll have a glass of red," Wetzon said.

"Whatever," Nina said. She was wearing a dark blue business suit with a silk blouse in a busy blue paisley. Her makeup was subtle.

Wetzon had gone home after lunch with Laura Lee and found a message on her answering machine from Silvestri, asking that she meet him and Nina Wayne at John's in the Village at seven-thirty.

The line in front of John's (no slices sold here) that usually straggled out onto the sidewalk was not in evidence this night before Thanksgiving. In fact, the Bleecker Street pizzeria many, including Wetzon, felt was the best in New York had a few empty tables tonight.

But the air was redolent with Sinatra over the jukebox and with melting mozzarella and tomatoes, garlic, and charred crusts. And one pie after another was paddled in and out of the brick oven as quickly as they were prepared. The atmosphere took Wetzon back over twenty-five years to a dive called the Golden Grill, where she'd had her first taste of something called tomato pie.

There was something about pizza and old-fashioned pizzerias that gave Wetzon a sense of well-being, better than Valium any day. At this moment in her life she was supremely happy sitting here in one of

John's slightly uncomfortable wooden booths, elbows on the table, breathing pizza, Silvestri's thigh pressed against hers.

The salads were enormous mounds of greens, studded with mushrooms and tomatoes in a sharp vinaigrette, and quickly the table was crowded with plates and glasses.

In the booth behind them two actors and a civilian were having an intense discussion about the new Woody Allen movie, the actors dissecting the technique of the various performers. Not content to stop there, they moved on to the camera work, the script and, of course, the director. All the while, the civilian kept protesting plaintively that she'd liked the movie.

The pies, their parchment-thin crusts with charred edges, were set up on raised platforms over their beers and salad plates. They began eating at once, the women letting Silvestri put slices on their plates, waiting for him to initiate talk about the case. For why else should they be here together?

Why else indeed?

Silvestri took a notepad from the inside pocket of his jacket and set it on the table. "I've talked to almost all the principals—I'll run them down one at a time—but I'll tell you right now, except for Peter Koenig, they stonewalled me. And I'm not so sure about Koenig. He seemed too good to be true and almost overly anxious to help."

"Stonewalled? What do you mean?" Nina was eating her slice with a knife and fork.

"I mean as in stonewalled. You know, the three monkeys, see no, hear no, say less."

Wetzon was not surprised, and said so. "No one wants to think that any of us could have killed her. Did you figure out when it might have happened?" She folded her slice slightly and chomped. How odd it felt to be eating with such relish and discussing the horrible death of a friend. Did all the mundanities of life carry on, or was she becoming callous?

"Probably not long after the show closed, in 1977. Right, Nina?"

"It would fit what we've been able to learn from the remains."

"*Combinations* closed the end of the third week in May, in 1977," Wetzon said. "Business fell off and they kept posting the closing notice and taking it down." When she saw they didn't understand, she explained, "The producers of a show that might close have to put up a two-week closing notice or Equity says they're liable for two weeks' salary. They were afraid of the falloff in business that always happens after Memorial Day, so they finally closed it."

"That means Terri was probably murdered sometime—and this is an approximation—between May twenty-fifth and mid-June, in 1977, because the lease on the apartment continued to be in Poppy Morris's name until June fifteenth, and then was not renewed."

"Okay," Wetzon said, "so what did Poppy have to say about it?"

"She's the only one I haven't been able to talk to. The husband—Mort Hornberg—says she's been very busy with the big Thanksgiving party they give every year."

Wetzon gave a short laugh, almost like one of Smith's humpfs. "Poppy busy with the party? Give me a break. Poppy's never lifted her little finger to do anything in her life. She's—"

"So who plans the social calendar?" Nina said.

"Mort does. He's the social butterfly. Mort's one of those obsessive types who has to control everything. Poppy couldn't care less. In fact, I've had meetings at their apartment that ran through lunch and she never even offered anyone a cup of coffee or a drink or anything. Mort kept excusing himself, there'd be loud whispering, then he'd come back in and not be able to look at us. It makes Mort crazy because he worries about how things look and what people think of him."

"Hornberg claims he didn't know Terri very well. Says he was assistant director and stage manager on the show and only knew her in that capacity." Silvestri flipped over a page. "And never saw or heard from her after the show closed."

"What did he say about the lease being in Poppy's name?" Wetzon asked, spearing one of Silvestri's mushrooms.

"He said I'd have to ask her. He claims he didn't even meet Poppy until after *Combinations* closed. When I asked who Terri had been with before and during the show, he closed down on me. Protested he'd been busy and paid no attention, then gave me Peter Koenig. Didn't know his name, he said. Called him that actor who used to hang around her, who's in *Tacoma* something or other."

"*Tacoma Triptych,*" Wetzon said. "I saw it last night, and met Peter for a drink afterward."

"Les—" He had that look on his face as if he didn't trust her to make an intelligent decision on her own safety. "Dammit, you're not paranoid enough. Someone who killed once and got away with it could do it again. It would only be easier the second time."

"Oh, come on, Silvestri. It was at Joe Allen. There were a lot of people around, Silvestri, even Carlos." Silvestri gave her one of his so-you-say looks, but she went right on. "Mort hardly knew Terri, but after seventeen years he remembered Peter? Fascinating. Who else did you talk to?"

They started on the second pie, and Silvestri ordered three more beers. Sinatra was singing again, golden oldies.

"Phyllis Reynard. Foxy. What a piece of work. She looks like she's been sun-dried, tiny, but not frail. Dresses like she's on the make. On the make and collecting Social Security. She played cat and mouse with me. 'Terri sang like an angel,' " he mimicked, doing a surprisingly good rendition of Foxy's smokey voice. "And that's all she knew about her."

"Did you talk to JoJo by any chance?" Wetzon asked.

"JoJo?"

"JoJo Diamond. He was the conductor on *Combinations.* It was his first time out. Foxy liked his rangy odor and plucked him out of percussion, insisting she had to have him on the show. Davey had always worked with someone else, a guy named Jimmy Bronson, who had much more experience as a conductor."

"Excuse me." Nina had been listening intently. "JoJo? Foxy? These are names for grown-up people?"

"It's show biz, Nina," Wetzon drawled.

"How old is this JoJo?" Silvestri asked. "Foxy's age?"

"No way. JoJo was in his late twenties when he did *Combinations*. He was a loose dick around the company."

Nina laughed.

"Oh, yeah?" Silvestri said.

"Not me, Silvestri. I like my men clean and lean." She pressed her thigh against his.

"Did Foxy know he was a loose dick? Quaint expression, Les."

Sinatra segued into "Love and Marriage."

"She may have. I ran into her with Carlos yesterday and asked her about Terri. She went on about people who try to take something that's not theirs, getting what they deserve. Did she say that to you, too?"

Silvestri shook his head. "No. I guess I'll have to have a little talk with this JoJo Diamond. Is he conducting the revival?"

"Yes. Mort's office will know how to reach him, but I'll bet he's in the phone book. Did you talk to Medora Battle?"

"I did, but she insisted on someone being with her." He flipped through his notes. "Yeah. Ed Venderose."

"Yuk. What a creep. He was an apprentice on the show, just out of law school and having trouble passing the Bar. I don't remember that he was very close with the Battles. But obviously I didn't notice a lot of things then." She sighed.

"One of my people has followed up on the list of actors you gave me, Les. Everyone sort of remembers there was someone on the show Terri was having 'a thing with,' but no one knows who. At least, they're not saying. They all mentioned you, Les."

"Me?"

"Yeah. They said you'd know because you shared a dressing room with her and were her roommate on the road."

"Which leaves us nowhere because I don't remember anyone special. What the hell is the matter with me? She hinted about something when we were at Filene's, but I wasn't pushy . . ." Silvestri raised an eyebrow and she smiled. "I'm not the same person I was then. Now I push and have no shame."

That seemed to end all discussion, until Silvestri said, "Uh, Les," and waited.

"Yes?" She watched him uneasily. Something was up.

"Les, Nina is free tomorrow. I want you to take her with you to Mort Hornberg's party. They all know me and most of them haven't connected me with you. I'd like it to stay that way as long as possible. If I'm there, they'll clam up. Tell them Nina's a relative or something— and, Les, be a little obsessed about Terri. Maybe they'll loosen up."

"I *am* obsessed about Terri," Wetzon said. "But it's Thanksgiving. What are you going to do?"

"Spend the afternoon with Rita."

Oh, terrific, Wetzon thought, giving her lover what she hoped was an enigmatic look. Maybe I would like to spend the afternoon with you and Rita, too. But she didn't say it.

"What time is this event?" Nina asked. She was trying to read between the lines and seemed not quite sure how to proceed. "And what's the dress code?" When in doubt, talk clothes.

"Early afternoon, unless you want to be there with the kids. Mort's in the Majestic on Seventy-second and Central Park West. They get a grand view of the Macy's parade from the twenty-second floor. Then the nannies take the kiddies home for turkey, and the parents stay on for the main event." She moved away from Silvestri. He didn't deserve her thigh. "As for dress, anything goes, even jeans. The host, guaranteed, will be in well-pressed jeans and a blue cashmere sweater."

When there was nothing left on their plates, Silvestri signaled for the check. Wetzon and Nina put on their coats and began moving toward the door while Silvestri went off to pay the bill.

"Leslie?" Someone called from another booth, and an angular woman with chin-length brick-red hair waved to Wetzon.

"Louie!" Wetzon said, real pleasure in her voice.

Louie left her companions: a man with hoops in his ears and a shaved head, and another in a pinstriped suit and blue-striped shirt. The second had to be a lawyer, Wetzon thought. Wall Street people wear white shirts with their pinstripes.

"Louie, this is great," Wetzon said, hugging Louise Armstrong, her contractor. Louie had reconstructed Wetzon's apartment and become her friend. "It's been too long."

"It has, Leslie. You're looking wonderful, as always." Louie wore threadbare, paint-spattered jeans tucked into cowboy boots and a green plaid flannel shirt.

There was a soft "Ahem" just behind Wetzon. Nina.

"Oops, I'm sorry." Wetzon stood aside to include Nina. "This is Nina Wayne. Nina, this is my friend Louie Armstrong, a brilliant artist. She did the painting you liked in my living room. And she's the great contractor of all time."

For a quick second Nina's eyes flickered. The reserve Wetzon had begun to take for granted in Nina altered. Nina put out her hand and Louie took it. Suddenly Wetzon felt *de trop*.

"Pleased to meet you, Nina," Louie said. Her freckles stood out stark against her usually ruddy skin.

"I might be needing a contractor," Nina said.

Louie pulled a card from her shirt pocket and handed it to Nina.

As Wetzon watched, they seemed to have forgotten she was there. It was as if they were doing a slow waltz around one another, but neither had moved. Then Silvestri appeared behind them and the moment was over.

Wetzon had seen it happen often enough, this instantaneous magic. She'd seen it . . . it reminded her . . . she closed her eyes . . . yes. She'd seen a moment like this on the first day of rehearsals for *Combinations* all those years ago.

Between Terri Matthews and Rog Battle.

MEMORANDUM

To: Carlos Prince and Leslie Wetzon
From: Nancy Stein, Assistant to Mort Hornberg
Date: November 22, 1994
Re: *Combinations, in Concert*

We've added a property floater to cover lights and sound
equipment and general liability to our insurance policy at
an estimated cost of $250.

The Nederlanders will also cover anyone who is on their
payroll (union crews and front of house, etc.) for workers'
compensation. According to the contract, we (representing
Show Biz Shares) will be responsible for all personnel
involved in the event who are not presently in the regular
service of the Richard Rodgers Theatre.

Georgie Buckmeister (sound) and Angelo Iannatta (lights)
each get two pairs of tickets for the Friday performance.

Chapter Twenty-Six

THEY DROPPED NINA AT THE PATH TRAIN TO NEW JERSEY ON NINTH STREET
and drove uptown. It had flurried lightly while they were in John's, and
now the streets, when lights hit them, glittered like a carpet of stars. It
had something to do with the ground glass that was put into the paving
to make the mixture stronger.

There was no conversation in the car, as if she and Silvestri were
both building little barricades.

As they passed the back of Lincoln Center, Wetzon finally broke
the silence. "Do you want me to wear a wire, Silvestri?"

"Of course not." He sounded annoyed. "Les, it's highly unlikely
that we'll find this perp after seventeen years, but there's a chance if
someone Terri knew killed her, and that becomes more likely every
day, we may corner the guy and get him to confess."

"The *guy*, Silvestri? Couldn't a woman have done it?"

"It's possible. Guns are the great equalizer. Terri wasn't a peewee,
though. It wouldn't have been easy for a small woman to get her into
that trunk. At least not without help."

"So I guess that lets me and Foxy out, but what about Medora or
Poppy?"

"See what you can come up with tomorrow." A car was actually
pulling out across from Wetzon's building, and Silvestri backed into the
parking space it had vacated, turned off his lights, and put his keys in
his pocket.

"You coming up?"

"You want me to?"

"Don't be coy, Silvestri. Goddammit." She opened the door and got out.

"Let's take a walk." He got out of the car and locked it.

"A walk? Where?" She felt like a porcupine, swollen with bristles. He'd gotten out of going to Mort's party with her one more time.

"Just a way down Columbus." He had his arm around her shoulders and was drawing her along. "Come on, Les. Be a sport. I just want to show you something. You'll like it, I promise." His words came in little moist puffs.

The wind had turned winter wicked. Overhead, the half-moon was barely visible and stars winked in a cavernous sky. It was a beautiful night. Or at least it would have been if she weren't so pissed.

Traffic was backed up bumper to bumper on Columbus; headlight, blending into lamplight, imbued the sidewalks with an almost garish, celebratory aspect. Muffled noise came from the brightly lit restaurants. The smell of burning logs filled the air. Everyone fortunate enough to have a fireplace was using it tonight. But the sidewalks streamed with people, parents with children in strollers or sitting on shoulders, all bundled in winter gear, all heading downtown. A crowd stood in front of Dalton's coffee bar on Eighty-third Street holding cardboard containers, sipping everything from decaf to double espresso.

The West Side on this Thanksgiving Eve was filled to bursting, as if no one had left for the holiday. And, she thought, who would leave this wonderful place, ever? Certainly not Leslie Wetzon. It was in her blood.

The sky was black and there were cop cars everywhere. She knew where he was taking her.

As they approached the park around the Museum of Natural History, the streetlights caught the small remnants of golden foliage sitting like feathery crowns on the row of chestnut trees, which with their naturally peeled barks, gleamed ghostly like a chorus line of ancient femurs. Naked branches reached into the dark sky. She shivered inside her warm coat.

An endless procession of traffic rolled down Columbus, even though most who were leaving for the holiday had already left. Eighty-first Street was blocked by sawhorses. Two uniformed cops from the Twentieth Precinct stood watching the gathering throng. "You can stand and watch on the south side of the street," one of the cops said, motioning to the huge crowd behind the barricades. "On this side you have to keep moving."

"Hey, Silvestri!" the other cop called, waving, motioning for them to come around the blockade, where the sidewalk was a passing parade.

A brass band was playing oompahs, heavy on the drums.

Eighty-first Street between Columbus and Central Park West was lined with canvas, on which rested some giant, totally deflated balloons —you could recognize Garfield the Cat by his stripes—and some partially inflated. A huge white truck was pumping helium life into Woody Woodpecker. Barney waited his turn. The Cat in the Hat lay like a monster on its side, full of helium but not ready to float. Workers in orange were in the street, fixing netting, checking progress, holding string.

It was the annual preparation for Macy's Thanksgiving Day Parade.

"You can't stop and watch on this side!" someone shouted, but everyone did, shuffling feet, a moving pretense. Children, dogs, strollers, Pinkertons, cops in uniform, security guards, auxiliary police, Rollerbladers, moved back and forth in front of the elegant apartment buildings. Enterprising children from these buildings sold coffee from urns and home-baked cookies, and people were buying. Upstairs, every window was filled with people, staying warm, but with the best view in town.

Woody Woodpecker raised his head in front of her. The crowd across the street cheered. And then the dog struggled to his feet. Somehow she had lost Silvestri and found Beethoven.

Her nose was numb with cold. She covered it with her gloved hand

and peered around for Silvestri. She had wandered almost to Central Park West and the Beresford, that grand corner building where Alton Pinkus lived. No one had stopped her. Everyone was involved with the Mayor, wearing a red Macy's cap, standing with his wife, while their sophisticated offspring became children again, gaping at the huge balloons.

She began heading back, staying close to the buildings on the north side so as not to get in anyone's way. Across the street the Hayden Planetarium seemed surreal beyond the dense crowd, its glowing dome a backdrop to the dancing femurs.

The giant creatures floated high above her against the blackness of the sky, buoyed by the wind, casting ghostly shadows on the buildings. Oddly menacing.

A pulse raced in her throat and she shivered. She searched for the familiar slant of Silvestri's shoulders. Where was he? She'd assumed he was right behind her. Resting her back against the cold stone of one of the buildings, she felt disoriented. Two cans of beer. How can you get disoriented from two cans of beer? she asked herself.

"Magnificent, isn't it?"

A nice-looking man seemed to have been beamed down to stand beside her. He wore a tan suede jacket, good khakis, and tooled cowboy boots. His blond hair showed white at the temples. Something about him seemed familiar, yet she had never seen him before.

"Magnificent," she agreed, thrusting her hands into her pockets. He must have come out from one of the buildings, she thought, looking back toward the barricade for Silvestri.

"May I give you a word of advice?" the stranger said. He smiled with his lips closed, as if he were hiding some tooth problem. His eyes picked up the light, something wild.

"I— Huh?" She was already moving away from him. What was this feeling? Was he going to unzip his fly and expose himself?

Even so, she was surprised when he caught up with her. He put his cheek near hers; his scent was cloying. "Don't testify," he said.

Wetzon shot her elbow back hard into his ribs and heard him spit, "Bitch!" Then he shoved her and she stumbled backward.

"Lookit what that man did, Mommy," a child said.

"I saw that," someone else said. "People are *so* rude these days."

An elderly woman asked, "What happened? Are you all right?"

"I'm fine," Wetzon said, looking back for him. All she saw was the bulky figure of Barney, the purple dinosaur, grinning down at her.

MEMORANDUM

To: Carlos Prince and Leslie Wetzon
From: Ed Venderose, General Manager
Date: November 22, 1994
Re: *Combinations, in Concert*

Please see that I have all ticket orders in my hands for each
of the two performances by December 10th. We expect sales
to be brisk and the box office to go clean very quickly.

Chapter Twenty-Seven

FROM OUTSIDE, THE TWENTIETH PRECINCT HOUSE HAD NO PERSONALITY whatever. It could have been a school were it not for all the NYC blue-and-white cop cars everywhere, not to mention the unmarked cars parked all over the block on Eighty-second Street and on Columbus and Amsterdam.

Everything inside was unadorned in an almost self-conscious way.

Wetzon flipped through page after page of mug shots, reluctantly. Some sixth sense told her she wouldn't find the man who'd threatened her here. "Silvestri, this is a waste of time, believe me," she said half-heartedly, trying to keep the whine from her voice. What was it that had been familiar about the man? Why couldn't she put her finger on it?

"Just keep looking, Les." He didn't even try to keep the edge of exasperation from his voice, as if this were her fault. And she—who still couldn't wholly forgive him for excluding her from his Thanksgiving—was nursing a slow burn.

Detective Lisa Seidman, in a serviceable charcoal-gray suit and an open-collared pink-striped shirt, set a cardboard cup of black mud on the table to Wetzon's right. "That's the best we can do, I'm afraid. Caffeine you can slice." Lisa was taller than Wetzon, with the broad shoulders and lean hips of a swimmer. Her thick black hair skimmed her collar.

Silvestri pulled up a chair and sat down across from Wetzon. "They need her testimony to prove the case," he told Seidman, picking up on the dialogue he'd begun with Seidman when they arrived at the precinct house almost an hour before.

"If she's that important, why didn't they put someone on her?" Seidman said.

Wetzon looked up from the multitude of faces, black, white, Hispanic, who'd begun to look like people she saw every day on the street. If you rode the subway twice a day, to and from the office, and you were bombarded with at least one hundred faces each way and different faces, too, you were on overload. How could you ever remember anyone specifically?

Silvestri and Seidman were talking about her as if she weren't there —or worse—as if she were deaf and dumb. She interjected, "I told Marissa Peiser it wouldn't do any good. They'd get to me if they wanted to."

Silvestri slammed his fist on the table. "Why the fuck didn't you mention it to *me?*"

Wetzon blocked him out. She listened as two detectives talked to a woman whose car had been vandalized. "Do you have anyone mad at you, ma'am?" one asked.

"Because you're so easy to talk to, Silvestri," Wetzon said sweetly. There were still five books waiting for her to look at. She smacked the book shut. "He's not here and I'm tired. I want to go home." Her adrenaline had pumped her up at first but now it had dissipated; all she craved was sleep. She stood and reached for her coat, which was folded over the back of a nearby chair. *Do you have anyone mad at you, ma'am,* she said to herself. And answered: *The usual assortment, I guess.*

"Les, goddammit, sit down. Let's get this over with." Silvestri was so angry his face was red. What the fuck did he have to be angry about? He was cutting her off for Thanksgiving.

"It would be better, Ms. Wetzon, to go through all the books now," Lisa Seidman said, "while your memory is fresh." Her face was impassive.

"Well, okay, I guess," Wetzon said. "Especially since you're so nice about it." She sent Silvestri some loathing to go with his attitude, sat down, and opened the book again, flipping through the pages until she reached the place where she'd stopped. Silvestri left the room. If he didn't come back, she wouldn't care. She just wanted to sleep.

A sharp-nosed mustached cliché, wearing an eyepatch, all his hair on the lower portion of his face, caught her attention. *Riccardo Durban, alias Dead Eye Rick.* Get a life, Rick, she thought, and went on turning the pages, studying the faces. They meant nothing to her. Finally, she closed the last book. "I'm sorry, but thank you."

Silvestri hadn't returned, so she shook hands with Detective Seidman. "You probably won't find him, will you?"

"It's unlikely. But if you see him again, call me. Here's my card. And I would reconsider, if I were you, accepting the offer of protection."

"Thanks," Wetzon said again, putting on her coat. She tucked Detective Seidman's card into her pocket.

Downstairs, Silvestri was talking to the desk sergeant. They looked up as she approached and stopped talking, watching her.

"I didn't find him," she said. She kept walking, right out the door.

The air was scented with pine needles and honey-roasted nuts from a vendor on Columbus.

They walked without touching, splitting apart for people going in the opposite direction. She looked sideways at Silvestri's frozen face, made more so by the spotty light from the streetlamps. "Why are you so angry with me?"

After a long pause during which she thought he wasn't going to respond, he said stiffly, "Who says I'm angry with you?"

"Forget it," she said. "Communication's not your long suit."

They walked the rest of the way without speaking. In front of her building he said, "It's late, so—"

"Isn't it, though." She marched through the door Mario was holding open for her without looking back and got on the waiting elevator. What good was it loving someone who caused her so much pain?

Unlocking her door, she reached down and scooped up Izz, burying her face in the soft fur. Unconditional love. That was the best.

She dropped her clothing on a chair and scrubbed her face clean of makeup. Purposely, she did not bother to check her answering machine; she had no interest in talking with anyone.

As she was pulling on one of Silvestri's T-shirts, she remembered that hidden away in her cupboard was a huge chunk of dark chocolate from Li-Lac in the Village. She'd been saving it for a special occasion. This was it.

She sat down on her kitchen stool, removed the chocolate from its bag, and set it on the butcher-block counter, thinking to cut it in half, but changed her mind. She definitely deserved the whole thing.

It was over. She and Silvestri. She knew this somehow. Cops. Why had she gotten involved and stayed involved with someone like Silvestri? It was masochistic, or was it adversarial? Something. She hated what it did to her. Here she was snapping at her beloved Carlos, vilifying Smith. Oh, hell, Smith deserved vilification, if that was a word. She sighed. The chocolate melted inside her mouth, giving her a soothing rush. Cops, she thought. Cops . . .

A shard of thought crossed her mind. She pushed it away. She was very tired. Being tired led to ridiculous connections. She put her head down on the counter and dozed. The thought returned and throbbed in her forehead.

Izz came tearing into the foyer from the bedroom, wagging her tail. When the key turned in the lock, Wetzon sat up.

Silvestri stepped into the apartment and closed the door. He patted the squirming dog and looked over at her. "Hi," he said.

"Hi." She got off the stool like a sleepwalker and came to him. He was holding out his arms and she walked right into them.

"Dammit, Les." His cold breath tickled her ear. "I love you so much, you make me crazy."

"Dammit, Silvestri," she responded. "Ditto."

He kissed her. "You taste of chocolate."

"I ate all of it. There's nothing left."

"Too bad." He took off his jacket and hooked it on the doorknob.

"Why does this happen? Why don't you talk to me?" She watched him undo the harness and place his gun on the counter.

"I'm a cop," he said. "This is who I am."

The shard flickered back. She tried to hold it. Something about the man who had threatened her.

Silvestri pulled her to him again. "I don't want to lose you, Les. So when these things happen to you—"

She pushed the shard away. Whatever it was could wait till tomorrow.

MEMORANDUM

To: Carlos Prince and Leslie Wetzon
From: Nancy Stein, Assistant to Mort Hornberg
Date: November 23, 1994
Re: *Combinations, in Concert*

Ed brought up the question of security. The Richard
Rodgers normally has a guard on duty from 12–6:00 PM.
The budget already contains provision for an additional 5
hours (from 6–11:00 PM).

However, Show Biz Shares has now scheduled a reception
for after the performance, which means we'll probably need
to add an extra hour for the security guard. The cost for this
is $35 plus benefits.

Chapter Twenty-Eight

THE SUN WAS BUTTERY, LEAKING THROUGH THE WOODEN BLINDS. WETZON stretched her body under the quilt. Her nose was cold. She pulled the quilt over her head and breathed in Silvestri's smell.

Somewhere far away the kettle whistled and then the clatter began. Silvestri always clattered in the kitchen. It was an Italian thing, he said. She could hear him talking to Izz. See, even someone as self-contained as Silvestri carried on conversations with animals.

She curled up and dozed, her mantra pirouetting to her even breathing. Unorthodox meditation, but orthodox was anathema to her. Yes. Yes. Richard Hartmann was trying to keep her from testifying against him to the grand jury. Smith was totally self-involved, missing an important human link. Terri had been killed by someone Wetzon knew, someone who'd been living with murder on his—or her—conscience for seventeen years. Life with Silvestri was an emotional-roller-coaster affair, with no end for, she knew, either of them.

Spin, dip, pivot, breathe. She shot up and threw off the quilt.

The man who had threatened her was a cop.

That was why she hadn't seen him in the mug shot books and why she'd known instinctively she wouldn't. Maybe Hartmann worked with an investigator. Of course he worked with an investigator. All criminal attorneys do. Or maybe this was a rogue cop for hire . . .

She smelled coffee, the sharp distinctive espresso that was Starbucks. Silvestri opened the blinds and the sun spilled through; colored dots of light exploded like a kaleidoscope. He cut the lovely stream of dust motes unceremoniously by handing her a mug. Then he sat down on the bed facing her. He was wearing Jockeys and the white singlet he favored. He said, "Les, about yesterday . . ."

"Yes?"

"Give me some time—"

"Give me a break—" She stopped. He looked so tortured she said "What the hell" with a shrug. She breathed in the steam from the mug, then took a tentative sip. "Do you know, Silvestri, you always blame *me* when someone tries to hurt me? Is it me? Or is it you? I don't think it's the Detective Silvestri doing it, because I've never heard you blame the victim."

He listened without interrupting, without the fierceness of the blaming anger that always infuriated her. When she fell silent, he said, "You're right. I want to keep you safe—"

"From the world, Silvestri? You can't. I could get run over by a truck on my way to work in the morning. Get over it." She smiled, set the mug down on the chest next to the bed, leaned toward him, and kissed him. "But not completely."

He groaned, set his mug on the floor, put his arms around her. "You don't know how much I love you."

"You could tell me once in a while," she whispered into his neck.

His beeper went off with such a loud intrusive noise they both laughed.

"On Thanksgiving Day?" she said.

"Don't move," he said. He picked up the phone and called in. "Silvestri." Listening, he looked over at her. "Yeah?" He listened again. She knew that look on his face. She'd lost him. "Let me think about it." He hung up and made as if to stand.

Sighing, Wetzon pulled the covers over her head, which was when he burrowed in with her. "Now, where were we?" His kiss was Colgate and espresso.

"Tell me."

"What? You want to know about the phone call?"

"Um. No."

He laughed, ran his hands slowly up her spine, then pulled off her T-shirt. "Really?"

"Well, maybe later. Tell me—"

"Yes?"

"Forget it," she said, horrified. She'd been about to ask him to tell her how much he loved her.

"Oh, Les," he said, as if he knew.

THE SOUND, THAT OF LAPPING WATER, WOKE HER. SHE REACHED FOR Silvestri; he wasn't there, but the bed was still warm where he'd been. The water sound stopped. The lapping sound continued. She peered over the edge of the bed. On the floor Izz was slurping up what was left of Silvestri's coffee.

"Izz!" Wetzon scooped up the protesting fur ball. "You're going to be wired. What kind of dog drinks coffee?"

Izz's muzzle and tongue slobbered, dripping espresso over the quilt. "Lovely, lovely," Wetzon muttered, blotting it up with tissues.

The shower started. From the bathroom came the sound of Silvestri singing. Singing? "Jesus," she said, putting the dog aside. She sat up; it was after ten.

She slipped into her T-shirt and padded down the hall to the kitchen. Silvestri had made enough coffee for an army. The sun filled the kitchen with pure warm light, glancing off the French wall tiles in streaks of blue and yellow and gold, tricking her eyes. In mid-pour she froze, coffeepot in hand. The man who had threatened her last night. His eyes. She set the pot back on the stove.

He'd had two different colored eyes. One blue, the other greenish. Why hadn't she remembered this yesterday?

"Nina will be here in an hour," Silvestri said. He stood in the doorway, clean-shaven, dressed in jeans and a navy turtleneck. "What're you looking at?"

"I'd like to jump your bones again," she said, "but I'm busy now." She put her arms around his waist and breathed him in. "The man who threatened me last night—"

"You remembered something!"

"Yeah. He's a cop."

Silvestri stared at her, disbelief on his face. "What makes you so sure he was a cop?"

"Intuition, Silvestri. That's the one thing we women have all over you men. Besides, I know a few cops, and if you know a few, you can sense them."

"Stereotypes, huh?" His arms tightened about her. "So what about this cop?"

"He had two different colored eyes. One blue, one green."

Silvestri put his hands on her shoulders and held her away from him. "You're certain about this?"

She couldn't suppress the excitement in her voice. "You know him, Silvestri?"

"Maybe. I'm going to call in."

He was still on the phone when she got out of the shower, and she could still hear him a short time later, just before she turned the dryer on her hair. Combing with her fingers, nape to crown, she caught a glimpse of Silvestri standing in the doorway. She shut down the dryer and flipped her hair back.

"His name is Joe Daly. He was with the 7-3 until last month. He's a dirty cop, Les."

MEMORANDUM

To: Foxy Reynard, Medora Battle, Carlos Prince, Leslie
    Wetzon, JoJo Diamond, et al.
From: Ed Venderose, General Manager
Date: November 23, 1994
Re: *Combinations, in Concert*

The performances are scheduled for Thursday, December 22
and Friday, December 23rd, at 8:00 PM.

Rehearsals begin on Friday, December 16th, with a break
on Sunday, the 18th.

Rehearsal space will be at the Minskoff, and Carlos Prince
and Mort Hornberg will be there for all rehearsals. There
will be a dress rehearsal on Wednesday, December 21st
from 10 AM to 1 PM. A wardrobe and hair and make-up
person will be at the dress rehearsal. Rich Berlin has
offered to do hair for the two performances for no fee.

On Tuesday, December 20th, from 11AM to 1PM the press
will be invited to attend a rehearsal. You are all asked to be
there. The cast, hair and makeup people will be called at
10:30 AM. The orchestra will rehearse on stage, Wednesday,
the 21st, from 10AM–1PM and from 2PM–5PM.

Chapter Twenty-Nine

"Carlos, that's a tough schedule."

"It's not as if you haven't done it before, Birdie."

"Yeah, when I was young. I can't wait to tell Smith I won't be around for two weeks."

They sat around Wetzon's dining table, sated. Sparse crumbs on plates and an all-but-empty container of cream cheese that still hinted of scallions were what was left of the bagels and fixings Silvestri had picked up at Barney Greengrass (The Sturgeon King) around the corner on Amsterdam. Only coffee remained, and not much of it.

Nina Wayne had arrived promptly, wearing black leather jeans, high-heeled boots, and a rust hand-knit sweater that grazed her waist. Her coat was quilted black leather, soft as brushed silk.

"Watch that drool, Silvestri," Wetzon said after Nina had excused herself and headed down the hall to the bathroom, Izz on her heels. Should she warn Nina that Izz had the disconcerting habit of jumping on any lap? Naaa. She considered Silvestri. "I guess you like tall women with tight asses in black leather."

Silvestri laughed. He with the turquoise eyes. "I like women," he said. "Especially prickly little ones with great legs and—"

"Leave it at that, please." She felt the pull, wanted to crawl across the table and attach herself to him. Sexual Velcro, she thought. But when the *tap, tap, tap* of Nina's heels came again, Wetzon was in the kitchen loading the dishwasher and Silvestri was at the dining table pouring the last bit of coffee into their mugs.

Nina came into the kitchen smiling, Izz contentedly nestled in the crook of her arm.

"I guess she jumped you," Wetzon said.

"You guess right. She's adorable, though I'm a cat person myself."

Wetzon wiped down the butcher-block counter with a sponge. "I'm allergic to cats. And cats seem so . . . superior and self-contained. They don't need you."

"They are and some do," Nina said. "Besides . . ." She was walking back to the dining room and tossed off the next comment so quickly that Wetzon, following her, wasn't quite sure she'd heard right. Had Nina really said "Besides, lesbians always have cats"?

Silvestri had taken a folder from his briefcase and was leafing through papers, each with a name at the top left.

"Who do you want to start with?" Wetzon asked, sitting.

Nina, already seated, turned her chair just so, giving herself a perfect view of Louie's painting.

"Mort Hornberg," Silvestri said. "Total stone wall. We don't have much. Said he hardly knew Terri, but remembered the first name of the actor she was going with."

"Peter Koenig," Wetzon said.

"Memory is an odd, unpredictable thing," Nina said. "Sometimes we remember things that don't seem to have any significance."

"And then again," Wetzon added, "Mort has always found young men very attractive, so he might have remembered Peter's name for a reason."

"To your knowledge, Les, did Terri ever speak of Hornberg in other than a work-related capacity?"

Wetzon shook her head.

"Okay, let's move on to Peter Koenig. As opposed to Mort Hornberg, he couldn't have been more cooperative. He was almost too good to be true. He says he met Terri in college. He was a year ahead of her and was already in New York when she got here. She looked him up. So he and Terri are together until she gets the part in *Combinations* in 1976. Am I right, Les?"

"I think so, but you're taking his word for it. Remember, I didn't know Terri very well before *Combinations*. It was my first Broadway show, but not hers. And from what I saw and the few things she said to me, if there had been anything between them, it was over."

"Which he admits. So he leaves New York either just before, or just after, she's murdered."

"And," Wetzon said, "stays away for seventeen years thinking she's still alive but uncommunicative."

"Rather," Nina said.

"He contacted me because he was back in New York and thought he'd look her up. Thought I'd know where she was." Wetzon chewed on her lower lip. "My gut instinct is I don't like him, Silvestri. I didn't like him then and I don't like him now. He gets in your face and he's too slick."

"Motive," Nina said. "Terri broke it off with him and he was angry. And jealous."

"He has a permit to carry a gun."

Silvestri's eyes widened. "How do you know, Les?"

"I saw it the other night when he took out his credit card to pay for drinks. It's grayish and was slightly larger than his other cards. It says 'Pistol License.'"

Silvestri jotted a note on the paper in front of him, then looked up. "Does Actors Equity keep a record of members' blood types?"

"Blood types?" Wetzon looked at Nina, who was listening with interest.

"Yeah."

"I don't think Equity is allowed to; it's all confidential, but over the years when there was a blood drive and we gave blood, it was always through Equity. These days, with computers, someone might know how to access records of my blood type, Carlos's, and Peter's. And even Mort's."

"Mort Hornberg at Actors Equity? I thought he was a director."

"He was a stage manager then, and they're repped by Equity."

"Foxy Reynard," Silvestri said, shuffling his papers. "Old girl with young stud. Very jealous. She blew me off."

"Jesus, Silvestri, I'd hardly call JoJo young, or a stud. He's an over-weight slob who still behaves like a rock musician though he's pushing fifty. And he ain't Paul McCartney, or even Mick, by any stretch of the imagination. We always figured him for dirty underwear. I guess Foxy didn't like him looking at other women, especially young pretty ones like Terri."

"Or you?" Nina said.

"Ha! JoJo hit on me a few times, but he's not my type. And I'm not his. He digs tits and ass." She grinned at Silvestri. "No, I don't think JoJo did it. Don't you need an all-consuming passion to commit mur-der? He's only passionate about one thing: JoJo. No, it wasn't JoJo."

Nina took a sip of coffee. "Why not?"

"I've been thinking about this a lot. Whoever he was, he was more important than JoJo. That's why Terri and this guy kept their relation-ship so secret. And here's something else. I'm betting Foxy didn't do it either. How could Foxy, who barely weighs a hundred pounds, have gotten Terri's dead weight into the trunk and the trunk into the base-ment?"

"With help," Silvestri said. "Say, JoJo?"

Wetzon shook her head. "Foxy's smarter than that."

"Les, smart has nothing to do with committing murder. Half the guys at Attica are as smart as you and me."

"I suppose JoJo could have shot her, but it doesn't make sense. Foxy made certain everyone knew he was her dolly."

"I had a brief conversation with him yesterday. 'Beautiful voice, pretty girl, never saw her socially.' He claims he never saw her again after the play closed."

"Moving right along," Nina said.

"Medora Battle. Her husband, Roger, died seventeen years ago, around the same time as Terri did. Coincidence?"

"Heart attack," Wetzon said.

"What kind of relationship was it?" Nina asked. The sun came through the blinds and slatted their faces. Wetzon got up and tilted the blinds away from them.

"Between Medora and Rog? Close, I think. They worked well together. They'd already had two big Broadway musicals that were still running. They were hot. Everyone always said Rog was the real talent. The proof was that Medora never did another show after he died, and maybe Medora thought she couldn't write without him either. But I just found out that Medora Battle is the pseudonymous author of *Tacoma Triptych,* which opens on Broadway the first week in January."

"How'd you find that out?"

"Smith's son, Mark, is at Harvard with Medora and Rog's daughter."

"So they were the perfect married couple?"

"Is anyone, Silvestri? I don't know. I suppose they had the usual disagreements, especially because they worked together, too. Rog, though, was more social—outgoing. You can see it in the pictures. On the other hand, Rog was also supposed to have a girl on every show, and there was a story about Medora and her mother physically attacking one of these girls on a subway platform."

"When?"

"Before I came to New York. Otherwise, I would know more about it. And I think Rog liked Terri."

"You saw them together?"

"Not really. Only in rehearsal. Never alone. And usually something like that leaks out because on the road everyone is a yenta."

"But you *know* he liked her." There was an edge to his voice.

"Silvestri—"

"Intuition, Silvestri," Nina said. "Admit it. We have it."

"Are you two ganging up on me?"

"*Moi?*" Wetzon said, hand to her breast.

"*Moi?*" Nina made the same motion.

"Enough," Silvestri said. "I surrender. Does your incredible intuition tell you Medora was the jealous type?"

"I never noticed. We were all working hard. They had a young daughter, about two, and a boy a couple of years older. They were parents and partners, and as partners they had this wonderful career that brought in fame and big bucks."

"Which Terri might have been jeopardizing."

"Terri wasn't like that," Wetzon said. "She would never have broken up a marriage, especially one with young children." Oh, God, she thought, what was it Terri had said to her in Filene's? *I never say never anymore.*

"You wouldn't, Les, but you can't speak for her."

"Passion is like a fever in the blood," Nina said. "It doesn't always make sense, and when you're in its throes, you don't always do the right thing."

Wetzon squinted at Nina. She was so interesting. "I suppose. But honestly, I don't think Rog Battle could evoke that in anyone. He was kind of white bread, beige. Beige hair, metal-framed glasses, medium height. Not fat, not thin, narrow shoulders. No chest." Silvestri had his head down making notes, so she added in her most sultry voice, "Nothing like you, Silvestri."

"Thanks, Les," he said solemnly. "I needed that. Next on my list is Poppy Morris Hornberg, who I get to interview tomorrow. What can you tell me about her, Les?"

"That she loves being Mrs. Mort Hornberg and would kill before she would ever give it up. But she hadn't even met Mort at that time, I don't think. Ask her. She must have known Terri, because Terri was living in her apartment."

"We'll see what we can come up with today, Silvestri," Nina said.

Silvestri closed his folder. "Davey Lewin," he said. "Anything?"

Wetzon shook her head. "Davey was a very nice guy, but he had a known substance-abuse problem. No secret that he was gay, and back then, it often was. He had a lover. They're both dead now. What about Carlos and me, Silvestri?"

"What about Carlos and you?"

"Aren't we suspects?"

"I've talked with Carlos and I've talked with you, and I'm eliminating both of you." He slipped the folder back into his attaché.

"Gee, thanks. Listen, it occurs to me you ought to talk to Ed Venderose. He's now the general manager on the benefit, but he was an apprentice on the original show."

She spelled Venderose for him. "Anything else?" he said.

"Yes. Why were you asking about blood types, Silvestri?" She looked at Nina. "Is this something for you?"

Nina hooded her eyes.

"That call this morning, Les—"

"What about it?"

"The FBI serology lab typed Terri's blood as O, verified by the hospital records in Cincinnati. But they found evidence of another blood type."

"I don't get it. You can't have two blood types, can you?"

"It's not possible. We think she may have put up a fight and the killer left some of his blood on her clothing."

"That's why you were asking me about whether Equity kept blood type records."

"Right."

"But isn't it a little like looking for a needle in a haystack, Silvestri?"

"Not this time. The blood type we found is A_2, about as rare as they come."

MEMORANDUM

To: Carlos Prince and Leslie Wetzon
From: Nancy Stein, Assistant to Mort Hornberg
Date: November 23, 1994
Re: *Combinations, in Concert*

The program deadline is a week from Friday. Please send
me your latest bios and a photo right away.

I am also coordinating food during the rehearsal period, and
am asking the Edison Café if they will donate or, at the
very least, do it at cost.

Chapter Thirty

"CARLOS, DID YOU SEE THE LATEST FROM EL HORNBERG?"

"Birdie, great minds. I was just about to call you. I can't believe the chutzpah."

"Chutzpah is an understatement. It's obscene. He's promoting free food when he's going to make all that money on the TV version."

WATCHING NINA ACROSS MORT HORNBERG'S PALATIAL LIVING ROOM, HER honey-colored hair hanging loose and curly past her shoulders, talking to Medora Battle, Wetzon decided Nina Wayne was an original. She raised her bottle of Beck's and saluted her. Nina looked no more like Nina Wayne, forensic anthropologist, than Wetzon herself did.

Wetzon snaked by the determined buffet line, which spilled over from the dining room. Performers were always ravenous, and there were plenty of them here tonight. Some were even actors. A cluster of people stood around the piano, and someone was playing the score of *Hotshot: The Musical,* Mort's big smash.

Under the picture windows was a jungle of greens and purples in ceramic pots. Wetzon worked a bit of toe space among them and looked out at Central Park. The Park was almost still. Some wind rippled through the last holdouts of the fall foliage, but no cars. She could see clear through to Fifth Avenue.

Below her, Strawberry Fields, the John Lennon memorial, was visible because the trees had shed their final leaves and gone to winter bare almost overnight as the temperatures dropped.

Only the truly obsessed, of which New York had more than its share, were circling the reservoir on Thanksgiving Day. But in truth, the City was on holiday, and many of the young upwardly mobile professionals had gone home to Minneapolis, Cleveland, and Baltimore.

"I like your friend," Medora said to Wetzon's back.

Wetzon turned to face her. "Nina's a big fan of the show, especially yours and Rog's work." Now that she knew that Medora was the author of *Tacoma Triptych*, she wondered how she had not guessed it immediately at the theatre the other night.

"I wanted to apologize for my rudeness," Medora said.

Rog had been dead seventeen years, and Medora now looked more like Rog than Rog would have if he had lived. She was Rog's height, which was tall for a woman, with narrow shoulders. Her tan hair was streaked with white. She was still a stick in clothing, and although the shapeless silver-flecked knit she wore was stylish and looked expensive, it did nothing to enhance either her looks or her figure. The gray gum-soled Arche shoes made her ankles thick.

"It's okay," Wetzon said. "You wanted to protect your secret, and I sort of blundered into it."

Medora's lips twitched, an involuntary tic, not the ghost of a smile. It was something Wetzon remembered Rog having had. "You know then." She fiddled with the gold bracelet on her wrist.

"I hope you win the big one, Medora."

"Thank you, Leslie. Isn't it awful about that little Terri Matthews?" She signaled a black-tied waiter with her chin and took a glass of champagne from his proffered tray.

"No, thank you," Wetzon told the waiter when he held the tray out to her. Champagne did not agree with her and she was not seduced by the elegance of the rented tulip glasses or Mort's favorite Bollinger label. To Medora, she said, "Yes, awful."

"Did you know her well, Leslie?" Medora's eyes teared behind her gold-framed glasses, and the tic returned.

"Only through the show. How about you and Rog, Medora? Did you get to know her outside the show?"

"Not at all. Of course, I do remember she was very accommodating."

Accommodating? Now that was a peculiar choice of a word. It gave Wetzon pause.

"Who was very accommodating, Medora?" Ed Venderose filled the space like the pumped-up creatures from Macy's parade, like an evil Barney.

"Terri Matthews, Edward. Leslie and I were just reminiscing, weren't we, Leslie?"

Wetzon nodded. "Don't you have a matinee, Ed . . . ward?"

His eyes were stones. "I do, Leslie. I just wanted to speak to Medora alone, if you don't mind."

"Why should I mind? Oh, incidentally, did you happen to know Terri well, Ed . . . ward? We're thinking that maybe one of us would do a little vignette on each of our late friends. Is there anything in particular you remember about her?"

"Nothing good."

"Turned you down, huh, Ed . . . ward?"

"What do you know about anything, Leslie?" Venderose practically spit the words at her.

Medora threw Wetzon an apologetic, if spastic, smile as Ed hustled her away. Could they possibly be lovers? Hell, anything was possible. If so, that would be a real odd couple. But then, Silvestri and Wetzon were also an odd couple, totally mismatched. . . . On the other hand, if couples were perfectly matched, as Medora and Rog had seemed to be, wouldn't that be boring? And Ed Venderose had always been ambitious. He would hook his wagon to a star . . . but who would have him except maybe a fallen star? Soon to be resurrected. Stay tuned.

A draft of gin-flavored breath brushed her cheek. "Having a good time, Leslie, darling? Why aren't you drinking champagne? Waiter." Without listening to her negative response, Mort began signaling frantically for a waiter. When one appeared, he set his empty glass on the tray and took another. "You should have been here this morning for the parade. The floats were terrific and the kids loved it." Mort's nose was

red and his eyes were too bright. His cashmere sweater was tucked
tightly into his jeans, calling attention to, instead of disguising, his slop-
ing shoulders and little pot belly. She wanted to say to him, "Mort, join
a health club, hire a personal trainer." But she didn't.

"Sorry I missed it then. Incidentally, why the hell is Ed Venderose
on the show?"

"Leslie. Darling." Mort looked shocked, or pretended to. "What
are you talking about? Nancy tries very hard, but believe me, the girl
just doesn't have it. And she's not in the union. We have to keep
everything—how do you say?—kosher."

"How do I say? You ought to know what kosher is, Mort. But it
wouldn't be kosher because Ed is a pig. Couldn't you at least have
asked Carlos and me first?"

"Leslie." He pressed his palm against his chest. He was doing his
sincere act. "You know if I had *any* idea that you didn't want Ed, I
would never have brought him on board. But Medora specifically requested— Besides, a lot of people are pigs, darling. Your Wall Street
friends as well, according to what I read in the papers."

"Hey, Mort!" A flashy Hollywood type sidled up, eager to get a
piece of the maestro. His pants were too tight across his buns and he
wasn't wearing socks, just loafers with tassels. He sniffled into a hand-
kerchief.

"Never mind, Mort. It's done." Wetzon took his arm and steered
him away from the slick job, flagrantly Armani-ed. "I want you to meet
my friend Nina." She guided him skillfully through the clumps of
guests, each of whom wanted a word with the host, to where Nina
stood chatting with JoJo and Carlos. Arthur Margolies, Carlos's lover,
was having a *tête-à-tête* with Elaine Stritch, who appeared to be in the
middle of one of her stories, for she was waving her hands around,
cackling. "So I said, 'My God, you can't go to him for *motivation*,' "
Stritch croaked. Everyone laughed.

"Nina, this is Mort Hornberg. Mort, this is my friend Nina Wayne."

"Delighted," Nina said, offering her hand. "I am a great admirer of
your work."

Mort was immediately charmed. He held on to Nina's hand, leaning over it so long that Wetzon was afraid he would kiss it. "Well," he said, "let's get something to eat and talk about it. You don't mind, guys, if I steal this lovely lady away from you?"

"Oh, dear," Nina said. "And I wanted to hear the end of JoJo's story about how *Combinations* came together."

"JoJo? What does JoJo know? He only conducted the orchestra. *I* called the show. I worked closely with Davey Lewin, Nina. We were like *that*." Mort held up two entwined fingers.

"I'm dying to hear all about it, Mort." Nina winked at JoJo, who looked as if he could strangle Mort. She took Mort's arm, and off they went.

"Don't believe everything you hear," Carlos called. He put his arm around Wetzon, who snuggled up against him. "Love you, Birdie."

"She'll be sorry," JoJo growled. "All he does is talk." He stuck his thumbs in the pockets of his jeans, his hips thrust forward.

Interesting body language, Wetzon thought. "She's not looking for what you think she's looking for, JoJo."

JoJo turned his attention to a tall blonde in a sequined T-shirt. "How've you been, Leslie?" he said without interest.

"Are you talking to me, JoJo, or is that blonde you have your eye on also named Leslie?"

"Birdie, darling, na, na, na." Carlos shook his finger at her, but he was starting to convulse.

Now she had JoJo's attention. He said, "I think you've missed me all these years, Leslie. Admit it."

Wetzon turned her sweetest smile on JoJo, and gave Carlos a little poke with her elbow. "Not at all, JoJo. But I kind of remember you and Terri Matthews had something going."

JoJo grinned. His teeth were discolored. "Not me, kiddo. We had something going on *Night Music,* but then Foxy came into my life, so I dropped her. I thought we might rekindle on *Combinations,* but I guess she was still mad. She turned me down flat. Just like you. Think I don't remember? We all kind of thought you two were getting it on."

"When women turn you down, JoJo, I bet you always say they're lesbians. Maybe they're just not attracted to you. Hard to believe, isn't it?" She caught a glimpse of Foxy standing near the French doors leading to the dining room, a glass of champagne in her hand, dark eyes searching. "I think your handler is looking for you."

"Carlos, call off your attack . . . poodle," JoJo said.

"JoJo, damn it, Terri was having an affair with someone on the show. I thought you might remember something about Terri that could tell us who it was." She could feel herself getting hot.

"Birdie, darling, it's Thanksgiving. Let's keep this light."

"Come on, JoJo, you must remember something about her."

"Her?"

"Terri. You know damn well who I mean."

"You know what I remember about her? She had an attitude. She thought she was better than everybody." Something had broken loose. Anger. Pain?

"Not Terri," Wetzon said. *Not the Terri I knew.*

"Darling," Foxy came up behind JoJo, claiming him. "Would you get me a little something to munch on?"

Carlos looked around for Arthur. Stritch had a small audience listening to her *Showboat* stories, but Arthur was not one of them.

"There he is, and look who he's talking to."

"Who is that? Looks like another lawyer."

"It is. Sondheim's. Let's leave them to talk about contracts and get some food. How about it, Dear Heart?"

Wetzon nodded.

"Darling." Foxy tried again, tugging JoJo's arm. JoJo hadn't moved.

"In a minute," he snapped. "Leslie, you just didn't know Terri as well as you think you did. Terri was one of the guys in the beginning, but believe me, she changed after she started babysitting for the Battles."

• • •

MEMORANDUM

To: Carlos Prince, Leslie Wetzon, Medora Battle, Foxy
    Reynard, et al.
From: Ed Venderose, General Manager
Date: November 23, 1994
Re: *Combinations, in Concert*

The show will be called by the Production Stage Manager
from the back of the house and we'll need at least two
assistants. We are currently looking for volunteers, so if you
have any suggestions, please call me as soon as possible.

The first performance will be a black tie event. Mort will be
informing the cast through Nancy.

Chapter Thirty-One

CARLOS SAID, "*I HAVE A FEW SUGGESTIONS, O FABULOUS PERSON WITH SOUR expression.*"

Wetzon responded, "*I don't want to hear them right now, thank you very much. Do you suppose the volunteers get anything for the TV version?*"

"*Not if Mort can help it,*" Carlos said.

"I SWEAR TO GOD I DON'T REMEMBER ANYTHING ABOUT TERRI BABYSITTING the Battle kids, but as soon as JoJo said it, it sounded right." Wetzon held the drumstick swathed in a paper napkin and chewed on it. She was standing with Nina, who was waiting to use the bathroom in the foyer.

Chita Rivera was coming down the stairs, laughing at something Fred Ebb was telling her. "Try upstairs, Leslie," she called, then stopped to embrace Rita Moreno.

At the baby grand, Foxy and John Kander were sitting, doodling.

"Let's try it," Wetzon said. "There are at least two more upstairs."

Upstairs it was quieter, or perhaps it was the thick mauve carpeting that kept it so.

"I haven't met Foxy or Mrs. Mort," Nina said.

"I was beginning to wonder where Poppy is myself. With Mort running around being the hostess with the mostess, Poppy might have felt redundant."

"That Mort's a piece of work, Leslie."

"You don't have to tell me. Did you get anything out of him?"

"Not much. He loves everybody."

"Today maybe."

"Let's see if this—" Wetzon tried the door. It was locked. She knocked. "Anyone in there?"

When there was no response, Nina shrugged and followed Wetzon down the hall to the master bedroom. Funny, gurgling sounds were coming from behind a closed door just off the staircase. "It must be little Maudie," Wetzon said. "Let's have a look." Smiling, she opened the door.

Sunlight ricocheted around the room, which was decorated as a nursery. Maudie was lying on her back in her crib, her chubby little legs up in the air, fat little hands reaching for the dramatic Mylar mobile hanging above her crib. But Maudie wasn't making the gurgling sounds. Those came from a highly touted playwright and an older, celebrated, supposedly heterosexual film actor, who lay on the floor near the crib *in flagrante delicto,* out of the infant's line of sight.

"Jesus," Nina said. She and Wetzon backed out of the room and stared at each other. "Where is the mother?"

"If not Poppy, what about the nanny?"

Nina pointed over the railing. "The nanny is that blond bimbo in the sequined T-shirt talking to JoJo."

"What a surprise. I'll catch up with her downstairs."

A door away, the master bedroom was drowning in Sister Parish chintz, pink chintz no less, with flowers and leaves. A canopied bed loaded down with a plentitude of pillows of every size and shape conceivable was almost a guarantee for discomfort.

The bathroom door opened and a man and woman stepped out, entwined. They paid no attention to Nina or Wetzon.

"Look at this," Nina called after stepping inside. The black marble counter was scattered with powder. Nina wet her finger, touched the powder, brought it to her tongue. She rolled her eyes at Wetzon and closed the door.

"I am no longer shocked," Wetzon commented afterward as they stood in the hall looking down into the living room below, which was a thick snarl of people. The noise floated up muffled, then showered over them like confetti.

"That's my partner," Wetzon said. She pointed Smith out to Nina. Smith was wearing dark glasses. "And the tall guy with the unnatural suntan and gold chains is Joel Kidde, the big talent agent. The young man with them is Smith's son, Mark."

"Do you see Mrs. Mort?"

"No. I wonder where she is. Maybe she went out to a movie. She's capable of that."

Nina laughed. "She couldn't be that bad."

"Oh, no?"

"Do you miss it?"

"Miss what?"

"Dancing. The Life."

"Sometimes. I miss the camaraderie of dancers. I miss the unreasonable joy of performing, letting my body lead, and not my head. It is complicated . . ."

They walked down the stairs. "Do you see Foxy?" Nina asked.

"Try the little woman in black with the Indian jewelry sitting at the piano with John Kander."

"Ah."

"One more hour," Wetzon said, "is about all I can take."

They split up at the foot of the stairs, Nina heading for the piano. Wetzon looked around for the nanny, ducked past Garth Drabinsky, who was pontificating to a group of young men on the future of the musical theatre.

"Hi, Leslie." Sunny Browning squeezed by Steve Sondheim to shake Wetzon's hand. "If the future of the musical theatre is Garth Drabinsky, we're in trouble. He throws money around like birdseed. His company is a public company. This is your field, Leslie. Doesn't he have to do financial reports? Doesn't he have to itemize expenses? How does he get away with it?"

"I don't know, Sunny."

"Well, his investors are stupid if they don't call him to account. Although I have to give it to him. He promoted that lavish opening night party at the Rainbow Room for *Showboat,* most paid for by the city of Natchez."

"It's a Canadian company traded on the Toronto Exchange so I can't see the SEC getting involved." Anyway, Wetzon thought, if Drabinsky wasn't on top at the moment, probably his competitors wouldn't find fault with him. Sniping was part of the culture in the Theatre.

"A producer has to know how to say no. He obviously says yes, yes, yes, yes, yes, more, more, more, more."

"Well, Hal Prince must love it."

"I guess." She looked depressed. "Doc Simon is going Off-Broadway with his new show. Manny Azenberg is the smartest of all of us. He knows what he's doing."

"Leslie! Excuse me, I didn't mean to interrupt. I just want to give my old buddy a great big hug." Bonnie McHugh had about three layers of foundation on her face. Her hair was an unnatural shade of red.

Old buddy, Wetzon thought. Really. She introduced Sunny to Bonnie, then said, "How are you, Bonnie? Are you back in New York for the concert?" Makeup and all, Bonnie had a new face. And a new chin.

"No, darling. Don't you know? I'm moving back. I bought a loft in TriBeCa. I'm going to do a musical next season for Andrew." She paused, then added, "Lloyd Webber." She was wearing a lacy black body suit designed to show so much cleavage that implants were obvious to anyone who'd ever shared a dressing room with her. Her skirt barely covered her black lace panties. Doc Martens clunkers and black hose that stopped about mid-thigh, leaving about six inches of flesh in the open, completed the ensemble.

"Bonnie!" Mort shouted. "Darling! Stay right there. Uncle Mort is coming."

Wetzon slipped away. She had just caught sight of the blond nanny, who was letting JoJo feel her up in full view of everyone. She came up

behind the nanny and whispered, "You'd better get your ass back to
Maudie because something unpleasant is going on in the nursery."

The nanny looked rattled. She tore herself away from JoJo and
headed for the stairs, unsteady on her spike heels.

In the dining room a few latecomers were heaping their plates.
Wetzon took a slice of sweet potato pie and a cup of coffee, then looked
around for a place to sit or lean. She wedged herself into a spot next to
the French doors, only a few feet from where Smith and Joel were
talking to Neil Simon, and tried to catch Smith's eye behind her
shades.

Smith looked odd. She was talking animatedly, but she hadn't removed her dark glasses. And there was a small discoloration on her
chin that she had carefully covered over with makeup. Had Joel hit
her? Not likely somehow. Now Hartmann, that was quite another
story.

Twoey, standing head and shoulders over everyone, waved to
Wetzon and began to weave his way over. His eyes were sparkling
behind his glasses. He looked very happy. "There you are, babes," he
said, giving her a kiss. "I was looking for you."

"Well, here I am," she said.

"Are you down, Leslie? You can't be. I won't let you." Twoey took
the plate from her hand and gave it to a passing waiter, who was
traveling back to the kitchen with an empty champagne bottle. Then
guiding her with an arm on her shoulders, he brought her over to
Smith and Joel Kidde.

"Zenie!" Twoey said, twirling Smith around and giving her a hearty
kiss on her lips. "What's with the shades?"

Smith straightened her dark glasses and pursed her lips. "Sugar,"
she said.

"Uh-oh," Twoey said. "I'm in big trouble now." He said it lightly,
but he gave Wetzon a questioning look.

"We were just talking about *Angels in America*," Joel said.

"Yeah," Twoey said. "Rocco told me. He got his loan out but the
New York production lost over six hundred thou."

"I told them to put it in an eleven-hundred-seat house, but they didn't listen to me. What do I know? I'm only an agent," Joel said.

"More than an agent," Smith murmured.

Twoey stared at her for a moment, then said, "The Walter Kerr was the wrong theatre. It's only got about nine hundred forty-five seats, no one wants to sit in its second balcony, and the stage is too shallow for a play with all that scenery."

When the producer, Marty Richards, joined them, Wetzon slipped away unnoticed. She followed the servers through the swinging door into the kitchen. A maid stood at the sink rinsing dishes, another was taking pies from the oven. Someone was slicing a ham; someone else was scraping leftovers into an immense green garbage bag.

The kitchen was huge, lined with white, windowed cabinets. Granite counters and a center cooking island were the other outstanding features. Off the kitchen on one side was a pantry, and on the other, a breakfast nook with a butcher-block table and four chairs. Under the window in the breakfast nook was an upholstered window seat, hidden from sight unless you came right into the room, which was how Wetzon found Poppy Hornberg.

Poppy was sitting, knees up, on the window seat, immersed in *Searching for Mercy Street,* Linda Gray Sexton's autobiography. Her fingers delivered pieces of cold turkey from a plate near her bare feet to her mouth. Her other hand played with strands of her hair. The pages of the book were spotted with grease and turkey debris, as was the bosom of her black velvet Laura Ashley dress. She wore no makeup. Her hair made Wetzon think Poppy had plugged herself into an electrical outlet with wet fingers. She looked up when Wetzon said her name.

"Oh, hello, Leslie." There was no welcome in her voice.

"Hiding out?"

"You might say. It's certainly not my idea to have all these strangers I don't care about and who certainly don't care about me in my house."

"I wanted to talk to you before I left."

Poppy was immediately defensive. "About what?"

Okay, Wetzon thought. You'll get no diplomatic questions from me. "I wanted to ask you about Terri Matthews."

"I don't want to talk about her."

"You're going to have to talk to the police, Poppy. I heard you and Terri were roommates at one time." She was fishing, but maybe she'd catch something. "Which means you might know something about why she was murdered."

Poppy's fragile skin blotched. She closed her book, but not before, to Wetzon's horror, she marked her place by folding the page in half. "I don't have to tell you anything," she said.

"True."

"Mort says your boyfriend's a cop."

"You'll meet him tomorrow. Actually, you might find I'm easier to talk to."

Poppy licked her fingers and dried them on her velvet dress.

Wetzon said, "If you knew her well enough to be her roommate, don't you care that she was murdered?"

"Not very much." A tear suddenly dribbled down her cheek.

Wetzon pulled over a chair. "Tell me about it."

Another tear spilled. Poppy sighed. "I was in my senior year at NYU. I had a part-time job with Oliver Smith, painting sets, but it didn't pay much. I needed help with the rent. Someone in the theatre department knew her, knew she was looking for an apartment. We met and got along fine. Then she moved in and everything got messy and I left."

In the kitchen someone dropped a pot on the quarry-tile floor and both Wetzon and Poppy jumped. The book fell to the floor. Poppy bent over and picked it up.

"What made you leave?" Wetzon asked.

"Richard Heflin. Did you know him? I was crazy about him. I met him way before I met Mort."

"He died a long time ago, didn't he? In California."

Poppy nodded. "He had Hodgkin's, and twenty years ago people still died of it. He wasn't sick then. That happened later. Terri knew how much he meant to me. I told her everything. She was like my big sister." Poppy wiped her cheeks with the back of her hand, like a child. "I found them together. They told me I had to move out because they wanted to be together. It was horrible. I moved uptown so I wouldn't ever have to run into them. I thought she went to California with him. I read his obituary in the *Times* just like everyone else. It never mentioned Terri."

"You must have been very angry."

"I'm still angry. It doesn't go away. But isn't it funny how fate works? Someone I didn't even know helped me out. Someone else she hurt."

"How?"

Poppy picked turkey from under her fingernails and licked her fingers. "By killing her, of course. Because if I'd had a gun, I would have done it myself."

MEMORANDUM

To: Carlos Prince and Leslie Wetzon
From: Nancy Stein, Assistant to Mort Hornberg
Date: November 23, 1994
Re: *Combinations, in Concert*

The rates for the musicians provided in the budget reflect
the Local 802 single engagement contract, not Broadway
rates. Ed Venderose is very pessimistic about getting any
concession to these rates from 802 but is willing to
accompany someone to the union to request a concession.

Chapter Thirty-Two

"AND THAT SOMEONE MEANS YOU, O KIND AND GENTLE CHOREOGRAPHER,"
Wetzon said.

"Why me?" Carlos said plaintively. "Why not Mort? He has more
clout than I do."

"Poor, sweet dear, because Mort figures egg looks better on your
face than on his."

WETZON FOUND CARLOS WITH MARK SMITH AT THE FOOD TABLE, NOW LADEN
with desserts, dishing. Actually, Carlos was trashing everyone with lusty
gusto and Mark was laughing.

Listening with half an ear to Carlos's rapid monologue, she cruised
the array of sweets, which went well beyond the traditional pumpkin
and apple pies. In fact, was that . . . ? Yes. Wetzon zeroed in on and
snagged the last, lone, sweating butter brownie, which testified to its
Greenberg bakery origins.

"It's a major sin," Carlos was saying.

"Thish ish a major shin," Wetzon said, mouth full of brownie.

"I'll have a bite of that before you demolish it, Birdie."

"In your dreamsh," she said, finishing it. "I make it a cardinal rule
never ever to share chocolate."

"Selfish bitch." Carlos grinned. "You see, Mark. You have to watch
these women. They run the world."

Mark laughed. "Have you met my mother?"

" 'Tis true," Wetzon said. "What's the major sin you were going on about?"

"Bonnie's mode of dress. She looks like a Hollywood ho."

This time Mark's laugh was a trifle too loud. Wetzon gave him a quick glance. She hoped he wasn't partaking of any white powder. She said to Carlos, "Why Hollywood?"

"Alliteration, my sweet." He made kissy lips at her and poked a small custard tart crowned with a glazed fig.

Mark's eyes darted around as if he was looking for someone. He seemed edgy.

"How do you like your first Mort Hornberg Thanksgiving, Mark?"

Carlos threw her a sardonic look and moved aside for someone who wanted a closer look at the tarts.

"Wetzon, have you seen Mom?"

"You mean the lady in the dark glasses?"

"He punched her." Mark's eyes grew moist.

Wetzon sighed. "Who? Hartmann?"

"I think so. She won't tell me. You know Mom. If he touches her again, I'll kill him."

Drawing him aside, Wetzon said, "No, you won't. I'll talk to her. You go back to Boston. Hartmann's going to jail. I'm giving grand jury testimony that'll put him away for a long time. Mark, I want you to promise me that you won't do anything crazy."

He looked down at her, weighing her words, then nodded. "I'll try," he said. "Oh, there's April."

"April Battle?"

"Yeah. We're driving back together on Sunday. You know her, don't you?"

Wetzon stood on tiptoe to see where Mark was pointing, but all she could see were talking heads. She gave up.

"I'd love to meet her."

"I'll bring her over," Mark said.

"Now this is eternal proof of what a wonderfully magnanimous personage I am," Carlos said. He was offering her half of an oversized dark chocolate truffle. "Of course, if you feel you *must* turn it down—"

"Never." It was in her mouth in less than a second.

"There's this chocolate mousse thing, very dark and dense-looking . . ."

"Chocolate mousse thing? Dark and dense? Lead me to it."

"The other side of the coffee urn. It's calling to us . . . listen . . ." He made his voice shrill. " 'Birdie . . . Carlos . . .' "

They filled their plates with generous portions of the chocolate mousse thing and stood eating, looking down at Central Park West. The street was dotted with remnants of the parade, blown helter-skelter by the sharp November wind. Traffic was beginning to flow again.

"What's wrong, Birdie? Where's Silvestri?"

"With his mother."

He looked at her, mock aghast. "And you gave that up for Mort's party?"

"No."

"Uh-oh. Don't tell me. You weren't invited."

"You got it."

"Oh, Birdie." He put his arm around her.

"I think he keeps me at arm's length because he's still punishing me about Alton."

"Why not have it out with him, then? Clear the air."

"Because I don't seem to be able to break through my own passivity."

"Maybe you don't want to."

"Carlos, my love, I think I'm having some kind of crisis."

"Not you, Birdie."

"Don't make fun. I'm serious. I seem to be living in a weird Pollyanna trance. I don't see the bad things in people."

"Like who? Me?"

She poked him. "No, not you. You're a splendid creature, through and through. I mean, for example, Terri. A few minutes ago Poppy told me Terri stole a boyfriend and an apartment from her."

"Oh, my. It's the apartment part that makes Terri truly evil."
Wetzon sighed.

"This must be serious."

"She seemed not to be able to keep her hands off anyone's man."

"What about yours?"

"If you remember, darling, I didn't have one. I was happily, or unhappily, celibate."

"Well, let's consider the source. Look who's telling you about her. Foxy, for godsakes. And Poppy—"

"Poppy wasn't lying."

"Now, Birdie, don't tell me you don't think Poppy's a wee bit pathological. I mean—not to show at her own party?"

"Not in this instance. Did you see any of this in Terri? Tell the truth. Wasn't she this nice girl from the Midwest?"

"No, Dear Heart. There are no nice girls from the Midwest—or anywhere for that matter—in the business. Terri was just another very eager gypsy on the make. Nothing wrong with that."

"Is that what I was, too?" Her voice came out thin and scratchy.

Carlos set their empty plates on the floor and put his arms around her, holding her close. "Oh, Birdie, never you. You never quite got the hayseed out of your hair. If it weren't for *moi,* you would have gotten trampled to death."

"Hey, hey, what's going on here?" Mort called. "What's all this lovey-dovey stuff?"

They looked up. Mort was standing near the piano with Nina Wayne and Mark, beckoning to them. With Mark was a tall young woman whose fair hair was cut impossibly close to her scalp. Her high cheekbones and angular features were stunning, especially considering she wore no makeup.

As Wetzon and Carlos came closer, Wetzon realized that this must be April Battle. She wore black leggings, a black blazer, a black turtleneck, and combat boots. Except for her height, April bore little resemblance to either parent.

"So go on, Nina," Mort was saying. "Just what is this mysterious thing you do?"

Wetzon, startled, held her breath. She looked at Nina, who was smiling reassuringly.

"I'm a doctor, and I'm associated with the National Institutes of Health."

Wetzon breathed again.

"Can you believe it?" Mort cried, as if to say how odd it was for an attractive woman to be a doctor.

The girl, April, rolled her eyes at Mark.

"I'm visiting Leslie for Thanksgiving, but I'm also here because I'm consulting on a project that's been in the works for years. Everything is going on a database."

"What kind of project?" Mark asked.

"Blood," Nina said. Her pronouncement produced a profound silence. "It's my field. I'm up to my elbows in it," she added, looking pleased.

Then Mort said, "Blood. What's a nice girl like you doing up to her elbows in blood?"

"Actually, it's blood typing that we're working on. We want to pinpoint everyone in the country with rare blood types. Then in an emergency the database is available with all the information. We're working through a group called the Blood Club."

"You mean like Rh-negative?" Carlos said.

"Yes, and A_2, which only about seven percent of the population have. It's very important to register people. So, my friends, if you know of anyone with a rare blood type, either tell me or—"

"Really? Only seven percent?" April said.

"That's right."

"And this database will make it easier to get the right blood to people who need it?"

"Yes. Do you know someone, April?"

"Yes, I do." April moved away slightly, unconsciously, setting herself apart from the others. "Me," she said.

MEMORANDUM

To: Carlos Prince and Leslie Wetzon
From: Ed Venderose, General Manager
Date: November 23, 1994
Re: *Combinations, in Concert*

There is a potential additional Box Office cost for a third
Box Office person (required by contract). I am going to talk
to the Treasurer about some accommodation for the cause,
but right now I feel we should get a third person in the Box
Office starting Monday, when the tickets go on sale. Since
time is so short, I have gone ahead and done this. The cost
is an additional $1000 per week including benefits. If we
sell out in the first week, we may be able to reduce our
costs. I'll get back to you after I deal with the Treasurer.

Chapter Thirty-Three

"HELLO, YOU HAVE REACHED OUR MECHANICAL DEVICE THAT ANSWERS OUR telephone when we're not available. Please leave your message after the rude sound and know that we're dying to talk to you." A long hoarse beep.

"Hello? Carlos? Are you there? Damnation. You're not. Well, this is my message. This is going to be the most expensive two performances for charity ever. I hope you know that. And the next time I let you talk me into producing anything, may I spend the rest of my life recruiting stockbrokers on Wall Street."

THEY STOOD ON COLUMBUS AVENUE STARING AT CHARIVARI'S CUTTING-EDGE-of-fashion windows. The wind plowed disorderly furrows in the nap of Wetzon's raccoon coat. Her face was numb with cold.

"So, April Battle would have been around two when Terri died?" Nina pulled her scarf up over her chin.

Wetzon nodded. "Do you inherit blood type the way you inherit eye color?"

"Something like that."

"And April's is A_2?"

"It was a little hard to talk, so she gave me her number at school."

"The FBI found evidence of A_2 . . ."

"On thread fragments of Terri's jeans."

"And Terri's blood type was O."

"Right."

They watched as a family—three children, two parents, and an elderly woman—got out of a limousine, bucking the wind, and entered the apartment building next to Charivari. The limousine driver took voluminous Zabar's bags out of the trunk and entered the lobby after them, then came out, got in the limo, and drove off.

"So," Wetzon said, "either Rog or Medora—" She stopped. "I'm sorry, I'm on overload. I have to quit. Do you want to come uptown with me?"

Nina shook her head. "I have an appointment. Tell Silvestri and we'll hash it through tomorrow."

They parted, Nina heading for the IRT on Broadway. Wetzon plunged her gloved hands into her pockets and trudged up Columbus, head down against the wind. People who'd been downtown for the parade and the festivities in front of Macy's were now straggling home. Children were cranky and adults tired and testy. Sunlight was slipping away. Like her self-confidence.

The stock market was rattled by higher interest rates and the Fed's abject fear of inflation. People were drawing money out of stocks for CDs and bonds. Treasuries were looking like a better return than stocks. PaineWebber had bought Kidder, further shrinking the Street, and Rosenkind Luwisher, Smith and Wetzon's biggest client, had all but said that it planned to do without headhunters.

Although Wetzon was certain that Rosenkind Luwisher would find this a mistake and backpedal, in the meantime, did it make sense to continue in the business? Did it make sense to bring in a star head-hunter? Wetzon, for one, would not want to take Rosenkind Luwisher back as a client when they ultimately discovered they couldn't recruit for themselves. Unless, of course, they groveled.

She laughed aloud, and a child so bundled into winter gear his arms were immobile stopped to stare at her.

"Come along, Jeffrey," his mother said, smiling nervously at Wetzon.

"Is she a crazy lady, Mama?" the child asked.

"I just may very well be," Wetzon told him, but Mama had rushed Jeffrey off, so there Wetzon was, talking to herself again.

And what about Smith? For the second time since Wetzon had known her, Smith was in a relationship that was out of control, but this time, at least, she was trying to extricate herself from it.

Richard Hartmann, Esq., was a very busy fellow. He hired people to take potshots at Wetzon and he punched Smith in the face.

Sirens began clanging, and in a short time two fire trucks came into view racing east on Eighty-sixth Street. Puffs of smoke were squeezing through the boarded-up windows of a tenement on the corner of Columbus that was in the process of being renovated. Firemen climbed out and two went upstairs, shouting.

A little crowd gathered to watch, but Wetzon moved on. Wait one bloody minute, she thought. There was nothing wrong with my judgment about Hartmann. I knew he was a scumbag the minute I met him.

Maybe it was women she was a poor judge of. Maybe she tended to trust women more than men.

That revelation brought her to the lobby of her building, where Rafael was standing in the middle of the sidewalk watching the firemen. He greeted her with good wishes for the holiday and held the door for her. An electric menorah, for the Jewish tenants, sat on a central table in the lobby, ready to be lit, for Hanukkah started on Monday at sundown. Early this year.

Her face tingled from the abrupt change in temperature. "Has Mr. Silvestri gone up yet?" she asked her doorman.

"I didn't see him and I been on all afternoon."

When she opened her door, there was no effusive greeting from Izz. No Izz to lavish unconditional love on her. And Izz's leash was gone, but not her knitted sweater, which Silvestri maintained made Izz look like a pussy.

So, he takes my dog to his mother's and not me, she thought. Then stopped herself. Now you're really crazy, Leslie Wetzon. You're actually jealous of a little dog.

She turned on all the lights. One message blinked at her from the answering machine. She played it back.

"Leslie." It was Peter Koenig's resonant voice. "I have two shows today. Can we talk tomorrow at some point? There's something bothering me about all this." He left his number.

Stripping off her party clothes, Wetzon pulled on her leggings and sweats. Silvestri, she knew, would check Actors Equity, or elsewhere, on blood types for Peter, Mort, and the entire original company. Even Davey Lewin might be represented, because he'd been a gypsy originally. And if Equity didn't have it or couldn't give it, they were stuck. Except for this development with April Battle.

Regardless, tomorrow no one would be in, so it would all have to wait until Monday.

She turned on the jazz station from Newark and did barre work for about twenty minutes accompanied by the Modern Jazz Quartet, an oldie but a goodie. Then she turned off the radio and put *Combinations* into the CD player, letting it run through while she improvised. When her number came up, she soft-socked it in deference to her downstairs neighbors. Ah, the joys of multiple-dwelling life.

Suddenly exhausted, Wetzon shut everything down. She padded into the bedroom and lay on the bed, pulling the quilt over her.

SHE COULD SMELL L'AIR DU TEMPS. IT WAS DARK, BUT LESLIE KNEW TERRI was in their room on the other bed, her back to her. Terri was on the phone, talking in excited whispers. That's what had awakened Leslie, the excitement in Terri's voice. It's not right to listen, she told herself, blocking out the words.

But, foolish girl, herself said, standing apart, *if you listen, you might learn who the murderer is.*

Go away, Leslie said. *If it was Rog, what good is it to know now? Rog is dead.*

• • •

THE PHONE WAS RINGING A LONG WAY OFF. WETZON ROLLED OVER, FACE IN her pillow. Just as the ringing finally stopped, Izz walked across Wetzon's back and, digging at the pillow, stuck her cold, wet nose into Wetzon's warm neck.

"Go away, wicked dog," she murmured.

"Les?" Silvestri lay down on top of the quilt and threw his arm over her.

"You brought in the cold," she complained, not moving.

"Who cares?" he whispered.

"There it is in a nutshell," she said to the pillow.

"Not true."

"You keep me at arm's length while I'm kicking and screaming trying to get close to you."

He drew back the quilt and put his arms around her. "I love you, Les."

"But you haven't forgiven me Alton Pinkus, have you, Silvestri? And you should. It's been over a long time."

He was silent. "I know," he said finally. His heart thumped against her ear.

"Are you brooding?" She kissed him under his chin.

"I don't brood."

"Ha! Wanna bet? Who was that on the phone?"

"Your partner."

"Oh? What did she want?"

"She's at Lenox Hill Hospital ER."

Wetzon sat up. "Is she all right?"

"Oh, she's fine. It's Joel Kidde. I told her we'd come and sit with her."

"What happened? His heart?"

Silvestri shook his head. "Two goons beat the shit out of him to-night in front of her building."

MEMORANDUM

To: Mort Hornberg, Carlos Prince, Leslie Wetzon, et al.
From: Edward Venderose, General Manager
Date: November 23, 1994
Re: *Combinations, in Concert*

The load-in will be two 8-hour days on Monday and
Tuesday, the 19th and 20th. There may be another 4 hours
on deck Wednesday night.

Please let me have all bills for expenses you will not
personally absorb. I will be forwarding them to Show Biz
Shares, who will pay the bills out of the net. It is my hope
that you will absorb all out-of-pocket expenses as part of
your donation.

Chapter Thirty-Four

"Birdie, darling, Fat Eddie hopes we will absorb all of our expenses. I definitely detect Mort's fine hand in this."

"Are we naive? Wouldn't you think all the expenses incurred would be picked up by the TV production? I'd love to leak this to the press."

"Hello, hello, is this the New York Times? *Good. I'd like to speak to Alex Witchel."*

THEY HEARD SMITH FIRST, THEN SAW HER BEFORE SHE SAW THEM. SHE WAS having a mini breakdown without removing her huge dark glasses or her mink coat. Or, for that matter, the Hermès scarf covering her hair à la Jackie O.

An embattled orderly was trying to calm Smith without success. He could not even get her attention. The whole ER was in turmoil, with patients and families and frazzled medical staff all yelling at one another and at Smith. The din in the overcrowded space was unreal, and Smith stood in the middle of it, howling.

"Silvestri, NYPD," Silvestri said briskly, flashing his shield. The turmoil began to subside. The yelling stopped. People withdrew from the action, sat down.

Wetzon saw Smith's glasses train on them.

"Smith," Wetzon said, "it's okay now. We're here." She held out her arms, and Smith, flailing, went right past Wetzon and threw herself at Silvestri.

"Xenia," Silvestri said, a dumbfounded expression on his face.

"Mmph, mmph, mmph," Smith blubbered into Silvestri's left lapel.

He patted her back awkwardly, looking at Wetzon, who shrugged. *She's all yours, sweetheart,* Wetzon, noir detective, mouthed.

"Xenia," Silvestri said, "are you hurt? Do you need medical treatment?"

Smith shook her head without removing it from Silvestri's chest.

"Then why don't you stay with Les while I find out how Joel is doing." Gently, Silvestri loosened himself from Smith's grasp.

"Come along, Smith," Wetzon said, taking her partner's hand and backing through a swinging door. She pulled Smith with her into a wide, well-lit corridor of some length. No place to sit, but the linoleum was waxed and spotless. And inviting.

Silvestri followed them. "What was the name of the A.D.A., Les? Something Peiser?"

"Marissa."

"Okay. I'll be back."

"What are we doing here?" Smith said in a plaintive voice.

"We're going to camp out on the floor and wait for Silvestri. That's right, bend your knees and plant your tush on the linoleum." Wetzon was rewarded with a tremulous smile. "You want to talk about it?" She put her arm around Smith. Sitting like this, their backs against the wall, they were the same height.

Smith rested her head against Wetzon. "It was awful," she said. "One kept his hand over my mouth—he said I had to watch—while the other beat Joel with a humongous flashlight and then kept kicking him when he was lying all bloody on the sidewalk." She swallowed a sob. "He wet himself."

"Joel?"

She nodded. "My doorman called the police. The one kicking Joel said something like 'This is what you get when you mess with someone else's property.' "

"Christ, you're someone else's property? How did this happen to you, Smith?"

"I tried to break it off—"

"And I see what you got." Wetzon handed her a tissue and Smith patted her cheeks dry. "I suppose in his own warped way Hartmann is crazy in love with you."

Smith turned her head so that her shaded eyes met Wetzon's head-on. "They all are. You know that, sweetie pie. But no one has ever behaved in such an uncivilized way about it."

Wetzon tried not to smile. It was so typically Smith. "Smith," she said, "you have to admit that part of your attraction to Hartmann was that he's dangerous. And unpredictable."

"Unlike Twoey," Smith murmured. "Twoey was altogether too predictable. Until he left Wall Street for the Theatre."

Wetzon gave Smith a sidelong glance. What was she up to? "I've always said Twoey was special."

Smith got to her feet and shook out her mink. "I'd better call Mark. He went somewhere with April to serve hot meals to the homeless, but he must be home by now."

"You raised a wonderful boy."

"I raised a bleeding-heart liberal for pitysakes." She held her hand out to Wetzon and pulled her to her feet. "You're a good friend, sugar, and I suppose I've been a little hard on Dick Tracy. When I called, he didn't even hesitate. He just said you'd both be right over." She felt in her coat pockets. "Do you have any change?"

Wetzon handed her a quarter. Maybe Smith was learning humility, the hard way, she thought. But then, Smith always did everything the hard way.

They left the quiet of the corridor for the ER, which, if anything, was busier than before. A child was screaming "Mom—my, Mom—my!" over and over. There were no vacant seats in the waiting area.

A trashy young black woman in four-inch platform boots and six hoops of various sizes through one side of her nose was yelling and cursing into the only working phone. Blood ran down her arm from an ugly cut near her bare shoulder. Her kinky curls were bleached yellow.

"Humpf," Smith said in a loud voice, folding her arms and staring at the spectacle. "They let all kinds in here. I thought this was a private hosp—"

The woman gave a fierce tug and yanked the receiver from the box. With an alacrity that was shocking, she went for Smith, wielding the phone like a club. Smith shrieked as Wetzon pushed her out of the way. The ruckus that ensued had everyone screaming until a security guard, wearing rubber gloves, pinioned the woman's arms, forcing her to drop the receiver, and a nurse shot her with a hypodermic. She continued to hurl curses at Smith even as they walked her out of sight.

Good God, Wetzon thought, how many times over the years had Smith made her want to do that herself?

"I've got to get out of here," Smith said in a strained voice, kicking the receiver out of her path.

Wetzon touched Smith's elbow. "Let's go outside for some air. Silvestri should be back any minute."

Smith didn't protest. She said, "I could use a cigarette."

"You don't smoke."

"What difference does that make?"

The frigid air hit them like a soothing cloth. Their breaths made slower and slower puffs in the night air. An ambulance blasting lights and sirens rolled up to the ER entrance. Detached now, they watched the frenzied activity begin anew as the patient was moved from ambulance to emergency room.

"Les?" Silvestri stood near the door. "Xenia, Joel's been in surgery. They had to get a plastics guy for his face—"

"Poor Joel," Wetzon murmured.

Smith did not react, as if she hadn't heard.

"He's got some internal bleeding, but in general he's very lucky. You can go up and see—"

"I want to go home," Smith said. "He peed all over himself. I don't want to see him."

"Well, okay." Silvestri looked at Wetzon and shook his head. "The hell with it," he said. "I'm tired, too, and so is Les." He went out to the curb and flagged down a cab making the turn from Lexington.

Wetzon waited in the cab, dozing while Silvestri saw Smith into her apartment.

"What a piece of work," he said, getting back in the cab. He gave the driver Wetzon's address, and she curled up against him. "Spoke to Marissa Peiser. I set up a meeting with her for Sunday."

She gave him a long look. "Silvestri, I'm not sure I have the guts to go through with the grand jury stuff." The cab was racing through the Park via the Eighty-sixth Street transverse; there was hardly any traffic.

"You won't have to."

She sat up. "What are you talking about? I won't have to?"

"Hartmann made a deal. They're giving him immunity."

MEMORANDUM

To: Carlos Prince and Leslie Wetzon
From: Edward Venderose, General Manager
Date: November 23, 1994
Re: *Combinations, in Concert*

At the top of the show the *Combinations* sign will be in
neon script mounted on a mirror. It will fly in and fly right
back out. In the beginning of the show four photographs
(Davey Lewin, Rog Battle, Larry Lawrence, and Terri
Matthews) will fly in. They'll measure 6 feet by 3½ feet.

As you know, the backdrop will be the New York skyline
designed by Eliot Larson for the revival of *It's a Bird . . .
It's a Plane . . . It's Superman.* I've cleared it with Eliot,
who will be paid a small fee by the TV producers.

Chapter Thirty-Five

"Carlos, my love, I'm thinking I'm going to fly in and fly back out. And in glorious neon, too. How would you like that?"

"Birdie, darling, neon is your thing. I'm thinking I would like to add Mort Hornberg's photo to the other four."

"He would have to be dead, dear one."

"I think that could be arranged."

BLEARY-EYED, COLD, AND A LITTLE SHELL-SHOCKED FROM THE GLUTTONY OF the day before, people dribbled in to Sarabeth's. Too much to eat, too much to drink, too much togetherness.

Having no close relatives except several cousins somewhere in the Midwest she hadn't heard from in years, Wetzon looked on holidays with mixed feelings. Regret? A little. Envy? Some. And definitely, a smidgen of relief. She knew interfamilial relationships could be, often were, difficult and fraught with treacherous potholes, especially on holidays.

Laura Lee steadfastly maintained that family gatherings were always like Anne Tyler's *Dinner at the Homesick Restaurant.* Eager anticipation and careful planning always gave way to unintended slights, bruised feelings and, finally, an explosion that left everyone damaged. But every year, as if cursed by the gods to endlessly repeat the event, the whole process with all its emotion and stress would be replayed.

Still, spending a show-biz Thanksgiving at Mort Hornberg's was

not any better. It was actually worse. Wetzon had returned home feeling empty and alone.

"More coffee?" A skinny waiter with an ever-so-slight mince was
poised to pour caffeine into Wetzon's half-empty cup.

"Decaf," she said.

He spun away and returned with the orange-collared carafe, filling
her cup with a flourish.

There was little animation at the tables. The Upper West Side
intelligentsia who did breakfast regularly at Sarabeth's sat glaze-eyed,
staring into their Baby Bears, which was how oatmeal appeared on the
menu.

Wetzon sat on a banquette near the back of the restaurant thinking, with some chagrin, more about Richard Hartmann than Terri
Matthews.

So Hartmann had made a deal. What kind of deal? And how did
Wetzon fit into it, if at all? What was Hartmann going to talk about in
exchange for—? She warmed her cold fingers on the sides of the cup.
He was going to tell them about his clients. The authorities would then
have to keep him out of prison, where he'd certainly be murdered, and
off the streets, where the same thing would happen. They'd give him a
new identity. But Hartmann was so enamored of his own identity it
would never work.

She saw Peter Koenig enter. He was wearing a very English-look-
ing tweed cap and a soft brown trenchcoat, its belt tightly knotted
around his waist. It emphasized the breadth of his shoulders. He was a
good-looking guy, no doubt about it. He made heads at the tables near
the door turn slightly as he stopped to talk to a woman at the bakery
counter. After a gasp of surprise, the woman came around the counter
and gave him a hug.

"Old friend?" Wetzon asked when Peter finally got to her table.
He'd been waylaid by people at two other tables and by a waiter, all
congratulating him on his performance in *Tacoma Triptych*.

He pulled out the chair and sat down, smiling. He was all pumped up from the praise. "Dee and I both studied with Uta . . . twenty years ago. God," he said. "Twenty years."

Uta Hagen and her husband, Herbert Berghof, had taught acting at H.B. Studio in the Village to several generations of American actors. Twenty years ago it was Uta, Sandy (Meisner), Stella (Adler), and the Actors' Studio. Legends all. Their like would never again be seen in the Theatre.

"I'll have coffee," Peter told the hovering waiter. "Orange juice and"—he studied the menu—"the oatmeal and a toasted English."

"Just the toasted English for me," Wetzon said. Sarabeth made her own English muffins, which were taller and better than any commercial ones. "I take it the show is going well?" Was Peter carrying a gun right now? Wetzon wondered. Maybe she should just ask him straight out.

"Great. Oliver Stone wants me for his next—"

"Did Streisand buy your play?"

"No. Michael Douglas did."

"Does that mean he'll do your role?"

Peter shrugged. "Thanks," he said as the waiter brought the orange juice and filled his coffee cup.

"Muffins and oatmeal coming," the waiter said.

Peter smiled at her. "Have you made any progress finding Terri's mystery lover?"

"Some. Not much, I'm afraid. If we stick to the people connected to *Combinations* . . . at least four, including Davey, were gay. I don't know how many were bi. It could have been JoJo."

"JoJo? JoJo Diamond? I doubt it." Wetzon could hear the disdain in Peter's voice. He wouldn't accept the fact that Terri would turn him down for a pig like JoJo. He popped a pill in his mouth and washed it down with juice. "Vitamin," he said.

"Why not JoJo?"

"He wasn't important enough. Neither was Mort, but I doubt that he was interested anyway. I had the sense that it was someone with more . . ."

"That leaves only one person, you know. Rog Battle."

"Rog Battle. I suppose . . ." But he looked doubtful.

"Then again, Rog Battle died right after the show closed, maybe even before Terri did."

"So that theory doesn't make sense."

"The police think she was killed between the time the show closed and the lease on the apartment was up—a window of about three weeks."

"I saw her the last time around the tenth of June."

"Do you carry a gun, Peter? I noticed the license in your wallet when we were at Joe Allen."

"And you told that detective. So that's how he knew." He leaned away from her, "You betrayed me" written all over his face.

"I may have mentioned it in passing," she said, faintly embarrassed.

"I haven't carried a gun in years. My degree was in pharmacology. I used to pick up hours here and there at different pharmacies. The gun was to keep me from getting killed in a robbery. I got rid of it years ago, before I left the city. The license is way out of date."

"Then why do you still carry it?"

"For the cops." He laughed. "It's gotten me out of more speeding tickets."

"Did Terri own a gun?"

"Not that I know of—but she used to practice with me, so she knew how to handle one."

Wetzon took a sip of coffee. "You said when you called me that there was something you didn't understand?"

"Yes."

"About Terri's death?"

"More about her life. Leslie, you roomed with her on the road. You were out three weeks—right?"

"Right." What was he getting at?

"Then you must know something about this guy she was involved with. You're holding back."

She was indignant. "I'm not holding anything back. Why would I? I don't remember anyone specific. What an outrageous thing to say."

"I'm not saying you're doing it on purpose." A huge bowl of oatmeal topped with sliced bananas and strawberries was set in front of him, along with an English muffin. The other muffin went to Wetzon.

Conversation stopped while they spread butter and the orange-apricot marmalade that Sarabeth was famous for. Peter splashed milk into the bowl. "Maybe you buried it," he said.

"Buried it? Buried what?"

"I'm going to talk to that detective again this afternoon, and I want to propose something, with your permission."

She eyed him with suspicion. What the hell was he talking about? Was he suggesting a lie detector test? Ridiculous. "What the hell is this about, Peter?" She took a big bite out of her muffin.

"Look, I may have been the last person—besides the murderer—to see Terri alive. I was in her apartment. She was packing her trunk. Don't tell me she didn't leave something of him lying around."

"But you said you didn't see anything."

"Leslie, I have this idea. I did the part once in a show. I'm going to suggest something to that detective, what's his face, Silvestri. I want you to agree so I can tell him we'll both do it."

"Do what?" she said, exasperated.

"Get hypnotized."

MEMORANDUM

To: Carlos Prince, Medora Battle, Foxy Reynard, JoJo
    Diamond, and Leslie Wetzon
From: Nancy Stein, Assistant to Mort Hornberg
Date: November 23, 1994
Re: *Combinations, in Concert*

Please don't forget the meeting at Mort's office on Monday,
November 28th, at five o'clock. Mort asks that you please
not be late, as he's booked on a seven o'clock flight to the
Coast.

Chapter Thirty-Six

"DANG BLAST IT," CARLOS SAID. "THE WHOLE WORLD HAS TO REVOLVE *around Mort's schedule.*"

"Dang blast it?" Wetzon said. "What century is this?"

"Oh, well, I suppose, we should count ourselves lucky the meeting *isn't going to be held at the VIP Lounge at Kennedy.*"

AFTER A TWO-HOUR SESSION AT THE DANCE STUDIO ON WEST SIXTY-FIRST Street, Wetzon and Carlos strolled up Columbus Avenue to Cooper's coffee bar. It was a cold Sunday morning. The shop was empty except for the counter person, a young Asian woman reading Plato's *Republic* with obvious enjoyment, and a fleshy woman in bicycle pants and a short ski jacket who was working the *Times* magazine crossword puzzle with a ballpoint pen.

Carlos paid for their coffees and they took the containers to a ledge and sat on the high stools.

"I'm probably going to need one more session, but I think I've got it." She watched two tourists on the sidewalk trying to decide whether to come into the shop.

"You'll be fine, Birdie." He took her chin and turned her head to him. "Give us a look at you." She made a face at him. "Eeeeek! She's turned me to stone!"

"Oh, Carlos. You know, you and I are a better match than Silvestri and I are. How did it happen?"

The tourists came in talking rapid German, got coffee, and sat down with their cameras and guidebooks to review the passing parade on Columbus.

"Dear Heart, the joys of life are all about mismatching. It would be such a bore if two lovers agreed on everything."

"Really?"

"Think on it."

"I'm mulling it over."

"I'll leave you to mull, then. We have a brunch in SoHo."

"Before you flee, just one question. Was Davey Lewin bisexual?"

"Davey? Our Davey? Ohmigod!" Carlos began to laugh. The woman in the bicycle pants looked up. "Here, Birdie, come on out before I embarrass both of us." He pulled her out of the shop. "You're thinking maybe Davey had a thing with Terri and killed her?" His laughter broke him up again.

"You're not answering my question," she growled.

"Okay, okay. Here's my answer. Davey bisexual? Never. No way. Not Davey. He was a dear, but believe me, he was one of the girls."

"Maybe he wanted to have little Daveys. That's happened before."

"Little Daveys? Get a grip, Birdie. Davey didn't have a thing about procreating. If there was one thing Davey was not, it was a breeder. Besides, didn't you say Terri was shot?"

"Yes." She was defensive suddenly, starting to feel grumpy.

"Well, Davey's father was a gun freak. Tried to get Davey into it. Davey hated guns; he would never—"

"Okay, stop." She held up her hands. "I get it."

"I've gotta go." He planted a kiss on her lips, then whispered in her ear, "One little note, darling, speaking of breeders. Just remember, it's not too late to make little Birdies."

She took a swipe at him, but he ducked and was off down the street waving over his shoulder.

Little Birdies, Wetzon thought. I'll kill him. She walked up Columbus to Seventy-sixth Street. Here on the school playground the year-round Sunday farmers' and flea markets were in full session, bulging with shoppers.

Both pale-petaled and red-petaled poinsettias sat plump in their pots along the metal fence that marked off the schoolyard. People were lined up to purchase them. The smell of hot, spiced apple cider pricked the cold, damp air, making Wetzon's eyes itch and her nose run. The sky was overcast. A little colder and it would snow. She pulled her beret down over her ears and blew her nose.

She bought six unblemished Northern Spy apples at one stall, some mesclun and two sweet potatoes at another. On the ground a vendor had arranged on a sheet an assortment of handmade herbal wreaths. Baked fruit pies, muffins and Pennsylvania Dutch pretzels, forced narcissus, which Wetzon had once tried to grow, but failed. She had never had much luck with plants. As Carlos always said, she had a black thumb. Yet she bought two poinsettias, one for herself and one for Marissa Peiser. A poinsettia had a limited life, so she would not be responsible for its death.

Little Birdies, huh, she was thinking when she unlocked her door. Well, Leslie Wetzon didn't have a thing for kids either. Maybe that was Silvestri's problem.

Silvestri and Izz were lying on the sofa watching the McLaughlin Group fight it out over Clinton policy.

"Hi," she said, laying her coat and hat on a chair. When neither Izz nor Silvestri moved, she added, "Did you have a nice workout, Les? Yes, darling, I did. Thank you for asking." She unpacked the beige-petaled poinsettia and set it on the coffee table.

Silvestri turned down the sound. Why not, it was a commercial anyway, she thought. "Very nice," he said.

"Feels like Christmas. Feels like snow." She ruffled Izz's fur, ran her fingers over Silvestri's brow.

"Hey," he said, catching her hand and pulling her down. He sniffed. "You smell great."

"That's sweat, Silvestri."

"*Your* sweat mixed with *your* perfume."

"I'm going to take a shower."

"Oh, darn," he said, his face solemn, his eyes laughing at her.

"Oh, darn? Well, I guess I could delay it."

Silvestri set the dog on the floor. "Get lost, Izz," he said.

Marissa Peiser lived on West 104th Street and West End Avenue in what had to be one of the last rentals on the Upper West Side. The seventies and eighties had seen the conversion of almost every apartment building on the East and West Sides to co-ops. Silvestri dropped Wetzon and the poinsettia off in front of the building and went to find a parking place. The cold was bone-chilling.

She shared the elevator with two exhausted little boys in blue knit caps sprawled snoozing in a double stroller and their equally exhausted parents. A tan cocker spaniel was leashed to the stroller. When Wetzon got off on the fifth floor, the cocker spaniel, whose name was Sadie, tried to follow her, jerking the stroller and waking the boys, who immediately began to shriek.

"Little Birdies, indeed," Wetzon grumbled under her breath as the doors closed on the tumult.

The creature who answered Peiser's door was almost unrecognizable to Wetzon. Her hair was slipping out of a ponytail, and she was wearing jeans and a Cornell sweatshirt, both stained, wet, and greasy in various spots. So, come to think of it, was her face.

"I'm sorry," Peiser said, distracted. "I thought I'd be finished by now, but I'm not really good at this. Come on in." She held the door open for Wetzon. "Just drop your coat on that chair."

"What are you doing?" Wetzon stood in a large foyer, to the left of which was a dropped living room and to the right, a dining room. Every surface—floor, sofa, table—was covered with stacks of papers and books.

"It's Hanukkah tonight, and my parents are coming to dinner. I'm in the middle of potato latkes."

"Is this appropriate?" Wetzon held out the bag with the poinsettia.

"Oh, how nice. Sure. Thank you." Peiser set it down on the

crowded dining room table—an oak job with heavy carved hairy feet and claws—plastic bag and all. "Come on back to the kitchen."

Following her, Wetzon said, "Silvestri's looking for a parking place."

"You can let him in. I have to finish this." On the counter was a bowl of grated potatoes sitting in water. Peiser plunged her hands into the water, came up with fistfuls of potatoes, and squeezed the moisture from them, setting them in another bowl. When she finished the process, she added eggs and flour and baking powder, scooped the mixture by the tablespoonful and dropped clumps into a pan of hot oil, where they began to brown immediately, filling the kitchen with a scent that made Wetzon's mouth water. "Leslie, if you set up a double layer of paper towels on that plate, we can drain them." Peiser flipped the latkes over with a slotted spatula. The oil hugged the latkes, sizzling around them. "When Silvestri gets here, I'll stop. We can have a snack and talk."

"But you won't have enough for your dinner."

Peiser laughed. "Open the oven door."

The door to the oven was warm; when Wetzon opened it, she saw each shelf was crammed with latkes on cookie sheets.

Silvestri arrived as Peiser was setting a heaping plate of latkes and a bowl of sour cream on the dining room table, pushing aside the briefcase and papers and legal pads. Wetzon carried in plates, forks, and napkins.

"Boy, that smells good," Silvestri said. He reached for a latke and it disappeared in his mouth.

Peiser poured coffee into mugs. "It's decaf, Leslie. I'm sorry I had to get you up here, but you wanted some answers and I thought it would be easier to talk here. Off the record." She put latkes on each plate and passed the sour cream.

"You made a deal with Hartmann," Wetzon said. She didn't think she could eat, but Silvestri was having no problem spreading sour cream and dispatching one after another.

"*We* didn't. The FBI moved in on us. He agreed to name names."

"He's going to get away with laundering money."

"Among other things. We've been told in no uncertain terms to stay out of it."

"What's the deal?" Silvestri said. "If the Feebs let Hartmann out on the street, he's as good as dead."

"They've got him stashed away in a hotel under another name."

"Oh, great," Wetzon said. "So he can still send two goons to beat people up." She cut a latke in quarters and ate one. It was crunchy on the outside and tender within.

"I heard what happened to Joel Kidde, Leslie. I understand Hartmann's been warned."

"But what does the FBI care about a private citizen when Hartmann's going to give them so much?"

"I'm sorry, Leslie."

"Oh, hell," Wetzon said, setting her fork down. "I feel as if I'm walking the plank and you're sawing it off behind me."

"Let's go home," Silvestri said. He got her coat from the foyer and put it on her shoulders.

"You'll be all right, Leslie. He's not going to try anything now. He'd be crazy to."

"Right." Wetzon opened the door and walked away.

"I'm sorry," Peiser said, holding out her hand.

"Forget it. I know how it is." Silvestri shook her hand and went after Wetzon.

They sat in the car not saying anything. He put his arm around her. "For what it's worth, I don't think he'll try anything now. There's no reason for it."

"He's crazy, Silvestri, and mean. He would hurt me for spite. Revenge. I got him into this. I'm scared because I don't know what direction he'll come from."

"I have a couple of retired buddies. They've gone private. I'll get someone to look out for you when I'm not around."

"I'll be okay," she said stiffly.

"Aw, come on, Les."

She put her head on his shoulder. "How do these things happen to me?"

"You're a magnet," he said. He kissed her nose, then started the car and pulled out on West End Avenue.

"So I guess Hartmann gets off, and we never find out who killed Terri."

Silvestri made a left on Eighty-sixth Street. "I've been thinking about what Koenig suggested. And I'm game if you are."

"Game?"

He made a U and pulled up in front of her building. "Yeah. I think there's a chance you and Koenig might remember something if you go under. I've seen it work before. So if you want to try, I'll set it up. At the very least you'll know you've done everything you can. What do you say?"

She let it lie there between them for a while. Finally she said, "Why not?"

MEMORANDUM

To: Carlos Prince and Leslie Wetzon
From: Ed Venderose, General Manager
Date: November 26, 1994
Re: *Combinations, in Concert*

We have two options available to us regarding the floor. 1) The floor will be covered with Marley to prevent high heels from getting stuck in tracks. Cost of Marley and installation needs to be priced. I'll do it when I get the go-ahead. 2) The cast will be supplied with dance shoes and we'll have to have a 4-hour prop call Thursday evening (this means overtime) to rebuff the floor. Get back to me quickly on this. Mort favors Marley. It'll look better on TV.

Chapter Thirty-Seven

"WHAT DO YOU FAVOR, CARLOS, DEAR HEART?"

"Mort's head on a silver platter?"

"Besides that."

"Marley, of course. It will look so much better on TV."

"I HAD A LITTLE CHAT WITH TOM KEEGEN. HE SWEARS HE DOESN'T OWN A gun. Denied everything," Metzger said. "He's a weaselly guy, but I'm inclined to believe him."

"You are?"

"Yeah. He also said he was sorry to lose Darlene, because she was so hard to train; but if she was unhappy with him, it's just as well she found another place."

"Gee, how magnanimous of him."

"And he said to tell you and your partner that she's not worth the trouble."

"What the hell does that mean?"

Metzger chuckled. "I'm just the delivery boy, Leslie. Don't shoot me."

"I'm sorry. You're right. Thanks, Artie." She hung up the phone.

"What was that all about?" Smith asked from behind her dark glasses. *Vanity Fair* lay open on her desk and she was flipping through the pages.

"Artie Metzger talked to Tom Keegen. Keegen denied he took a shot at Darlene and wishes us good luck with her. Artie thinks maybe Hartmann had someone do it to scare me off testifying."

"Humpf," Smith said. She was the old Smith again in a chic, fitted black pinstriped suit, sheer black hose, and her Bally slingbacks. Well, almost her old self. Wetzon noticed that her hands trembled when they picked up the mug of coffee in front of her.

"The other thing you should know is that I'm not going to testify after all because—"

"Thank God," Smith interrupted. She set her mug down.

"Because Hartmann made a deal with the FBI. He's going to name names."

"Oh, no!"

"Right. I don't think his friends are going to be as generous with their support as they have been in the past. I'm glad you're finished with him."

"He's going to rat on them," Smith said, awe in her voice.

The phone rang. Wetzon placed her hand on the receiver, but the ringing stopped and the hold light began to blink. "*Rat* is a good word, I think."

"That's so damn brave of him." Smith spoke with more animation than Wetzon had heard from her in the last days.

"Brave? Hardly. He's trying to save his ass. He'll be lucky if he *has* an ass after his friends find out. There could be a contract out on him as we speak."

A knock on the door and Max appeared, still in his tweed overcoat. "Jay Kipper for you, Wetzon. He's returning your call."

"I think we should have our staff meeting now," Smith said.

"Just let me take this, Smith. It's about Howie Minton."

"Howie Minton! We're still trying to place him? I can't believe it. When did we introduce him to Loeb Dawkins?"

"About a year ago, maybe a little more."

"And he can't come to a decision, for pitysakes? He can never come to a decision. Why do we waste our time?"

"Listen, Smith, it's not as if brokers are breaking down our doors to beg us to place them. This time I thought it was for real. Howie's manager was fired and his new manager was not feeding him business the way the old manager used to. Jay has been great with him, found him an assistant, set up a breakfast with the regional guy. Jay's ego hasn't gotten in the way."

"Take the goddam call."

Wetzon punched the blinking button and lifted the receiver. "Hi, Jay."

"Hi, Wetzon."

"I'm just checking on what's happening with Howie."

"Tell you the truth, Wetzon, I'm giving up on him. I call him, he says he'll call back, he doesn't, I call him again. I have to close my legs."

"Oh, Jay, I'm sorry. Let me call him and get a reading of what's going on." She hung up the phone.

"So." Smith said. "More of the same from Howie Minton."

Wetzon nodded. "Jay says he has to close his legs."

"Close—his—legs," Smith repeated slowly.

"Yes. Don't you find something vaguely demeaning about that turn of phrase?"

"Everything on Wall Street is vaguely and sometimes blatantly demeaning to women. We can't let it bog us down. We have to get past it; otherwise, we're out of business."

Smith was right. If Wetzon had pointed it out to Jay, who was actually very pleasant to work with and an excellent recruiter able to close on most of the brokers Wetzon introduced, it would destroy the relationship.

Over the years Howie Minton's suspect sheet had grown from one dog-eared page to twelve, stapled together in the left-hand corner. Wetzon set it aside. "I'm just not psyched to call Howie now. Do you want to have the staff meeting?"

"Yes. We also have that meeting at Mort's this afternoon."

"We? Why are you coming to our production meeting?"

"I don't see why you have to be so ungracious, sweetie pie. Mort invited me. Joel isn't well enough yet and there are many things to be discussed on the television filming, especially in the technical area. Of course, I'm the novice because Mort has done this before, but that lovely man Edward Venderose has been most helpful." Smith rose and opened their door. "Staff meeting, everyone," she announced, as if they had a staff of ten.

"In other words, Ed is line producing." No wonder Mort had brought him on, but why should the stage version have to pick up his salary? If the TV production paid him, it would net-net more money for Show Biz Shares. Damn, she would call Mort on this.

Wetzon gave Darlene her chair and sat on her desk while Max rolled his chair in from the reception area. The phones were unnaturally quiet. Wetzon hoped this wasn't a further omen of the climate on the Street. The markets were nervous waiting for the latest employment figures and concerned about the Fed's next move.

"The meeting will come to order," Smith said, although no one was talking. "I'm asking each of you to help design a working plan for the new year, which is almost upon us, with individual goals. Very little will be accomplished between now and the first of the year. We know that, don't we, Wetzon?"

"True. From today until January second is the most social time of the year in New York. There are parties almost every night. Christmas parties, dinners, cocktails, office parties—by the way, hold the twentieth for ours—brunches, luncheons, and open houses."

Max asked, "Does that mean no one will go out on appointments?"

Darlene was picking at her nail polish. She said in a bored tone, "Of course not." What had happened, Wetzon wondered, to the very insecure persona she had shown them when she started? Had it all been an act?

"Most companies wind down their business," Smith told Max. "On Wall Street the major selling to realize losses is about finished. Clients are starting to worry about taxes. Business is slow."

"But if your timing is right," Wetzon said, "they will interview."

Darlene crossed her legs. She was wearing herringbone hose and four-inch heels. Her short skirt inched up to mid-thigh. "I have four interviews set up in Boston," she said.

"Good work," Wetzon said. "You should know that Keegen has backed off. No more restraining orders. The court threw it out. And Keegen denied trying to kill you."

"And you believe him?" Darlene said, wounded.

"Not necessarily. I'm just saying that if he was responsible for taking that potshot at you, he's been warned off. Detective Metzger doesn't think you have anything to worry about."

Darlene gave Wetzon a triumphant smile, then turned to Smith. "So I can call everyone I used to talk to?"

Smith nodded. "Yes, but I think you should be our regional director of recruiting. What do you think, Wetzon? Wetzon can keep New York, New Jersey, Connecticut, and Pennsylvania, and you can have the rest of the country, Darlene."

"Sounds good to me," Wetzon said. The way business was shaping up, Darlene could have the whole goddam country.

"What about me?" Max asked, easing open his jacket so they were sure to see his bull-and-bear suspenders.

"Dearest Max," Smith gushed. "You are the best cold caller we've ever had. We're going to give you a new title. What do you think, Wetzon?"

Wetzon closed one eye and smiled at Max. She and Smith both knew that a fancy title and a token would get you on the subway. George Abbott, the late, legendary Broadway director-producer, had said it best. "Give them billing," he said. "They'll always take billing over money."

Wetzon said, "How about Assistant Vice President for Telemarketing?"

"Oh," Max said, blinking rapidly. "I really like that."

Smith's lips twitched. "It's yours, then, dear Max. We'll have some new cards printed, won't we, Wetzon?" She smiled her Cheshire cat smile and suddenly Wetzon felt cheap.

The ringing of the phone broke up the staff meeting, and then a second call came in hard on the first. Darlene rose and, with a wave, tottered out of the room.

"For you, Wetzon," Max said. "On two. Detective Silvestri."

Sitting down at her desk, Wetzon felt the surge of adrenaline she always felt when she heard Silvestri's name. She pressed the second button. "Hi."

"Les," he said. "Are you sure you want to go through with this hypnosis thing?"

"I thought you felt it was a good idea?"

"I did and I do, so long as you use it as an exploration into the past and not as a way of taking more blame on yourself. None of this was your fault."

Easy for you to say, she thought. She said, "I wish—oh, hell, I wasn't hot to do it at first, but Peter may be right. It's hard to believe that neither one of us saw or heard anything."

"It was a long time ago."

"I could have blocked it out."

"Or maybe you didn't think it was important enough to remember."

"That's kind of interesting."

"There's this guy, Tom McLean. He's a detective sergeant, retired. He's at John Jay, on the teaching staff. I've worked with him before and he's good."

God, she thought. It's here. She said, "I didn't expect it this soon."

"I set an appointment for Koenig on Monday, the fifth. He wanted to get it over with before his opening."

"I can understand that."

Silvestri must have heard the hesitation in her voice. "You don't have to do it, Les. Remember, this is not official police business. There's nothing legal about this, so we won't have a problem with enhanced memory, which always comes up with hypnosis at a trial. It's basically for you, Les, and maybe, just maybe, something useful will come up on Terri Matthews's murder. Then you'll be able to put it behind you."

"I know. I agreed to do it, so I'm not going back on my word. But let's not rush into it, okay?"

"Okay," he said. "Write this in your book. I set an appointment for you with Tom McLean for December ninth, at two-thirty. That's a week from this Friday."

"So soon?" She sighed. "It's about trust, I suppose. It's hard for me to think about letting go."

"Tell me about it," he said. She could hear the smile in his voice.

MEMORANDUM

To: Medora, Foxy, Carlos, Leslie, et al.
From: Ed Venderose, General Manager
Date: November 26, 1994
Re: *Combinations, in Concert*

Although United Scenic Artists is not insisting that a
member of the union sign off on the costumes, I've asked
Peg Button if she would donate her fee, with the
understanding that if indeed the TV version happens, she
will be reimbursed.

Chapter Thirty-Eight

"Birdie, do you notice how everyone is getting something out of this except us? This is supposed to be a goddam charity affair, and it's turning out like the United Way."

"I am pissed enough to promise you that I will get down on my hands and knees and beg The Village Voice *to do an exposé."*

"And, darling, get me some of my stuff," Mort called.

Clutching her black notebook to her breast, Nancy stopped in mid-run from the little galley kitchen, panic on her face, and burst into tears. Mort had sent her back and forth for legal pads, for pens, for chairs, for coffee or Cokes for everyone, and now, finally, for his "stuff."

Wetzon patted Nancy's shoulder, then stuck her head into Mort's office. "Give her a break, Mort. She's not Wonder Woman."

"That's the trouble," Mort groused. His feet were on his desk and he was leaning back in his chair talking to Carlos, who gave Wetzon one of his fish eyes.

Medora was sitting on the sofa bonding with Smith. They were acting like old friends, with Smith actually patting Medora's hand. Indeed, with both of their progeny about the same age and attending Harvard, they probably had more in common than anyone else in the room.

Standing near the door, Foxy was giving Ed Venderose her ticket requests and instructions.

Where was JoJo? Wetzon wondered.

"Grab a seat, Leslie," Mort said. "Don't make problems. Nancy and I understand each other, don't we, Nancy darling?"

Nancy, a cup and saucer in each hand, winced as she came into the room. JoJo followed carrying three cans of Coke. He passed one to Smith, one to Foxy, and kept one for himself.

Nancy and JoJo, Wetzon thought. Why not? JoJo was generous to a fault. On *Hotshot,* he'd bestowed his largesse on none other than Poppy Hornberg.

Carlos and Wetzon took the coffee, which smelled and tasted like kerosene. Had Nancy managed to spill some of Mort's Fernet Branca into the coffee?

"So, okay. Let's iron out any last-minute glitches," Mort said after Nancy brought him his glass of dark, syrupy liquid. "Why are you standing there?" he told her. "Close the door and let's get started."

Nancy's chin trembled as she took the empty chair next to Wetzon. She opened the black notebook and began to write.

Carlos said, "The first thing to talk about is Ed and I went to see Local 802 about a concession on the number of musicians. They turned us down cold. They said it was because of the TV production, but I think it wouldn't have mattered."

"Well, that's not a surprise, although, I must say, they are not as adamant as they used to be. Still, we're stuck with three walkers?"

"We are."

"Walkers?" Smith said.

"They are nonplaying musicians added to the payroll because the union contract on a particular house requires a certain number," Ed said. "They used to have to come to the theatre and sign in, now they don't have to show up at all."

"And they get paid anyway?" Smith gave Wetzon her I-told-you-the-Theatre-needs-me look.

"They certainly do," Mort said.

"And our other situation," Ed said, "is Bonnie McHugh's hairdresser. He won't negotiate and he won't do anyone else's hair."

"So let's not use him at all," Foxy said.

Ed responded, "She won't do the show without him. He must be shtupping her good."

"I hate to disappoint you, Ed," Carlos announced with hardly concealed glee, "but for your information, Bonnie is a lesbian."

"Oh, for pitysakes," Smith said.

Well, Wetzon thought. And how come I didn't know that? On the other hand, Carlos tended to think everyone in the world was gay.

Ed said, "You think everyone is gay."

"Au contraire," Carlos said, not letting Wetzon catch his eye. "Xenia's not, Medora's not, and we wouldn't have you."

"That's enough," Mort said. "You've all met Xenia, haven't you?" He beamed at Smith. "As you probably know, Xenia and I are going to produce the TV production with Joel Kidde. We're doing it as a documentary. Someone'll go around with a microphone and a handheld during rehearsals and then backstage during and after the performance. It was my idea. Isn't that terrific?"

Terrific, Wetzon thought. Even she had to admit it was an interesting idea, but then, Mort had not originated it. The concert version of *Follies* a few years back had done just that to ease the transition from the proscenium to the small screen.

"I'm thinking," JoJo said, "if we have to pay these musicians, I can use them. We'll enhance the orchestra. It'll sound better on TV."

"Good fellow," Mort said.

"And you can charge it to Show Biz Shares," Wetzon said, "so it will leave more money for all of us."

Mort eyed her warily. She knew he couldn't tell if she was being sarcastic or not.

"Somehow," Medora said faintly, "that doesn't sound right."

"Thank you," Carlos said. "I think we've all forgotten this is a benefit. We're raising money to take care of those in our community who are HIV or have AIDS, and we're honoring our dead."

Foxy began to applaud slowly.

"Well," Smith said, still hiding behind her dark glasses, "I would like to add something, and I'm sure I speak for Mort and Joel. The TV production company will pick up all extra costs, so long as it doesn't get out of hand."

"The TV production company should pick up *all* the costs," Wetzon said.

"I don't think that's such a good idea," Mort interjected as Smith was about to respond. "It's okay to be charitable, but we also have to take care of ourselves. We have a chance here to make a lot of money."

"Yes, of course," Wetzon said. "We mustn't forget that."

"I knew you'd come around, darling," Mort said. "Let's see now. Ed has given you the rehearsal schedule. Carlos and I are going to be very busy that week, so if any problems come up, talk to Ed. Anything I've left out, Ed?"

Ed shook his head, but Nancy said, "*People* magazine. They're probably going to come in for the dress."

"Speaking of dress, unless I've tuned out, no one's discussed wardrobe," Wetzon said.

"Oh, I thought you knew," Mort said. "We've got black stretch jumpsuits for everyone from Donna Karan, bless her, and we'll accessorize with scarves, jackets, and stuff. Peg Button will do it. And our Nancy will coordinate everything."

"Oh, my, it's late. I have to go." Medora stood up and everyone else did likewise.

"Clean up in here, there's a good girl," Mort told Nancy.

"Bet that didn't come in the job description," Carlos whispered to Wetzon.

"Count on it," Wetzon said. "Mort, by the way, I've been meaning to ask you about the sound and light equipment companies, like Boomer, Inc."

He stared at her. "What do you want to know?"

"Who owns them?"

"What kind of question is that?" He'd gotten very red.

"A good question I thought."

"Well, I do. And it's perfectly legal."

"How nice. Then you are going to donate the use of the materials and not charge anything but labor against the production costs, aren't you, you sweet thing?"

"Well, of course," he said. "That's what I was going to do anyway."

Wetzon saluted him and left the room. She stopped to look at the photographs again on the walls in Nancy's office, feeling a little teary-eyed with nostalgia, when Smith ambled by, slipping into her mink. "Where are you off to?" Wetzon asked her partner.

"I'm going with Medora."

"And where is Medora going?"

"Medora, where are we going?"

"The Dramatists Guild," Medora said. "It's the penthouse in this building. You're perfectly welcome to come along, Leslie. They're making a small party in honor of Rog. He would have been sixty today. We're setting up a work/study program at NYU for young playwrights in his name."

"That's a wonderful memorial, Medora. We should all attend the party," Wetzon said. "Why didn't you tell us?"

"So much is happening right now, it just slipped my mind." She wiped a tear away with a tissue. "You know, I used to think that *Combinations* had bad karma. Rog was the first to go, then it seems little Terri, although we didn't know about her, then the rest over the years."

Wetzon said, "But it's time Rog was honored. Especially now, with the concert and your new play about to open." How could something like that just slip her mind? Could it be that Medora didn't want to remember Rog? What a horrible thought, she told herself.

"I wholeheartedly agree," Carlos said. He'd obviously overheard most of the conversation.

"So sad," Smith murmured, her tongue making *tsk, tsk* noises against her teeth. "For someone of such talent to be cut down in his prime." She put her arm around Medora and they continued toward the door.

"Waiting for a bus, Birdie, darling?" Carlos's voice broke into Wetzon's reverie.

"No. Thinking. Why did Medora make such a point of saying Rog died first? What if Rog wasn't the first? What if Terri was? We have no way to pinpoint the exact day of Terri's death. If Terri died first . . ."

"Methinks you've gone overboard on all this," Carlos said. "Be careful."

"Oh, la," Wetzon said, kissing her fingers at him. "See ya."

She heard Carlos say to Mort, "Have you been in to see *Hotshot* lately?"

"No. I never look back."

"Well, I can't be so cavalier and neither should you," Carlos said. "We have a responsibility to our audience to see that the show is as good as it was when it opened. I was in last night and took out all the improvements." He was talking about the extra pieces of business actors added to their roles as a show ran—a real problem on a long run.

Mort's voice rose slightly. "Fuck the audience," he said.

MEDORA HAD STOPPED TO SPEAK TO FOXY, GIVING WETZON A SOMEWHAT private moment with Smith, who was waiting to one side. "Get her to tell you what Rog died of," she said to Smith.

"I'll do nothing of the kind," Smith said.

"Then I guess you don't want to share in Peter Koenig's retainer."

"Oh, for pitysakes," Smith said as Medora joined her. Wetzon let them walk ahead of her to the elevators.

When she caught up to them, Medora was saying to Smith, "He'd been at a meeting and came home upset about something. He wouldn't tell me what. He went to bed early and had a massive heart attack in his sleep. I found him. The children were so young. It was really a terrible time for me. If it weren't for Edward—he was the only one—I probably wouldn't have gotten through it." She gave Smith a thin smile, then looked around. "Where is Edward? He's coming with us."

"I think he's on his way. Someone told me that Terri babysat for you," Wetzon said.

"She did once in a while." The elevator signaled DOWN and the doors opened. "I think we should wait for Ed."

"This is down anyway. I thought you were going up to the penthouse."

"So we are." Medora smiled. Smith pressed the UP button.

"I've heard such contradictory things about Terri lately. Did she help you after Rog died?"

"Oh, of course she did," Medora said altogether too quickly. "I'm sure she did. I wonder if I should go back for Edward."

"You guys go ahead. I'll tell Ed where you are. I forgot to remind Carlos of something." The arrow flashed green for UP, but Wetzon was already on her way back to Mort's office.

In the reception area Ed Venderose was taking a list of ticket orders from Nancy. "Medora said she'd meet you upstairs at the Guild," Wetzon told him.

"Okay, that's it," Ed said to Nancy. "I'm heading over to the box office after the party upstairs, so I'll talk to you later."

"Tell me something, Ed," Wetzon said. "Do you remember Terri helping Medora out with the kids after Rog died?"

"Terri Matthews? Boy, you're on some kind of trip with all of this, aren't you, Leslie?"

Wetzon sighed. "Just give me a direct answer, Ed." He seemed determined to make her fight for everything she wanted to know. As if he were protecting someone . . .

"All right. Here it is direct. No way. It was kind of funny how everyone disappeared at the time, but I wasn't surprised about Terri. She was a selfish bitch. The only one she was interested in was herself. And Rog."

MEMORANDUM

To: Medora, Foxy, Carlos, Wetzon, et al.
From: Ed Venderose, General Manager
Date: November 29, 1994
Re: *Combinations, in Concert*

I think you'll all be very pleased to know that ticket sales
on the first day the box office was open have been very
brisk. At this rate it is very possible we'll go clean very
quickly.

Chapter Thirty-Nine

"Ah," Wetzon said, "now that's a lovely sign of things to come, don't you think, Carlos, love?"

"Yes, we just might be able to save a box office salary. Those guys get more money than my gypsies. Equity minimum creeps up and the other unions outpace us. An ordinary reedman in the pit comes in and reads music for a couple of hours, doesn't have his blood in the show, gets more than our people who are dancing their hearts out."

"Ya know, Wetzon," Hale Hamilton, the good old Southern boy broker drawled, "Ah been really lucky in this business. Ah love Mutha Merrill, Ah love my clients. Ah thank ya for keepin' in touch, but Ah'm as happy as a two-dick dog."

Wetzon cradled the receiver. "So it goes," she said. She turned to her partner, who was putting a top coat on her mauve nail polish. "Hale Hamilton's as happy as a two-dick dog."

Smith stopped in mid-motion and rolled her head around so that the dark glasses stared at Wetzon.

Wetzon continued. "I ask myself, am I happy as a two-dick dog?"

The nail brush dropped into the bottle. Smith slowly removed her glasses. The skin around her eye was only slightly yellowish. With a little more powder, someone who didn't know, wouldn't.

Grinning at her partner, Wetzon said, "Welcome back." Then, "Are you?"

"Am I what?" Smith fluttered her fingers in the air to dry the polish.

Wetzon let the words roll off her tongue; their essence made her tipsy. "Happy as a two-dick dog."

"I truly believe you deal with the scum of the earth."

"Me? You do, too. In your own immortal words, we make our living dealing with pond scum."

"I don't know . . . maybe it's time for a sabbatical."

"Seriously, Smith, confession time. Are you happy, as a two-dick dog or otherwise?"

"Not really. Are you?"

Wetzon was silent, thinking. "Not really. Isn't it strange? We both have plenty of money, we run a successful business, people admire us, we're reasonably attractive, you have a wonderful son. And we're not happy. Why is that?"

Smith sighed. "I'm in love with Dick Hartmann," she said in a tiny voice.

"But—"

Smith held her palm up to Wetzon. "Please don't comment."

Wetzon nodded. "Okay. My turn? I feel as if I'm Silvestri's back-street mistress, someone he'd never introduce to his family."

Now Smith nodded. "We need a pick-me-up." She stood. "It's after four, so let's go."

"Go where?"

"Get your coat." Smith was suddenly all movement, throwing on her what-becomes-a-legend-most mink, hustling Wetzon into her own coat.

Light was fading rapidly when they hit the street. The buildings were sharply etched against a darkening sky.

"We'll have to walk," Smith said, obviously delighted with herself. Coltish, already way ahead of Wetzon, she barely missed running down a woman carrying two huge shopping bags from Saks.

Wetzon caught up with Smith on Second Avenue. "Why are we in such a rush?"

"We don't want to be late."

"I feel as if I'm with the White Rabbit," Wetzon murmured, and fell behind again because she stopped in front of Steve Sondheim's house, swept off her beret with a flourish, and bowed deeply.

"Oh, for pitysakes!" The White Rabbit's screech lassoed her and pulled her forward.

"Saks? We're going to Saks?" Wetzon said.

The sidewalks were suddenly dense with people. Tourists, all speaking different languages, the bridge and tunnel crowd, and even some locals.

"Hurry," Smith said.

"Where are all these people coming from? Who are they?" Wetzon felt herself beginning to be swept up in the excitement.

On Fifth Avenue, crowds were lined up in front of Saks's windows, listening to actors reading a children's story as animated figures in the windows illustrated the reading.

Booksellers vied for space with the Salvation Army Santa and his well. Bells jingled lightly and jangled sharply. The Promenade, or Channel Gardens, which led to the Rockefeller Center skating rink, was a confection, decorated with spun-gold angels, heralding.

The tree was visible then. A Norway spruce so immense that even unlit, it was majestic.

"Shouldn't we get out of this crush?" Wetzon asked, finding her way blocked everywhere by sheer humanity.

"Don't dawdle," Smith called. She crossed Fiftieth Street and disappeared.

Wetzon pushed her way through the crowds to the International Building at 630 Fifth Avenue. Among the milling mob of tourists, Smith's head floated as if she had no body. Wetzon looked up at the giant sculpture of Atlas balancing the world on his shoulders that marked the front of the building. She said, "And where is Smith taking me, Arnold?" Laura Lee always referred to the International Building as "the one with Arnold in the front." Arnold for Schwarzenegger. "And why would I want to go there?"

She'd guessed finally that Smith was taking her to Richard Hartmann's law offices, which overlooked Rockefeller Plaza.

"Isn't that so?" She repeated her guess when she caught up with Smith.

"Don't be ridiculous," Smith snapped. "He's not there. Bill Veeder invited me personally to the tree-lighting party, and I don't see why we shouldn't take advantage of it." She pulled Wetzon into the lobby. "When did you last see the tree lighting?"

"In person? Never. Always on television. But—"

"The partners' offices all overlook the Plaza, and Bill Veeder is a very attractive man."

Wetzon groaned. She felt her will dissipating under Smith's intensity. Well, hell, it was Christmas. Joy to the world, peace on earth, and goodwill toward . . . And besides, she was here already, and Hartmann was hidden away somewhere. She didn't even know his law partners. They could be honest, couldn't they? "Okay," she said, "let's do it."

They edged onto the express elevator with a horde of others, including several children, poor things, who immediately disappeared among the hems of the adult coats. Smith reached across a sable-steeped, blue-haired woman to press 41. "Pardon," she said in a French accent, all the while sizing up the coat. Wetzon choked back a laugh and got a curled lip from Smith. From the thirtieth floor on, people got off on each floor, and the elevator emptied out completely on the fortieth.

"You know, sweetie," Smith said, "you're getting so judgmental. It's not becoming. It makes you very spinsterish, and you certainly can't afford to let it show on your face at your age." Smith's eyes had the peculiar, delighted glint that she always got when she was offering Wetzon advice in the form of criticism.

"You're such a good pal," Wetzon said as they got off the elevator.

"I'm telling you for your own good—"

A Christmas wreath covered the door, which was partially open, so that you could hardly read the name Hartmann, Veeder and Kalin, P.C. Music spilled out from within, along with laughter and the piping voices of children.

Wetzon followed Smith into the festivities.

A receptionist in a red dress, with a corsage of white and silver bells on her tremendous bosom, was talking on the phone and sipping champagne. She smiled at Smith and said, "Merry Christmas."

There was now a towering balsam, fully decorated, where Wetzon remembered a man-eating plant had sat. The receptionist hung up the phone and said, "Go right in, Ms. Smith." She waved to the bleached walnut door set into glass bricks that led the way to the inner offices of the law firm.

They entered a wide, curving hallway. A bar had been set up near the conference room, and secretaries and associates mingled with partners.

"Xenia!" Greeting them was a tall, craggy-faced man with sharp blue eyes and almost white hair. A dead ringer for Paul Newman. "So good to see you. Merry Christmas." He kissed Smith first on one cheek and then the other.

"Bill, you sweet thing," Smith gushed. "This is my partner, Leslie Wetzon."

"Welcome, Leslie Wetzon. Welcome. Come, hang up your coats and have some champagne." Bill Veeder's words were warm, but his ice-blue eyes appraised her. He held out his hand. "Come," he repeated. "It's a holiday. Peace and goodwill."

She shook his hand. He had a firm, dry handshake. A subtle woodsy aftershave scent surrounded him.

Veeder said, "All the windows on this side overlook the Plaza. Caviar's in the conference room. Well, you know your way around, Xenia. Make yourselves comfortable."

They hung up their coats among a jungle of furs and made for the bar, where two associates were liberally pouring champagne into fluted plastic glasses. Smith introduced them to Wetzon by name.

Leaving Smith to charm the young lawyers, Wetzon took a glass of club soda and wandered off in search of caviar. The conference table was covered with a paper cloth on which rested what was left of three massive brioches. Some ingenious person had designed each so that it was sliced into finger sandwiches, filled, and put back in the exact shape of the brioche. Very elegant. The sandwiches were filled with caviar and cream cheese, with prosciutto and mozzarella, with Gorgonzola and chutney. A lot of well-dressed types were digging into the food as if they'd come in from the Long March. On the sideboard were stacks of *Journals* and Law Reviews, along with dirty glasses and crumb-covered plates.

"Don't be shy," a voice said. Bill Veeder touched her elbow lightly, took a paper plate from a stack, and handed it to her.

"Oh, I'm not shy," Wetzon said. "*Cautious* is a better word, I think. I always study the lay of the land before I jump in." She set down the club soda and filled the plate with stacks of little sandwiches, mostly caviar. She loved caviar.

"You're not drinking," he said.

"I don't drink champagne."

He looked at her thoughtfully, then said, "Come on." Keeping his hand on her elbow, he guided her out of the conference room and down the hall, where all the doors were open and the offices filled with people clustering near the windows. There was one closed door. He opened it, escorted her inside, and closed the door again.

The room was extremely masculine. A taupe rug with a flat nap and a design of tiny brown diamonds covered the floor. Mahogany bookshelves, glass-enclosed, a beautiful broad Stickley desk with brass trim, brown leather chairs, and a taupe-and-brown sofa with a glass-topped coffee table filled the space. The vertical blinds were open.

"You've kidnapped me," she said. She set the plate down on the coffee table on top of Tom Clancy's latest hardcover, picked up a couple of caviar sandwiches, and walked over to the window, eating. She was getting crumbs on his rug, but she didn't care. He read Tom Clancy. Down on the Plaza, skaters were performing on the ice.

Bill Veeder reached around her and opened the window. His scent made her dizzy. At once choral voices floated up to them. Bits of carols. ". . . Hark the . . ." and "Oh, Holy Night . . ."

Behind her she heard the clink of ice against glass. Turning, she saw he was holding two glasses. He gave one to her. "I thought you might enjoy a very special single malt," he said.

"I might."

He touched his glass to hers. "Your health, Leslie Wetzon."

She felt chilled suddenly. "And yours, Bill Veeder." She took a sip of the scotch after he did. It wouldn't do not to be careful in the enemy camp. She held it in her mouth for a moment, then swallowed. It was the best she'd ever tasted.

The singing had stopped and someone was talking.

A discreet sound, almost unrecognizable, came from the phone. Veeder looked down at it, picked it up. "Yes." He moved the sleeve of his French cuff and checked his Piaget. "Yes," he said again. He studied Wetzon as if she were a picture puzzle, taking her apart, putting her pieces together again one at a time. Wetzon turned her back on him. It was a male-female thing. Or maybe it was a predator-prey thing, but whatever it was, it was making her uncomfortable. He said, "Xenia? Yes. Well, I'll leave you, then." He hung up the phone.

Wetzon moved away from the window. "I think it's time for me to go."

"Not yet," he said, gently blocking her path. "You haven't seen the tree." He brought her back to the window.

From below a cheer rose like a mushroom cloud. The enormous tree burst into light, and the cheer caught them and held them together briefly, in an almost loving embrace.

"Merry Christmas, Ms. Wetzon."

"Merry Christmas, Mr. Veeder."

They drank, watching each other. She set her glass down on his beautiful desk and left the room.

She was no dope. This was a setup of some sort to put Smith together with Hartmann. Smith was not finished with Hartmann. Not by a long shot.

And this could only mean that Hartmann was not finished with Wetzon either.

• • •

MEMORANDUM

To: Carlos, Leslie, Medora, Foxy, JoJo, et al.
From: Edward Venderose, General Manager
Date: December 3, 1994
Re: *Combinations, in Concert*

You are aware that Peg Button has agreed to sign off on
costumes. United Scenic Artists doesn't care if Nancy is
costume coordinator because it's only for 2 performances,
but we feel a union member should do the job. I am happy
to tell you that Peg volunteered to do the accessories as
well. I know you'll agree with me that she's a classy dame.

Chapter Forty

"AND I'M HAPPY TO TELL YOU PEG IS DEFINITELY A CLASSY DAME," CARLOS said. "I bet she turns her fee back to Show Biz Shares, too."

"I'm sure you're right, but can you believe Mort? He was going to have Nancy coordinate costumes. And for free, no doubt, since he's paying her salary anyway."

"Do you think that was also part of the job description, Birdie?" Carlos said, raising one brow and lowering the other eyelid.

Wetzon touched her finger to his supercilious nose. "You're a classy dame, too, darling," she said.

THEY WERE SITTING AT THE ROUND TABLE IN THE WINDOW OF CAFÉ CON Leche: Silvestri and Peter Koenig. She saw them before they saw her. Peter's face was flushed. He was talking and talking. Silvestri was listening, nodding, sphinx-faced.

She doubled back and headed over to Broadway. Silvestri had insisted that Peter and Wetzon not discuss the routine of the hypnosis sessions with each other until both were completed, so she took a hike over to Broadway, if one block could be called a hike.

The trees and shrubs on the center island all along upper Broadway wore dusters of little glowing lights, part of the celebration that was Broadway at Christmas. Wetzon crossed the street. In front of Zabar's someone was clanging a bell, asking for donations for the homeless; Christmas carols came from a van piping music onto the street; tables were stacked with bestsellers (probably ripped off from publishing companies), which were being sold by vendors for half price.

She went into Zabar's. At six o'clock, even holiday time, it wasn't terribly crowded, at the very least you could still walk around without bumping into masses of people. She picked up two pounds of coffee beans, a package of sliced Scottish salmon, six bagels, a sopressata sausage, scallion cream cheese, a chunk of Gruyère, a dozen eggs, and a container of rice pudding. When she felt off-kilter and her soul was raw, rice pudding soothed.

You could always tell what kind of party the person ahead of you on line was giving by the contents of the shopping cart or basket. The woman directly in front of her wore down-at-the-heel running shoes, grubby trousers, a faded blue down jacket full of nicks with feathers seeping through. Her shopping cart was stuffed to the brim with bags of bagels and bialys and packages screaming smoked fish. A modest holiday brunch? The checker rang up a total of almost two hundred dollars, and the woman dropped a gold American Express card on the counter.

One of the best things about the West Side was that you could run out of your apartment in old clothes and no makeup and no one would hold it against you. The West Side was easy.

She paid for her groceries and returned to the restaurant on Amsterdam. Silvestri was alone now, making notes in his little notepad, the angle of his jaw softened. His hair in the back just touched his collar. The more he lost in front, the longer he let it grow in back. But it couldn't be too much longer because although One Police Plaza was ambivalent about hair, there were limits. Unless you were undercover, a pigtail was a definite negative.

He was all she wanted, she thought as she stood in the dark watching him through the window. Then he looked up and caught her, a peculiar expression on his face for just an instant before it faded.

"Hi," she said, coming into the restaurant. He put his notepad in his inside pocket and rose. The man behind the counter, who was wiping up, stared. He'd seen the gun. He looked Silvestri over carefully, then went back to wiping. A cop was a cop.

Silvestri gave her a perfunctory kiss, or tried to, but it didn't work like that for either of them. He held the chair for her as the counterman removed the empty coffee mugs, wiped down the table, and left them with menus.

"Nina's joining us in a bit," Silvestri said.

"How did it go with Peter?"

"Let's wait till Nina gets here so I don't have to say it twice."

"Fine. Order me a glass of Merlot." She went to the ladies' room, breathing in the heavy garlic mist as she passed the kitchen.

When she got back, Nina was there and three glasses of red were on the table. Nina smiled at Wetzon.

"Let's order first," Silvestri said, "then we can talk." His notepad was on the table again.

Wetzon and Nina ordered the shrimp and rice, and Silvestri had the roast pork and a platter of plantains. The waiter left them a plate of crisp wedges of garlic toast.

"Do you want to start, Nina?" Silvestri asked.

"After you." Nina was wearing the same very tailored business suit Wetzon had seen her in before, her hair in the severe, but somehow sexy, chignon. Nina helped herself to a slice of toast and drank some wine. "How did the hypnosis go?"

Silvestri's eyes clouded. "Fairly well. I don't want to go into too much detail right now because Les has—"

"Friday afternoon," Wetzon said. "Dump-da-dump-ta."

"Okay, just tell me if Peter remembered anything that might be helpful?"

"Maybe." Silvestri flipped through pages until he found his place, took a swallow of wine, then ate a slice of the garlic toast. "Koenig's session showed Terri more nervous with him than he remembered. Her trunk was open in her living room and she was packing."

"Did she tell him where she was going?" Wetzon said.

"She wasn't leaving town. She was moving to another apartment."

"Go on," Nina said.

"She kept looking at her watch, as if she was expecting someone."

"As we postulated: the celebrity lover," Nina said.

"There was some mail scattered on her coffee table. Bills—New
York Telephone, Con Edison—and a pile of letters under a red rubber
band. The top envelope was addressed to Terri with no return address."

"Maybe it was on the back," Wetzon said.

"Maybe. She was rushing him out and he was upset. She told him
—and this seems to be exactly what she said—that there was no place
for him in her life. He thought he recognized the handwriting, but he
couldn't make the connection and lost it."

Wetzon groaned. "Oh, come on, the handwriting? Doesn't that
sound hokey, Silvestri? Are you sure he wasn't making this whole thing
up to throw suspicion elsewhere?"

"We haven't ruled Koenig out, Les, but there's no concrete evidence pointing—"

"His blood, what about his blood?"

"Here's where I come in," Nina said, then stopped to let the waiter
set down their dinner plates.

On the street the lights from the Christmas decorations in the
restaurants and shops along Amsterdam Avenue radiated and reflected
off each other like a chain reaction in the darkness. The sidewalks were
busy with people shopping, coming home from work, shopping, searching for a place to dine, shopping.

They checked out one another's plates and began to eat.

"Peter Koenig's blood type is AB," Silvestri said.

"I spoke to April Battle," Nina said. "Genetically, April is A_2A_2. She
had to inherit an A_2 from at least one parent who might be A_2A_2 or
A_2A_1, or A_2O or A_2B."

"I'm lost," Wetzon said.

"Go on," Silvestri said. Did she see a smirk on his face?

Nina smiled. "Simply, here it is. April Battle's mother, Medora, has blood type O. April inherited her rare blood type from her father. It was Rog Battle who had the A_2A_2."

MEMORANDUM

To: Carlos, Medora, Foxy, Leslie, JoJo, cast and crew
From: Edward Venderose, General Manager
Date: Thursday, December 7, 1994
Re: *Combinations, in Concert*

Your memory may need refreshing about rehearsals, so here it is, finalized:

Rehearsals begin Friday, December 16th, at 10:00, run the 17th, break Sunday, the 18th, commence again Monday, the 19th, at 10:00, all at the Minskoff.

Mort and Carlos are expected to be there throughout.

We move to the Richard Rodgers on Tuesday, December 20th, at 10:00. The press has been invited to the rehearsal. We'll run the show from 11:00 to 1:00.

Wednesday, the 21st, we have the dress from 10:00–1:00. Wardrobe and the hair person will be there.

The orchestra will be in the pit for the dress and will continue through final rehearsal from 2:00–5:00.

Cheers. Focus on this: At least it's a limited run.

Chapter Forty-One

"WOULDN'T IT BE SMARTER TO INVITE THE PRESS TO THE DRESS SO WE'D BE IN *costume? I'm going to call Mort and suggest it."*

"Don't bother, Birdie. I already did. Gotham Magazine *took the dress. They've invited an audience. It's Christmastime, Noel, Noel. The publisher's paying back all the favors."*

"Wait a minute. For free? They're not paying? Are they contributing something to Show Biz Shares?"

Carlos shrugged. "It's publicity, darling."

"It's not going to sell one ticket. We both know that. It's publicity for the goddam TV show."

SHE WAS SO TIRED WHEN SHE CAME FROM THE REHEARSAL STUDIO THAT SHE caught a cab on Broadway. Carlos, that supremely social creature, had gone off to yet another party, this one at his guild. He had invited her to go with him but she had declined. Wetzon considered the membership to be a cranky and competitive group of unrecalcitrant ESTies and lily-livered cowards. She would not spend a millisecond in their self-congratulatory company.

Attending their party would contaminate her and make her hiss and boo. Christmas was for goodwill, not hissing and booing.

She got out of the cab across the street from her building feeling almost deliciously satiated from the rehearsal. She was languid, buoyed several inches off the ground. Her endorphins were in full furl. The front door wore a large wreath that jiggled when Mario, the doorman, held it open for her. A lushly decorated Christmas tree filled a corner of the lobby. Near the mailboxes a UPS man was just starting to unload dozens of packages.

Gathering up her mail, she floated onto the elevator. On the twelfth floor one of her neighbors had set a huge poinsettia on the white lacquer sideboard that decorated the hallway shared by four apartments. The area was pungent with garlic. Silvestri was home early.

She opened the door and received the little package that was Izz full in her arms. The new Beatles album was turned up high and Silvestri was flipping mushrooms in the sauté pan.

"Heaven," she said.

"Linguine al fungi." He grinned at her through the steam. "Or something like that. Fifteen minutes. Pour the wine, bread's on the table."

She set the little dog down, hung up her coat, and dropped her briefcase and purse on the floor for Izz to inspect. Then she came into the kitchen and inhaled. "Who are you and what are you doing in my kitchen?" She locked her hands around his middle and rested her head on his back. He was so unpredictable.

"Your lover, come to ravish you. But first, the aphrodisiac." He tossed the mushrooms with almost professional aplomb.

"Oh, sure," she said.

He pulled her around and kissed her nose. "I want to walk you through what to expect tomorrow."

"So you're bribing me with fungi because you know I'm a sucker for mushrooms, is that it?"

"Something like that. Then afterward I ravish you."

"Okay. I think I'll dress for the occasion, then."

She took the bottle of Burgundy and left him to his cooking. She loved him when he was like this.

The table was set with linen napkins and candles. She did one of Smith's *humpf*s, poured the wine, and lit the candles, then went down the hall to her bedroom and took off her suit. Under it she still wore her dance clothes. He hadn't even noticed her leggings and ankle warmers hanging below her suit skirt.

He was waiting for her, pasta apportioned, salad on the side, when she returned. "What a wonderful wife you'll make some lucky person someday, Silvestri. Now if only you did laundry. . . ."

"I don't do laundry or windows," he said, "but I—"

"Never mind. Business first or I'll be a wreck tomorrow."

The meal and the dance session combined to make her mellow. After they cleared the table and put the scant leftovers away, for Silvestri was a midnight snacker, Wetzon carried cups and her carafe of Starbucks' hair-raising decaf into the living room.

"Where do we begin?" She filled the cups and sat on the chair opposite while he and Izz reclined on the sofa.

"Are you afraid of this, Les?"

She shook her head. "Not afraid exactly. Apprehensive. Will you be there with me?"

"If you want."

"I do. Why don't you tell me about this McLean person? He's okay?"

"He's a good guy. He's a professional, a clinical psychologist, a criminologist, and an ex-cop."

"Which means he's still a cop."

"One of the best."

"I guess I'm afraid he'll dig around in my psyche and—"

"He won't. He's just going to take you back to a specific time. Nothing else. Tom's a real pro. You'll like him. I gave him the case file and I told him about you."

"Whadja tell him, Silvestri?" She hated to hear people were talking about her. It made her feel somehow diminished.

"That you're a smart-ass and a hardhead," he said. "What do you think I told him?"

"You wouldn't have said that, because, my love, you're a real pro, too. Are we going to do it in his office?"

"Yes. Same place he did Koenig. All you have to do is meet me in the lobby of the John Jay Administration Building at two-fifteen tomorrow and I'll take you up."

"Silvestri, I've been doing a lot of thinking about this. . . . I'll bet Terri was already dead when Rog died."

"What makes you say that? Do you know something you haven't told me?"

"Gut instinct. Maybe Rog killed Terri. Maybe we ought to get a court order and get his body exhumed. What if his death wasn't natural?"

"But what's his motive for killing her, Les? Or someone else's motive for killing him? And getting an exhumation order won't be easy. Let's take first things first. Get tomorrow over with."

"Maybe he was going to leave Medora and—"

"Then Medora would have a better motive to kill them both."

She stood up. "You're right. I'm going to take a shower."

"Not yet," he said, following her.

The telephone rang.

"Don't answer that," he said.

Her answering machine saved her from a decision. A moment later an agitated voice said, "Leslie? I must talk with you. Your friend, that blood doctor, has been harassing April. You think I don't know what you're doing?" Medora was shrieking now. "Stay away from my daughter and stay out of my life!" The phone call ended with a slam as sharp as a gunshot.

Silvestri looked at her. "Well, we sure hit a nerve," he said.

MEMORANDUM

To: Carlos, Medora, Foxy, Leslie, JoJo, cast and crew
From: Edward Venderose, General Manager
Date: December 8, 1994
Re: *Combinations, in Concert*

Here's some good news we can all breathe a sigh of relief about. The *Combinations, in Concert* benefit is completely sold out. The box office is closed, which means we're saving plenty of money.

If you still need tickets, or know anyone who wants to buy tickets, please let Nancy know right away.

Chapter Forty-Two

"WHAT DOES THIS MEAN?" SILVESTRI SAID, LOOKING OVER WETZON'S shoulder. "Sold out is sold out in normal language."

"The Theatre doesn't use normal language. In the Theatre, Silvestri, sold out is never completely sold out. The box office can always come up with something, and so can the general manager. They squirrel tickets away all the time for celebrities. I mean, what if the Prez and his entourage want to come . . . ?"

"And if they don't get sold, these phantom tickets?"

"On a hit show, Silvestri, they always get sold."

THEY MET AT THE JOHN JAY ADMINISTRATION BUILDING SHORTLY AFTER TWO o'clock.

Silvestri hadn't stopped talking, but she hardly heard him. It was as if she were already in a hypnotic trance.

"Tom McLean," he was saying. "From D.C. . . . a retired detective sergeant . . . clinical psychologist and criminologist . . . in constant demand . . ."

Wetzon looked sideways at him. Why was he babbling on like this? Finally, as they got on the elevator, she said, "Are you nervous or something, Silvestri?"

He pressed 6, exchanged how's-it-goings with two other detective types, and didn't respond to her question until the elevator emptied on the fourth floor. Then he squeezed her hand. "Whaddaya know, kid?" he said.

"I know you're acting as if maybe I'll say or do something that'll embarrass you, Silvestri."

He looked at her, shocked. Then the elevator stopped and they stepped out. He was still holding her hand.

"Do I make you feel like that?"

She nodded.

"Jesus, Les. I'm sorry. I don't mean to." His brow furrowed with concern.

"You're so busy protecting yourself from me, Silvestri."

"Okay, Les, I hear you. We'll talk about it later. Right now this is not about me. You have to clear your mind and be relaxed for the session to take." He was looking down at her; his lips moved as if he had something else to say.

Just say it, Silvestri, she thought. *Say it.*

And just like that, he did. He said, "I love you, Les. I want you to be safe."

THE FIRST THING WETZON NOTICED ABOUT TOM MCLEAN WAS HIS EYES. THEY were medium brown and velvety. Kind eyes. He looked like a doctor, stocky in dark gray checked suit, white shirt, and red paisley tie. A Norman Rockwell doctor, only younger. Tom McLean was probably in his late forties or early fifties. His face had just the right amount of wear and tear.

"Come on in and make yourself comfortable, Leslie," he said. He had a firm handshake and warm hands. His high forehead showed a mildly receding hairline, black, peppered with gray. Her hands were icy, but he made no comment. He indicated a large leather easy chair that squished when she sank into its comforting depths.

"Would it be all right if Silvestri stayed?"

"Would you like that?"

She nodded, suddenly feeling like Alice, that she was shrinking, and she hadn't even eaten anything. "Yes, I would."

"Well, okay, Silvestri, hang up the coats in that closet. I'd like you to sit over there." He pointed to a chair well out of Wetzon's line of sight. "Beeper off?"

Silvestri said, "I know the routine."

"Do you need to use the bathroom, Leslie?" McLean asked. "We're going to be here for a while."

"No, I'm fine." Silvestri had alerted her. The session had to be done on an empty bladder.

The room had the feel of a study. It was lined with books, and something by Bach was just barely audible. Her feet rested on a faded oriental in subdued browns. Tom McLean sat at his uncluttered cherry-wood desk. He gave her a reassuring smile.

The afternoon sun pushed against the closed blinds, making the room a cocoon. It could have been any season, even summer.

McLean said, "Relax, Leslie. You're in good hands. I've done over a thousand of these interviews."

"Silvestri told me," she said, wishing he'd get on with it.

"I want you to feel you can say anything to me. I want you to feel so comfortable with me that you will drop your guard. I'm going to turn the lights down a little and I want you to loosen any clothing that is binding you."

She was wearing a business suit. Hell, everything bound her. Compromising, she took off her jacket and laid it on a side table, then sank back into the chair. He'd turned the lights down without rising from his chair.

"You're not bothered by elevators, are you, Leslie?"

"Only when I have to wait a long time for them."

"Good. I'm going to guide you into a natural condition of relaxation. This is not a sleep and you will not be in a trance." His voice was deep and almost melodious, but riveting. She could not turn away. "You will be comfortable within yourself. You will never be out of control. You can stop it at any time. I'm only going to ask you about this one event that we agreed on prior to today. Is that okay with you?"

"Yes."

"And I'm going to use this tape recorder because it's important to capture exactly what I say and your response."

"Okay." She realized with some awe that she would have said okay to him whatever he asked her.

"You're not from New York, are you, Leslie?"

"No. I grew up on a farm near the Jersey shore, but I've lived here for almost twenty years."

"Do you ever miss it?"

"Miss what? The farm?" When he nodded, she said, "Never. I felt buried alive there. Trapped."

"Tell me what you do when you relax."

"Barre work. Did Silvestri tell you? I was a dancer." She smiled. "I was a really good dancer."

"Broadway?"

"Yes."

"Do you do anything else to relax? Something less physical perhaps, something that makes you happy?"

"Yoga, but that's still physical. I guess I'm a physical person. But I also do TM, transcendental meditation. And sometimes I make a big mug of coffee, put my feet up on the sofa, play Mozart, and read a novel."

"Who do you read?"

"Doctorow or Jane Smiley or Anne Tyler. If I know I don't have to answer the phone and deal with some crisis in my business, that makes me incredibly happy." His eyes invited her to say more, but she didn't.

"We're going to eliminate your body, Leslie, to get to your mind. Your body is going to become a dull, heavy lump. You will hear your heartbeat, feel your blood flowing through your muscles." He was speaking slowly and evenly, and she felt she was sinking deeper into the chair.

"We're going to work together now to get you to the point where you really want to remember. We're going to go through a series of mental exercises, walk to different places, that will take you away from

yourself and cause your energy to focus away from your daily routine."
His voice was deep and smooth; it washed over her like warm sunshine.
"Then, when you're very comfortable, we're going to bring forward
your memories of this particular event and project them on a TV
screen. We'll be able to watch your memory play on TV, so that you'll
also be an observer."

"Oh," she said, vaguely disappointed. "You're not going to put me
into the memory, to relive it?"

"It is my experience that if you're a third party you'll remember
much more. It'll be like watching an old movie. What we're doing here
is very important. It's what you owe your friend. Are you comfortable
with this, Leslie?"

"Yes." She had spoken, hadn't she? But she could hardly hear herself. The chair beneath her was a warm soft lap, and she was sinking
back into a soft bosom as her body relaxed.

"I'm going to ask you to remember, Leslie. Do you want to do
this?"

"Yes," she said, her eyes on his. He was so kind. She felt the last
threads of resistance ooze from her fingertips.

"You're going to consciously command yourself to do this, to relax
and do as I ask you to do. You may be worried. Tell me if you are. Tell
me if you can do what I ask you to do?"

Her breathing was slowing, becoming deeper. She marveled, still
observing. "Yes," she breathed, but she wasn't sure she said it out loud.

"I want you to put your hands flat on your thighs, with your fingers
spread out," McLean said. His voice came to her in a gentle baritone,
repeating, "You feel yourself sinking slowly deeper into the chair. Con-
centrate on my voice, Leslie. I want you to focus on the tip of your ring
finger on your right hand. Watch your fingertip."

She stared at her fingertip with its pearl-polished oval nail. It was a
nice fingertip.

"Now, Leslie, you're going to gather together all your inner
strength and energy. In the process, you're going to have a very pleasant experience because you're going to learn how to relax by concen-

trating on my voice and you're going to do as I tell you. Watch your fingertip . . . listen to my voice . . . do as I tell you."

Time expanded slowly like an accordion making no sound.

"Watch your fingertip . . . listen to my voice . . . do as I tell you . . ."

She felt herself floating, unable to keep her eyes open, yet there was a spectacular light show racing through her brain, and voices, everyone talking at once as if all the telephone lines in the City had crossed.

His voice came in a monotone. "You have lights and voices exploding in your brain. Let them. Don't try to keep them out. Your eyelids are getting heavy now and your breathing has slowed. You feel yourself relaxing. Take a deep breath and release tension. Your body is growing heavy. In a minute you'll feel your eyes begin to close. Let them close, Leslie. Listen to my voice. Do as I say."

Her eyes closed as he spoke, yet she wasn't asleep. She could smell the leather of the chair, hear her own breathing.

"Your mind is very clear now, Leslie. Empty of thoughts. Listen to my voice. Do as I ask you to do."

She was suspended, floating, with only his voice as her anchor. She could hear her even breathing. All the tensions of her life were ebbing slowly from her. She was at peace.

"Imagine yourself walking slowly on a sandy beach. It is late afternoon. See yourself walking."

She is suddenly a teenager again, walking on the beach at Seaside, feeling her toes grip the warm sand.

"You're alone, Leslie, walking . . . slowly . . . gently. The sand is warm. You hear the rolling rhythm of the waves. As you walk, each step makes you more and more relaxed. Your eyelids are heavy . . . your muscles are heavy. Your body is relaxing more with each step. Your breathing is getting slower and slower. You are not afraid because you have nothing to fear."

Her footsteps slow until she is barely moving. She can smell the salt air, the seaweed, the Coppertone lotion mingles with sun and sweat.

She can no longer hear the waves, but only Tom McLean's voice reaching her, reassuring her. She knows she would follow him anywhere.

"In the distance," he said, "you see a tower of yellow stone. It is covered with ivy. You come closer and closer to it and you enter the building. There is an elevator waiting for you. You get on and press 'ten.' On the tenth floor there is a room especially prepared for your perfect peace. As you pass through each floor, you will feel yourself relaxing more and more. By the third floor, you will feel peace; by the fourth, your eyes are closing."

She listens to his voice saying the numbers slowly one after the other, floor after floor, wave after wave.

"You are now on the tenth floor and you get off the elevator and walk to the center of the room. You are surrounded by warm light. There's your chair waiting for you. Sit down, Leslie, lean back, listen to the ocean. Every last bit of tension is leaving you."

Deflating. She is deflating. As if she has no bones at all. No bones, no bones. Bones.

"Imagine I'm tying a helium-filled balloon on your right wrist. Now I'm going to let go of the balloon and you'll feel a tug and gently . . . one . . . two . . . three . . . your hand is rising. Let it rise, and as it rises, you will feel the last bit of tension slowly leave your body."

She feels the tug then, feels her right hand rise, rise . . . rise. Her eyelids are too heavy to open.

He said, "Leslie, you are doing so well. You're going to have a wonderful experience. Now I'm going to disconnect the balloon and your hand is going to float back down and rest on your thigh."

His voice has stopped. She listens for it, wants it back, then it is there again and she follows it.

"Now, Leslie, imagine you are sitting in the warm comfortable room and you're watching a TV screen. Turn the selector till it stops on March 18, 1976. You are working in your first Broadway show and you are in Boston for the tryout. You are in the small hotel room you are sharing with your friend Terri Matthews. It is the night before the opening in Boston. Can you see yourself?"

The room is shabby. Terri has moved the furniture around so that the beds are not side by side. The faint odor of mildew mixes with hairspray, and L'Air du Temps, Terri's perfume, permeates the air. Rain slams on the window, drips like black tears, leaks through the rotted frame.

She stares at the picture. "It's so dark." She can't find herself and is afraid. "Where?" she said. "Where? Where am I?"

MORTON HORNBERG PRODUCTIONS
234 West Forty-fourth Street
New York, New York 10036

December 9, 1994

Mr. Conrad Berry
Executive Director
Show Biz Shares
163 West 46th Street
New York, New York 10036

Dear Connie:

Re: *Combinations, In Concert*

Enclosed please find our fully executed contract for the above-captioned event.

Thank you for your cooperation.

Best Regards,

Edward Venderose

Edward Venderose
General Manager

EV/ns
Enclosure
By Hand
CC: Carlos Prince and Leslie Wetzon

Chapter Forty-Three

"CARLOS, DON'T LAUGH. CONTRACTS MEAN IT'S OFFICIAL. I'M STARTING TO GET *nervous. I'm not a twenty-three-year-old being twinkle toes on Broadway. I'll be forty in January. I haven't been on a stage in almost ten years."*

"Darling, not to worry. Write this down." He rattled off a phone number.

"Whose is it? Wait. I know this number. It's Chita's." Chita Rivera was every gypsy's role model. She was still dancing at sixty, despite the terrible accident after which doctors said she'd never dance again.

"So," Carlos drawled. "Need I say more?"

"BE PATIENT, LESLIE. THERE'S NOTHING TO BE AFRAID OF. IT'S NIGHT. THAT'S why it's dark. Let your eyes get used to the darkness."

She heard herself breathing slowly, deeply. "There are two beds," she said. "Terri's moved hers so that it's across the room. Leslie's is under the window and it's raining in on her . . . me. It's raining in on me. I'm in bed. It's cold. The room has no heat. It's always cold in Boston."

"Yes, it is. It's the night before the opening. Have you been out with the other actors?"

"We all went out for some beers and Chinese. I can smell the ribs. They were so good."

"Was Terri with you?"

"I think so . . . no . . . wait . . . she was supposed to come but she never showed. I was really tired and didn't hang out after dinner. I went back to the room."

"Is Terri in the room when you get back?"

"No. She's not here."

"Isn't that odd?"

"No. Not really. She's been sort of disappearing since we got here. She told me she has friends here."

"You were sleeping, Leslie. Did something wake you?"

"The rain." She sighed. "It's coming in on me and I'm cold . . . but I don't think that's what wakes me."

"What is it, Leslie? What wakes you?"

"Cigarettes. I smell the smoke. Maybe that wakes me."

"Are you alone in the room?"

"No."

"What happens next? Who is there with you? Is it Terri?"

"I'm cold. I'm only in a T-shirt."

"Do you hear anything?"

"Yes. It's Terri. She's sick. Groaning."

"What do you do?"

"I start to say something . . . but . . ."

"What, Leslie? Something stops you from speaking to Terri. Slow it down. Freeze the frame."

"She's not alone."

"Who is she with?"

"I don't know. I don't want to know. Oh, God, it's happening again."

"What is happening again?"

"What if she picked someone up—like the Boston Strangler. What if . . . no."

"Terri's done this before?"

"No."

"What do you do?"

"Nothing."

"Why?"

"I think I know who she's with."

"Who is it, Leslie?"

"There's that funny light filtering through the rain from the street-lamp outside. It misses me and hits the floor. Black loafers with tassels. I see them."

"Are they Terri's shoes?"

"No. It's raining hard. It's coming in on me."

"Who is with Terri, Leslie?"

"I don't want to hear them doing it. Why do I have to be part of it? It's so personal. I'm not like that. It's not fair of her to bring him here to our room."

"You know who it is, don't you, Leslie?"

"He has a wife and two little kids. . . ."

"Do you hear anything they say?"

"No. I don't want to hear."

"What do you do, Leslie?"

"I lie down and pull the blanket over my head and hold my hands over my ears the way I used to. I finally fall asleep."

"What happens in the morning?"

"The sun is out. It's so bright it wakes me up."

"Is there anyone in the room?"

"No. It was all a dream. Terri is coming out of the shower wrapped in a towel. She says, 'Oh, there you are, lazybones.' She's so cheerful."

"Do you say anything about the night before?"

"I say, 'Terri, did you have someone up here last night?' "

"She is looking at me as if I'm crazy. I'm not sure it wasn't all a dream. She says, 'You'd better get going. We have a nine-thirty call.' "

"What do you do?"

"I get up. I'm starving. I smell buttered toast and coffee. I tell her to wait for me and I take a quick shower. Terri is pulling on black tights, then an iridescent leotard with a run in it. She picks up something from the floor and slips it on her wrist. Something I haven't seen before . . . or maybe . . ."

"Describe it, Leslie."

"I . . . I'm trying. . . . I can't see it clearly."

"Then go on. What do you do after that?"

"I get in the shower."

"Leslie, is there anything else that happened in the room that night that you want to tell me about?"

"No."

"All right, Leslie. You did a very good job. We're going to end now. In a few minutes I'm going to ask you to awaken. I'm going to say 'One, two, three, four,' and on 'four' you will awake completely refreshed. You will feel as if you have had a very relaxing sleep, and the memory of what happened in that hotel room will be clear. Now, turn the TV off, close your eyes, and let your body float. You are very relaxed, very comfortable."

She turned the picture off, lay back, and floated.

"Now in a minute I'm going to count 'One, two, three, four,' and on 'four' I'm going to ask you to awaken. You will feel completely refreshed. One . . . two . . . three . . . awaken, Leslie."

She opened her eyes, blinking. She felt disoriented, unable to move.

"Sit quietly, Leslie," Tom McLean said. "Relax. Don't force it. It takes a minute or two."

Her hands began to move of their own accord. She stretched. "Good grief," she said.

"How do you feel?"

She smiled at him. "As if I just woke up from the best sleep I've had in years."

"Is there anything you want to ask me?"

"Give me a minute or so." She stretched again. "I love this chair."

He was smiling. "How long have you been sitting in it?"

"A minute or two . . . I don't know."

"It's been forty minutes, Leslie."

She was stunned. "I don't believe it."

"Tell me how you feel, what you remember about sitting in the room watching the moment play back. You can join us now if you like, Silvestri."

Silvestri's hand rested on the top of her head, then he took the other leather chair.

McLean said, "Tell us, Leslie. It will all come back to you."

She closed her eyes, saw it all, opened them. "It was there for me to see so clearly," she said. "How could I have missed it?"

MEMORANDUM

To: Carlos, Leslie, Medora, Foxy, JoJo, company
From: Edward Venderose, General Manager
Date: December 8, 1994
Re: *Combinations, in Concert*

Please give close attention to the Thursday (22nd) rehearsal
call. I have included only a four-hour call for wardrobe,
based on the idea of a dress rehearsal from 10 to 1. If
wardrobe is needed beyond that time, you may want to
extend this to a full eight-hour call BUT at additional cost.

Chapter Forty-Four

"Hello, Nancy? This is Leslie. This four-hour wardrobe call? Do we really need that much time? Aren't we all going to be in DKNY jumpsuits?"

"Peg Button'll be there with a trunk of accessories. She says she needs the time. Incidentally, she's got a black sequined vest for you."

"Sequins? My God, they'll be popping off and underfoot during my whole number. Ask her if she can find an alternative. Like bugle beads."

"So what do you think, Silvestri?" Tom McLean said. "I feel certain we got it."

"Yeah," Silvestri concurred. He was standing to one side talking to McLean in a low voice. Wetzon could barely hear him. "How do you feel, Les?" He offered his hand and pulled her out of the chair.

She emerged almost reluctantly. "I'm perfectly fine." She smiled at Tom McLean, held on to Silvestri's hand. "Guaranteed, you've never seen me so relaxed. This man is a witch doctor. He's cast a spell over me."

"Do you have any questions about any of this?" McLean asked.

"A big one. Could it be a false memory?" Wetzon said. "Why didn't I remember before? Was it because of Medora and that I thought it wasn't right, what was happening, so I blocked it?"

"That's possible," McLean said. "What did you mean when you said it was happening to you again?"

"I said that?"

"Yes."

"I don't know."

"Leslie, sometimes a memory will reappear after hypnosis—hours, days, weeks, even."

"You mean like what Terri picked up from the floor?"

"That, and other things."

Silvestri said, "I'll have another talk with Medora Battle, then go over it with someone at the D.A.'s office on Monday."

THEY WALKED UPTOWN BECAUSE SHE WANTED TO. IT WAS COLD. WINTER AIR. But she was made of feathers, light and free. Only her hand in his kept her on the ground.

"Wouldn't it be wonderful," she said, "if I could keep this feeling for the show?"

He was amused. "I could ask Tom to come over and give you a fix before you went on."

She stopped. "Silvestri, I have an idea. I'll invite him. What do you think? Would it be out of line?"

"No."

"I'll ask him what night, Thursday or Friday? I ordered four tickets for each night. Which reminds me, which night do you want to come?"

"Both."

"Both? Really?"

"Don't you want me there? Or did you promise a seat to some other guy?"

"I do want you there, and there is no other guy, and you know it. You've never seen me onstage. If I'm going to make a fool of myself, you might as well witness it."

He laughed. "You'll be fine. You always are."

They were walking again now, faster.

"I was just twenty-two," she said. "I was having so many new experiences it was as if I was being bombarded with feelings I couldn't handle. So I just closed down. I don't know what upsets me more, that

Terri was having an affair with Rog or that I didn't know it. I liked Terri. But there were two little kids involved."

"What if Terri was making it with both Battle and Koenig?"

"That would have shocked Leslie Wetzon, girl dancer, working on her first Broadway show, but eighteen years later, why not?"

"Of course, it could have happened, and Koenig will have to be the one to tell us. But my gut tells me he's not lying."

"God, Silvestri, did I say I *was* naive? What if Terri was going off with Rog, and Medora found out and shot her?"

"And what about Rog? Did she kill him, too?"

"She could have. Don't you want to try to get his body exhumed now?"

"I want to have one more easy conversation with Medora Battle, get what I can. I don't want her to lawyer up. I can get the record of where he's buried from downtown."

"She's got *Tacoma Triptych* opening in four weeks. And *Combinations.* If she gets an inkling of what you're doing, she'll try to stop you."

"I don't stop easily."

Broadway was a forest of evergreens of varying sizes and shapes. Lincoln Center, always ablaze in lights, added its own tree sparkling on the plaza, which Beverly Sills herself had lit on Monday.

"I said it was happening again, didn't I?" Wetzon's eyes teared.

"You did."

"Because it had happened before." She sighed. "I was away from home for the first time, a very young seventeen. My college roommate used to sneak guys up to the room. I'd pull the covers over my head and pretend I couldn't hear."

"Which is why you blocked the memory of Terri and Rog Battle." Silvestri sniffed the air. "Smells like snow."

"Yup," she said.

"Do you want to get a tree?" he asked casually.

She closed one eye, cocked her head and looked at him. "We? Us? Get a tree . . . together?"

This time he was the one who said "Yup."

"That's pretty daring of you, Silvestri. Choosing a tree together? Hmmmmm. Are you sure you want to take that responsibility? Why, it's almost like getting engaged."

He chucked her under the chin. "Sometimes a tree is just a tree," he said.

They settled on a fat fir about Wetzon's height with the help of a young woman with a twangy Australian accent who had set up her business in front of the supermarket, probably giving the manager a cut on each tree sold. Silvestri dickered her down to forty dollars, swung the fir over his shoulder, and carried it home.

"You'll find the stand in a plastic bag under the bed. Just clear away the dust balls," Wetzon told him.

The phone rang as she was measuring coffee into the paper filter. "Hello?" She wedged the receiver between shoulder and ear.

She recognized immediately the sounds that greeted her. Back-stage noise. Splendid to the ear of a stage performer. Distinct from all other background sounds. "Hi, Leslie, it's Peter. Can you hear me? There's so much noise here."

"You're calling from the theatre. What do you expect?" She glanced at her watch. It was half-hour. The last thirty minutes before curtain.

"I have only a minute. I just tried to get that Silvestri, but if he calls now, I'm not going to be able to talk to him. Did you have your session with McLean?"

"Yes." She was being cautious. She heard Silvestri rumble past with the stand for the tree.

"Did you remember anything?"

"Odds and ends. Nothing definitive, I'm afraid." The water began to boil and she poured it into a measuring cup and from there into the filter.

"Well, look. I'll talk fast. In my session I saw an envelope addressed to Terri. It was part of a pile of what looked like letters. The handwriting meant something to me, but I couldn't remember why. Well, I remembered—and it's weird."

"How weird?" As he explained, she listened without comment. When he was finished, she agreed it was weird and told him she'd try to reach Silvestri for him, then hung up.

In the living room Silvestri's beeper went off while he was working on the tree. "Fuck," she heard him say.

When she came into the room, he was on his knees fitting the tree into the stand while Izz, a wise dog, sat several feet away, watching.

"I've got to call in," he said.

"I know what it's about. Wanna hear?"

"Be my guest. What do you think? Is it straight?"

"It's tilting a little to the left. Peter Koenig just called. He couldn't reach you. He said he recognized the handwriting on that envelope in Terri's apartment. He got an invitation to a Christmas Day open house in the same handwriting.

"Who sent him the invite?" He stood up and brushed off his hands. The tree was standing straight.

"Medora Battle."

MEMORANDUM

To: Carlos Prince and Leslie Wetzon
From: Edward Venderose, General Manager
Date: December 10, 1994
Re: *Combinations, in Concert*

Not included in the budget are the direct expenses of Show
Biz Shares reception following the Friday evening
performance. Obviously, catering, coat check, etc., is being
arranged by Show Biz Shares. As the Nederlanders are
waiving the lobby rental, our expenses are minimal. They
may include additional time for security, as well as porter
and matron, depending on the length of the reception. Right
now we're budgeted up to eleven o'clock.

Chapter Forty-Five

"CARLOS, WOULDN'T IT BE SMART TO ALERT THE COMPANY AND GUESTS THAT WE have to be out by eleven? Otherwise, we might have stragglers. You or Mort could do it on Friday before we start rehearsals."

"Good thinking, Birdie, but we'll let old pompous Ed do it. I'm sure he'll have other announcements to make. He can tack this one on."

WETZON SET THE SMALL SPRUCE ON MAX'S DESK. IT WAS ONLY ABOUT THREE feet high and came with a ready-made stand. Their reception area was too small for a bigger tree.

Only Darlene's coat was in the closet. Smith's mink wasn't there. "Smith's not in yet?" she called to Darlene, who came out of her cubbyhole.

"She said she had some personal business and would call in." Darlene was wearing red-framed glasses that kept sliding down her tiny nose. When she poked them up, her eyes behind the lenses managed to look startled, as if each time the glasses slid up her nose it was a surprise.

"Okay," Wetzon said, filling her mug. "Let's go over what you have."

They carried their coffee into the room Wetzon shared with Smith. Darlene had a manila folder under her arm. She pulled over Smith's chair, sat, and opened the folder.

Wetzon smiled. Smith would have a fit if she saw how comfortable Darlene was getting. And in Smith's chair.

With the folder open in her lap, Darlene took a theatrical pause. "I —we have a firm start date in Boston. December thirtieth. Adam Gans. He's coming from A. G. Edwards and he does almost six hundred thou."

Wetzon was pleased. With their six percent fee, $36,000, even divided in half, would throw Smith and Wetzon $18,000. "Very, very nice. And very nice for you, Darlene."

"We have a tentative start date of January sixth for two brokers from Prudential. They're partners." There was that pregnant pause again. "Together they do one mil two."

"Well, Darlene, I'm overwhelmed. Smith told me you were phenomenal and she was right. Wait till she hears."

"I tried to tell Smith when she called in, but she said she had an appointment and would talk to me later."

"What else are you working on?"

"I have six more interviewing in Boston."

"Great. Loeb Dawkins needs about two and a half to three mil in production to get the office on its feet, so we're more than halfway there."

"We're there. They're going forward because two of their own brokers who do in the high six are transferring from the Wellesley office. One will be producing manager. There's room for seven more after the other three start, so I'm proceeding. The office opens officially on January third."

"This is wonderful. It means we start the year with a bang."

The phone rang and Darlene answered it from Smith's desk. "Smith and Wetzon, good morning. Darlene Ford speaking." Her voice was crisp and professional, with just the right whisper of warmth. She was making sure clients and candidates knew who she was. "Ms. Smith's out of the office, but we expect to hear from her. May I take a message?" Darlene scribbled a name and number on a pink message pad that Wetzon handed her.

She'd discover soon enough that Smith never returned a call, but

Wetzon wasn't about to tell her. And Smith would discover that Darlene was not a pliant piece of clay that Smith could mold. It appeared that Darlene had a sizable ego of her own. What fun it would be to watch the two of them dance around each other.

Max stuck his head in the door. He was wearing a tweed topcoat and—God help us, Wetzon thought—a matching deerstalker hat.

"Good morning, Wetzon. Good morning, dear," he said to Darlene, then he disappeared, although he could be heard puttering about, probably dealing with the tree Wetzon had planted on his desk. Darlene rolled her eyes at Wetzon.

"You'll get used to him. He means well. And he can be quite effective."

"I want to thank you," Darlene said.

"For what?"

"For not standing over me. I really appreciate that. Tom Keegen and Harold listened in to my phone calls. They never let me breathe."

Max interrupted them. "There's a call for you, Wetzon. Doug Culver."

Dougie Culver. Now what did he want? Wetzon waved good-bye to Max and Darlene and motioned for the door to be closed behind them, then picked up the phone. "Dougie, what a nice surprise. I thought you guys had written off headhunters, or are you just calling to wish us a Merry Christmas?" Had Rosenkind Luwisher learned so fast that their managers didn't know how to recruit a fly with honey?

"Merry Christmas, Wetzon. We have written y'all off, so to speak. Actually, we are in the process of hiring someone to work internally, and you—"

"And you're calling to ask me to help you find someone so you can put me out of business, Dougie? Shocking."

"No, Wetzon, not at all. I'm askin' you to join us here at Rosenkind Luwisher as our internal recruiter."

Wetzon almost dropped the phone. "What?"

"Of course we realize we're askin' you to leave a successful business, so we will put together a very attractive financial package for you," Dougie continued, then realized he was not getting a response. "Hello? Wetzon?"

She tried to speak but couldn't find her voice. Finally, she said, "Dougie, I'm extremely flattered, but—"

"Don't give us an answer yet. Think about it and get back to us. Real soon, y'hear? I'll put all the figures together for you."

The phone was cradled but she didn't remember doing it. Break up Smith and Wetzon? Isn't that what she herself had been considering half-seriously? The firm could go on, but it would have to be renamed. Well, Smith had Darlene now. But Smith wanted to go into show business. And then there was the notion of Leslie Wetzon as a corporate animal. Uh-uh. If Wetzon joined Rosenkind Luwisher, she would lose her independence. She would exist on their whim . . . they could even fire her.

She picked up the phone and punched in Smith's home number, letting the phone ring twenty times before recradling it. Where was Smith anyway? Maybe she'd gone shopping. That's where Wetzon should be. She still had Carlos, Arthur, and Laura Lee to shop for. Not to mention Smith and Mark. And Silvestri. Hell, if Smith could take a personal day, so could Wetzon. She'd do it this afternoon.

The door opened. "Wetzon?"

"Max?"

"Call for you. Norman Mizrachi."

What a strange day this was. Norman Mizrachi was an ultra-Orthodox Jewish broker. He wore a yarmulke, and the fringe of his prayer shawl hung from under his suit. He'd been at Bruns Securities for at least two decades. This was a first; he'd never called her before. She was surprised he even knew her number. "Hi, Norman," she said into the phone.

"Wetzon." His labored breathing sounded more like Zero Mostel than Zero Mostel had. "You know I have never understood why any broker would have need of a headhunter."

"So you've told me often enough."

"I still don't see it, but right now I don't have the time to do this myself. I am marrying off my daughter next week—"

"Congratulations." *That, you bonehead, is exactly why brokers need headhunters.* Time was the most valuable commodity on the Street.

"I could use a big check. You know what's going on out there."

"You'd get a big check, Norman, but why all of a sudden do you want to go? It has to be more than a big check. You've been at Bruns over twenty years."

"Twenty-two years, Wetzon, but the firm has changed."

"We know that. The Street has changed."

"Let me tell you, Wetzon, Marty Donnelly, when he ran this company, sent all his million-dollar producers a bottle of the best scotch for the holidays. You know what Logan Wickersham sent us? Right to the house, too."

"Noooo."

"An enormous ham."

"Unbelievable."

"Yes. A ham. And let me tell you, I'm not the only Jewish broker around here doing over a mil."

"Okay, Norman. Let me ask you a few quick questions about your business and the environment that would make you most comfortable, then I'll go away and do some homework and get back to you."

She was still jotting notes on their conversation after she hung up the phone. It was amazing. Management all over the Street continued to resent paying headhunters, yet they had no idea how to keep their brokers happy. It looked as if she would be in business for a while. If she wanted to be.

She tried Smith again. No answer. Stretching, she looked out the back windows at their wintery garden. Mr. Diamontidou, their super, had strung every tree and bush with tiny lights. Over the top? Maybe. But it was lovely.

All this business with Terri's awful death had unsettled her. Had she been sleepwalking through her life? Was she still sleepwalking?

Carlos. He always knew how to jolly her out of any upset. She punched out his number but got his machine. She didn't leave a message.

She walked over to Saks and became the demon shopper. A taupe chenille scarf for Laura Lee, a black chenille sweater with silver threads for Smith. Cashmere sweaters for Mark and Silvestri. Carlos wanted fuzzy earmuffs; he got white mink, for the man who has everything. Gloves for Arthur. That took only half an hour. It took another hour to get a salesclerk to take her charge.

Over to Barnes & Noble. She asked a young clerk for the Joseph Papp biography.

"Who is Joseph Papp?" he said.

Now that was depressing. *"Sic transit gloria mundi,"* she muttered. The clerk gaped at her as if she were a nutcase. "A little Latin expression," she explained. That only seemed to prove that his judgment of her was right, so she left him and managed to find the book herself amid a lot of other theatre books. The Winchell biography was perfect for Arthur, and she thought Silvestri might like Stephen Hunter's *Dirty White Boys,* even though it was a novel. They'd both loved his last one, *Point of Impact.*

Loaded with packages, she went back to Saks and the bank of phones near the Fiftieth Street entrance. It was four o'clock. She called the office.

"Max? I'm not coming back. Are there any problems? Has Smith called in?"

"Aaah . . . no . . . aaah . . ."

"What is it?"

"Mark called. He seemed a little upset. He wanted to talk to you."

"Give me his number."

"He said he'd call back."

She thought for a moment. How depressed was Smith about Hartmann? Would she do anything stupid . . . like . . . "Max, I'm going up to Smith's. If Mark calls back, tell him to try me there."

With four shopping bags, she struggled out of the store, intending to catch a cab going up Madison, but a cab pulled up right in front of her and two women got out.

"That's my cab," a man yelled from across the street near St. Patrick's. He was waving his arms. "That's mine!" He was overweight and his color was florid.

Wetzon got into the cab and slammed the door. "Seventy-seventh and Third," she told the driver as the red-faced man began pounding on the window, snarling at her. She locked the door but rolled the window down an inch. "I'm sorry," she said, "I have an emergency."

"Bitch!" he screamed, forcing his fingers through the small window space.

"Get away from my cab or I call the cops!" the Russian driver yelled. He pulled away slowly with the man still clutching the window. "You break my window and I kill you!" he shouted. The cab jerked forward suddenly, leaving the man behind, glowering in the middle of the street.

Was it a full moon? Wetzon wondered. Or was it some energy she was giving off?

She had a set of Smith's keys on her key chain, so she was able to let herself into the apartment. She stood in the shadows and called, "Smith?"

The apartment was empty. It was more than empty. It felt hollow. She turned on the light and walked around. The rooms had an abandoned feel to them, as if nobody lived there, in spite of Smith's furniture.

In the living room under the coffee table Wetzon found a single Tarot card. The Tower. Lightning had hit the Tower and people were falling out of it. The card in her hand trembled, or maybe her hand did. That was when the phone began to ring.

She picked it up. "Mark?"

"Yes. Is she there?" He sounded frightened.

"No. What's wrong?"

"Wetzon, it's him. You got to stop him."

"Who, Mark? Wait a minute. Slow down."

"Hartmann. She's running away with him."

"Mark, I don't see how. Hartmann is in protective custody. He's a Federal witness."

"Wetzon, you've got to stop Mom. She called me and said I was a man now and I'd be all right. Wetzon—she said she was calling to say good-bye."

MEMORANDUM

To: Carlos Prince and Leslie Wetzon
From: Nancy Stein, Assistant to Mort Hornberg
Date: December 11, 1994
Re: *Combinations, in Concert*

Ed asked me to let you know that we are using the Marley floor and that it will be delivered on Wednesday at 11 A.M. Showtech has given us permission to cut it to fit the Richard Rodgers stage, but it's Ed's impression that they are not charging us anything.

Chapter Forty-Six

"BIRDIE, I CAN'T BELIEVE THAT MORT KEEPS ON PROMOTING FREE STUFF. Doesn't anybody know about the TV special? Should I maybe pick up the phone and leak it to the Post?"

"When everyone who contributed finds out Mort's going to make a ton of money on this, they'll tar and feather him and ride him out of town on a rail. Or something like that."

"Hmmmm, now there's an interesting image. I guess we shouldn't interfere with fate. What do you think?"

WETZON WENT THROUGH THE APARTMENT AGAIN, WITH MORE CARE THIS TIME. Smith's mink was not in her hall closet. The only thing left in her jewelry box was the gold back of an earring, lying forlorn on the green suede. There must be something here that would tell Wetzon where Smith had gone, if it wasn't already too late. Hartmann would be heading for Brazil or some other country without an extradition policy with the United States.

Smith's bed was made—that in itself should have alerted Wetzon that something was wrong. Smith was a lousy housekeeper.

She sat down on the bed and called Silvestri. He was out of his office. She left her name and Smith's number.

Where the hell would Smith be meeting the scumbag? What to do? She dialed again.

"Peiser." Marissa's voice was muffled by munching sounds. Her lunch?

"Marissa?"

"Yes." Caution in her voice. The munching stopped.

"This is Leslie Wetzon. I have reason to believe that Richard Hartmann is going to leave the country. He may already have left."

A swallow, then, "How do you know?"

"I think my partner is going with him. Jesus, what a fool."

Marissa didn't ask who was the fool, Hartmann or Smith. She asked, "What do you want me to do? The Feds are responsible for him now."

"Please, please, can you find out where he's supposed to be this afternoon? I'm begging you."

"Okay. I'm going to put you on hold, or do you want me to call you back?"

"No, please, I'd rather hold, if you don't mind." If she waited for Marissa to call her back, she'd go crazy. No, it was better to hold.

The silent apartment depressed her, closed in on her. Would Smith really be stupid enough . . . ? Hell and damnation, she thought, I can't keep trying to save Smith from herself.

She slipped out of her shoes and lay on the bed, phone resting on the pillow near her ear. Damn Smith. To take a perfectly good life and throw it away.

Then a chilling thought struck her. If Smith were gone, what would happen to Smith and Wetzon? Wetzon would be free to take the job with Rosenkind Luwisher, then, wouldn't she?

Where was Peiser, dammit? Dead sound told her they were still connected. The brokerage firms entertained you with music and news while you were on hold. She sat up, felt around for her shoes. Found one, stuck her foot in it. Where was the other? Under the bed? She knelt. There it was on its side. She reached under. No dust balls, but a crumpled piece of paper. She sat down on the bed again and flattened it out.

"Hello, Leslie?"

"Yes. What did you find out?" She was staring at Smith's writing.

"Hartmann had an absessed tooth. They took him to his dentist."

"Do they know he's going to make a break for it?"

"They do now."

"Damn. His dentist, is he at 200 Park?" Smith had written *GC*, and under it, *escal 5:00.* 200 Park was the MetLife Building, connected by escalator to Grand Central Station. It was already four-forty.

"How did you know?"

"Tell you later. Right now I've got to try to stop them."

"Leslie, stay out of this. Let the Feebs handle it."

"I'm not going to let Smith throw her life away." She hung up before Marissa could say anything more, left her packages, locked the door, and ran for the elevator.

At rush hour the fastest way to Grand Central Station was the subway on Lexington Avenue. She was scarcely aware of the cold and that her coat was open. She'd left her gloves in Smith's apartment.

Token from change purse, down the steps, lickety-split, out of my way, *out of my way,* token in slot and through the turnstile just as a No. 6 rumbled into the station. Wetzon stepped on. No seats, but she was too nervous to sit anyway. At the Hunter College stop, at Sixty-eighth Street, a score or more of young people got on, packing the train.

Move it, move it, she thought.

Fifty-ninth Street and Bloomingdale's, half the riders got off, more people got on. It was taking too long, dammit, close those doors. The doors close. The doors open. Close. Open. *Close the goddam doors.* When they finally rolled into Grand Central, Wetzon dodged and danced through the crowd, up one steep flight of stairs, up more stairs, running to the main room of the station, where the escalators rode to and from 200 Park Avenue, once the Pan Am Building, now the Met-Life Building.

The main floor of the station was swirling with people, holiday shoppers, kids home from school, waiting for trains to take them back to Westchester, N.Y., or Fairfield County, Conn., two of the richest areas in the country. Christmas decorations hung from every available windowpane and hook. A cluster of schoolchildren were singing carols to an organ accompaniment.

Hundreds of feet overhead, the last gasp of afternoon light seeped through the multitude of small windows around the landmark's domed ceiling. Where was Smith? Why don't I just give it up, she thought. I can't tell her who is bad or good anymore. She wouldn't know a good person if he wore wings.

Wetzon's eyes were on the escalator. She made her way to the foot of the moving stairs.

Christmas music almost obliterated the *pop, pop, pop,* and then the shrieks. People plunged from the escalator in all directions, leaping, screaming, bumping into one another, jumping, running, falling.

But one person didn't move. He was sprawled backward on the moving staircase as if he were resting, his eyes wide, coming closer and closer. His face was twisted in a grotesque smile. Why was he smiling? He'd played mean and lost. Some of his mob clients obviously didn't cozy up to the fact that he had turned responsible citizen and was naming names.

Hartmann's mouth opened as if to greet her, but produced instead a geyser of blood. "Good-bye, Richard Hartmann," Wetzon murmured.

Someone screamed.

"Out of the way. Move back!" someone shouted.

More screaming. "Look at him! Look at him!" The moving staircase shuddered and came to a halt.

"Get back, miss." He was FBI. The plain suit, the short neat hair.

The tumult was deafening. Everyone was screaming now. Above it all, a voice howled, "Oh, God, did you see that? Did you see—"

A man on a bullhorn told people to stay calm, to move back. He said that EMS workers in blue jackets were trying to get through the crowd.

Where was Smith? Wetzon raised her voice and added to the cacophony. "Smith!" But she couldn't even hear herself. She began to push away from the crowd. Hartmann had been alone on the escalator. Where was Smith?

Her knees began to wobble. She braced her hand on the wall near

Zaro's. It was amazing. People was standing around buying cakes and breads to take home as if nothing had happened.

She began walking, looking for Smith in the stalls of the Christmas bazaar, the bookstores, not knowing, or caring, where she was going. She felt a little crazy, panicked. It was as if she'd gotten caught up in a maze and couldn't get out. *Where was Smith? Had they killed her too?*

The sign said OYSTER BAR; the arrow pointed downward. She took the incline into the tunnel, and there it was, clean and bright, the Oyster Bar, an oasis for wonderful clam chowder in winter and soft-shell crab sandwiches in summer.

She pulled open the door. A few people were at the counters, with more in the dining room.

Turning toward the bar, she saw several men, but her eyes skimmed over them to the lone woman in the black mink coat. At the woman's feet were two Vuitton suitcases and a Bergdorf shopping bag. A platter of empty bluepoints was on the bar in front of her, as was a half-filled martini glass.

"Smith?" Wetzon said.

Smith turned. A rueful smile played over her face. "I couldn't do it," she said.

MEMORANDUM

To: The *Combinations in Concert* Company
From: Mort Hornberg
Date: December 15, 1994

Well, gang, here we go. In a few days we'll have an audience
and it'll be wonderful. Give it your all. Of course, I know
you will. Just remember, it's a party, so have a good time.

Oh, and by the way, we've agreed to be part of a
documentary on the show, and the Thursday night
performance will be filmed for Lifetime. You'll all be getting
two weeks' AFTRA minimum for this, and quite a showcase
of your talents.

Chapter Forty-Seven

"Lifetime, Carlos! Ted Turner lost. And do you notice how he says it's a documentary? Some documentary when they're going to film the whole performance!"

"Notice something else, Birdie?"

"You mean his condescending 'quite a showcase of your talents,' like you ought to be so grateful to the extraordinary Mort Hornberg?"

"Nooo. Doesn't he seem to have forgotten that he has two partners on this production? He's not speaking for me, thee, and he. He's just speaking for he."

"Get the cast point of view," Wetzon heard someone say.

The man carrying the camera was young, bearded, hair in a ponytail. Another man spoke into a microphone in vaguely intimate, syrupy tones: *"Combinations* was first staged in 1976." He pointed his microphone at Wetzon. "Did you have any inkling you were working in a musical that would change the direction of the Broadway musical theatre?"

Wetzon, in gray leggings, a gray plaid flannel shirt over her black leotard, was stretching one leg against the sidewall near the door to the rehearsal room.

"It was my first Broadway show," she said, glad she had her good side to the handheld camera. "I thought it was wonderful. The book was by Rog and Medora Battle. They'd had three previous hits." She switched legs. "But then—"

The interviewers were no longer there. They'd moved on to point the camera at Bonnie McHugh. Well, why not?

Rehearsals had begun in the morning with Mort and Carlos talking to the company. Then Ed Venderose made all of his unnecessarily long, pompous announcements. And finally, the TV crew had arrived and begun wandering through rehearsals asking questions.

It had been an emotional experience, seeing everyone again. Some she hadn't seen in seventeen years. Margie Nicholson, one of the singer-dancers, had put on quite a bit of weight. Hidden in the layers of fat was a lithe young woman with a belting voice. The voice was still there.

Two pianos were set at either end of the studio, both working at once. JoJo was putting Bob Rosen, whose curly hair was now totally white, through his ballad.

"It was a musical without a conventional plot," Mort said to the camera. He'd parked his glasses on his scant-haired dome. "Only some-one with the genius of Davey Lewin would have had the guts to do it at that time. I watched, absorbed"—smiling sheepishly—"and learned." The camera left Mort and panned the room, searching for its next victim.

Carlos waved Wetzon over to the other piano, where Vicki Howard, who was doing Terri's old part, and Bonnie McHugh stood. A young rehearsal pianist was dipping into "Monogamy Is Not for Me." Foxy sat on the bench beside him beating time. Like a backseat driver, Wetzon thought. Nearby, Medora was talking to Mort, who nodded, nodded, then put his arm around her.

Cardboard coffee cups were all over the floor. The plastic chairs that had neatly lined the long wall when the company arrived were now every which way. Hands held cups but not for long: everyone was moving.

The camera and microphone drifted over to where Medora stood with Mort. "Did you and your husband start out to write something unconventional?"

Medora looked startled by the interruption, but quickly collected herself. "Not at all. We wanted to write about a disintegrating marriage. *Combinations* is really about finding who you are. Davey saw the play as a metaphor for relationships. Before we knew it, we were writing little scenes. That's when Davey brought Foxy in and she began setting the little scenes to music, and well, there you are." Medora flung out her hand and the hammered-gold cuff caught the light.

"Musical theatre," Mort said, "is all about collaboration. We all work together to produce something that none of us could do separately."

"It's talent mixed with chemistry," Carlos said to the camera. "Let's get going here, ladies."

The pianist began to play. The women took their places—old patterns never forgotten—Leslie in the center. Bonnie, Leslie, and Vicki. Three white girls imitating the Supremes.

"Goddam, that was fun," Bonnie said when they came to a slightly ragged finish. She was heavy on the eye makeup, and her rehearsal clothes were too new and too color-coordinated. She took off her shirt and tied it around her waist. Her pink leotard was cut to her navel.

Across the room parallel with the windows were eight standing microphones, which no one was using. The rehearsal room was otherwise a clutter of shopping bags, music stands, sweaters, thermos bottles, shoes, and canvas bags. Laughter. A shriek of joy.

Sound surrounded them: pianos, talking, vocalizing. And through it all, the excitement and energy of putting on a show, a show that had developed a cult following, a show the critics now admired. No one remembered the mixed reviews the original had received, or how it had limped along at the box office during its final weeks and gone out brilliantly to a packed closing night.

"It's hysterical what's going on here," Bonnie was telling the camera. "Trying to put together a whole musical in four days."

Singing—not all the same numbers—filled the huge room.

"Like doing a sitcom?" the polished voice asked Bonnie.

"Much harder." She thrust her tits forward. "I think it would be easier to start a new musical from scratch."

"Are you thinking of coming back to the Theatre?"

"Oh, how I would love it, but there's so much . . . you know . . . crap around. It would have to be something terribly special, like *Combinations.*"

Wetzon, listening, wondered why Bonnie didn't mention she was coming back to Broadway. Was she saving it for a big announcement, one she didn't have to share with this event?

JoJo came over, rested his hand on Foxy's shoulder, rubbed the back of her neck. "How's it going?"

Foxy frowned. "The voices are . . ."

Wetzon looked at Bonnie and Vicki. Foxy was right. They needed work. Singing had never been her strong suit.

"It'll be fine," Carlos said. "Not to worry."

"We'll work on it," JoJo said, trying to step out of the cameraman's way until he realized they wanted him.

"What did you think when you signed on for the show?"

"When we started this show," JoJo said into the camera, "I was the rehearsal pianist. Ray Honnicker was musical director. I had no experience as a conductor. Ray got sick and couldn't continue, and all of a sudden Foxy"—he smiled at Foxy—"and Davey picked me up, gave me a stick, and set me down on the podium. I've been here ever since."

When they broke for lunch, the camera followed them. A table had been set up just inside the entrance to the studio, and the Polish Tea Room, otherwise known as the Edison Café, supplied sandwiches, fruit, and coffee.

Bright two-sheets celebrating many plays and musicals were mounted on the walls.

Wetzon took a sandwich from the platter marked TUNA and refilled her cardboard cup with coffee.

Foxy was telling the camera, "It's called rehearsal."

Mort said, "Foxy's not afraid to try something new. The marriage of words and music on this show was a breakthrough for her and for the musical theatre."

Finding an empty spot on the floor, Wetzon sat, splaying her legs out in front of her. The camera and microphone appeared in front of her as she was about to bite into her sandwich. "Don't you guys eat?" she said.

"How do you feel after this first morning?"

"In less than a week we're going to be performing in front of a real audience. It's an incredible thought."

Vicki Howard was vocalizing, sitting at one of the pianos, accompanying herself. Bonnie was working through her small routine, after she'd made sure the camera was catching her.

Wetzon finished most of her sandwich and threw the rest away. She refilled her cup and looked around. She didn't see Carlos. Or Mort.

The sun came through the long south-facing windows, patching the floor. Wetzon lay down flat in the sun and closed her eyes. The noise became muted. The sun was bright on her eyelids. She rested her forearm over her eyes. She smelled sweat, good sweat, and tuna fish and coffee. And something else . . . L'Air du Temps. She felt a tiny inner jolt.

A shadow fell across her. She opened her eyes, seeing nothing at first except sunlight. Then Medora Battle came into focus, looking down at her.

"I know this is going to disappoint you, Leslie," Medora said. "But as I told your boyfriend, Rog was very specific about what he wanted. So when he died, I had him cremated. I scattered his ashes in the Hudson."

TELEGRAM

COMBINATIONS, IN CONCERT COMPANY AND CREW

RICHARD RODGERS THEATRE

226 WEST 46TH STREET

NEW YORK, NY 10036

I AM PROUD AND THRILLED TO HAVE PLAYED A SMALL PART IN WHAT YOU ARE
RECREATING.

MY ADMIRATION AND GOOD WISHES,

EDWARD VENDEROSE

Chapter Forty-Eight

"GRACIOUS GOOD WISHES FROM EDWARD VENDEROSE," WETZON SAID, reading the telegram pinned to the backstage bulletin board. "Somehow I have this feeling he got a free ride. Didn't you think Nancy was doing an okay job?"

"I try to stay out of intramural politics, Leslie," Foxy said. "You must know that Medora insisted on Ed's joining the production."

"STAND IN FRONT OF THE MICROPHONES," MORT SAID. "AND DON'T MOVE around too much because we'll lose you." He demonstrated. It was late Tuesday afternoon and they were all exhausted. "Leslie, we'll have two low mikes—"

"Three," Carlos said, winking at her. He'd been so busy with the technical stuff that they'd exchanged about two sentences, some shrugs, and a wink, in as many days.

"—pointing down," Mort continued, "to catch your taps."

"And every mistake," Wetzon said.

She saw Foxy sitting at the nearest piano, JoJo hovering beside her. Only Medora was not around.

The cast was nervous. Half of them, like Wetzon herself, were no longer in the business. And Bonnie and Kenny Klein had been in L.A. for years doing sitcoms.

"We'll be in the theatre tomorrow and the orchestra will be in for some of the time, so you'll get a real sense of how it'll be on Thursday night," JoJo said.

"Any other notes from anybody?" Getting no response, Mort continued, "See my girl before you leave today. She's got your costumes and shoes." Then, *sotto voce*, "Let's all hope she got it right. It would be a first." Mort's tone was pleasant enough, but the meaning was not attractive. "Capezio's donated jazz shoes. Just make sure they fit before you leave today. Leslie, for your number—"

"I'm wearing my own, Mort, thank you very much." She gathered up her purse and sack of sundries, then waited her turn for her jumpsuit.

Nancy's skin was yellowish. She'd lost weight. She seemed always on the verge of tears, and who could blame her? "Is it worth it?" Wetzon asked when she collected her package.

"Is what worth it?" Nancy's eyes focused on something, someone, behind Wetzon.

Wetzon turned. JoJo. "Be careful," she said, only for Nancy's ears.

But hell, Nancy was young, perhaps trusting and naive, and ambitious. A dangerous combination. Wetzon had been there, too, eons ago.

"How do you feel it's going?" the syrupy voice asked, sneaking up on Wetzon.

"Considering the short time we have to put this together and the fact that some of us have not done theatre in a long time"—she looked directly into the camera and smiled—"we're having a wonderful time."

And she was, too.

Smith was making a remarkable recovery. At some point Wetzon would have to tell her about the offer from Rosenkind Luwisher. Or would she? She had thought it through and had come to a conclusion that satisfied her. Yesterday she'd called Dougie Culver and turned the offer down. He'd been surprised, but pleasant.

There was just no point in giving up her freedom, such as it was. Not now. And she had to face facts. She did not follow the rules and she couldn't keep her mouth shut. She would not make a good employee.

On Forty-fifth Street she headed toward Eighth Avenue to catch the Broadway bus. The sun was gone and the wind had picked up. She pulled her beret down over her ears. The subway would be faster.

Retracing her steps, she cut through Shubert Alley, all done up in Christmas greens. God, that looked like Silvestri standing in front of the Shubert with Mort and a man in a tan trenchcoat. It was. She slowed her steps.

"Here's your girlfriend," Mort said. "You might as well bring her, too." He turned and crossed the street, stopping to talk with producer Liz McCann, who had a suite of offices in the same building as Mort. He left Silvestri with the other man, whom Wetzon had never seen before.

Wetzon sidled up to Silvestri. "What's going on? Something on the cremation of Roger Battle?"

"This is Gordon Bogdon, Les. He's with the D.A.'s office."

Wetzon shook hands with Bogdon, a clean-cut man in his early thirties. His fine pale hair flew all over the place in the sharp wind.

They crossed the street and stood in front of Sardi's. Silvestri said, "Medora Battle's lawyer has called a news conference for six o'clock in Hornberg's office."

"Her lawyer? Oh, she must be going to announce that she's the author of *Tacoma Triptych*, but why would she do that in Mort's office?"

"There's more to it than that; otherwise, they wouldn't have asked me to come," Silvestri said. "And I wouldn't have asked Gordon here."

"Maybe she's going to confess. And to think if I'd taken the Broadway bus, I would have gone home and missed everything."

"Somehow," Silvestri said, ignoring her spikiness, "somehow I find that hard to believe. We have absolutely nothing on her. The blood wasn't hers. We haven't found any letters linking her to Terri. We have nothing that puts her in that apartment—or that building—ever."

"And Peter Koenig's memory of it isn't good enough?"

"Not good enough," Gordon Bogdon said, emphasizing each word. "Can't be used in a court of law."

She tucked her arm into Silvestri's. "So let's go up and hear what she has to say."

Mort's entire reception area was filled with folding chairs. The flaky receptionist, wearing her coat and hat and a sullen expression, was lining up the chairs in rows. Several people whom Wetzon did not recognize were already there, as were some she did. Pia Lindstrom from NBC. Alex Witchel from the *Times*. There were others from the *Times*, too. And *Variety*, the *News*, and the *Post*. More kept arriving. No surprise. There wasn't much hard news in the Theatre these days.

The door to Nancy's office opened and Nancy appeared. She checked the status of the chairs, swept everything off the reception desk into a drawer, and put a second chair behind the desk. "You don't have to hang around, Susan," she told the receptionist. And Susan didn't.

Wetzon took a seat in the last row and Silvestri and Bogdon sat in front of her.

At ten after six Medora appeared, flanked by her daughter, April, and a nice-looking young man. The son, Wetzon thought. They were followed by a short woman in a red suit, her roundish cheeks framed by a frizz of rich brown hair. Her face carried more years than her hair color implied. A huge brown velvet beret—her signature—clung to the back of her head. Bella Weissberg. Weissberg's law firm represented a huge chunk of the theatre community. No surprise that she represented Medora Battle.

Bella Weissberg took her place standing next to Medora behind the receptionist's desk. "Thank you for coming on such short notice," she began. "I'm Bella Weissberg. I represent Medora Battle, and I represent the Estate of Roger Battle. My client Medora Battle would like to make an announcement, and then she will read a statement. Any questions will be addressed to me in writing, please." She sat down.

Mort appeared in the doorway, accompanied by another man.

"Aha," Wetzon said.

Silvestri leaned his head back. "Who's that?"

"Richard Winkler. The producer of *Tacoma Triptych*."

April—who looked more and more distressed—and her brother sat down in the front row. Nancy remained behind Mort.

"I want to thank everyone for coming. I know we gave you little notice, but things don't always go as planned." Medora's smile was fleeting. "The time has come for me to own up to *Tacoma Triptych.*"

Dennis Cunningham stirred in his seat, exchanged a look with Pia Lindstrom.

"Yes," Medora continued. "I am the mysterious playwright."

Someone who looked like Price Berkley from the *Theatrical Index* asked, "Why did you feel you had to use a pseudonym?"

"Price Berkley," Wetzon whispered to Silvestri. "Theatre person, journalist, entrepreneur."

"It seemed right at the time." Medora blinked several times as if she had something in her eye. "For years everyone said that I couldn't write without Rog, and I was terrified that they might be right. I've had a writing block since he died. Now I'm free of it and I want to own up to my work. I'm very proud of *Tacoma Triptych.*"

"Good for you, Medora," a woman in the back said. Liz Smith.

"What made—"

Bella Weissberg got to her feet. "We don't want to take too much time with this. Everyone is very busy. So, if you have any questions, Medora will be very happy to talk to you individually and answer your questions. You can make an appointment through my secretary tomorrow." She rattled off her phone number. "Now my client would like to read a statement. She will answer no questions about this at any time. Are you ready, Medora?"

Medora nodded. Weissberg sat down. Medora took a piece of white paper from her purse, unfolded it, put on a pair of glasses. She cleared her throat.

"In the spring of 1977 I became aware through some letters I found that Rog, my husband, was having an affair with one of the performers in *Combinations,* Terri Matthews. When I confronted him with what I'd found, Rog was very upset. He told me he'd made a terrible mistake, that he didn't want to destroy our family. He went down to the Village to break it off with Terri." Her voice had been getting steadily gruffer. Now she paused, took a tissue from her pocket, and blew her nose. "I'm sorry. This is very painful for me. Rog was to call me afterward, but two, then three, hours passed and I didn't hear from him. Something had gone wrong. I got in a cab and went down there."

Although Medora now spoke in a monotone, she kept her eyes on the paper she read from. Her cheeks were wet. No sound came from her audience.

"What happened next I have been living with for over seventeen years. Now I must release it. What I found in that apartment was devastating. Rog lay on the floor covered with blood. Terri was dead. There was a gun between them. I kicked it away. I'd thought Rog was dead, but he wasn't. He was in a terrible state. Some of the blood was hers, some his. He said she had struck out at him when he'd told her it was over. She'd hit him in the nose and he'd bled heavily. Terri had then produced a gun and threatened to kill herself with it. She threatened to kill him, too. He'd struggled with her. The gun went off. The bullet made a small hole in her head. He knew she was dead. And I knew she was dead."

A murmur like a hum raced through the room, then subsided. Medora cleared her throat. "What happened next was entirely my fault. I wanted to protect my family. My children were so young. The publicity would have been horrible. And Terri was dead. I didn't see what good it would do to call the police. I knew she had no family. No one would miss her. I got Rog cleaned up and we put Terri in the trunk and, between us, we carried the trunk down to the basement. Then we cleaned up the apartment and made it look as if she'd moved out."

She folded the paper, putting it back in her purse, then she reached across the desk for her children's hands, clasping them.

"I gave Rog a Valium and took a sleeping pill myself. What I didn't know was that Rog would take the rest of the container of Valium and then drink most of a bottle of vodka."

Wetzon touched Silvestri's shoulder. "Let's go," she whispered.

Medora said, "The combination of liquor and pills was too much for Rog. By the time I woke in the morning, he was dead." A shudder went through her body.

April and her brother took Medora in their arms and held her.

Silvestri rose and, with Bogdon, followed Wetzon from the room. In the corridor he studied her face. Then he said, "You don't believe her, Les?"

"No. Do you?"

"No. Gordon?"

"We can probably charge her with concealing a crime, but it's seventeen years later. And if you're thinking that there's a chance she killed Terri Matthews herself, there's not one damn thing we can do about it."

TELEGRAM

COMBINATIONS, IN CONCERT COMPANY

RICHARD RODGERS THEATRE

226 WEST 46TH STREET

NEW YORK, NY 10036

THANKS FOR MAKING THIS WONDERFUL NIGHT POSSIBLE. GOD BLESS US ONE AND ALL.

MERDE, DARLINGS.

                      AND LOVE,

                      LESLIE AND CARLOS

Chapter Forty-Nine

"It's you and me together, Birdie. We are grand. I want you to think about this seriously. Could you leave the Barracuda? I'm serious now."

"Oh, Carlos. Leave Smith? Would I? Could I? Will I? Guess."

"Birdie, get a life. This is not Follies.*"*

The minicam and the microphone caught it all. There was singing in the corridors, vocalizing, the *mi-mi-mis* and the *la-la-las* blending. The orchestra onstage tuning up.

Everyone glittered.

Peg Button's accessories came with glitter dust. Scarves flowed like molten gold. Red silk bow ties were sprinkled with sparkles. They all had shiny black top hats and pink neon canes. For the "Monogamy" number, Wetzon, Bonnie, and Vicki had shimmering gold pleated micro miniskirts to wear over their jumpsuits. And Wetzon had a jet vest with short tails for her tap solo.

"So the nun says to the Mother Superior, 'God knows, only two things are happening around here. . . .'" Bonnie cackled from the girls' dressing room. " 'And I'm doing all the dusting. . . .'"

Wetzon straightened Carlos's bow tie, which wasn't awry at all.

"How do you feel now that the big day has finally arrived," Carlos said, mimicking the intimate—and yes, superior—tone of the Questioner. Carlos made his fist into a microphone and poked it in Wetzon's face.

"Geddowdahere, you're telling me this is opening night?" Wetzon said in a thick New York accent.

"Cut," Carlos snapped. Then to the phantom engineer, he said, "Pity. You can take the girl out of the chorus but you can't take the chorus out of the girl."

"Ta-*da!*" Wetzon did a quick tap, shuffle, step, step, and bowed.

"So when the orchestra gets louder," JoJo said, "just move closer to the mike."

Vicki stopped Wetzon in the wings to give her a careful hug, so as not to muss their makeup. "Thank you for giving me a chance to do this. I've got my life back." The ubiquitous minicam caught it all.

"It's all right, Vicki," Wetzon said, showing the camera her back.

"I've been praying for Terri's soul," Vicki said. "I lit a candle for her today."

"I think maybe we all have in some way or other."

"Half hour!" the assistant stage manager called, then circulated. "Half hour!"

"Everything is going to be open—outside mikes, everything," Mort said to the minicam person, who had dressed for the occasion in a black T-shirt and black cords.

"Sweetie pie, don't you look cute in your little jumpsuit."

Wetzon turned. A radiant Smith in a black sequined strapless tube. Over her magnificent shoulders, a black velvet opera cloak. So tall and elegant was she that Wetzon immediately felt the unattractive little girl in the wrong party dress.

Go away, Smith, she thought. I don't need you right now. She said, "What are you doing backstage? They've already called half hour."

"Protecting my investment, sugar." Smith beckoned to the minicam operator, and when he strolled over, she purred, "Be sure to get the performers just before they go on. We want to see the nerves of an opening night."

Carlos, heading toward them, caught a glimpse of Smith and did a complete about-face. Wetzon laughed. "Bye, Smith." She started after Carlos.

"Wait, babycakes. I forgot to tell you something." Smith's lips formed a pout. "You never even asked about the office."

"Darn." Wetzon stuck her tongue in her cheek and slapped her hand against her thigh. "It completely slipped my mind."

"Well, I have an interesting piece of news for you, Miss Thinks-She's-So-Funny."

"What's the news?"

"Rosenkind Luwisher. Guess who they hired as their inside recruiter?"

Wetzon looked at her partner. Did Smith know?

Impatient, Smith said, "I knew you'd never guess, not in a million years. Harold. They hired Harold."

Wetzon was shocked. "Our Harold?" That was hardly a compliment to Wetzon.

"Well, once our Harold."

"They hired Harold Alpert away from Tom Keegen?" Wetzon began to laugh.

Smith giggled. "I knew you'd love it." Her attention had stayed on Wetzon long enough, it seemed, for she said, "Oh, there's Joel. Bye now, sweetie. Break a leg."

"We say *merde* now, Smith."

"Oh," Smith said brightly, "Okay, *merde* a leg, sugarplum." She blew a kiss at Wetzon and was off.

"Would I leave her? Could I leave her?" Wetzon sang under her breath. "Yes. Will I? Ha!"

"Fifteen minutes," the assistant stage manager called.

Wetzon headed back to the dressing room for one last check on her makeup, but Mort was in there having one of his long-overdue tantrums.

"You're overpaid," Mort snarled, shaking his finger at Nancy.

"Manny pays his girl *half* what I pay you and she's on call *twenty-four* hours."

A small sound like a moan came from Nancy.

"Don't give me any of that crap about your having a life! If you work for me you don't get your own life. I'm going to close down my office and put you and that dumb girl on the phone on the unemployment line. You don't know how good you have it!"

Wetzon heard Nancy's strangled sob. She banged on the door, even though it was already ajar. "Must you, Mort?" The room looked as if it had been trashed, for all the clothes and packages and makeup cases lying about. Damp flesh-colored panty hose hung over the back of a chair. "I have never heard Nancy complain about anything—ever. And let me tell you, from where I stand she has *plenty* to complain about."

Mort was in a tux with a green velvet bow tie. Nancy looked like his twin. How could they have worn the same outfit, down to the color of their ties? It had to be somebody's joke.

"Still suffering from our Joan of Arc complex, are we, Leslie?" Mort simpered.

"Places!" the assistant stage manager yelled. "Mort, where are you?"

Mort spun around and went off toward stage left, where he would make his entrance and welcome the audience. He was to do a tribute to the dead members of the company, whose enlarged photographs already hung in full view. The photographs would then be withdrawn and the overture would begin.

Wetzon strolled to the wings, stage left, and took up her position with the others. Mort finished speaking. There was applause, and the orchestra began the overture. The actors lined up stage left and stage right, as assigned, ready to take their places in front of the microphones for the opening number.

The lights were dazzling as Wetzon stepped out behind Bonnie; the applause rose up and embraced them. Her hands were cold and her heart pounded. The microphone loomed up in front of her; listening to the applause, she felt more alive than she had been in years. And more terrified. That lovely terror she had almost forgotten.

Her eyes couldn't acclimate, for the spots isolated them onstage, but she heard and sensed a packed house. She knew where Silvestri was sitting. He was there. She didn't have to see him.

The actors tipped their hats to the audience and began to sing.

THEY CAME OFF AND ON FOR THE NUMBERS, TOOK THEIR BOWS; THE CHEERS became roars.

Everything moved inexorably toward her "Time Machine" solo, and then front and center, it was there.

They cheered her when she took her place in front of the lowered microphones, but they were cheering everything now. The brasses led. She touched her heels to the floor. The music lifted her, carried her, dropped her, twirling, and finally left her to finish the number in dead silence, but for the taps. Pirouette, slowly, slower, slower, stop.

Then, somehow, she was off. How had she gotten to the wings? She'd forgotten Silvestri, Smith, even Terri. Forgotten everything but the steps, the stage, and the music.

"You were fabulous, Birdie!" Carlos swept her into a great bear hug. "Go take your bow." He pushed her out onstage and the whole audience stood up and cheered. She bowed and retreated, finding it hard to breathe. Her heart was thumping against her ribs.

"Has there ever been a night like this?" Bob Rosen demanded, his cheeks flushed. He kept patting Wetzon on the back.

Wetzon smiled. "Goddammit, it is fun, isn't it?"

Then the finale rode in on them, and it was over. And, truly, she would never be the same. How many people get a chance to repeat a triumph eighteen years later?

"It went wonderfully, gang!" Mort shouted. "Super!"

When they took their bows, people brought bouquets of flowers to the apron of the stage. The company turned and flung their arms to

JoJo and bowed to him, and applauded him. JoJo bowed and applauded the company.

Medora and Foxy came onstage. They, too, received bouquets of roses.

Backstage they were opening champagne, passing the bottle around; it foamed over plastic glasses, their hands, the floor. Everyone was laughing, high. Applause, the sounds of clapping, the love spreading from the audience to the players, was a drug, an upper.

Wetzon edged away. She wanted to savor this, nurture it, and not share the moment.

"Of course there's a life after *Combinations*, and I'm here to tell you," Bonnie said to the minicam.

"Great work, Leslie," Foxy said. "I'm glad we'll have it on tape."

"I couldn't have done it without your gorgeous score. It was a joy to dance to." Wetzon realized, shocked, there were tears in Foxy's eyes.

Foxy leaned over and kissed her cheek. "Thank you, Leslie, dear. That means a lot to me." She moved on to Carlos.

"You were wonderful, Leslie," Medora said quietly. "Better than ever." She held out her hand and Wetzon took it. Medora's diamond earrings caught the light; her gold bracelet glimmered.

Wetzon shuddered, involuntarily. "Thank you," she said. She felt strange. Sweat ran down the inside of her jumpsuit, down the back of her neck. She headed for the dressing room. *Go away, Medora,* she thought. *Leave me alone.*

"HE HAS A WIFE AND TWO LITTLE KIDS. . . ."

"Do you hear anything they say?"

"No. I don't want to hear."

"What do you do, Leslie?"

"I lie down and pull the blanket over my head and hold my hands over my ears. . . . I finally fall asleep."

"What happens in the morning?"

"The sun is out. It's so bright it wakes me up."

"Is there anyone in the room?"

"No. It was all a dream. Terri is coming out of the shower wrapped in a towel. She says, 'Oh, there you are, lazybones.' She's so cheerful."

"Do you say anything about the night before?"

"I say, 'Terri, did you have someone up here last night?' "

"She is looking at me as if I'm crazy. I'm not sure it wasn't all a dream. She says, 'You'd better get going. We have a nine-thirty call.' "

"What do you do?"

"I get up. I'm starving. I smell buttered toast and coffee. I tell her to wait for me and I take a quick shower. Terri is pulling on black tights, then an iridescent leotard with a run in it. She picks up something from the floor and slips it on her wrist. Something I haven't seen before . . . or maybe I have."

"Describe it, Leslie."

SHE HADN'T BEEN ABLE TO THEN, BUT NOW SHE SAW IT CLEARLY, AS IF IT HAD flashed on a screen in her brain. It was a bracelet, a gold cuff. How could I have missed it? she thought. Was I really that naive? She had thought all along that it was Rog with Terri that night, but she was wrong. It wasn't Rog at all.

Medora followed her into the dressing room. No one was there. They were all in the wings drinking champagne.

"I hope you're satisfied, now that you know what really happened to Terri," Medora said.

Wetzon leaned back against the dressing table. There was powder everywhere, and glitter dust. "You certainly didn't tell us in your statement."

Medora folded her arms. She was wearing a long black silk skirt and a fitted red velvet jacket with black braid. "You don't believe me, Leslie? That hurts me."

"Does it, Medora? I think you're a fine writer. After all, you wrote the scenario."

"Medora?" Ed Venderose's voice came from somewhere in the corridor. Medora didn't respond.

Should I feel threatened, Wetzon thought. With everyone around?

"There was no scenario," Medora said.

"Oh, no? Try this. You and Rog were both in love with Terri and she chose . . . Rog. Did you kill Rog, too, Medora?"

"Les?" This time it was Silvestri's voice that came to them.

"I was leaving Rog," Medora said. "We were going to make a life together with the children, Terri and I."

"Medora," Ed called, concern in his voice. "Where are you?"

"Okay, so Terri changed her mind. She chose Rog," Wetzon said.

Medora shook her head. "No. It was Rog's gun. He couldn't stand the thought of losing her."

"Les?" Now Silvestri sounded concerned.

"Or you?"

"Or me." Medora sighed. "He killed her and then panicked. He called me. I went down there. Rog was gone. Terri was dead. I didn't know what to do."

"You took your letters, your love letters."

"How do you—? Yes. I'd written her so many letters that year. She'd saved every one." Tears began to creep down Medora's cheeks, streaking her makeup.

"Medora?" Ed was close by.

"How did you get Terri into the trunk?"

"I helped her." Ed stood in the doorway. His face was pasty. "Then I brought her home." Medora reached out to him and he took her hand.

"Where was Rog?"

"I don't know," Medora said. "I only know that he came home sometime during the night and killed himself in his own bed so that I would find him in the morning. Are you satisfied now?"

Wetzon bowed her head. Ed took Medora away.

Turning to the mirror, Wetzon saw her eye makeup building up to make a run down her cheeks. Silvestri's image filled the mirror behind hers. His face told her he'd overheard a lot of what had been said.

"So that's it," she said.

"Yup," he said.

She smiled at him in the mirror. The mascara had made a break for it. "Now about my number . . ." she said.

"Les," he said, then stopped.

"I guess I kinda knocked you out, huh, Silvestri? Maybe even killed you?"

He came closer, took her shoulders, turned her to him.

She said, "Well, come on, guy, speak up. We all like a little praise once in a while, you know."

When he crushed her against his white shirt, she thought about the mess her mascara was making. "Silvestri—"

"Shut up, Les," he whispered in her hair.

It was a grand night for singing, a grand night for dancing, and a grand night for the American musical theatre. "Combinations" is back, even so briefly, and even in a concert form, to let us know how barren the musical theatre has become, as T-shirts and mugs are more important than the material on the stage.

Bravo, "Combinations"!

—From *The New York Times*
December 23, 1994
By Andrew Elofison

Chapter Fifty

THE WIND TORTURED THE UPPER WEST SIDE AND THE RAIN RATTLED Wetzon's windows.

"It's not supposed to rain on Christmas Eve, Izz," she said. The dog looked up at her and yawned. "It's supposed to snow. Not much. Just enough for a white Christmas."

She had turned down dinner with Carlos and Arthur; she'd rejected Christmas eve at Xenia Smith's. Because Silvestri had said he'd be home tonight. But it was already six o'clock and he wasn't there. Had she lost him to Rita again?

The *Combinations, in Concert* benefit had been a smashing success, and she should have been exhausted after two performances. She'd spent the day resting, puttering around, throwing things away. She'd nibbled on Carlos's Christmas bread, made from his secret recipe, which he delivered to all his friends every year with much fanfare. She was still flying, hyper on performance adrenaline.

The book was closed on Terri. What was the truth? She would never know for sure. And maybe, just maybe, she didn't want to know. Too many years had passed. Medora had loved Terri; of that Wetzon was certain.

Lying on her mat in the sponge position, she slowed her breathing. All made up and nowhere to go, she thought.

So, she could still be twinkle-toes over Broadway. For two nights at least. She listened to her body. No complaints yet, just a twinge here and there.

Carlos was determined they should work together, but could she go back to the Theatre and die a little each time a show failed? Uh-uh. No. It was easier on the heart and soul, not to mention Arthur's favorite word, *kishkas,* to stay on Wall Street.

This year the bond market fell out of bed, Kidder Peabody disappeared forever under a scandal, Prudential shook but didn't crumble, and Rosenkind Luwisher had eliminated headhunters from their budgets. Still, it would do.

She became aware that she could no longer hear the wind. She sat up in time to see Izz fly off the sofa, shrieking, and run to the door. "The master has arrived," Wetzon said, wondering what he would make of Wetzon leaping off the sofa, shrieking, to greet his arrival.

Silvestri set two shopping bags down near the tree and added some packages to the others already there.

"Do you want to go out?" he said.

"It might be nice. Where?"

"Oh, we'll find a place." He headed for the bedroom and she followed. "I'm getting into the shower."

"Is it still raining?"

"No, but it's cold."

She put on a long jersey skirt, boots, and a red turtleneck, then piled her hair on top of her head, tying it with a wide, shiny red ribbon. The full-length mirror in the bedroom gave her back chic. Okay.

Her stomach squeaked. She was hungry. In the fridge was a container of goat cheese in herbs and olive oil that she'd bought at the farmers' market on Union Square. A left-over chunk of sourdough sat in a bag on her counter. She sliced the bread and stuck it in the toaster oven until it was brown, then spread the slices with the goat cheese.

"Eating again, huh?"

"Wow," she said, looking him up and down. Silvestri was all dressed up. A sharp navy suit, blue-and-white-striped shirt, and a red tie with a Bogart and Bergman scene from *Casablanca* handpainted on it. "What kind of tie is that?"

"*Casablanca.*" He flapped it around. "Don't you like it? Rita gave it to me."

"Oh." She crossed her eyes and handed him a piece of bread with goat cheese. "It's gorgeous."

He laughed. "Liar. Rita didn't give it to me. The guys downtown did. Come on, grab your coat and let's go."

"Where?"

"Why do you always ask so many questions?"

"I'm curious."

They walked down Columbus Avenue.

"Don't walk so fast," Silvestri said.

"I'm cold."

Behind the Museum of Natural History, a group of carolers sang "Joy to the World" and "Good King Wenceslas," and everyone on the street stopped to sing along. Silvestri and Wetzon stayed through "Little Drummer Boy." Then Silvestri hailed a cab.

"Where are we going?" she asked again when they were sitting in the cab.

"Lord and Taylor," he told the driver, who was wearing a red Santa hat with a saggy tail that ended in a white pom-pom. "That's Thirty-eighth and Fifth, and take your time."

"Lord and Taylor? It's seven o'clock, Silvestri. Lord and Taylor has been closed for at least an hour."

"I know," he said. And that was all he said.

Fifth Avenue was brilliant with lights. They passed a horse-drawn carriage filled with children, tourists probably. In front of Tiffany's a Santa climbed into a Rolls-Royce packed with presents and pulled away from the curb.

A red double-decker bus moved along their right side, then the lions in front of the New York Public Library reappeared. The lions had wreaths around their stone necks.

"Come on," Silvestri said after he paid the driver. "Merry Christmas."

They stood in front of the store. She said, "I told you it was closed."
Even on Christmas Eve, especially on Christmas Eve, people lined up
to look at the decorated store windows.

"I want to see the windows," he said, not paying any attention to
her crankiness.

"I'm hungry."

"In time."

The windows celebrated Norman Rockwell and an American
Christmas. When they finished looking at each and every one of them,
she had a catch in her throat. "Okay," she said, "that was lovely. Now
can we eat?"

He was walking her up Fifth Avenue now. "Merry Christmas,"
people said as they passed. A red Cadillac went by, festooned with
tinsel. On its roof were a sleigh and reindeer. A menorah was positioned above the headlights. Christmas music spilled out onto the
street, and everyone smiled and smiled.

"Merry Christmas!" someone called from a hay wagon, and the air
was suddenly filled with flying candy canes in cellophane. Silvestri
snared one and gave it to her.

"How do you feel now?"

"Super," she said. "But famished."

The Saks windows she'd seen and Silvestri wasn't impressed with
them, but across the way Rockefeller Center throbbed with music and
light: the towering tree in the Plaza, the giant red ornaments on the
side streets, and the whirling ice-skaters. The night was filled with
music.

St. Patrick's was lit up and the doors were open. Later, this ca-
thedral and the others all over the city would be filled for midnight
Mass.

She stood watching the skaters while the music flowed around her.
"O come, all ye faithful." She looked up at Silvestri. She had so much
to be grateful for. Health, success, friends. A beautiful home in the
most wonderful city in the world. Love. She squeezed Silvestri's hand
and began to cry.

"Hey, now," he said. "That hungry? No need to cry about it. I'll feed you."

She shook her head. "You wouldn't understand."

"Try me," he said, but they were walking again.

"Where are we going?"

"You'll see."

On Fifty-fourth Street, they turned east, crossed Madison, neared the Elysée Hotel.

"The Monkey Bar," she said. "The Monkey Bar!" She was suddenly thrilled. It was the new "in" place, having only reopened a couple of months ago. She stopped and stared at him. It was so unlike Silvestri to even know about it. Maybe Carlos had told him.

He looked at his watch. "Come on, let's go in."

"My God, Silvestri, you're full of surprises."

They checked their coats, and she left him at the dark, crowded bar with the monkey murals and the grand piano while she went to fix her hair and replace her lipstick, which she'd eaten off.

She fussed a little with her hair and smoothed her foundation with a piece of damp paper towel.

Even more people were clumped around the bar when she came out, and it was noisy. Where was Silvestri? There he was. He had his arm around a redhead in a tight black dress . . . as if the redhead was his girl.

Damnation, she thought. What nerve. A chippy with a nice ass and great legs. Blast. And he was laughing, would you believe. The chippy was telling him some story and he was laughing. Wetzon was furious. What she should do was just get her coat, get in a cab, and go home. No way. She wasn't going to run away, but this had to take the cake for chutzpah. What was she doing with her life anyway?

Turn around, bitch, she thought, willing the bitch to turn around. But it was Silvestri who turned. His face lit up. "Les!" He held his hand out to her. "Come over here."

She came over slowly. "Silvestri, goddammit," she said, "who do—"

He was staring at her. He began to laugh, was doubled over with laughter. "Les," he said, catching his breath, then starting to laugh again.

The chippy turned and smiled at Wetzon. Only she was no chippy. "I don't understand," Wetzon said. "Will you stop laughing, Silvestri?"

He gave up trying. "Les," he said. "This is Rita."